Andrew Hammond began his working life in a cheap suit, sitting in the bowels of York Magistrates' Court, interviewing repeat offenders who always said they 'didn't do it'. After several years in the legal profession, Andrew re-trained as a school teacher. CRYPT is Andrew's first fictional series but he has written over forty educational textbooks for a host of publishers and he can spot the difference between an adjectival and adverbial phrase at fifty paces (if only someone would ask him to). He now leads a double life: in term-time he is a respectable Headmaster of a school in Hampshire; in the holidays he escapes to his farm in Suffolk and writes gruesome horror stories. He lives with his wife, Andie, and their four angels – Henry, Nell, Ed and Katherine – none of whom are old enough yet to read 'Daddy's scary books'. But one day . . .

By Andrew Hammond

CRYPT: *The Gallows Curse*
CRYPT: *Traitor's Revenge*
CRYPT: *Mask of Death*

Look out for the 4th CRYPT book, coming March 2013

For Noogie

CRYPT
COVERT RESPONSE YOUTH PARANORMAL TEAM

MASK OF
DEATH

ANDREW HAMMOND

headline

First published in 2012 by
HEADLINE PUBLISHING GROUP

1

Cataloguing in Publication Data is available from the British Library

ISBN 978 0 7553 7823 4

Typeset in Goudy Old Style by Avon DataSet Ltd,
Bidford-on-Avon, Warwickshire

Printed and bound in Great Britain by
Clays Ltd, St Ives plc

Headline's policy is to use papers that are natural, renewable and
recyclable products and made from wood grown in sustainable forests.
The logging and manufacturing processes are expected to conform to the
environmental regulations of the country of origin.

HEADLINE PUBLISHING GROUP
An Hachette UK Company
338 Euston Road
London NW1 3BH

www.headline.co.uk
www.hachette.co.uk

GHOSTS ARE THE STUFF OF FICTION, RIGHT?

WRONG.

THE GOVERNMENT JUST DOESN'T WANT YOU TO KNOW ABOUT THEM...

THIS IS THE TOP SECRET CLASSIFIED HISTORY OF CRYPT.

In 2007, American billionaire and IT guru Jason Goode bought himself an English castle; it's what every rich man needs. He commissioned a new skyscraper too, to be built right in the heart of London. A futuristic cone-shaped building with thirty-eight floors and a revolving penthouse, it would be the new headquarters for his global enterprise, Goode Technology PLC.

He and his wife Tara were looking forward to their first Christmas at the castle with Jamie, their thirteen-year-old son, home from boarding school. It all seemed so perfect.

Six weeks later Goode returned home one night to find a horror scene: the castle lit up with blue flashing lights, police everywhere.

His wife was dead. His staff were out for the night; his son was the only suspect.

Jamie was taken into custody and eventually found guilty of killing his mother. They said he'd pushed her from the battlements during a heated argument. He was sent away to a young offenders' institution.

But throughout the trial, his claims about what really happened never changed:

'The ghosts did it, Dad.'

His father had to believe him. From that day on, Jason Goode vowed to prove the existence of ghosts and clear his son's name.

They said Goode was mad – driven to obsession by the grief of losing his family. Plans for the new London headquarters were put on hold. He lost interest in work. People said he'd given up on life.

But one man stood by him – lifelong friend and eminent scientist Professor Giles Bonati. Friends since their student days at Cambridge, Bonati knew Goode hadn't lost his mind. They began researching the science of disembodied spirits.

Not only did they prove scientifically how ghosts can access our world, they uncovered a startling truth too: that some teenagers have stronger connections to ghosts than any other age group. They have high extrasensory perception (ESP), which means they can see ghosts where others can't.

So was Jamie telling the truth after all?

Goode and Bonati set up the Paranormal Investigation Team (PIT), based in the cellars of Goode's private castle. It was a small experimental project at first, but it grew. Requests came in for its teenage agents to visit hauntings across the region.

But fear of the paranormal was building thanks to the PIT. Hoax calls were coming in whenever people heard a creak in the attic. Amateur ghost hunters began to follow the teenagers and interfere with their work. But it didn't stop there. Goode and Bonati quickly discovered a further truth – something which even they had not bargained for. As more and more people pitched up at hauntings to watch the agents in action, so the ghosts became stronger. It seemed as though the greater the panic and hysteria at a scene, the more powerful the paranormal activity became. There was no denying it: the ghosts fed off human fear.

So where would this lead?

To prevent the situation from escalating out of control, Goode was ordered to disband the PIT and stop frightening people. Reporters tried to expose the team as a fraud. People could rest easy in their beds – there was no such thing as ghosts. Goode had to face the awful truth that his son was a liar – and a murderer. The alternative was too frightening for the public to accept.

So that's what they were told.

But in private, things were quite different. Goode had been approached by MI5.

The British security services had been secretly investigating paranormal incidents for years. When crimes are reported without any rational human explanation, MI5 must explore all other possibilities, including the paranormal. But funding was tight and results were limited.

Maybe teenagers were the answer.

So they proposed a deal. Goode could continue his paranormal investigations, but to prevent more hoax calls and widespread panic, he had to do so under the cover and protection of MI5.

They suggested the perfect venue for this joint operation – Goode's London headquarters. The skyscraper was not yet finished. There was still time. A subterranean suite of hi-tech laboratories could be built in the foundations. A new, covert organisation could be established – bigger and better than before, a joint enterprise between Goode Technology and the British security services.

But before Jason Goode agreed to the plan, he made a special request of his own. He would finish the building, convert the underground car park into a suite of laboratories and living accommodation, allow MI5 to control operations, help them recruit the best teenage investigators they could find and finance any future plans they had for the organisation – all in return for one thing.

He wanted his son back.

After weeks of intense secret negotiations, the security services finally managed to broker the deal: provided he was monitored closely by the Covert Policing Command at Scotland Yard, and, for his own protection, was given a new identity, Jamie could be released. For now.

The deal was sealed. The Goode Tower was finished – a landmark piece of modern architecture, soaring above the Thames. And buried discreetly beneath its thirty-eight floors was the Covert Response Youth Paranormal Team.

The CRYPT. Its motto: *EXSPECTA INEXSPECTATA*. Expect the unexpected.

Jamie Goode was released from custody and is now the CRYPT's most respected agent.

And his new identity?

Meet Jud Lester, paranormal investigator.

CRYPT
COVERT RESPONSE YOUTH PARANORMAL TEAM

MASK OF
DEATH

CHAPTER 1

TUESDAY 2.16 A.M.

ST EDMUND'S HOSPITAL, LONDON

Adam McNeal's eyes shot open. Bloodshot and watery. Head pounding.

Like sharp needles, his screams stabbed the cushion of silence in this forgotten ward. But few people could hear him. It was a part of the hospital no one came to; that's why he'd been put there.

'They're coming!' he shouted, his body writhing around in the soggy bed.

No reply.

'Help me!'

His skin was postulated and weeping. Deep red and purple sores, like blackened bruises but yellow and pus-filled at the core, covered his pitiful body and clung like limpets to the embarrassing floral gown he'd been given, now stained and sodden.

The pillow beneath his sweaty hair was damp and as he sat bolt upright he left an imprint on it – the cradled shape of his poor, wretched head. He looked like a young child, caught up in some heat-oppressed night terror. He needed his mother to come and shake him out of it, tell him everything was OK, it was just a dream. Put a cold flannel on his neck, hold his hand and stroke his matted hair.

But Adam McNeal was forty-three.

And this was no nightmare. He was dying.

'Yaaagh . . . Go on . . . get away, get away from me . . .'

Under the sheet his legs were kicking again and his arms were stabbing out at the terrifying images that flickered like projector slides across his mind's eye. His flailing arms revealed painful black sores, growing like fungus beneath his armpits.

Sweat trickled down his forehead and seeped into the cracks and sores and scabs. His nose was darker than the rest of his face – blackened in parts, almost as if he'd bruised it. And beneath the sweaty hair at the base of his neck, there were more black spots forming.

'The ghosts! Get 'em away!' he screamed again. 'No. *No!* Don't take me. You can't have me! You can't have me, no! You can't . . . you . . .'

There was a hand at his wrist.

Another at his shoulder. He was pinned down.

The needle pierced his skin and within a few moments the thrashing and screaming waned. A few more convulsions and then his body was at rest. The sedative had worked its magic. For now.

Emily placed the needle back in its case and stared at him. She could feel tears forming in the corners of her eyes. He must have been so handsome, before – beneath the dark scabs and the sweaty rashes. His strong jaw, his straight nose, and those symmetrical lips that moved almost imperceptibly as his breathing slowly steadied itself.

It was tragic to see something so poisonous and ugly eating its way out of something so beautiful. She stroked his left hand, placed across his large, muscular chest. The ring on his finger was now lodged fast. Blackened skin had swollen up around the shiny silver band, and the nails at his fingertips were flaking off, revealing dark sores beneath.

Where was this going to end? Emily knew the answer to that.

The doctors had written him off already.

Tests were still ongoing to identify his disease and how to treat it, if they could, but you only had to look at this man now to know that he was on a downward spiral.

And as a nurse it was her job to be right there, up close, watching the metamorphosis – a tall, handsome man slowly becoming a disease-ridden corpse. Prince into beast.

Emily picked up the needle case and the bottle of sedative solution and left the room forlornly.

The door closed behind her and there was a smash of glass. The bottle had dropped from her hand and shattered on the hard tiled floor. Its contents formed a syrupy puddle around her feet as she stood there.

Terrified.

Lighting in the corridor was dim at this time of night – just the emergency exits and the odd spotlight turned low – but it was enough for her to see the shape approaching. It seemed to glide eerily over the tiles instead of walking. It was wearing a long black overcoat, or was it a robe of some kind?

But it wasn't the dark robe that scared Emily. Or its apparent lack of arms and feet, engulfed in black cloth. It was its face that struck terror into her stomach and caused her body to shake uncontrollably.

Shrouded in a black hood was a pearly white mask, shaped like a skull, with concave cheekbones and large black holes for eyes.

But it was the nose that freaked Emily out and she started crying as the figure came closer. She'd never seen anything like it. In the centre of its skeletal face where the nose should be was an elongated beak, animal-like, about ten inches long, pointing in her direction, like a dagger.

CHAPTER 2

THREE DAYS EARLIER

CALDER'S JEWELLERY STORE,

HATTON GARDEN, LONDON

Nicky Calder carefully placed the gleaming gold ring back into its snug position in the burgundy velvet display tray. The rows of jewellery inside the glass cabinets looked enticing. They had to. Tonight was opening night and he'd never get a captive audience like this again. They were coming to celebrate and drink champagne and be seen in this chic part of town. But Nicky knew different. They were coming to be fleeced. No one would be leaving without a stylish little paper bag with 'Calder's' emblazoned across it.

The door behind him clinked – that optimistic ring to say a customer had entered the lair. He turned and beamed at the guests wandering in. Outside he saw high-class taxis deposit upper-class guests wrapped in fur coats.

This was the night he'd been dreaming of for years. And it was finally happening. His new suit looked good, and the half hour he'd spent agonising over which shirt to wear had been worth it. The white, blousony top with oversized cuffs contrasted well with the sharp lines of his slim-fit navy-blue jacket. Nicky had a flamboyant dress sense and so did many of his friends in the clubs and bars he frequented. He'd been known to wear the odd bit of eyeliner now and again, and his foundation and concealer were a godsend after those frequent late nights spent dancing and drinking. His blond hair was thinning if you looked closely, but he kept it short and applied enough wax to create a tufty, Tin-Tin flick above his forehead. He was the wrong side of forty, just, but he didn't look it – unless you saw him at seven in the morning, when he looked the wrong side of fifty. He loved champagne and cigarettes, that was his problem.

'*Saluti! Benvenuti*, my darlings!' he said warmly. 'Come in, come in. Champagne?'

Some female guests giggled with undisguised excitement at Nicky's Italian accent, while their husbands rolled their eyes and clung tightly to their wallets in their pockets.

The shop was filling and Nicky was dancing across the room, air-kissing the cheeks of anyone he could find, while his assistants, Toni and Rachel, were offering fluted glasses of pink champagne from silver trays. They knew their brief – get as much of the stuff down the guests' necks as they could. Nicky didn't want to see anyone clutching an empty glass.

The small boutique in this famous jewellery quarter of London was awash with superlatives.

'Oh, it's divine, darling.'

'Simply stunning.'

'Look at this one, sweetie, it's a must.'

'Honey, just look at this. Don't you think it suits me? Oh, do say it does, darling.'

Nicky winked at Toni across the room and sneaked a quick smile. This was going to be a lucrative night.

CHAPTER 3

TUESDAY 4.00 A.M.

ST EDMUND'S HOSPITAL, LONDON

Dr Mike Withers rubbed his eyes wearily, got up from his desk and grabbed the clipboard. It was time to do the rounds. He loathed night shifts. By the time he'd finished and returned home, his wife would have got the kids up, fed them breakfast and bundled them off to school without even so much as a farewell hug for their daddy. And then there was the constant battle of trying to get some shut-eye while his wife tiptoed around downstairs trying to clear the chaos left behind by the children. There were no winners with a night shift.

He left his tiny room and began the long marathon of patient checks.

Twenty minutes later he was walking down the corridor into the quarantine ward, East Wing. This was an eerie place in the daylight and at night-time it assumed an even stranger atmosphere of neglect and hopelessness.

St Edmund's was one of those giant, red-brick Victorian hospitals. The solid block of building rose above the houses in this poorer district of London like a factory building. Its austere appearance lived up to expectations inside. Long, dimly lit corridors with Victorian tiles from floor to ceiling, like the kind you see in old swimming pools. The wards were no better. Funding was tight, after all.

One day, Withers thought, he would make a name for himself and join all those better-paid doctors at the more prestigious hospitals across the city. Do some private practice work too. Triple his salary and then set himself up as a private consultant to the rich.

But for now, he had to contend with the night shift at St Edmund's – the only hospital brave enough to take him on after medical school.

He tapped the pass code into the metal keypad by the double doors and kicked the scuffed metal footplate. The door swung open with an ominous creak.

'Emily?'

Why wasn't she sitting at the reception desk, playing solitaire on the computer, like she usually did?

Maybe she was actually checking patients, like he always told her to do whenever he visited this forgotten wing.

But there was something strange in the atmosphere tonight. Chilling even.

He walked past the empty desk and on, deeper into the section. He passed Ward A and peered through the closed door. He could see two beds, each with sleeping bodies in them. He'd check on those in a minute. Better to find Emily first so as not to give her a fright. He'd done that a few times in the past and he knew how easily scared she was.

'Emily?' he said again, softly.

Nothing.

Another room on his left. No one there. Just empty beds. A lone fly buzzed around an emergency light.

He checked the third room and saw three beds, one of them empty, one emitting the guttural snores of a suffering patient and the other with an old man sitting bolt upright.

'Hello,' Withers whispered. 'Everything all right?'

No answer. He could just make out in the dim light a strange expression on the old man's face. He was wide-eyed but speechless.

Probably dreaming, thought the doctor. So many of the patients suffered nightmares – the frightening consequences of the high temperatures they were running. Better to leave him, especially if he's not making any noise.

He decided he'd talk to Emily and get her to check on him in a moment. Bringing someone out of a nightmare was always laborious and required the kind of bedside nursing skills he'd always lacked.

He turned the corner and headed for the last room in the section – home of the new patient whom everyone had been talking about. The man with the unknown disease. Unknown until the tests arrived, at least. They should've been here by now, he thought.

It was a long corridor, dimly lit. But Withers could see there was something on the floor up ahead.

He stopped.

'Emily?'

He ran the last few steps, his heart beating like a machine gun inside his chest.

She was a mess.

The dirty white floor tiles were stained with dark brown puddles of congealed blood that led ominously from her neck.

Emily's throat had been cut. Her head was twisted round and facing the opposite end of the corridor. He saw a terrified expression etched forever on her face. Her lifeless eyes were wide and her mouth was open and bloodied.

He'd seen some things in his short time as a doctor but nothing quite like this. He put a hand to his mouth as he felt the bile rising inside. He placed his other hand against the wall to stop himself from keeling over.

He regained his composure and – pointlessly, he knew –

stooped to place a finger at her neck to check for a pulse. Nothing. Her skin was cold.

'Oh, God,' he said.

A sudden chill began at the base of his spine and trickled up his back, bringing a shiver to his scalp.

If someone has done this to Emily – could they still be here?

He spun round, his breath quickening. His eyes were darting defensively in every direction. Up and down the empty corridor. He turned round again.

No one.

There was one room left. He knew whose that was and held his hand over his nose like a mask; last time he was in there the stench from the poor man's skin was horrid.

He slowly pushed the door open. It was dark and cold. The freezing night air blew through him from the direction of the window. As he went to close it, his shoes crunched over broken glass and he saw jagged shards sticking out from the window frame like icicles. The window had been smashed. He peered through the gaping hole at the metal steps beyond – the rickety fire exit that led down to the shadowy car park below. His forehead felt icy cold.

He spun round to face the bed. The orange curtains that were pulled round it were flapping from the draught and they revealed brief glimpses of crumpled, sticky sheets.

'Hello?'

Nothing.

'Mr McNeal?'

Gingerly, he pulled the curtains apart and saw damp, sweaty sheets and patches of congealed, crusty blood.

But no patient.

Adam McNeal was gone.

CHAPTER 4

TUESDAY 6.11 A.M.

CRYPT, LONDON

This was an ungodly hour to be undergoing training, thought Jud as he swung his legs out of bed and promptly stood on a belt buckle. He winced at the pain jabbing into the sole of his foot. But at least it was waking him up.

His black hair was sticking up at the back – that wild, tufty crop you see on weary kids who pitch up at school without their hair combed and with stinking, sleepy breath. The ones who've so obviously been pulled out from beneath their duvet by an anxious mother, with one eye on the clock.

He rubbed his eyes – they still stung from a late night spent on the Xbox with Luc.

He gazed around the cesspit that he called his room – half-empty drinks cans, discarded clothes on the floor and a myriad of books and old magazines. He spied a half-eaten Twix bar stuck to his desk and grabbed it, devouring the remains in seconds. He screwed the wrapper into a ball and hurled it at the heaving bin in the corner. It uncurled itself before it reached its target and slowly drifted to the ground. Missed, as usual.

The radio alarm clock was still blasting out from the shelf

above his bed. Some crappy pop song from his dad's generation. He sat back on the bed, switched it off and lay back on the pillow. Just five more minutes. There was plenty of time.

The phone rang.

'Yeah?'

'It's Bex. You up?'

'No, Bex, I'm fast asleep. This is a recording.'

'You better be up. We're supposed to be in SPA 1 in twenty minutes.'

'That's ages. Chill.'

'Have you eaten yet?'

Jud stared at the empty Twix wrapper. 'Yeah, don't worry about me.'

'So I'll see you outside the SPA then?'

'I'll be there, swimming trunks and towel at the ready,' he joked.

'You're a funny guy,' she said sarcastically and hung up.

The SPAs, or Simulated Paranormal Activity rooms, couldn't have been more different to the soothing, steam-filled rooms their name suggested. Every agent, and especially experienced skulls like Jud, joked about the SPAs, but secretly they feared them. When you received notification from Bonati or Vorzek that it was your turn for a session, you knew it was time to follow the CRYPT motto and 'expect the unexpected'.

The simulated hauntings that Bonati and his staff conjured up in those rooms were enough to make the hairs on your entire body stand to attention, never mind the tufty bits at the back of your head. And send prickly shivers right up your spine.

And Jud was about to enter the SPA again. His turn to be scared out of his wits. Would he handle it?

Yeah, of course.

But he could have done without the early start. It was Bonati's little way of telling the agents he was still the boss. He set these training courses at ridiculous hours of the day just to keep them on their toes. As he often said, ghosts don't work nine to five, so why should the agents?

A few minutes later Jud was in Sector 3. He saw Bex waiting outside SPA 1.

'Another minute and I'd have gone in without you.'

'No you wouldn't,' said Jud, nonchalantly.

'Well, you know how everything's timed. If Bonati says the session begins at six thirty, we can't be late. We have to get in there. Got your equipment?'

'Yeah.'

'And your neutraliser?'

'Yes! You sound like my teacher or something. It's not a school trip, you know. What's up with you today?'

'Nothing,' said Bex. 'I just wanna get started, that's all.'

But Jud knew the reason for her anxiety. This wasn't the first SPA session they'd had together. Since Bonati had paired him up with Bex for her very first assignment – what they now called the Tyburn case – the professor had decided they worked well together and so Jud often found himself working with Bex. And she was like this every time they went into the SPA together. She'd boss him around, pretend she was relaxed and prepared, when they both knew she was nervous. That's why she fussed so. She liked being in control but when it came to the SPA, she never knew what to expect when the simulation started.

But that was just the point.

Jud typed the security code into the keypad and aligned his eye with the retina recognition scanner. The electric door soon slid across and they both entered the holding bay. They waited for the door behind them to shut again before the next one opened. Those few unsettling seconds of being trapped between doors were, if Jud was honest, the only part of the entire simulation that he disliked. The holding bay was the size of a small lift and those few seconds when both doors were closed felt like a lifetime. He could feel his stomach somersaulting as his mind played the usual trick of building the scenario of the doors being stuck and there he was, trapped in that tiny space forever.

Claustrophobia. He'd always battled with it.

But the internal door began sliding across and they were soon inside the main room.

They'd both been given the coordinates – the long code of digits to be keyed into the computer for the simulation to begin. Of course, Jud had left the note with the numbers on back in his room, but Bex had brought hers.

She keyed in the code. They had a few minutes before the simulation began. Just enough time to get themselves into the centre of the laboratory and set up the recording equipment.

The purpose of the SPA training sessions was twofold: firstly, to test their technical skills in detecting and recording changes in the environment, and secondly, to test their ESP. So they'd brought all the equipment they could muster into the SPA – their EMF meters, motion detectors, electrostatic locators, Geiger counters and, of course, their EM neutralisers.

They stood there poised. Jud could hear Bex's heavy breathing. She was tense. It was like those first few seconds in the dentist's chair when the dentist turns his back on you and you know he's about to turn round with a bloody great drill in his hand.

She gulped.

The lights in the room went off. They stood together, and allowed their senses to scan the darkness like lasers.

They felt an icy cold wind begin to blast at their feet. It rose gradually until their whole bodies shivered.

Then their eyes widened until they bulged out of their sockets, as a headless figure emerged from the shadows.

CHAPTER 5

TUESDAY 6.28 A.M.

GORE STREET, LONDON

The incongruous, rusty truck rumbled its way past the gleaming white buildings of Knightsbridge. Past the black Range Rovers and the Bentleys parked casually outside the million-pound apartments of their owners.

This was winners' row. All along the avenue, vines and wisterias grew skywards from the chic cellar gardens and entwined themselves around the shiny black railings that lined the pavement. Trees were dotted elegantly at discrete intervals down the road, not too many to make it cluttered, nor too few to make it sparse. A perfectly planned neighbourhood.

The smelly cart edged its way past the smart cars and drew up outside the next block of terraces. Pristine green wheelie bins stood to attention, waiting to be emptied.

The hazard warning lights from the truck bounced orange flashes off the buildings as, deep inside, residents pulled pillows over their heads and tried to grab another precious hour of sleep, some cursing those 'blasted bin men' outside (the very same people who'd cursed their absence when they'd decided to strike months before and the filthy rubbish was piling up).

Gavin parked the truck and waited for Mitch to get out and

wheel the bins to the giant grabber on the side – it was his turn.

One by one, Mitch wheeled each bin towards the van, their plastic wheels juddering over cracks and uneven slabs in the pavement. He pressed the giant red button, the hydraulics lurched into action and the giant grabber picked up the bins in turn like a claw, emptying their delicious contents into the waiting mouth on the side of the lorry and then slamming them down again on to the pavement with a thud that made the residents punch their pillows again.

As Mitch replaced one of the bins outside one apartment, his movements triggered the security light down in the cellar garden.

He glanced down at the wisteria and the clipped rose bushes and the quaint ceramic flowerpots in a row.

And then he saw her.

She was lying on her front, head face down in a small garden bed by the door. She was wearing some kind of posh frock. The hemline was gathered up past her knees and Mitch saw the tops of her stockings.

Was she drunk? Late home last night, perhaps, and collapsed before she'd even got inside? Silly tart, he thought.

'Hello?' he said.

No response.

'Hello? You all right, luv?'

His stomach was beginning to churn with nerves and a breathlessness had come over him.

He ran to the lorry and banged on the window.

'Oi, Gav! Come 'ere!'

Gavin got out.

'What d'ya want? Get a move on, mate, I wanna get home.'

'Come and look at this,' said Mitch with a grave expression.

The security light had plunged them into darkness but it was soon triggered again as they walked down the stone steps.

'Shit,' said Gavin. 'What the 'ell's been goin' on here then?'

'Hello? Can you hear me, luv?' said Mitch once again. But

there was no response. The woman didn't move. They could see black sores at the base of her neck. Bruises maybe? Cuts?

Gavin went to grab her.

'Woa!' said Mitch. 'You don't know what's happened to her. I don't think we should get involved. Let someone else find her.'

'What?' said Gavin, pausing to look at him. 'Don't be stupid. I wanna see if she's all right. Don't stand there, you idiot, give me a hand, man.'

Together they slowly lifted her body and turned her over.

'Oh, bloody hell. God, look at that,' said Gavin.

Her face had been lacerated, as if it had been slashed open with a knife. Patterns of congealed blood ran across her cheeks like a latticework of branches and twigs. And the pale skin around her eyes was so swollen and bruised, you couldn't see her eyeballs.

'She's bloody dead, ain't she?' said Mitch, shaking his head and staggering backwards. 'We've found a dead bloody body.'

They just stared at her in silence for a few seconds, neither one moving or daring to speak. Stared at the slashes around her throat and the chilling expression of fear printed indelibly across her face.

Gavin grabbed her left hand to feel for a pulse. But he quickly dropped it again.

'What?' said Mitch, twitching. 'What've you seen now?'

'Look at it,' said Gavin. 'Look at 'er 'and.'

Mitch bent down and saw it.

'What the hell?'

Her wedding finger was missing – just a red, pulpy socket and the white bone of the knuckle joint protruding through torn flesh. Her wrists were blackened in places, just like her neck. Dark, angry-looking scabs were visible.

A window rattled just above them and they jolted with fear then strained their necks to look up.

'It's the ghost!' shouted somebody somewhere above them.

'You what, love?' said Mitch, straining to look up.

'I said it was the *ghost*! I saw it!' the well-spoken but desperate voice came back.

They could just make out some grey hair and the top of a wrinkled forehead, leaning out of the window two floors up.

Other lights were slowly blinking on. Curtains were twitching.

'Love, I think you should keep it down,' said Mitch. 'Come down an' tell us if you want. But keep the noise down, yeah?'

'No!' she shouted, terrified. 'I'm not moving! There's ghosts about!'

'She's either sleepwalking or she's batty,' said Gavin, shaking his head.

'I don't need this,' said Mitch, staring at the body again. 'One shock is enough. We don't need some mad woman shouting about ghosts as well.'

'I said I saw it!' the old neighbour persisted. 'I *saw* the ghost. Don't you understand, young man? It had a black cloak.'

'You what, luv?'

'And a mask too!' she continued, finding her stride now. 'A white mask. It was horrible!' She was shrieking and they heard the wooden grinding of sash windows sliding upwards, revealing concerned-looking neighbours either side of her.

'Give it a rest, Doris!'

'Have you been drinking again, eh?'

'Take your pills, love and *shut up*!'

But down on the ground, Mitch and Gavin weren't laughing. There was something in the way she said it that made them begin to wonder if she really was telling them the truth. This old woman must've seen something for all the fuss she was making. Something terrifying.

They stared at the lifeless body lying still on the ground, like a broken statue. A grey, sallow face, wearing the startled, animated expression of a gargoyle.

CHAPTER 6

TUESDAY 6.43 A.M.

ST EDMUND'S HOSPITAL, LONDON

Detective Chief Inspector Khan walked across the rain-soaked car park towards the imposing, red-brick façade of St Edmund's.

He'd been up since some ridiculous hour. They all had. Half of his men would be in Knightsbridge by now, responding to a weird report of a dead body and a rambling old woman.

He could have gone with the others, but he felt drawn to this place – to this hospital.

He paused momentarily to look up at the windows. Which one was it? Third row up, over on the left maybe?

How long ago was it anyway? Maybe four years?

He remembered it as clear as anything. Gazing past the faded orange curtains out at the scruffy skyline. And waiting.

Waiting for his father to die.

It had been a slow and depressing deterioration. First the stroke, then some signs of recovery, then a second stroke, massive this time, and one from which his father never regained consciousness.

He remembered sitting for hours on end at the bedside, watching his father's chest move slowly up and down, and wondering whether it would go on doing so for hours, days, months or years.

Three weeks it was in the end. Three weeks of juggling work with hospital visits and then funeral arrangements and then probate and the endless squabbling with his two sisters over how much they should sell their parents' house for. His mother had long gone. His father had struggled on for a few more years, stubbornly insisting on remaining in the same house, despite its crumbling plaster, leaky water pipes and cracks in the walls.

They sold it for a pittance in the end.

And all the time he was beginning to suffer with the now familiar pains of a stomach ulcer. That was when his blood pressure had started to climb too. It had been such a stressful period in his life. He remembered he'd had a few harrowing investigations to contend with at the same time as dealing with his father's prolonged demise. His nerves were shot to pieces and his body virtually jangled with tablets for the ulcerated stomach and the high blood pressure.

And now here he was once again, in the same hospital, going to see another dead body, only this time, if the reports were to be believed, it was the body of a person far more cruelly dispatched than his father.

Great to be back, he thought and rolled his eyes as he trudged up the cracked steps and pushed open the glass doors. He felt a twinge of pain from his stomach as he entered the building and an acidic sensation rising up his throat.

Bloody hospitals, he thought to himself.

Inside he was met by a woman who introduced herself as the hospital manager. She looked about fifty, clearly upset and only recently out of bed by the looks of her. What little make-up she'd managed to put on barely concealed the bags under her eyes and her mascara had run at the edges from crying.

'This way, Inspector,' she said, her voice trembling. 'The first police officers here told us to leave everything as it is until you came, so it's . . . well, I mean it's . . .'

'A mess?' said Khan, showing little emotion.

'Yes, it is a mess, I'm sorry.' She was beginning to cry again. 'It's just that, well, Emily was one of our youngest.'

'The victim?'

'Yes, Emily Parker. She is one of our . . .' she paused and sniffed. 'She *was* one of our nurses. Dr Withers found her this morning in the East Wing.'

'OK. Well, we'll sort this out, get to the bottom of it, don't you worry about that.' Khan forced a smile. 'I know this place.'

'Oh yes?'

'Mm . . . my father died here.'

'Oh, I'm sorry.'

Khan shrugged his shoulders in resignation. 'It's one of those things. Comes to us all, I suppose.'

'Indeed.'

He followed her down long, white corridors, up sparse, echoing stairwells and finally into the quietest part of the building. Or it should have been. It was now full of police officers and hospital staff, all talking in loud whispers.

The manager pressed the buzzer beside the double doors that led into the East Wing.

A tired-looking doctor opened the door and greeted them, dressed in a white coat that clearly had not seen an iron for a long time.

'I'm Dr Withers,' he said.

'So you're the man who found her, yes?' said Khan.

'That's right,' said Withers, ushering them in.

'OK. Thank you. I'm DCI Khan. I'm here to—'

A shout was heard.

'What was that?'

'Oh, that's just the old boy in Ward B,' said Withers. 'Always having nightmares. He's just rambling again.'

Khan was surprised at the doctor's lack of sympathy.

'Shouldn't someone go to him?'

'No, don't worry, there'll be a nurse along soon. He's always doing that. Never sleeps easy. Usually wittering on about something. Old fool.'

Khan couldn't help wondering if this doctor had shown the same attitude to his own father in those last desperate weeks of his life. He objected to the way he'd just dismissed the old man like that.

But now wasn't the time. And perhaps the doctor was right – perhaps he was delirious.

They walked on, past Ward A. The shouts and cries from the old man were getting louder and as they passed his room, they saw him. He was sitting bolt upright.

'I saw it! I saw it!' he shouted.

Khan stared at the old man. 'Saw what?' he said.

'I told you, he's delirious,' said the doctor, beckoning him to move on. 'It happens all the time, Inspector. Let me show you the body. It's just up here.'

'No,' said Khan. 'The body can wait. It's not going anywhere. I want to talk to this patient.'

The doctor looked at the hospital manager and rolled his eyes. 'OK, OK. But don't imagine you're dealing with a reliable witness, Inspector.'

Khan walked into Ward B and sat at the end of the bed. He shuddered at the memory of doing exactly this with his own father.

'Saw what, my friend? What did you see?'

'The man in the mask! With the beak. I hated that beak. Hated it!'

Khan was trying to understand, but the old man wasn't making sense. Man with a beak?

'I told you, he's dreaming,' said Withers, getting impatient. He wanted to go home. It had been a long shift. 'This way, *please*.'

Khan rose from the bed. But he kept staring at the old patient. There was something in his face – in his eyes – that said to Khan he wasn't dreaming.

A nurse attended him and administered some kind of sedative.

'To help him sleep easy,' said Withers. 'It's what he needs.'

They left the room and approached the end of the corridor. As the assembled crowd of police officers and forensics in white boiler suits dispersed, Khan got his first glimpse of Emily.

And she was indeed a mess.

'She's just a kid,' said Khan, staring at the corpse.

'Yeah, she's young,' said the doctor. 'She had a bright future ahead of her.'

'So when did you find her?' said the inspector, shaking himself out of the trance that was consuming him.

'About four thirty this morning, I think.'

'And I hear you've got a patient who's disappeared, is that right?'

'Yes,' said Dr Withers. He looked towards the door which led into McNeal's room.

Khan moved towards it but Withers held him back quickly.

'Er, no, I'm sorry, Inspector. You need to be masked up first.'

'I beg your pardon?'

Whithers picked up two masks that had been placed on a table just inside the room. He offered one to Khan and began putting the other one over his own face.

'What is this?' said Khan. 'Why the masks? I thought you said the room was empty now.'

The doctor's voice was muffled slightly by the mask over his mouth, but Khan could make out his words – though he could hardly believe them.

'You see, Inspector, the missing patient, Adam McNeal, was showing signs of a strange and degenerative disease when he came in. I'm afraid he was delirious. None of us had seen symptoms quite like it before. So we sent off some blood samples for testing. The test results came in just before you arrived this morning. I don't know how to say this, I mean everyone's still in shock to see Emily, but the results of the test are just as shocking.'

'Go on,' said Khan, impatiently.

'Well, it seems McNeal was suffering from a disease not seen in this country for generations. I just don't understand it. I mean, it was effectively . . . plague.'

'*What?*' said Khan.

'Bubonic plague, to be exact.' The doctor spoke quietly and stared straight into Khan's eyes.

The inspector stood still and looked back. 'You're saying this man was suffering from the *Black Death*? Is that what you're saying?'

The doctor nodded ominously.

'And now,' said Khan, failing to hide his concern, 'and now you're seriously telling me that you don't know where he's gone? *Really?*'

Withers nodded again but averted Khan's gaze and looked out of the gaping hole where the window once was, at the sodden rooftops across the skyline and the dark clouds in the distance. Damp leaves were being blown inside by the rising wind that swept across the gloomy car park and swirled skywards.

'Yes, Inspector. I'm afraid he could be anywhere by now.'

CHAPTER 7

TUESDAY 6.51 A.M.

CRYPT

'Keep recording!' yelled Jud. 'Don't stop!'

'I can't,' cried Bex. 'I'm . . . too . . . *cold*.' She was shivering uncontrollably and her hands were shaking as she held the infrared camera.

The temperature in the room had dropped steadily since the simulation had begun and they couldn't take much more. But Jud knew that Bonati wouldn't let it continue for much longer.

The headless figure that had loomed out of the darkness towards them was now shifting shape. One minute it was no bigger than Bex, the next it towered over them like some inflated genie from a bottle. And it whipped up the air around it like some icy tornado.

The body was wrapped in a tatty dress, like some Tudor scullery maid's – muddy brown with a faded white tabard blotted with red bloodstains. The dark hem of its dress flapped as it swept past them.

At the neck was a white frill – or at least it would have been white once, it was now drenched in blood. And in the centre of the neck hole was a splintered bony stump. Sinews and veins were splayed around it like earthworms.

The figure kept moving and shifting, floating across the floor, encircling them.

Jud was trying to neutralise its energy. He held his EM neutraliser tightly and pointed it at the figure, wherever it moved.

The rest of their equipment was set up behind them. The EMF meter and the Geiger counter were wired up remotely to the laptop on the floor beside them and the readings were being downloaded.

SPA sessions were as much about recording data as they were about 'sensory management', as Bonati called it – keeping control of your senses and not letting your fear get the better of you. They *had* to keep recording.

'Jud!' Bex screamed. 'What's that?'

'What?' Jud spun round.

'There!'

'Where?'

'Look down! It's *on you!*'

She'd dropped the infrared camera. It hit the deck with an ominous crack.

'What the hell're you doing?' shouted Jud, angrily. 'Do you know how much those things are? If you break the equipment, we fail the SPA test. You do realise that don't—'

He stopped. The headless figure floated across the room and seemed to hang in the shadows a few feet away.

Jud looked down at his legs, in the direction of Bex's trembling finger.

And he could see the reason for her cries.

There was a small child.

Clinging on to his left leg. And gazing up at Jud. He felt nothing, no pressure, no gripping. But the apparition was there. He could see it.

It was a little girl. Her hair was black and straggly and it was clinging to her forehead, covering one eye. The visible eye was large and watery.

Her mouth was gaping open and dribbling. Jud could see just a few jagged teeth protruding from her gums. One was oversized, almost like a fang. Or a tusk.

As her head flopped backwards against Jud's leg, Bex could see there were red rings round her neck, like bruises. It was as if she'd been strangled.

Jud shook his leg gently. The little girl clung on, but the movement shook her hair and her other eye was exposed.

'Oh, God!' Bex cried. 'Look at that!'

The girl's eye was larger than the other one and opaque, like a skin-coloured marble.

Bex went to pull the figure off Jud.

'No!' he yelled.

She raised her hands towards its neck.

The girl's mouth extended wider – it was as if she was crying but there was no sound coming out. Was she mute?

'I said *no*! Leave her alone!' Jud shouted. 'She's not hurting me. She's desperate, Bex. We have to understand why she's here.'

'OK, OK,' said Bex.

Jud didn't move. He said more softly, 'She's here for a reason. That's how it works. She's connected to the headless one in some way. We've got to work out why she's here, Bex.'

He was trying to calm the girl with the ugly face – stroking her matted hair gently. Bex had backed away, keeping an eye on the headless figure that was still lingering a few feet away. She knew Jud was right, of course, but she still didn't like seeing him in danger like this. This ghost could turn at any time and go for Jud. She watched it closely. The girl's eyes were misshapen and uneven, and she was staring in the direction of the headless one.

'Her mother?' said Bex nervously.

'Could be,' said Jud.

'Maybe she saw it,' said Bex, picking up the camera slowly and seeing if it worked.

No response. Defunct.

'Saw what?' said Jud.

'Well, maybe this girl saw her mother's execution. Might explain the wailing.'

'You might be right. Is she talking to us?'

They watched the girl's misshapen face. Her ugly mouth was moving now. The gaping hole was changing shape as her lips tried to form words.

But no sound came.

The headless maid approached them again. It was swooping around Jud, and the little girl's head twisted and turned so she could see it. The dark folds of the maid's dress brushed across the little girl's face.

Then they heard a voice. It was deep – it wasn't a girl's voice. Couldn't have been.

'For . . . give . . . me. For . . .'

'Did you hear that?' said Jud.

'Yeah,' said Bex, wide-eyed.

'Forgive me . . . little one.'

'It's the mother's spirit,' said Jud. 'Has to be.'

'I heard it,' said Bex. 'She wants forgiveness.'

Jud was nodding his head. 'Did you kill her?' he said into the room.

Nothing.

'Did you take this girl's life?' he said again. 'Your daughter's?'

'She was the devil's . . . she wasn't mine. She didn't belong to me . . . to any of us . . .'

'So you strangled her?' he whispered into the darkness. 'You strangled your own daughter because of the way she looked?'

Silence.

'And you paid the price,' he said slowly. 'Beheaded.'

The little girl at Jud's knee dropped her head back and wailed a soundless wail. Great globules of tears formed around her sighted eye.

'But she forgives you,' said Jud. 'I said she forgive—'

The lights came on.

The apparitions drifted into the air. They were gone.

Jud and Bex shielded their eyes from the brightness.

'What the . . .' said Bex.

'It's OK. It's all right. The SPA's been aborted.'

Seconds later a voice came over the giant speakers built into the ceiling of the room.

'Jud, Bex, report to Briefing Room 1 – *immediately*.'

It was Bonati. And he sounded anxious.

CHAPTER 8

TUESDAY 7.09 A.M.

PICCADILLY LINE, SOUTH

KENSINGTON, LONDON

The body of a barely conscious Adam McNeal was slumped against a damp, cold brick wall. In the dark shadows a rat scurried over his still, bare feet and tugged momentarily at the torn hem of his striped pyjamas. There was no response from McNeal.

Locked inside the hard shell of his skull a flicker of consciousness began to stir. A gradual realisation that he was alive was dawning, though there was no discernable evidence to suggest he was anywhere other than hell. It was cold, it was pitch black and the air was rank with the smell of something so foul it made his throat retch as soon as the aroma hit the cavity at the back of his nostrils. He slowly opened his lips and clicked his tongue at the top of his dry mouth like an alcoholic the morning after a heavy bingeing.

The sores around his ears and at the base of his neck throbbed, and the scabs that were gathering around his wrists and hands bled in the darkness.

If this was death, it was worse than he'd ever expected and he began to sift through his living memories to identify the great wrong he'd committed to deserve such a punishment.

If this was life then he longed for death.

He opened his sticky, encrusted eyes but there was nothing to suggest he could see. It was black as pitch. Was he blind too?

He felt the damp cotton of his pyjamas and pinched through the material to see if he could feel any pain. His fingers squeezed harder and harder until a sensation of pain reached him. He *was* alive. Wasn't he? Or if he was pinching his leg in a dream, then the dream made sense, it hurt.

But why he was here, how he'd got here, and where the hell he was anyway were questions that would have to wait for any kind of answers.

He tested his legs. He could move them. He moved his head from side to side. It felt like the very worst hangover he'd ever endured. He was grateful for the lack of light – which would undoubtedly have worsened the throbbing behind his eyes.

There was a rumble in the distance. He felt it through his thighs and the small of his back, still slumped against the hard wall. The vibrations swelled and he braced himself for something that was approaching.

The noise grew, louder and louder – the roar of an engine of some kind. It was so intrusive it made McNeal wish for the lonely silence to return again.

Then panic engulfed him as the realisation dawned that the sound was too similar to a train roaring down a tunnel to be anything else. Was he about to be smashed into pieces?

Had he been dumped right in the path of a speeding train? Had he just woken up moments before his own death? Why? Why couldn't he have slept through it and never woken at all? If the train speeding in his direction was heading straight for him, then the impact would be so sudden, he'd never have regained consciousness and would have passed seamlessly from sleep to death. *He should've stayed asleep.*

But he was awake and consciously taking his final few breaths.

There was no point in getting up. He could hardly move anyway. The disease – whatever it was that was claiming his body – had robbed him of any energy, save that which he'd expended on panicking now. And he knew it would claim his life soon anyway. The train would do him a favour.

He let his head fall back on to the wall behind him and he allowed his body to free itself of the tension and fear that had built since waking.

The noise grew to a deafening pitch and he waited.

Soon it'll be over, and this weird, cruel nightmare that had engulfed the last few days of his life would finally, mercifully, come to an end.

The roar approached fever pitch and his eyes saw a light cascading into the dark corner in which he found himself. He turned and saw there was a gap in the wall behind him, a few feet from where he sat, through which the light was pouring. The headlights from the approaching train. Must be.

He wasn't in the direct path of a train. Whoever, or whatever, had brought him to this place had had the good grace to hide his body inside some cavity, away from the tracks. Some opening in the brick-walled tunnel, like a cave.

His eyes turned from the shaft of light to the interior of his safe haven to avoid being blinded by the train's headlights. The train sped past and gave him just two seconds of illumination.

It was a two-second horror show. The train's lights had lit up the dark hole in the wall in which he found himself and it had been the most terrifying sight of his life.

Body parts.

Skulls.

Stacked up like accessories in a macabre store.

The pile of bodies was so dense, he'd mistaken it for a wall – just like the one he was seated against. But it wasn't a wall, at least not one made of bricks. He was staring at rotting flesh and mottled bones and empty eye sockets and nose cavities and skeletal fingers and headless torsos. Remnants of real people, now buried deep underground, abandoned, forgotten about. Stacked up like seasoned wood in a shed.

The lights passed by and he was plunged again into darkness. The deathly blackness of a mass grave.

CHAPTER 9

TUESDAY 7.15 A.M.

CRYPT, LONDON

Briefing Room 1 was vast but it didn't seem so as Bex and Jud entered. Every agent in the building was there. Some looked sleepier than others. You could tell the ones who'd been working early, or those, like Jud and Bex, who'd been thrust from their beds and given the SPA treatment at some ungodly hour.

Jud saw Luc at the back of the room and made straight for him. He'd saved him a chair, as usual.

Bex was left to drift aimlessly to the nearest available chair at the front. She sat down before her legs gave way.

'You all right?' said a skull in the seat next to her.

'Yeah, I'm OK,' said Bex. 'Stacey, isn't it?'

'Yeah. And I know who *you* are,' Stacey whispered.

'What?'

'Oh, come on! Anyone who gets paired up with Jud Lester as often as you do is bound to get known around here. So what did you do to deserve it?'

There was something in the way Stacey said it that told Bex this girl wasn't suggesting it was a punishment to be paired up with Jud. Another jealous agent?

'Whatever,' Bex said and gazed at the open door, waiting for Bonati to enter.

Stacey looked away. She cursed herself inside for opening her mouth. But this was the first time she'd sat so close to little Miss Perfect and she'd not been able to hide her jealousy. Stacey wasn't the only girl who wished she could be paired with Jud, just once at least. But this new girl on the block, with her fancy looks and too much confidence for Stacey's liking – well, she acted like she owned the guy.

Stacey was about to ask if Bex had come from the SPAs – why else would she look like she'd seen a ghost at this time in the morning? – but Bonati entered the room, followed by Vorzek, and a hush fell on the assembled group.

'Morning. Thank you for coming,' said the professor, making straight for the podium at the front. 'I'll get straight to the point.'

The agents sat up immediately when they saw a third person enter the room. It was Jason Goode.

'OK, this must be serious,' Stacey whispered. It was unusual to see the owner of Goode Technology PLC in person. Though Goode funded the entire CRYPT enterprise, he was rarely in the country, let alone on the premises; to see him so unexpectedly caused a stir.

And there was something different in Bonati's voice. They all noticed it as soon as he began. He was speaking quickly and there was a breathlessness to him – perhaps he'd run down the corridor, not wanting to be late. Unlikely. Or was he *nervous*? The professor was never nervous! Not even around Jason Goode, whom he'd known since they were at college together.

'Something's up,' whispered Luc to Jud. 'You can sense it.'

Vorzek and Goode stood to Bonati's left, just inside the doorway, and scanned the faces of the zombies and skulls in front of them. Goode clocked Jud's eye and allowed an almost imperceptible lifting of one eyebrow. It was as close to 'Hello' as they were ever going to get in these situations.

It was always so torturous seeing one another – father and son – but being unable to express anything more than a subtle raise of an eyebrow or a nod of the head.

Although, as they both knew, being alone together usually proved just as awkward. Since Jud's release from prison he'd spent so little time with his father, at least in the role he would have preferred – Jamie. So when they were able to chat more honestly with each other they had so little to say and the conversation was always punctuated by awkward pauses and banal phrases like, 'Well, how's it going, J?' or 'How's work, Dad? Been busy?'

As he stared at Goode now, Jud swept any homesickness or feelings of affection back into their rightful corner, buried deep in the shadows of his consciousness. He'd moved beyond that now. Had to. Self-preservation was vital. His mother was gone forever, and his father was a stranger to him.

And that was that. Move on.

He turned his attention to Bonati, who was still looking anxious.

'You'll be wondering why I've dragged you out of your beds,' said Bonati, his expression serious.

'You're kidding,' Jud whispered to Luc. 'I've already been to hell and back this morning.'

Luc smiled sympathetically.

'Well,' Bonati continued, 'it's been an eventful night, it seems. I've had a call from MI5. And I have some grave news for you.'

CHAPTER 10

TUESDAY 8.21 A.M.

KNIGHTSBRIDGE, LONDON

Two black Honda Fireblades turned a corner and screeched up Gore Street. Blue flashing lights told their riders where to go. It was obvious. Ticker tape stretched across the road and there was an ambulance and two police cars parked nearby.

A crowd of people was gathering. Some were still dressed in dressing gowns and fluffy slippers; others were in suits and ties, ready for work. All wore worried expressions.

The bikes halted at the scene and their riders dismounted.

'So, no chance of investigating in silence then,' said Grace, taking off her helmet and placing it on the black leather seat.

'No, but then what did you expect?' said Luc.

A police officer joined them.

'Can I help you?' she said. Her mood looked far from helpful.

'Yeah, we're from MI5. We're here to—'

'No need to explain,' said the officer. 'I've been briefed to expect you. I just didn't realise you'd be so—'

'So *young*?' said Grace.

'Well, er, no, I mean . . .' She looked embarrassed now.

'Whatever,' said Luc. 'Just show us to the body, please.'

The officer led them down the steps and into the tiny

basement garden, now crowded with officers, paramedics and pathologists in white boiler suits.

'Miss Charlotte Maughan,' said the officer, gazing in the direction of the corpse. 'Lives alone. Aged forty-one.'

Grace saw the dead woman's face and stopped.

'You OK?' said Luc.

'Yes, of course I'm OK,' snapped Grace.

'It's just that I saw you pause.'

'I'm taking it in, sensing this place!' said Grace. 'Isn't that what we're supposed to do?'

'OK, OK. Let's try and get some space around here.' Luc turned to the female officer who'd brought them down. 'Can we have a few minutes down here alone?'

She wanted to snap, 'Don't be ridiculous,' but she had been expecting them to say that. DCI Khan had already called and told her to expect some 'special agents', as he called them. He'd not said much more than that, only that they would need to conduct their tests alone.

She spoke to the others present and reluctantly they turned, shot Luc and Grace disapproving glances and headed up the steps on to the street.

'Ten minutes,' said a man in a white boiler suit. 'Then the body's mine. Try not to destroy the evidence, won't you?'

Luc knelt down to the corpse. Bonati had been quite correct in the briefing room. He'd warned them that it was not going to be pretty. But he'd also said that the body at St Edmund's was even worse. Luc wondered what Jud and Bex would be seeing now.

'She's been slashed,' he said to Grace.

'Yeah. Knife?'

'Of course it's not a knife!' came a voice from above. They turned and saw the man in the white boiler suit – the pathologist – shaking his head at them. 'Look at the width of the gashes. It's not a blade that's done that.'

'So what is it?' Luc shouted up. He'd had enough of this man's arrogance.

'I thought that's what you're here to tell us,' the man said. 'I heard you were the experts.'

CRYPT agents were used to such disrespect. The relationship between the CRYPT and the authorities who joined them at crime scenes was always a difficult one. Police officers and medical experts rarely took them seriously. Those who knew who they were – as this man might do – usually teased them for being so young. They often said they'd come from the 'crib' not the CRYPT, an unsubtle reference to their youthful faces. And those who didn't know who they were could be even less hospitable. No one liked being told by senior commanders that 'special agents' were attending and they should just 'leave them to it'.

But CRYPT agents had to be young. That was the point. Despite the teasing, the 'grown-ups', as they liked to think of themselves, knew very well that the extrasensory perception of these teenagers made them invaluable. And although the CRYPT remained a covert and elusive branch of MI5, they were developing a reputation in the inner circles of power for cracking cases with a hundred per cent efficiency. They'd not failed yet to identify the paranormal causes behind some brutal crimes and be able to end the hauntings quickly.

Besides, you had to admire their courage. Even the man in the white boiler suit giving them a condescending look would have run a mile if a ghost had appeared.

They watched as the same officer who had greeted them talked to the man in the white suit and soon enough they were gone from the railings.

Alone at last.

Alone with the brutally mutilated body of a woman dressed for a night out. Her elegance was a cruel contrast to the desperate way she'd been found, according to the officers, lying face down in a flower bed with her dress hitched up past her knees.

She was now flat out on the hard concrete, staring at the sky. They noticed there were dark scabs at the top of her forehead, near her hairline. Bruises?

And at her wrists too. Dark, weepy sores, like some itchy skin complaint. Scabs that wouldn't go away.

Luc lifted her hand, and saw the fleshy socket, now hardened, where the finger once was. Bonati had said in the briefing that this was a strange feature of the killing. And it did look weird now.

'Don't touch that!' shouted Grace.

'What?'

'The hand. Leave it!'

'Why?' said Luc, placing the cold, stiffened hand back on to the body. 'Do you feel something, Grace?'

'Yes. When you did that. When you picked up that hand. I felt it in *my* hand.'

'What do you mean?'

She lifted up her left hand and showed him. 'Here, I felt a jabbing pain just here.' She was pointing to her knuckle just below her wedding ring finger.

'Really?' said Luc. 'What do you think it means?'

Grace shook her head gently, a pensive expression on her face. 'I don't know. But it has to be significant. Whatever it was that visited this place in the night, it was after that finger.'

She stepped closer to the dead woman and examined her face: her thin, pursed lips, her greying skin, her bruised, swollen eyes. Grace could hardly make out the pupils, but she saw something in those eyes. And she knew what it was. She'd seen it before.

Pure terror.

'I don't know what this woman saw, Luc, but it wasn't human.'

'I agree,' he said. 'And I have a feeling we're going to find out just what it was.'

CHAPTER 11

TUESDAY 8.50 A.M.

CHELSEA SQUARE, LONDON

'Come on, come on!' Antonia said, not in a voice that Tamara could hear but one that gave vent to her frustration.

Why did this happen every time? Tamara was such a lazybones, a sleepyhead, a bedbug. Antonia called her friend all the usual clichés. Basically, she just didn't like getting out of bed in the morning.

And that was particularly bad for Antonia because she was her best friend and the one charged with taking Tamara shopping every Saturday morning.

She pressed the buzzer again, checking she had the right one out of a long line of identical buzzers – Flat 11, yes.

No voice emerged through the little metal box. Tamara was still in bed, no question.

Antonia chided herself for even bothering to buzz first – when had Tamara ever been up and ready? That's why she'd given her a spare set of keys. But the lift was usually busy and the stairs were tiring. Maybe one day Tamara would answer the buzzer, say, 'Hi, I'm on my way down,' and spare Antonia the pain of trudging up to the flat and then all the way back down again.

She placed the shiny Yale key in the lock and turned. She was in. The building, like the other ones either side of it in this leafy and exclusive part of Chelsea, was a large, Georgian terraced house. Like so many buildings in London, it would have been a fine and impressive family home once, servants beavering away in the kitchens downstairs, lords and ladies conversing politely upstairs. But today it was yet another block of private flats – luxury apartments, as the local agents liked to call them. Though the way of life of the Victorian gentry had vanished long ago, the grandeur of the entrance hall remained. High ceilings, marble columns, beautiful tiled floors, large sash windows.

Antonia felt sure that most of the residents were proprietorial about the place, pretending it was all theirs. You couldn't help it. That was just the point, and the reason why these 'luxury apartments' were among the most expensive in all of Chelsea – and Chelsea was seriously expensive to begin with.

But not Tamara, she was different. Although she probably had more money than everyone in the building put together – her father owned his own shipping company and she was his only child – Tamara didn't give the impression of being heiress to a fortune. She was kooky and funky. She worked hard in the job she had – her father had arranged some PR job in the city for her – and to her credit she was making the most of it. She worked hard and she played hard.

But on Saturdays, trying to get her out of bed? Impossible.

The lift was free, thank goodness. It 'pinged' softly when it reached Tamara's floor and the doors slid aside, revealing another impressive marble corridor and her best friend's front door down the end on the right.

Antonia knocked.

Nothing.

She knocked again. 'Hello?'

Typical! she thought. Just like every Saturday. Still in bed snoring, while I've been halfway across London already.

She placed the second key in the lock and turned it.

There was a smell that filled her nostrils as soon as the door opened.

Was that burnt toast?

She knew her friend had always had a penchant for late-night toast frenzies. It went back to their time together at uni. They'd chomp their way through half a loaf on a good night. Or bad night for their waistlines.

'Tammy? You up?'

There was no answer from her friend's bedroom.

The flat was a bit of a mess, but that wasn't unusual. If Tamara was the lively, kooky one in the friendship, Antonia was the motherly one. She was forever tidying her mate's apartment, and it looked like today was no different.

She'd get her out of bed first, put the coffee on – Tamara had a particularly gorgeous coffee machine which Antonia envied – and then set to work tidying up her abandoned clothes while her friend showered and changed.

It was a familiar routine every shopping day.

For dignity's sake she knocked on Tamara's bedroom door. She didn't want to catch her in the buff.

No answer.

She gently pushed open the door.

Her eyes widened and her mouth dropped open and she let out a scream that was like an animal's – the kind you hear from vixens in the night.

Tammy was spread across the bed, still wearing her evening clothes.

But Antonia knew she was dead.

Her head was slumped at right angles to her body and there was a giant gash across her neck. The white satin sheets were crimson. And the terror-struck expression on her face chilled Antonia to the bone.

This wasn't happening. This was a nightmare. She'd wake up soon. Wouldn't she?

Oh God.

Antonia was in a spin. Her heart was pounding as though it was about to burst out of her ribcage.

The tears were flowing now. Great salty drops rolling down her cheeks. Tammy was her soulmate, her partner in crime, her shopping buddy and the only one she could tell her secrets to.

And now she lay mutilated and torn.

What the hell had gone on in this flat?

And then it struck her in the pit of her stomach. Was the perpetrator still here?

She quickly shut the door and stood against it, staring back at the macabre scene. It was like something out of a horror film. Her friend's skin was grey. And the blood. There was so much of it. Tammy looked pitiful. Like a slab of meat on a white marble butcher's block.

If her slashed and broken neck wasn't shocking enough, Antonia noticed the state of Tammy's right hand. Her middle finger had gone, leaving nothing but a soggy, fleshy socket, oozing blood.

CHAPTER 12

TUESDAY 9.01 A.M.

ST EDMUND'S HOSPITAL, LONDON

Jud felt weird. There was something strangely familiar about the place. Maybe it was the stark white walls and the long empty corridors. Or the smell. Or the gloomy atmosphere, but something was serving as a reminder to him.

A reminder of a past life. Jamie Goode, locked up in the young offenders' institution.

A frustration was creeping into him, like a shadow slowly descending. A claustrophobia.

As he and Bex followed the tired and irritable Dr Withers down the corridor, deeper into the remotest part of the hospital, he couldn't help but remember those long, lonely days spent wishing the ghosts had claimed him instead of his mother.

The time in prison had seemed distant of late, but this place was bringing it back into sharp focus. And Jud was disappointed to see himself so unsettled. He thought he was over it.

But deep down he knew he'd never get over something like that. Wrongly accused of taking your own mother's life? Sent away to an institution, your life in tatters? Could anyone recover from that?

It was the remoteness of the place that came back to him now. You could have been anywhere on the planet. All the usual indicators – the shops, the signposts, the crowds, the streets – had been removed from Jamie. Or he had been removed from them, that was the point. Imprisoned both for his own safety – the public's reaction to a boy killing his own mother had been one of revulsion and hatred – and for the apparent safety of the public themselves. As if Jamie was a threat to the public!

He didn't do it in the first place.

Now, walking down this loveless corridor in the oldest part of the rundown hospital, Jud could almost hear the mantra re-entering his head and rattling around inside it, just as it did back then, in prison.

'The ghosts did it! The ghosts did it!'

No one had believed him except his father and the professor.

He suddenly became aware he was clenching his fists by his side. And his jaw was clenched too. Bex couldn't help but notice as she walked alongside him.

'You all right?'

'What? Er . . . yeah. Of course I'm all right. Why?'

'You just look tense, that's all. I thought maybe it was the vaccination—'

'I'm fine!' Jud interrupted her with a frown that said, 'Leave it'.

They'd each received a vaccination before coming to St Edmund's. Khan had briefed Bonati on the condition of the man now missing from the East Wing and he was taking no chances. The hospital staff, police officers, and now his own CRYPT agents were being vaccinated. The briefing that morning had ended with each of the agents filing out of the room and receiving injections in the sickbay before they went on their ways. A rude awakening for many of the sleepy ones, only recently out of bed.

Jud's arm ached now, but otherwise he was fine.

'You OK?' he said to Bex, more kindly this time. He felt bad for snapping at her. It wasn't her fault they were in this depressing place. She'd not been keen to come either. Or keen to have the vaccination, for that matter. She hated injections.

'Yeah, I'm OK,' she said. 'My shoulder feels a bit tender, but it's nothing compared to what I think we're about to see.'

They returned to silence again, as Jud looked forward to yet another gruesome haunting to distract him from the horrors that still lurked inside his own mind.

Within a few minutes they were outside the double doors that led to the East Wing. They watched Withers key in the pass code, the doors released and they kicked the metal footplates open.

Bex stopped.

'You feel that?' she said to Jud.

'Yeah. This place is alive with energy. Something's been here and it wasn't visiting to say hello. It was angry.'

The doctor looked incredulously at them. 'What are you talking about?'

Jud dismissed the conversation quickly. 'Oh, nothing, we've just been to so many crime scenes it's almost like we can sense what's gone on there. Keeps us amused.'

'Oh, right. I see.' Dr Withers wasn't sure if these kids were for real. The police had told him that crime scene investigators would be arriving to take fingerprints, photographs and any other evidence they could find to piece together what had happened. 'Isn't that what you guys do anyway?' the doctor had asked but the officers had told him that these agents were different. While the police focused on finding the perpetrators, the agents focused on the crime scene itself. It was just another dimension to the investigation. Nothing to worry about.

Bex stopped in her tracks.

'What was that?' She'd heard a desperate shout.

'Oh, that's just the old boy in Ward B,' said Withers. 'He's been having nightmares. He's rambling *again*! He's the bane of my life!'

Withers' insensitivity made Jud feel like punching him in the face but he decided perhaps now wasn't the time.

Jud and Bex knew about this man already. He was the reason they were there, though the doctor didn't know it. Bonati's briefing earlier that morning had told them how DCI Khan had visited the place and heard someone rambling about a ghost.

And if the doctor had known what Khan and the agents knew now, he wouldn't have dismissed it so easily.

When, in the early hours, the inspector had received reports of a body in Knightsbridge, his officers on the scene had said some old woman had talked about seeing a masked ghost. Was it the same one?

This was no delirious rambling. There had to be something in it. So Khan had followed the usual channels – called MI5 and they in turn had briefed Bonati.

And now here they were, leading agents Jud and Bex, to meet the guy in person, see for themselves the terror fixed across his face.

Up ahead they could see the slumped figure of a body on the floor – the dead nurse. They knew there was much work to be done – taking readings for any electromagnetism or residues of electrostatic energy on the body or around it. But the old man was potentially an eyewitness. He was too important to ignore. The body could wait.

They entered Ward B.

'What're you doing?' said Withers. 'I mean, what is it with this man? First the inspector, now you guys. Anyone would think there wasn't a dead body just up there, you all seem more interested in this patient. We can't leave poor Emily there forever.'

'I understand, Doctor. We'll see her in a moment, sir,' said Jud.

'The ghost!' The old man was shouting again. His head was shaking and his body was rocking on the bed. 'The man with the beak! I saw 'im. I saw what he *did*!'

'So it wasn't the missing patient?' said Dr Withers, now joining them at the bedside.

'No! Of course it wasn't 'im!' he said. 'I could've told you that, couldn't I?'

'Well, go on then,' said Jud. 'Tell us exactly what you saw.'

CHAPTER 13

TUESDAY 9.48 A.M.

BONATI'S OFFICE, CRYPT, LONDON

'It's what?' said Bonati, incredulously.

'It's happened again,' said Khan.

The professor got up from his chair and paced the floor of his cluttered office.

'Where?'

'Chelsea. A young woman. She was found by her friend this morning.'

'Same injuries?'

'Pretty much,' said Khan. 'Throat cut. Finger missing.'

'And anyone see any ghosts this time?'

The inspector shook his head. 'That's not to say there weren't any, though.'

'No, thank you, Inspector. I know that. Any news on the missing patient?'

The inspector shook his head, miserably. 'The missing suspect, you mean. No, not as far as I know.'

'I'd reserve judgement on that if I were you. I suspect he was more victim than perpetrator,' said Bonati.

'I guess that's for you to find out, isn't it?' said Khan. 'We'll do our job and you do yours, Professor.'

'But it doesn't change the fact that we've got someone on the loose in London with a highly contagious disease. People at the British Medical Association are worried, I can tell you.'

'Don't I know it,' said Khan. 'Who do you think I called after I'd left St Edmund's? You've spoken to the BMA as well then?'

'Yes, of course. How do you think I got the agents vaccinated so quickly? We hooked up with St Thomas's and they sent the vaccinations over.'

'Well done. I gather the PM's called a meeting with the Health Minister and the BMA. They'll be coordinating efforts as we speak, no doubt.'

'OK. Well, at least it's not the 1600s,' said Bonati. 'We've got some antibiotics. But have we got enough, should this thing spread, do you think?'

Khan shrugged. 'I don't know. We've got to contain this. Bubonic plague is the classic kind of fast-spreading disease you'd see in a bioterror attack, so I guess the government have already got the medicine stockpiled.'

'And you said that your officers reported seeing black sores on the body at Knightsbridge too, yes?'

Khan nodded his head. 'And on this girl in Chelsea, apparently.'

'There's something really worrying about this one, Inspector. It's different to other cases. There're too many factors here. The ghost sightings, the missing fingers, the plague symptoms. If – and it's a very big if, mind – if the ghosts are in some way connected to this outbreak of bubonic plague, then God help us. It could spread like wildfire. There are no limits where the paranormal is concerned. But I've never seen anything quite like this before. Scaring the public, attacking the public even, I've seen ghosts do it all, but I've never seen disembodied spirits *carrying* a disease that spreads to humans. This is *serious*.'

The two men looked at each other in silence. A palpable sense of foreboding had swept into the room like an invisible odour.

A sudden buzz from the phone on Bonati's desk broke the eerie silence.

'Yes?' he snapped. 'Oh, sorry, it's you, Jason.' He looked at Khan and rolled his eyes. 'What? *Now*? Well, I've got Khan here with me. When? Who was it? All right, all right. We'll see you in five.' He replaced the phone on the desk and turned to Khan. 'Jason wants to see us.'

'Both of us?'

'Yes. Now. He says he's just received a phone call. He won't tell me what it's about until we're face to face.'

'Blimey. Well, whoever just called him, they sure as hell haven't called me yet.'

'Or me,' said Bonati. 'There's very little that escapes my notice in this city, just like you, Inspector. So if Jason knows something we don't know, I'm not sure I want to hear it.'

'Mm . . .' said Khan, a worried look etched into his tired face. 'Me neither.'

A few minutes later they were exiting the lift on the thirty-eighth floor of Goode Tower – Jason Goode's own penthouse. They walked slowly down the marble corridor, Bonati taking care to walk as far from the floor-to-ceiling windows as he could manage. His vertigo had not eased despite so many trips up here. If anything, it was getting worse.

The automatic doors to Goode's suite opened before they'd had chance to ring the buzzer. The whole place was lined with CCTV and Jason had already seen them arrive. He often found it amusing watching his old friend exit the lift and walk wearily down the corridor, his legs shaking and his face twitching nervously, trying to avoid any glimpses of the cavernous drop below.

But as the doors swung open, they could see that Goode was in no mood for jokes today. He was sitting at his desk, a large, glass-topped structure fashioned in a sweeping curve that seemed to dwarf him. The black executive chair was taller than his back and it enclosed his body like a photo frame.

'What's happened, Jason?' Bonati came straight to the point as he sat down in one of the giant leather sofas opposite the desk.

'Morning, Khan,' said Goode, ignoring the professor. 'Nice to see you again. Do sit down.'

The inspector sat next to Bonati, resting on the edge of the seat and chewing his nails.

'Well?' said Bonati, impatiently.

'OK, Giles. I'll tell you what's happened. I've had a call from the DG.'

'The Director General of MI5?' said Bonati.

'The very same.'

'Why? What does he want?'

'It seems there's yet another victim for us to contend with now. Another haunting.'

'Yes,' said Bonati. 'At Chelsea. I know. Khan's just told me.'

'No. Let me finish,' said Goode. 'It's not at Chelsea. It's . . . well, it's at a classified location.'

'Look, what is this, Jason? You're talking in riddles. Tell me what's going on!'

Goode shifted in his chair and fiddled with a silver fountain pen on his desk. Then he looked uneasily out of the giant window across the room. The cityscape moved almost imperceptibly from left to right as the giant penthouse turned through its slow revolution.

'I shall tell you the location in a second, but it's classified to everyone else. No one needs to know where it happened.'

'Where *what* happened?' said Khan, beginning to share Bonati's impatience.

'A woman has received a visitation from a spirit, it seems. She survived, but she's unwell – very unwell, I'd say. She's showing signs of this damn plague we're hearing so much about.'

'OK, but why should the Director General of MI5 call you to tell you that, Jason? Why is he personally involved?' said Bonati.

Goode placed his pen down on the desk and stared straight at the two men.

'Because this time, gentlemen, the victim . . . is his wife.'

CHAPTER 14

TUESDAY 10.48 A.M.

PICCADILLY LINE, SOUTH

KENSINGTON, LONDON

Adam McNeal was dying. But he was stubborn too, always had been, and he was determined that this should not be his final resting place, a dark, unidentified mass grave of decomposing bodies hidden somewhere beneath London.

He may have been single, with little or no family to speak of; he may have received no visitors in the hospital, and it had seemed like no one cared whether he was alive or dead, but *he* cared where he was going to die.

And it wasn't here.

The two attempts he'd made so far to leave the deathly cave built into the side of the tube tunnel had been foiled. It had taken him all his energy to rise to his feet. The disease was stripping him of strength. But he had finally made it to the opening in the wall – twice now – and each time he had been about to set foot on the tracks a rumble in the distance and a flickering light had told him a train was approaching and he had thrown his body backwards into the cavity once again.

Two failed attempts at escaping. And now, as he sat in the same spot again, slumped against the wall, he knew he had to face the fact that he may never escape this place.

But he was going to try.

Slowly, he bent his legs upwards and staggered to his feet. His head felt like glass; the soaring temperature of his body was reaching critical point and he knew he was going to pass out again soon. He'd been slipping in and out of consciousness since first waking down there. But he was not to be defeated. He was not going to be another skeleton on the pile.

Another rumble, a rising din and a few seconds later another set of blinding lights swept past, lighting up the macabre scene.

Why were these bodies here? How long had they been dumped here? By the looks of them, many, many years. But the smell was rancid. Decaying human flesh must surely be the very worst smell on earth. He knew that now. He'd thrown up several times already, though it had been just bile. There was nothing inside him. His body was withering away. Cruel then that it still brought on the violent, painful convulsions of nausea, even when there was nothing to throw up.

He held on to the wall and straightened his back further until he was almost upright. He couldn't stand up fully, the ceiling of the space was too low and, in any case, his spine ripped and pulled in pain as he stood up.

He clambered his way back towards the opening. What had he got to lose? This time he would launch himself on to the tracks and try to find a station. If a train hit him, fine.

As he stepped cautiously out of the opening and lowered his foot on to the metal track he heard something.

It wasn't a train.

It was the terrified scream of a woman.

He looked in the direction of the sound, along the wall to his left, deeper into the tunnel.

There it was again.

Getting nearer.

He paused. Should he go back into the cave of bodies, wait for a train to end it all, or go and see what was causing the scream?

He went for the latter and edged his way further into the tunnel, trying valiantly to cling to the wall in the faint hope that, should a train come hurtling past, there would be enough of a gap to spare his life – or what was left of it.

As he trudged on he could see a faint spread of light cascading towards him, from what must have been wall lights further up ahead – the lights of a platform perhaps.

And then he saw it. Fear struck him like a blow in the solar plexus, winding him and leaving him gasping for air. A dark figure, up ahead.

In the dim light he could see the white, elongated beak. As the figure approached he could see the black eye sockets and the angular, white mask. The body was engulfed in a black shroud but McNeal could see it was clutching something, or dragging it.

And whatever it was, it was screaming for its life.

A young woman. Incoherent with terror. Kicking and screaming and lashing out, but to no avail. The figure was strong and resolute. It gripped the woman like a vice and just kept walking, undeterred, towards McNeal and the cave behind him. The final resting place for another unwilling occupant.

McNeal breathed deeply and kept on walking. He was going to save her. He had nothing to lose. Nothing at all.

CHAPTER 15

TUESDAY 11.00 A.M.

BRIEFING ROOM 1, CRYPT, LONDON

'Thank you, everyone, settle down, settle down. There's much to discuss and very little time.'

The briefing room was alive with speculation. The agents had returned promptly: Luc and Grace from Knightsbridge, Jud and Bex from St Edmund's, and the two skulls, Nik and Stacey, had come from the flat in Chelsea, where they'd met officers investigating the killing of Tamara Lytton.

'Now listen,' said Bonati, abruptly. 'I want to thank you for getting to the locations so promptly and gathering evidence. You'll appreciate time is of the essence. We need to hear from all of you, and quickly. I want to hear progress. I need to know we're getting to the bottom of this. And I'll tell you why. I'm seeing the Director General of MI5 shortly. Frankly, I should be there now, but I want to have something to report when I get there. I want to be able to tell him not to worry as we're making progress – that's why I've called you together again.'

'The DG?' said Jud, surprised. 'Why's *he* involved, sir?'

Bonati looked at the door behind him, to check it was shut. His eyes shifted furtively across the room. He didn't know what he was scanning for, the room was totally secure and was filled with nothing but reliable agents, but he knew the classified information he was about to share was so significant, any leaks would be a disaster. He glanced in Khan's direction. The inspector gave him a knowing nod to suggest 'go ahead'.

'Well, it seems we have another victim to add to our growing list. Although fortunately this time the person concerned has not died . . . yet.'

The professor filled them in with the latest news of the DG's wife.

There were incredulous gasps. The wife of the DG? It didn't seem real. Organisations like MI5 and MI6 were so anonymous, it was easy to forget that they were staffed by ordinary, fallible and vulnerable human beings.

'But when, where?'

'What time was this?'

'Is anyone with her now?'

Questions were fired at the professor like arrows from all directions across the room.

'One at a time, please,' he said, calmly. 'Let's keep our sensible heads on, shall we? Yes, of course someone is with her now. I've sent Dr Vorzek and a couple of skulls over there already. I shall be joining them, with Jud and Bex, please, as soon as this meeting is finished.'

Nik and Stacey looked at each other and rolled their eyes surreptitiously. 'Typical,' Nik whispered. 'The royal bloody couple.'

Khan smiled at the churlish comment.

Bonati had heard it too but he had no intention of wasting precious time discussing such childish jealousies. Jud and Bex's track record proved they were the best agents they'd got, no question. So there was no point in debating it now. And today he was going to need the very best. The DG would settle for nothing less.

'But before we go, I'm determined to have more to tell the

DG. I've got to show we're on top of this. So tell me what you've found.' He turned to Luc and Grace. 'Right, let's have you first. Tell us what you found in Knightsbridge.'

The next twenty minutes were filled with each pair of agents reporting what they'd seen and sensed at each location.

Everyone agreed there was real terror etched across the victims' faces. And the readings were significant. The bodies had all given off high levels of electromagnetic and electrostatic energy. Nik said it was a wonder she wasn't lit up like a Christmas tree, the amount of radiation Tamara Lytton had given off.

Few appreciated his gallows humour.

There was evidence to suggest that each corpse had had direct physical contact with a disembodied spirit. Such high levels of radiation in the vicinity pointed to that conclusion.

Besides, there were the strange reports from the eyewitnesses – the old man at the hospital and the female resident at Gore Street – both describing the same kind of ghost. Even the agents themselves, hardened by countless encounters with disembodied spirits, felt a slight chill when they allowed theirs minds to piece together the descriptions: tall figure, black shroud, white mask and that disturbing, beak-like nose protruding from the face.

Bonati confirmed that this was what the DG's wife had claimed she'd seen in the night too.

'So how come she survived, when the others didn't, sir?' said Grace.

'Good question. And no doubt we'll find out when we get there, though I suspect it's because the ghost was disturbed. The DG got home late perhaps and his movements unsettled the spirit. I don't know.'

'There's a pattern emerging,' said Jud.

'Go on,' said Bonati.

'Well, think about it. The others, this girl from Chelsea, the woman in Knightsbridge and now the DG's wife. What do they all have in common?'

Everyone looked at him expectantly but said nothing. The question was rhetorical. When Jud was on the scent of something, you didn't interrupt him with your own theories.

'They're not short of money, are they?' he continued. 'I mean, the DG's address may be classified but it's not going to be some tenement block in Peckham now, is it?'

'OK,' said Bonati. 'So?'

'No, hang on,' interrupted Stacey. 'The nurse at St Edmund's Hospital. You're not telling me *she* was loaded, are you?'

'Well,' said Jud, 'according to the eyewitness at the hospital, the ghost was after someone else and the poor nurse got in the way.'

'Of course,' said Bonati. 'The missing patient.'

'But we don't yet know if he was wealthy, do we, sir?' said Luc.

Bonati turned to Khan. 'Inspector?'

'Yes, it seems Adam McNeal was very wealthy indeed. Lived in Kensington. Single. Lots of spending money, I'd guess.'

'Look, why does this matter?' said Nik, impatiently. 'I mean, are you saying the ghost was targeting rich toffs or something?'

There was a small ripple of sniggers but few people were interested in Nik's attempts at point-scoring. They could see in Jud's piercing eyes that he was on to something. And he was never wrong.

'No,' snapped Jud. 'I'm just trying to find some common ground here. A connection. And it's true that all the victims were wealthy. I don't know what that means but it seems more than a coincidence.'

'Maybe,' said Bonati. 'And the missing fingers?'

'Well, we know that one thing rich people like to wear is expensive jewellery, sir,' said Bex, keen to support Jud's emerging theory.

Nik laughed. 'Great, so the ghost is a jewel thief, is that the theory, Lester? I mean, what the hell is a ghost gonna do with rings, huh?'

Jud didn't take the bait. He was used to Nik's teasing. He just looked at him calmly and said, 'Any better ideas, Einstein?'

'Well, there's the sores and the scabs,' said Grace. 'Don't forget that. We've said that we saw black scabs on the victims' bodies at Knightsbridge and Nik and Stacey saw them on the body at Chelsea. And we know the missing man at St Edmund's was covered.'

'Stacey's right,' said Luc. 'And the ones we saw on the woman at Knightsbridge didn't look like they'd been caused by the attack somehow. They looked older than that. Maybe a few days.'

'Now that *is* interesting,' said the professor, 'because I understand from MI5 that the DG's wife is showing similar symptoms.'

'She is?' said Bex, incredulously. 'So it's *really* serious.'

'Well, we don't know for sure. But believe me, she's drugged up to the eyeballs with antibiotics, just in case.' He looked at his watch. 'And it's time we visited her. Jud, Bex, let's go.' He stood up. 'The rest of you, I want you to research the bubonic plague. I want to know how it started, where it started and when. I want a bloody history lecture when I get back.'

Khan stood up too. 'And I'll get my officers on to this jewellery connection.' He gave a supportive nod in Jud's direction. 'You never know. I'll check to see if any of the victims had bought expensive rings recently. Worth a try.'

CHAPTER 16

TUESDAY 11.08 A.M.

PICCADILLY LINE, SOUTH

KENSINGTON, LONDON

McNeal paused to take a breath. The air was damp and musty, tainted with the smell of rotting corpses from the macabre cave behind him.

He was still moving towards the figure, which was looming ever closer. The woman's screams were now conjoined into one long animal-like wail that echoed around the brick tunnel.

Quite how he was going to rescue the woman, or whether a train would soon come and end it for him anyway, he wasn't sure. But he had nothing to lose.

As the masked ghost came within striking distance, McNeal went for it. Though the ghost was a foreboding shape, McNeal was himself a large man, taller than average and thickset, or had been once, before the ravages of the disease had taken their toll. But the anger inside him, and the determination to help, had brought a new-found strength from somewhere deep inside him. He had nothing to lose.

He threw himself on the figure, ducking beneath that terrifying, elongated beak that shot out of the front of its mask like an ivory horn.

He had unsettled the ghost, no question. Though it was blessed with the strength of ten men, it was unsteady on its feet, the weight of the woman under its arm making it difficult to stay upright in the tiny space between the metal train tracks and the curved walls of the tunnel.

It toppled slightly. McNeal pushed harder. The ghost fell on to the tracks. A strange, clicking sound was emitted from its mouth, half human whisper, half mechanical, and it chilled McNeal to the bone.

The young woman had taken advantage of the ghost's fall and struggled free.

'Here! Hold my hand!' shouted McNeal.

The woman, unnerved, looked at him. His face was blistered with pus-filled sores. His hair was matted and his clothes wreaked of the same rank smell that had been wafting towards her seconds ago.

'I thought you were dead, like the rest of them,' said the woman, shaking uncontrollably.

'What do you mean?' said McNeal, incredulously, pulling her towards him.

'I saw you before . . . down in the cave.' She was pointing a trembling finger over his shoulder as she clutched on to his body for comfort. 'It's where I was dumped too. God knows how I got there, I don't remember. But when I came to, I tried to get out this way, through the tunnel.'

'And you were caught?'

'Yeah. I heard the ghost behind me – it must've come out of the tunnel moments after I left the cave and followed me.' She glanced at the ghostly figure sprawled out over the tracks and shuddered. 'What's going on?' she said imploringly, like a lost child.

McNeal shook his head. 'I don't know how we got here, or why, but all I know is we've gotta get out. *Now*.'

As he said it they watched the ghost stir on the tracks. Quickly McNeal stepped off the platform and kicked and stamped feverishly on the ghost. His head was pounding, he was sweating profusely and he felt an overwhelming urge to throw up again, but still he fought on, stabbing at the black figure on the floor with his blistered feet. There was a crunch of something bone-like as the figure's frame crumpled under his feet like broken sticks. But still it was moving, its determination seemed impregnable.

There was a low, resonant growl far off in the distance and it sent vibrations humming down the tracks towards them.

'A train!' said McNeal, abandoning the ghost and grabbing the woman by the arm. 'Come on! This way!'

The woman couldn't move. Something was holding her foot.

She glanced down and saw the vice-like grip of a skeletal hand clamped round her left ankle.

The ghost was still defiant. Its frame rose up and it turned to face them. The long nose and the black eye sockets were chilling in the gloomy half-light.

'Ignore it. Stay close to the wall!' shouted McNeal. 'And breathe in!'

The noise rose and the whole scene was lit up by the bright headlamps of the tube train. There was the sound of screeching as brakes were applied.

But it was too late. There was no way the train could be stopped so quickly.

The woman closed her eyes and squeezed herself up against the tunnel wall. The ghost's grip on her ankle had loosened as it tried to stagger to its feet. But there was no time for them to flee. The relative safety of the cave was several metres back down the tracks but the train was now just feet away.

So this was it. They braced themselves. There was no way the gap would be wide enough. The train would have them, along with the ghost.

The screeching and grinding rose to a deafening pitch but the train didn't stop, it kept moving.

Inside the cab, the driver was stiff with fear, his eyes wide and transfixed by the sight in front of him – a white masked figure pressed up against the glass, its black, eyeless sockets staring at him. Its long beak-like nose had snapped at the end and out of it leaked a dark, green fluid that spread across the train window like algae.

The ghost's body had folded and broken like brittle sticks once again. Only this time it was dragged along the tunnel, past McNeal and the terrified girl next to him. As the carriages passed them, with just inches to spare, an icy wind blew into their faces. But they were alive. There was room. They'd survived, for now at least.

Inside the train, passengers were comforting one another. The sound of the screeching of brakes and the juddering of the carriages had led them all to believe a crash was imminent.

Some crouched down in their seats, while others sank to the floor and clasped their knees up to their heads for cover. Only a handful of passengers caught sight of the outline of two people, hiding in the darkness, pale, sickly faces screwed up tight as they waited for impact.

What the hell were they doing there? Was this the reason for the brakes?

'It's OK!' someone yelled inside a carriage as it pulled passed the sight. 'It can't be a crash, there's no other train. It must be suicide attempts. It's so selfish – I mean, if you want to commit suicide, why does it have to be down here?'

The train ground to a halt further along the tunnel. The driver was slumped over the steering controls, his heart pounding inside his chest.

McNeal turned to the woman at his side. She released a breath and slumped slowly to the floor, whimpering uncontrollably.

'It's OK,' he said. 'It's OK. We're safe. And they'll come and get us now.'

She looked up at him but kept sobbing and shivering.

'I'm Adam,' he said. 'Here, take my hand.'

She raised it up to him and he noticed the antique ring on her finger and the dark flesh that had swollen around it.

CHAPTER 17

TUESDAY 11.56 A.M.

SECRET LOCATION, LONDON

'Come in, come in,' said Sir Michael Walden, DG. Bonati led the way, followed by Bex and Jud.

'Michael, you've met Jud Lester before,' said Bonati.

'Of course,' said Walden, shaking his hand.

'And this is Rebecca De Verre,' said the professor. 'Another one of our top agents.'

Walden shook her hand. 'I'm glad you're here,' he said, nervous tension written across his face. You didn't have to have a sixth sense to see this man was worried.

He was dressed in navy suit trousers with a white shirt, open at the neck. It was the first time Bonati had ever seen him without a tie. His hair had not been combed to the usual standard and his eyes hung heavy.

'I'm working from home this morning,' Walden said anxiously as his soft shoes shuffled across polished floorboards to the great staircase. 'Didn't want to leave Debs' side, you see.'

He led them straight upstairs to the bedroom.

His wife looked worse than they'd imagined. Bex had assumed that the antibiotics might have kicked in already and there would be some colour to her cheeks. But there wasn't. She looked pale and lined. Bonati was especially surprised to see Debs like this. It was well known at MI5 that the DG's wife looked amazing for fifty, always well presented, made up and dressed in designer labels that offered a subtlety and elegance that was beyond most women twenty years her junior.

But now, without make-up, her hair damp from sweating and her eyes tired and worn, Debra Walden looked a shadow of the person who usually lit up MI5 social functions. And at her right temple were scabs, dark lesions that looked angry and sore. She raised a hand to wave to Bonati and they could see it, too, was covered in dark sores.

'Giles,' Debs said in a voice noticeably weak, her face slowly breaking into a cautious smile. 'Good of you to have come, but I'm OK, honest. I suppose Michael's been telling you I'm at death's door.' She turned to offer her husband a reassuring smile. 'He does worry about me, you know.'

Walden tried to shrug it off with a roll of his eyes, but Bonati knew he couldn't survive without her. For most of his adult life, Bonati had not regretted remaining a bachelor – until those rare occasions when he'd meet someone like Debra Walden and wonder how different things could have been if he'd married a woman like her. But Michael Walden and he went back a long way and Bonati was happy for his friend. The jealous moments rarely lasted long.

He shared his old friend's concern at seeing her like this, though he tried to hide it now. The last thing Debs needed was a couple of middle-aged men fussing over her.

'So, can you tell us what happened please, Lady Walden?' said Jud, straight to the point, as ever. 'What did you see and when?'

She turned to face him.

'Er, well, yes. It was last night,' she began, trying to lift herself up and rearrange the pillows behind her.

'Let me do that!' Walden rushed to her aid.

'Stop fussing,' she said to her husband – and not for the first time that morning, Bex suspected. The DG reminded Bex of her own father and there was something serene about this woman that was not unlike her mother too.

Walden helped his wife to sit upright and remained on the edge of the bed.

'Look,' she said. 'You and Bonati have much to catch up on, I'm sure. Why don't you take the professor downstairs and let me speak to these agents? We know they're going to be more use than the two of you!'

Reluctantly, Walden did what he was told and beckoned Bonati to follow him.

The door closed behind them and Jud and Bex sat on chairs on either side of the large four-poster. They had both noticed it was very cold in the room. Jud had stolen a glance between the drawn curtains and had noticed the windows were closed. There was no draught, but there was a definite chill in the room.

Bex took out her iPad and sat poised, ready to make notes. It was essential they recorded everything Debra said. Jud often said that small, incidental observations made by witnesses and victims could prove to be the most significant evidence of all.

'So, can you talk us through what happened?' asked Jud in his most sensitive voice. Bex was impressed.

'Well,' said Debra, rubbing a sore at her neck. 'It's kind of hazy. I've been poorly for a couple of days, you see. And I don't honestly know if it's the temperature making me delirious.'

'You say you've been ill for a few days,' said Jud. 'Why don't you talk about how the illness started and then we'll get to the events of last night. OK?'

Bex smiled in Jud's direction. Was he actually developing some patience at last?

'Right, well, I seem to remember waking up a couple of days ago feeling odd,' said Debra. 'We'd been out the night before. And I know I'd had a few glasses of champagne, but I'm used to that. This was unlike a hangover anyway. It was worse.'

'OK, go on,' said Jud.

Bex was making notes on her iPad.

'We'd been at this launch, you see. In Hatton Garden. Don't know how on earth Michael blagged an invite but it was a good do. Some jewellery shop just opened. Can't remember the name.'

Jud exchanged glances with Bex across the bed. It was just as Jud had said. Some casual preamble, like an introduction to what she was about to talk about, but Debra had already said something significant. A jewellery shop?

'Did you buy anything?' Jud said, trying to hide his keen interest.

'What? Oh, er, yes. Well, it was our wedding anniversary on Saturday. The trip to the launch was a bit of a surprise. Anyway, when we got there, Michael bought me this.'

She slowly moved across and picked up a ring from the bedside table.

'It's staggeringly beautiful,' said Bex.

'Thank you. Well, amazingly, it fitted. It's why we bought this one. But I can't wear it at the moment. This virus – or whatever it is – has affected my skin, and especially, would you believe it, on the finger I'd planned to wear it on. It was supposed to sit above my wedding ring, just here.'

She showed them her left hand. Her wedding ring finger was blackened and puffy. 'Looks horrible, doesn't it? I'm sorry.'

'No, no. Don't apologise,' said Bex. 'We're here to help. But I'm interested in this ring. Did you wear it at all?'

'Yes. I couldn't take it off, it was so beautiful. I wore it as soon as we'd bought it. I didn't even take it off to go to bed. I remember that because I had such a difficult job taking it off when I woke up next morning. My hand had swollen – you know, like they do when you get too hot in bed.'

'I know what you mean,' said Bex.

'Well, I just thought maybe it was the wrong size after all. But then my hands and my neck started to show these lesions.'

'So you woke up feeling strange, yes?' said Jud, keen to move the story on, see if there were any other hidden gems in what she'd got to say.

'Yes,' said Debra wearily. 'I woke up and my head was pounding. I was running a temperature. Michael got some aspirins for me and a glass of water. Well, I got out of bed and went downstairs eventually but I knew I wasn't right. You know that feeling you get when you're hot and clammy? You feel kind of dream-like?'

'Yes, of course,' said Jud.

'Well, I decided there and then that I shouldn't be out of bed, so I came back here and I've been here ever since. The doctors have been and gone. My rash, whatever it is, has got worse, but I'm told the medicine will keep it at bay. It's lucky we caught it when we did, that's what I'm told. Although to be honest I've not been told much else.'

Not surprised, thought Jud to himself. No one's going to tell you it's the bubonic plague, are they?

'And last night?' he said.

'Yes, last night. Well, Michael was out, as always, at some evening function. I was watching television in here until about ten o'clock and then turned it off to try to get some sleep. I was tossing and turning for a while. I turned the pillow over and over again, refreshing it to get the cool side, you know, but it didn't work. I was hot and clammy so I went to the bathroom for a flannel. When I came back I saw it—'

Her voice choked and she fell silent, overcome by painful memories of terror.

'Lady Walden?' said Bex, standing up. 'Are you OK?'

'Yes, yes,' she said, dabbing her eyes with a scrunched-up tissue. 'I'm OK, it's just . . . well, it was so *horrible*.'

'Go on,' said Jud anxiously.

'There was this . . . figure.' Her voice was trembling again. But she was determined to get through this. She knew, because

Michael had told her enough times, that these CRYPT agents knew their stuff and she was keen to tell them everything. But the vision that flashed through her mind was chilling.

'I'm sorry,' she said. 'This figure. It was dressed in some kind of dark cloak. But it wasn't all there.'

'How do you mean?' said Bex.

'Well, it didn't look . . . you know, completely solid. It was kind of cloudy. But I could definitely see it. I mean it wasn't some shadow. And it turned round.' She gazed into the room now, her hand over her mouth. 'Oh God, when it turned round. That face – that *mask!*'

'I know this is hard for you,' said Jud, 'but can you explain it to us in detail?'

'Yes, yes. I will. I'm sorry. It was so frightening. I mean, I've never seen anything like it. There was this white mask. And that nose. A long, pointed kind of beak.'

The agents were nodding. It was a description that conjured up an image they felt they knew intimately, without ever having seen it for themselves.

'Exactly where was it?' said Jud. 'I mean, where in this room? Can you remember?'

'Yes, of course I can.' She pointed to the en-suite bathroom opposite the bed. 'I came out of there and stood facing the bed. The figure was standing on this side of the bed, with its back to me.' She was pointing to the bedside cabinet on her left, where she kept her things.

'So what happened then?' said Bex.

'Well, I screamed. I mean, wouldn't you? And it was at that moment that Michael came home. He must have been trying to unlock the door quietly, because I didn't hear him. But I certainly heard him racing up the stairs. He burst in through that door but it was too late.'

'Too late?' said Jud.

'Yes. I mean I don't know if the sound of my husband's

footsteps startled it, or perhaps it was my scream, but it disappeared.'

'How?' said Bex, trying to keep pace with the story by typing frantically on her iPad.

'It just disappeared into the air. The room was dark of course. When my husband entered he put the light on straight away and saw me standing there, by the bathroom door, trembling.'

'So you described to him what you saw, and here we are,' said Bex tenderly.

'That's right. Do *you* think I'm going mad?'

'My God, no!' said Jud.

Bex said, 'If anyone's going to believe you, it's us.'

Jud turned to Bex. 'Look, I think we've heard everything we need from Lady Walden—'

'Oh, call me Debs, for goodness sake!'

'OK, well, I think that's enough stress for Debs now. Why don't you stay here for a little while and take some readings? We need to know if there's a trace of any energy still left in the room.'

'OK,' said Bex. 'And you?'

'I'll take my equipment and make a start taking readings on the landing outside and down the stairs. I'll help you set up first, then see you in the living room in about thirty minutes, OK?'

Bex nodded. She was already unpacking her instruments and setting them on the floor. She took her EMF meter and began scanning the bedroom. The needle was rising, quickly: 5mG, 12mG, 20, 36, 58. This was unusually high. There were electrical appliances in the room – the TV, the alarm clock – but nothing to emit these kinds of readings.

She moved towards the left side of the bed, towards Debra's bedside cabinet. Jud was just about to leave the room when Bex said, 'Wait! Look at this!'

The needle was going haywire – 121mG. There was nothing close by to explain such extraordinary levels of electromagnetic radiation.

Except the ring.

She hovered the hand-held meter over it and the needle rocketed to the end of the scale.

Jud quickly picked up Bex's Geiger probe and joined her by the bedside cabinet. He pointed the probe towards it. A series of loud clicks were emitted.

He saw the ring.

Debra let out a shriek. 'What's going on?' she said, nervously pulling the duvet up to her neck.

'It's nothing to worry about,' said Jud calmly. 'But I think we need to take this ring away for further tests. Is that OK?'

'What? Oh, er, yes! Of course. Take it if it helps the investigation.'

Jud fished around in his rucksack for a clear bag. He attached the usual plastic tag to the ring and placed it in the sealable bag as evidence. Then pocketing it, he made for the door.

'Good work, Bex. Now try the bathroom.'

He left to go downstairs with his rucksack slung over his shoulder.

Bex opened the bathroom door and flicked the light switch. 'I'll just check in here and then leave you in pea—'

She gasped.

And quickly shut the door again. It hit the frame with a thud that was heard by the people downstairs.

'What?' yelled Debs, her hands trembling as they gripped the duvet. 'What now? What've you seen?'

Jud was already at the door. 'What was that, Bex? What's happened?'

'It's in there!' she said.

'What is? You mean the *ghost*?' said Jud. Michael Walden and Bonati appeared behind him.

'Yes!' said Bex, nodding her head and panting with fear.

'Get back,' said Jud calmly. 'Sir Michael, can you take your wife downstairs please. Bex, stay here with the professor.'

Jud made straight for the door.

He opened it slowly. The light was still on.

'There's nothing—'

Wait a minute. His eyes caught something reflected in the mirror.

He opened the door further and entered. No fear.

And there it was.

It was not as tall as Jud had imagined. Barely his own height. It had its back to Jud – just a dark cloak was visible, like a black coat hanging on a peg.

What was it doing?

Jud made a tentative step towards it.

Without warning it began turning to face him and Jud saw the sight that had been chilling people to the bone.

The white mask. The black, eyeless sockets. And that beak. It was inhuman. Bird-like.

Jud stood still, just feet away, but braced and ready. He wasn't going to make the first move, but if the ghost was going to go for him, he was up for it. He tensed his fists at his sides. *Come on*, he was willing it. *Try me then.*

End this.

The figure remained eerily still. Something hidden deep behind the pale, gaunt mask was now focusing on Jud. It tilted its head to one side, then the other, like a bird intrigued by something.

Outside the room, Bex made a move in Jud's direction.

'No!' whispered Bonati, restraining her. 'Don't startle it. Jud knows what he's doing.'

Bex and Bonati gazed through the gap in the door and saw the reflected image of Jud's face in the mirror.

And then they saw his eyes widen.

CHAPTER 18

TUESDAY 12.28 P.M.

KING'S ROAD, CHELSEA, LONDON

DCI Khan was driving too fast and he knew it. But it was hard not to. The case was developing so rapidly, and spreading so far across London, it was too difficult to resist the temptation to drive at a matching speed.

And he did so love to drive fast.

He remembered those early days when he did a spell as a traffic cop in the 1980s. He missed the raw power and the sleek lines of the Rover SD1 – that iconic 'jam sandwich' police car. The 3.5L V8 could keep pace with just about any choice of car favoured by cheap criminals at the time. It outclassed them all.

But how times change. Here he was sat in a Ford Focus with all the luxuries of a shopping trolley. But he could still drive fast, he'd not lost that ability, and the Focus was nimble, with plenty of torque. It wasn't a Rover SD1, but then not even the traffic cops had those beasts these days, they had to settle for a Volvo estate.

He flicked the car through the traffic and paused at the traffic lights on the King's Road. He drummed his fingers on the steering wheel and allowed his eyes to wander from left to right.

Come on! Khan was impatient at the best of times, but this morning he was especially hurried. The revelations he and his colleagues had just discovered had made all the difference to this case. It no longer felt as if they were stumbling around in the dark, waiting for the next fatal haunting. They had a lead. A very real lead.

He'd discovered that McNeal from the hospital and the woman in Knightsbridge *and* the DG's wife all had something in common beyond the fact that they were victims of hauntings. They shared a love of jewellery, and they had all been to Calder's in the last week, the new jewellery store in Hatton Garden. He didn't know exactly why or how that affected the case, he only knew it was much more than a coincidence. It *had* to be significant.

And that's where Khan was heading, right after he'd made one more call. He'd made up his mind he was going to question the owner within an inch of his life. Might even take him in, depending on how accommodating he was. But first he wanted to see if the poor girl in Chelsea had visited the jeweller's too.

'*Come on!*' he shouted up at the sloth-like traffic lights. '*Change!*'

He knew he should have been at Calder's already, but he wanted more evidence. One more connection. If Tamara Lytton had been to the shop too – perhaps had been at the opening launch, like Lady Walden – then that was enough. Something was going on at Calder's. Something that Bonati and his crew had to investigate. And if Khan could make the agents' lives easier by removing the owner for a short while, then he would.

But not yet.

He pulled into Chelsea Square and parked outside the apartment block where Tamara had been found. He nodded to the police officer he'd stationed outside the front door. This was a serious crime scene and he didn't want anyone allowed in or out without his say-so.

He left the car and walked up the neatly clipped path, past the large magnolia tree to the giant, gloss black door with brass fixings.

'Well?' he said to the officer. 'Any visitors?'

'No, sir,' he said, 'just the usual crime scene investigators. Oh, and I think there's a forensic pathologist here.'

'Oh,' said Khan, 'we *are* honoured. He knew that two of the 'crime scene investigators' had been Nik and Stacey from the CRYPT, but this officer was deployed on a need-to-know basis and he didn't need to know.

Khan had little time for pathologists. And they usually had little time for him.

'What about the friend?' he asked. 'This Antonia Farr . . .'

'Farraday. Yes, she's still here, as you requested, sir. There's an officer with her now. She last saw her mate yesterday and then found her body this morning apparently.'

'Witnesses?'

'Yeah, we've checked. Farraday was seen by neighbours leaving yesterday and arriving this morning. She's clear. Very upset, though. Bit of a state.'

'Of course she bloody is!' said Khan. 'Wouldn't you be, son?'

If there was one thing Khan despised it was disrespect to victims or their relatives and friends. He knew that the officer probably hadn't meant it that way but he snapped all the same and tutted as he left him on the front step.

A few seconds later and he was upstairs, entering Tamara's flat.

He inspected the body first. Antonia was in the living room with the door shut. She could wait a few seconds. He needed to see the scene for himself.

'Jesus!' he said, on entering the bloodstained bedroom. 'Poor kid.'

A woman dressed in a white suit – one of three people similarly dressed in the room, and poring over the body for forensic evidence – turned and nodded.

'Yes, well, none of us is here for pleasure, Inspector.'

Khan frowned irritably. He'd met this pathologist before. Dr Marlowe. She was always so bloody patronising to him and his lowly colleagues.

'I realise it's not a pleasure trip for any of us, Doctor. She's a mess. We've got to find who or *what* did this.' He gazed past the pathologist at the young, beautiful face of the victim and the savage red tracks round her neck, from which blood had spilled on to the luxury satin sheets.

'What do you mean "who or what", Inspector?' said Marlowe. 'What do you think it was, a robot? I think we can safely say "who" and then get on and find them, yes? I'd have hoped you'd have found and arrested them by now! I mean it might help if you know you're looking for a person. There, I'll give you that, Inspector. I've helped you now. Go out and look for a *person*. That narrows it down a bit.' Dr Marlowe, splattered with blood, was in caustic mood. It had been a distressing visit and she resented having detectives standing there gawping at her while she pored over the mutilated body for evidence.

Khan was sorely tempted to explain that the reason he'd said 'who or what' was because it seemed increasingly likely that they were looking for a ghost not a person, but he resisted. Time was pressing and he wanted to get to Calder's as soon as possible.

Antonia was next door. Time to interview her.

He entered the living room and saw Tamara's friend perched on the edge of a modern-looking red sofa, being consoled by a female police officer. Another detective was in the room and had been asking her questions already, on Khan's instructions.

The heavy mascara Antonia was wearing had run with the tears that had flowed constantly since her brutal discovery. Her stomach ached from crying and her head was pounding. She'd paced the floor, she'd gazed solemnly out of the window, she'd reached for a drink and she'd sat, perched on the edge of the sofa, as she was now, but nothing had alleviated the pain.

And why oh why did she have to remain in this morbid place still? She'd wanted to leave for ages now but the police officers had insisted she remain.

And now, finally, here was the man they'd told her was coming. The reason for her having to wait in this prison of pain. This shabbily dressed inspector with a worn, miserable face.

'Antonia?' Khan said as gently as possible.

'Miss Farraday to you,' she snapped. 'Why is everyone trying to be my bloody friend? I had a best friend and I've lost her.' She began sobbing again and buried her head in her sweating hands.

'I'm sorry, madam,' said Khan, more formally now. 'Miss Farraday. Please accept my condolences. Miss Lytton's family have been informed. They'll be here soon.'

'Not while she's still in there!' shouted Antonia. 'I mean, for God's sake!'

'No, no, of course not. I mean, we'll take the body out before they're here.'

Antonia glared at Khan. 'She has a name you know.'

'Again, I'm sorry. Miss Lytton's body. Look, can I get you some tea?'

'Oh, of course, tea will solve everything, won't it?' said Antonia, staring at the carpet. 'I mean, that's what we Brits do, isn't it? As soon as a crisis comes along, we wash it away with tea. Well, I won't. I mean I can't! I'm never going to get over this.' She got up and went to the window again, sobbing. 'And I don't want any more *bloody* tea!'

Khan exchanged glances with the officer who'd been comforting Antonia on the sofa.

'Miss Farraday, I know it's been an awful shock for you and I'm so sorry to keep you here. I promise you can go in just a few more minutes. My officers will have covered everything, I'm sure, so I won't make you go through it all again.'

'Gee, thanks!'

'But there is just one question I have.' He beckoned for her to come and have a seat again. Reluctantly she trudged back to the sofa and flopped on to it dejectedly.

'Yes?'

'Well, do you know if Miss Lytton had bought any new jewellery recently?'

'*Jewellery?*' said Antonia. '*Jewellery?* What possible difference does it make now? I mean, why the hell do you ask?'

'So did she?' Khan ignored her question and kept on. He was sure he'd detected a faint movement in her eyes towards the direction of Tamara's bedroom just before she'd answered.

Was she nervous? Or had he imagined it?

Antonia shook her head. 'No, Inspector. At least, not to my knowledge. She would have shown me if she'd bought something. I saw her yesterday and she never mentioned anything. OK? Why, anyway?'

'Oh, nothing,' said Khan.

'So is that it?' said Antonia. 'I mean, is that what I've been sitting here for? Was that your only question?'

'Yes,' said Khan, calmly. 'My officers have informed me you have an alibi. You last saw her yesterday and then found her here this morning. Yes? We've checked with neighbours and people saw you arrive. You're free to go. But do stay in the area, if you don't mind. We may need to speak to you again. I'm sure you'll be very helpful if we have further questions, won't you, Miss Farraday? We know where to reach you.'

And with that Khan made for the door.

He nodded through the open bedroom door to the crime scene investigators and Dr Marlowe, whom he knew would not be disappointed to see him go.

He jogged down the grand staircase, the elaborate runner slipping slightly under his feet as his solid shoes touched the tip of each wooden stair. He reached the ground floor and marched across the black and white tiles towards the door. He was just about to open it and leave when he heard a voice from above.

'Inspector?'

He stopped. And turned.

'Inspector Khan? Wait please.'

It was Antonia.

He paused for her to reach the bottom of the staircase, then smiled. 'Miss Farraday. You wanted to say something?'

'Erm, well, I mean, I suppose I can help you. That is to say, I should've helped you earlier. I mean, I should've told you.'

Khan kept smiling. 'Go on?'

'Well, you see, I don't know, I just didn't want to have to tell you, especially not in front of others, but, well . . .'

Khan stood there patiently. He wasn't going to have to do any more talking, he could tell. She had not run all the way downstairs for nothing. He could detect there was something else in her eyes back up in the flat. And he knew she'd tell him in good time. It was a bonus that it was so soon.

'You see,' she continued, 'Tamara, Miss Lytton, *did* have a new piece of jewellery. Only the other day.'

'Go on,' said Khan.

'Yes, it was a ring. A very beautiful one. She showed it to me yesterday, or the day before – whenever it was. But it was recently. I mean, only in the last few days.'

'Right, I see. And why did you not want to tell me this earlier, Miss Farraday?'

'Yes, well, I'm sorry. It's just . . . I mean, it's the way she came by it, you see.' Antonia could see his face alter. 'Oh no, don't get me wrong,' she added, hurriedly. 'She didn't steal it! God, no. It was a present.'

'OK,' said Khan. 'So what's the problem with that?'

'Well, it's who bought it for her, that's the problem.'

Khan was beginning to lose patience now. He'd tried to remain calm and accommodating and non-threatening and everything those bloody psychologists and profilers told him to be at their latest training courses, but this was becoming tedious now. *Just spit it out!* he wanted to say.

'I see. And do you think you can tell me now, Miss Farraday?' he said, still trying to smile.

Antonia's eyes moved furtively across the hallway and out of the window beyond.

'Tamara was having an affair,' she said, sighing. Tears were welling up again. 'With a politician. A well-known one. And . . . well, for some reason he'd decided to buy it for her. Been to some launch of a new jewellery shop. A posh place, from what Tamara told me. That's how she got it.' She gazed out of the window over Khan's shoulder. And her face fell once again.

'Tamara was somebody's mistress, Inspector. She was dating a married man. The ring was a gift to keep her quiet, Inspector.'

It did more than that, he thought to himself.

CHAPTER 19

TUESDAY 12.48 P.M.

SECRET LOCATION, LONDON

The masked ghost went for Jud.

Its skeletal hands locked on to his arms. Vice-like they held him and began squeezing. As Jud wriggled and pushed he saw the ghost move a hand towards his jacket. It thrust its razor fingers into the pocket, ripping the seam as if it was tissue paper.

Bex ran in and launched herself at the ghost, knocking it crashing into the mirror above the sink. There was an almighty crack followed by a rapid shattering. Jagged shards flew in every direction. Jud tried to shield his face from bits of broken mirror piercing his skin. The ghost lay crumpled on the hard floor.

Bonati was at the door now.

'Rebecca, Jud! Get out – now!'

'No,' cried Jud. 'Don't worry, it's not after me.'

'Out!' shouted Bonati. 'Both of you. Follow me.'

He was in no mood for disobedience. For Jud to directly disobey an order was bad enough, but in the DG's own house? It didn't bear thinking about. He'd deal with him back at the CRYPT. For the moment, his prime objective was to prevent having two dead agents on his hands.

They followed him out of the room.

'I mean it, sir, it wasn't trying to kill me,' continued Jud. He turned to Bex, ignoring her glares warning him to keep his mouth shut. 'If you'd only stayed out like I told you to, Bex. We could've had real evidence.'

'So come on,' demanded Bonati. 'What was the ghost after then, if not your throat?'

Sir Michael had left his wife downstairs and re-entered the room. He was staring incredulously at the open bathroom door. He could just make out the outline of a figure, slumped in the corner beneath the sink. But it was fading. The edges of its cloaked body were merging with the air around it and a strange gaseous kind of plasma had enveloped it.

Jud paused to fish something out of his pocket.

'Answer the bloody question!' demanded Bonati.

'Mrs Walden's ring. I believe it was after this, sir. It was trying to grab it from my pocket when Bex came in. Honestly, it wasn't after *me*.'

They stood in silence and stared at Jud's hand holding the evidence bag containing the gold ring.

Bonati's phone shattered the quiet.

'Yes?' he said, irritably.

'It's Khan,' said a solemn voice at the end of the line. 'I've got bad news.'

'Really? Oh, you surprise me, Inspector,' the professor said sarcastically. 'Have you ever called with good news?'

'It's serious. We've had reports just in of another missing person.'

'What? When? Where?'

Jud looked at Bonati's face anxiously. He raised his eyebrows as if to say, 'What's happened?' but the professor was now listening intently.

'A mother in Kensington has turned up at the police station there in a terrible state. Apparently it's her daughter. She's been abducted.'

'Abducted? When? By whom?'

Khan's tone was portentous. 'Well, it's only just happened. She's saying they met up in Hyde Park. Her daughter's twenty-two years old and works as a graphic designer somewhere in Kensington. As I understand it, her mother had come in to meet her for lunch. Apparently – and reports are patchy at the moment, I'm told, because she's so hysterical – the mother was walking to meet her in the park but saw a figure take her before she could get there and help. It came out of the bushes and seized the daughter. Must've been seriously strong.'

'And did the woman give a description of the assailant, Inspector?' said Bonati.

'Yes. I'm afraid she did. She's already described the figure to us.' Khan's voice was low and deadly serious.

Bonati had already sensed where this was leading. Why else would Khan be informing him now if it had been an ordinary-looking person after all? 'It's not?' he said expectantly.

'It *is*,' said Khan. 'She said it had some sort of long black coat on, maybe a cloak. She couldn't see its face because it was wearing a kind of . . . pale mask, she said.'

CHAPTER 20

TUESDAY, 2.01 P.M.

CALDER'S JEWELLERY SHOP,

HATTON GARDEN, LONDON

Two unmarked police cars pulled into a row of disabled bays on the side of the road in Hatton Garden. Bonati, Khan, Bex and Jud got out of one, three officers left the other.

The visit, hurriedly planned in the front room of the DG's house just moments earlier, was not to be an all-out raid. The situation required more subtlety than that. And, as Jud had kept saying, the prime objective was to see if the jewellery in the store emitted the same kind of radiation as Lady Walden's ring had done. And the agents might detect something else in the room. But they'd never know if they went in guns blazing.

Khan and his men were on a different mission. They wanted to see the records: receipts, bills, anything they could lay their hands on that told them who had visited the shop in the last few days. The Waldens had told them about the invitation to the launch party. So there must have been a guest list. Khan was on the scent – he wanted that list and was determined to get it.

A few seconds later and they were outside the store.

No expense had been spared on the shop's refurbishment, that was clear. A rich, elaborate sign was freshly painted above the shop windows, through which the agents and officers could see theatrical velvet drapes, lavish armchairs and mahogany desks.

'You always know it's an expensive jeweller's when you see so few items of jewellery on display. It's a rip-off,' said Bex.

'It may be more than that,' said Jud. 'The stuff this guy sells might not just be pricey, it might be dangerous too.'

'Open minds, please,' said Bonati. 'Let's not pre-judge this place, or its owner, before we're certain there's a case here.'

As he said it, a flamboyantly dressed man in a blousony shirt and a shiny velvet jacket emerged from the shadows at the back of the shop. His hair was gelled fashionably into a spiky set of blond needles and in his thin hands, enveloped by immaculate cuffs with cufflinks that sparkled, he gently carried a dark blue tray of rings towards a glass cabinet.

The doorbell rang as Jud opened it.

Nicky Calder smiled warmly, though the number of people entering the shop seemed unsettling somehow.

'Good morning, gents,' he said, hospitably. 'Oh, and madam too!' he added as he saw Bex follow the group inside. Two officers had already disappeared around to the rear of the building and a third remained on the street outside. 'Can I help you?'

Khan was the first to speak. 'You certainly can.' He flashed his police identity card – and Jud watched Calder carefully as his eyebrows rose momentarily and a startled look flashed across his eyes, before his smile returned, revealing brilliant white teeth.

'And to what do I owe such attention, Inspector?'

'You recently held a launch party, I understand, Mr . . .'

'Calder. Nicky Calder. Yes, I certainly did. It was a very happy occasion. There have been no complaints, I trust? We were as quiet as mice, but one's neighbours can sometimes be over-sensitive, don't you think?'

'There have been no complaints about the event itself, Mr Calder.'

'That's a relief,' he said, though there were no signs of relief on his face. Bex noticed a very slight tremble to his hands now. He flashed a look at her and placed his hands behind his back.

'So why the interest in the launch party?' he said, casually.

'May I see the guest list?' said Khan.

'Certainly. I have nothing to hide, but I should like to know why you need—'

'Just the list, if you would,' interrupted Khan.

'Well, I should like to know why you need to see it first, Inspector. I don't wish to be obstructive, but I have my clients' privacy to protect. I think I'm entitled to an explanation at least.'

Khan's expression had altered. He looked straight at Calder. 'This is a multiple murder investigation, sir. We are attempting to piece together the last few hours of the victims, and we have reason to believe they were in attendance that night.'

Calder's face paled even more. 'I have nothing to hide here. The guests attended and they all left happily. If you are searching for answers here then—'

Khan interrupted again. 'The list please.'

Calder disappeared through a door in the rear corner of the shop.

'He won't do a runner, will he?' said Bex, anxiously.

'My men are outside,' said Khan. 'I'd like to see him try.'

Jud and Bex walked around the glass cabinets, peering at the blue velvet trays inside. The prices were staggering. The little white labels, attached to each ring with a delicate blue thread, were handwritten and few were below a thousand pounds and plenty showed prices much higher than this.

'You were right,' said Jud. 'No wonder he doesn't need to display many of these things. Sell one a week and he's made.'

'Detect anything?' said Bonati.

'The room is tense, there's no doubt,' said Jud, 'but it's hard to detect anything other than Calder's own nerves. There's more to this man than meets the eye.'

'Well, even I can see that,' said Khan. 'Maybe I should join the agency.'

There was a shuffle from the back of the room and Calder returned with a folder under his arm.

He moved to the large Georgian desk in the centre of the room and placed the folder on it. He leafed through its contents and found a typed list of names.

'There you are, Inspector. Always happy to oblige.'

As Khan began flicking down the list, Jud and Bex saw a cabinet with the key still in the lock. They gently opened it and pulled out a couple of rings. They each held one in their hands.

Jud felt it first. A dizziness was enveloping him, and a wrench that pulled at his stomach. He glanced across at Bex. She, too, looked unsteady and she leaned heavily against a cabinet behind her. The noise caused Calder to peer round Bonati and Khan to see what was going on.

'Put that back!' he snapped, launching himself in the direction of Bex.

Khan shook his head. Shouldn't have done that, he thought to himself.

Jud dropped the ring, blocked Calder's arm, grabbed it and wrenched it behind his back. He pushed him into the glass cabinet and from the other side Bonati and Khan saw his features squashed against the glass.

'OK, thank you!' said Bonati, barely concealing his anger. 'That's enough.'

Jud released him and stooped to pick up the ring. He walked to Bex and whispered, 'You felt it too, yeah?'

She nodded and looked at him, wide-eyed. 'Something's going on here.'

Calder straightened his suit and faced up to Khan.

'I demand to know what the hell this is about, Inspector. You come in here, you present me with no warrant. Your cabin boy here assaults me. You cannot possibly—'

But Khan had already found enough evidence to take him in for questioning. The list had confirmed their suspicions. They were all on there, buried in the long line of names:

Sir Michael and Lady Walden
Mr G. Hughes and Miss T. Lytton
Miss C. Maughan
Mr A. McNeal

Khan needed no other excuse.

'You can make your complaints when you're down the station, sir,' he said. 'This way please.'

'I beg your pardon?' said Calder abruptly. 'I'm not going anywhere. I've done nothing wrong.'

'You're helping us with our inquiries, sir. You're—'

'Wait!' interrupted Bonati, taking the list from Khan and quickly scanning it. 'There's another name on here that I think I know. It's Mr and Mrs A. *Cavendish*.'

'Grace Cavendish!' said Bex. 'It's not her parents, surely? What's her father's first name?'

'Alexander, I think,' said Bonati, gravely. He turned to Calder. 'Listen, this is very important. The Cavendishes, do you remember them? Do you remember what they look like?'

Calder just shrugged his shoulders. 'No.'

'Damn it, man, this is important. Mrs Cavendish has long blond hair. And I think Mr Cavendish is grey – quite slim. Glasses. Was it them? Come on!'

'Dunno.'

'But do they live in London, sir?' said Jud, unconvinced.

Bonati shook his head. 'No, I don't think so, but I do know Grace has an important birthday this week, doesn't she, Bex?'

'Yes. And her parents are down this week. They're taking her out today. I remember she told me she was looking forward to it. Oh my God.'

'Did a Mr Cavendish buy some jewellery, Calder?' shouted Jud.

'I have no idea. The receipts are with my accountant, I'm afraid.'

Jud was furious. Calder was obviously being obstructive and it took all of his restraint not to grab the guy and force the information out of him.

'Get him out of here!' said the professor to Khan. 'Let's hope we get more out of him at the station.'

'I've told you,' exclaimed Calder, resisting Khan's attempts to lead him out. 'I'm going nowhere! I've done nothing!'

'So you're refusing to come and help us with our inquiries, huh? I'll have you charged for that alone,' said Khan, in no mood for theatrics from this dramatic host. He signalled to the police officer who was watching from outside. The man entered the shop, made straight for Calder and bundled him out, no messing.

'You can't do this!' Calder was blurting. 'You can't simply walk in here and remove me from my own premises! What about the shop? I'll sue you for this. You see if I don't. Lost revenue. I'll sue you!'

'OK. Let me explain,' said Khan, out on the street. 'You can "volunteer" to come with us now, or we can return later today with an arrest warrant. What's it to be?'

Reluctantly, Calder accompanied them towards the car. He was still protesting to the officer as he held the door open for him.

Bonati turned to Bex. 'Do you know when Grace is meeting her parents?'

'Not sure. Tonight, I think.'

'OK. We've got time. Let's hope she's not about to receive some special jewellery as a birthday gift. We'll call her before she goes.'

'So how did you feel just then? Tell us what happened.'

'It was weird,' said Bex. 'I handled the ring and something happened. It was like an overwhelming nausea, as if I'd got a temperature or something. And a blinding headache too.'

'Yeah, me too,' said Jud. 'Exactly the same. It's like I felt sick suddenly. And my head was pounding.'

'Won't Grace feel this if she puts a ring on?'

'Let's hope so,' said Jud. 'But I don't want to risk it. She may not and then leave it on her finger. We've got to stop them giving it to her in the first place.'

'And what about the atmosphere in here?' said the professor. 'Can we focus on the shop please? Feel anything?'

'Well, this Calder guy was tense enough – I mean that was obvious when we entered. But there's not much beyond that,' said Jud. 'We'll get the instruments set up now and see what we find. I'm guessing there'll be some serious radiation coming from this jewellery.'

'OK, we'll leave you to it,' said Bonati. 'I'll go with Khan to the station. Jud, Bex, you get yourselves back to the CRYPT when you're done. And don't forget to warn Grace.'

'OK,' said Jud.

'I want another briefing later today,' said Bonati. 'I hope the other agents have been researching like I told them to. It's time to add all this up and see what we make.'

As Bonati left the building to join Khan on the pavement, the doorbell jangled once again but was soon followed by the ringing of Khan's mobile phone.

'Yes?'

It was an officer from Scotland Yard. 'There's been an incident, sir. On the tube, just near South Kensington station.'

'What's happened?' snapped Khan.

The detective at the end of the phone kept it brief. 'There's been a report of a near crash. Two attempted suicides.'

'OK. You can deal with that,' said Khan.

'But wait, sir,' said the officer. 'That's not all. The driver's saying he saw a third figure – crashed into it in fact. He says it was wearing some kind of black cloak and—'

'Don't tell me,' said Khan, glancing at Bonati who was waiting next to the car and staring at him inquisitively. 'A white mask with a long beak?'

'Well, yes, sir. Same description as before. There's a pattern here.'

'Oh, do you think so?' said Khan sarcastically. 'Well done, Holmes. Get over there now and find out all you can.'

'Already on my way, sir.'

Khan approached the car.

'You better find out why these bloody ghosts are here, Professor,' he said resolutely. 'Because it seems to me they're multiplying.'

'Another incident?'

'Yes. At South Ken station. Sounds you like you need to get an agent down there as well.'

'Will do. Though I'm running out of agents. This isn't the only case we're working on. I don't know what's wrong with this city. I've got agents over in Wandsworth at some disused factory; I've got others at a hotel in Shoreditch and about half a dozen at a giant warehouse in Clerkenwell, where the workers have downed tools and refused to go in until the ghosts have cleared off. And then there's the case up in Cambridge, in one of the colleges.

When you think about all the agents I've got working on this case too, Khan, if we weren't working under licence from M15, we'd be making a nice profit from these hauntings.'

'Well, you better add South Ken to your list.'

'Don't worry. I'll get on to Vorzek and see who's left to be deployed.'

Moments later the unmarked car swept past the shop window. Jud and Bex were left inside, unpacking their instruments.

Jud turned the 'Open' sign in the window to 'Closed' and he locked the door from the inside with the keys he'd found on the desk.

He pulled the blinds down over the windows and the room went dark.

First they took out their EMF meters and set them down, one on the desk in the centre, the other near a glass cabinet.

The needles were rising, indicating high levels of electromagnetic radiation, just as they'd detected in Lady Walden's bedroom: 10mG, 20, 32, 54 – then 105mG.

Something was stirring.

Jud took out the Geiger counter and pointed the probe into one of the glass display cabinets. There was a rapid clicking.

It had to be the rings; there was no other explanation that made sense.

Bex was just picking up her mobile to call Grace when she saw Jud taking another ring out of the cabinet.

'No, leave it!' said Bex. 'Don't be stupid.'

'I wanna know,' he said. 'It won't kill me.'

He went to put it on his finger.

'Don't put it on!' Bex shouted as she moved closer and tried to grab it off him.

'Hey, hey!' Jud said cheekily, still holding the ring in his hand. 'Anyone would think you cared or something.'

Bex flushed slightly, but still she persisted. 'I'm serious, Jud. Don't be stupid. We need you on this case.'

'What, and you think putting this ring on will kill me huh?' he was in one of his reckless moods. She'd seen it before, and it was becoming tiring now.

She stared at him as he rolled the ring around in his palm. What was it that made him so infuriating and yet so exciting to be with? Was it really bravery or some foolhardy self-destructive mode he had inside him? It almost seemed like he just didn't care what happened to him sometimes. Like he had some death wish or something.

The others at the CRYPT often said Jud had more courage than most of them put together. But Bex was beginning to doubt that. There were times when she'd seen fear in his face. He wasn't always that courageous. Especially when she wanted to get close to him, talk about his life, and his family. Get him to open up just a bit. He looked fearful then.

But now, playing with death in this way, rolling the ring around just like a dice – his 'courage' was becoming annoying.

'You don't need to put it on. Why risk it?' she said. 'Anyway, do you still feel something now it's in your hand, like we did before?'

'Yeah,' said Jud. 'I feel dizzy again, as if I've got a sweat on.'

'Your face looks pale,' said Bex.

'Shall I try holding some more?' he said, grinning.

'Oh sure, kill yourself.'

He reached into the cabinet and fished out three more rings. He held them in his hand and looked at Bex.

'Don't worry. I won't put them on!'

But Bex was worried. She could see how his face had whitened even more. Suddenly he wasn't smiling either. She saw his eyes roll upwards into his head before his eyelids closed. He fell back towards the cabinet. His weight knocked it over and there was an almighty crash as glass splintered across the floor. He landed on the fragments with a crunch.

'Jud!'

He wasn't responding.

'For God's sake, Jud! Talk to me.'

She knelt down, carefully dodging the splinters. 'You're such an idiot!' she said, panic-stricken, her stomach churning now and tears appearing at the corners of her tired eyes. 'Why? Why do you do this?'

He opened one eye slowly.

'Jud?'

'Er ... yeah. I'm here. I'm OK, I think,' he said, rubbing the back of his head. 'Ouch, I think I landed on some glass.'

'Of course you have, it's everywhere!' she said, helping him to his feet. 'What the hell happened then? Did you black out?'

'Must've done,' said Jud, flicking glass off his clothes. Pain was soaring in his left thigh. 'There's something in me,' he said. 'Is there a piece of glass there?' He turned round and let Bex lift his coat to see if there was something caught in his tight jeans. She knelt down and studied his legs. There was a piece of glass protruding from his left thigh. She carefully pulled it out. It was only a tiny fragment but enough to cause him pain. Suddenly she felt embarrassed to be so close to his body and stood up quickly.

'So what happened?' she said quickly. 'What did you feel?'

He was still rubbing his head where he'd landed against the cabinet. 'I don't know, Bex. It was kind of like a . . . a fog almost. Like a mist descended on me and took my breath away. Yes, that was it. Like I was being smothered. It felt hard to breathe all of a sudden. Blinding headache too. I guess I must have fainted.'

With a piece of paper from the folder on the desk she scooped up the rings he'd dropped and slid them inside a different cabinet. 'I don't want to touch the bloody things any more, and neither should you!'

'So how does this Calder handle them then? I mean, we can't be the only ones affected by them – look at what's been happening to the victims.'

'Perhaps he doesn't handle them himself – he just offers them to customers on the trays, sells them, and takes their money. He doesn't have to put the rings on, does he?'

'But when customers handle the jewellery, they don't fall over like I did,' said Jud.

'Well, no, but then they're not CRYPT agents, are they? We both know the kinds of experiences we can have while others are not affected. That's why we're agents. We feel stuff. It runs through us.'

Jud smiled at her. 'Great strapline, Bex. "Become an agent and *feel stuff*." But they *are* affected, that's just it, isn't it? I mean, ultimately.' He was staring into a different cabinet now, at the bright, polished jewels that twinkled back at him. 'Is there really a link between these things and the deaths of the people who wore them? It hardly seems believable, does it?'

Bex was more certain. 'Oh yes,' she said. 'It's believable. I don't know where these rings have come from, Jud, but there's one thing I'm certain of, they're cursed.'

Jud looked at her wide-eyed.

'Grace!' he said.

Chapter 21

TUESDAY 2.19 P.M.

SOUTH KENSINGTON TUBE

STATION, PICCADILLY LINE,

LONDON

Luc walked into the station foyer. It was almost empty, save for a handful of police officers, each clutching an MP5 semi-automatic carbine. It was the firearm of choice for most forces these days. Of German design, the Heckler & Koch 9mm sub-machine gun was very lightweight, considering the powerhouse of a carbine that it was.

Luc walked up to one of the armed officers and introduced himself. His badge was all that was needed, though, as per usual, it attracted a few raised eyebrows from the officers when they noticed how young the person holding the card looked. 'Special crime scene investigator, working for M15', was how Luc introduced himself. And it was enough.

'You're too late to see one of the witnesses,' said an officer.

'Which one?' said Luc.

'The driver. He's gone. We couldn't shut him up. They've

taken him off to hospital to sedate him. Hysterical, he was.'

From the patchy information that Luc had received from HQ, he didn't need to ask why the driver of the train had been hysterical.

'OK. Wouldn't you be?' he said cheekily, glancing at the machine guns and wishing he'd not said it.

The officers just shrugged their shoulders. 'Do we look like we're easily scared?' said one of them.

'Besides,' said the other. 'We've already been and inspected the place where this guy said he crashed into this masked man or whatever he was. And there's nothing there. No traces of a body at all. And believe me, son, we've seen some bodies on these tracks over the years.'

'But there was nothing there?' said Luc.

'No, mate. Nothing. No trace of blood. Bit weird, don't you think, considering the driver said he saw a body – wearing a mask – smash into his train and drop to the floor?'

Not weird at all thought Luc to himself – if you know it's a ghost.

'What about the two suicide attempts?' he said. 'Where've they gone?'

'Still here,' said one of the officers. 'We were told to keep them here as long as possible. I take it you're the person they're waiting for? The medics are not happy with you or with whoever your boss is. One of the doctors said they should've been in hospital ages ago.'

'OK,' said Luc. 'Well, I'll make sure I'm quick with them. I just need to talk to them – it's important.'

'It had better be,' said the officer. 'We've closed this whole bloody station and had to quarantine them over there. Be warned. It's not pretty.' He was pointing towards a small café at the other side of the cramped underground foyer.

Luc walked towards the building, cordoned off by police with the usual blue and white tape and cones. As he approached he could see through the windows figures dressed in white coats and wearing white masks over their faces.

He knew what that was. He'd already been warned by HQ. The two people found inside the tunnel here at South Kensington were suffering from the same disease as the others. And the paramedics and doctors and officers now attending to them couldn't take any chances. Not only had they received their vaccinations, they were wearing the precautionary masks and gloves.

Luc tapped on the window and a woman came out. She had piercing blue eyes that looked him up and down suspiciously from over the white mask around her nose and mouth.

'Yes?' she said in a muffled voice. Luc noticed the mask bob up and down over her face as her lips mouthed the words behind the thin layer of blue cotton.

He showed his badge once again and asked for a coat, mask and rubber gloves for himself. He was quickly given them and entered the café.

The two patients were lying on long bench seats, the kind you see in American diners. The table between them had been removed, and medics were attending to them. Luc was surprised to find the patients conscious and articulate. When the call came in for him to attend the scene, he'd had visions of two brutally injured people, already suffering from the plague and hours away from the same death that had claimed so many victims before them.

'Mr McNeal?' he said gently.

'Yes.'

Luc noticed his breathing was irregular and his face looked very sickly, though much of it was now covered in a white cream and there was a cold flannel at his forehead.

'Can I ask you about what happened down in the tunnel? How did you get here?'

McNeal spoke quietly but deliberately. Luc could see there

was real determination behind those eyes. 'If I tell you, as I've told the others, you probably won't believe me.'

'I think you'll be surprised,' said Luc. 'Why don't you try me and we'll see.'

'Well, I don't care if everyone says I'm mad or delirious, but it all started with the ghost – at the hospital.'

'I know it did,' said Luc, smiling sympathetically. 'It was the figure with the mask, wasn't it?'

'Yes,' said McNeal. 'Yes, it was. I remember it was pitch black. The sun hadn't even come up by then, and there was no one about. It was just so . . . weird. It's hard to explain. I mean . . . how we moved, through the dark streets. The ghost was so strong. It picked me up like a doll.'

'Me too,' said the woman lying on the bench opposite them. She could hear what they were saying and was anxious to tell her story too. Though her voice seemed weak, she presented the same determination as McNeal to tell the truth.

'And you are?' said Luc.

'Maxine,' she said softly. 'Maxine Sharp.'

'And you were brought here, to this place, by the same figure?' asked Luc.

'Yes. From not far away – just from Hyde Park. It's where I was meeting my mother, we were going to go for lunch. But this figure came at me – from out of the bushes or something. I swear, it just appeared. There was no warning. And then it grabbed me – I mean, really lifted me up. It must've carried me here.'

Something had been puzzling Luc from the outset and he felt now was the time to say it. 'But I don't understand,' he said gently to both of them. 'I mean, surely someone would have noticed you. They would have helped you. How did you get down into the tunnel without being noticed on the platform?'

They were both shaking their heads.

'We didn't just wander in through the entrance,' said McNeal.

'We escaped through the main shaft just now, but I don't think we were brought in that way. That's the weird thing. It's like there was another tunnel. We were underground. I don't remember coming in this way. There must be another way in – under this place. I don't know, maybe it leads out to the park as well. It was so dark when I came here and I was barely conscious.'

'Same with me,' said Maxine. 'We didn't cross any streets or anything like that. It seemed one moment I was in Hyde Park and the next I was underground somehow. This place is . . . horrible. I'm never coming back.'

'From what I can remember,' said McNeal, 'and you have to realise I don't think I couldn've been fully conscious, I was dragged underground somewhere. But I didn't come round until I was down there, in the cave.'

'*Cave?*' said Luc, surprised. 'What cave?'

'Down there, in the tunnel. Further along, past the station.' McNeal was pointing a blistered hand in the direction of the door.

'It's where we were dumped,' said Maxine. 'Like discarded rubbish.'

'Can you describe it for me?'

'It's the most evil place I've seen,' she continued. 'It's . . . well, I don't know what it is, it's some kind of *mass grave*.'

'So you saw other bodies in there?' said Luc.

'Other bodies? Man, we saw dozens of them,' said McNeal, struggling to sit up and resisting the attempts of the medics at his side to settle him down again. 'When I regained consciousness, I found myself in some kind of, I dunno, giant grave. The corpses must've been there for years. Maybe hundreds of years. It was mostly skulls and bones. But the smell and the . . .' He went silent for a moment and Luc noticed his eyes glaze over. His lip was trembling slightly. 'I don't want to talk about it just now, I'm sorry.' He was shaking his head and staring at Maxine who looked just as shaken. 'Maybe later.'

'That's enough,' said one of the doctors. 'We've done what your people told us to do. We've kept them here at the scene. You've questioned them and now it's time to get them off to hospital. Look, these people need the kind of treatment that only a hospital can provide, you understand? Now *please*, can we take them?'

'Yes, yes, of course,' said Luc. Eyewitnesses like these were absolutely crucial to an investigation, but whoever at Scotland Yard, or MI5, or even the CRYPT, had given the order to hold them here obviously had not realised how poorly they were.

The medics started to prepare the stretchers to take them out to the ambulances waiting on the street outside.

'Oh, one minute,' said Luc. 'Can I see your hands?'

'What?' McNeal and Sharp said almost in unison.

'Your hands. Please. Are you wearing any jewellery?'

Maxine Sharp she shook her head. 'I was, but it was removed just now – bloody painful actually, trying to get the ring off. The doctors had to use soap. Don't know why my finger has swollen so much.' Luc could see she was starting to cry. 'I mean, I don't know what's happening to me. I don't know what's—'

'Me too,' said McNeal. 'I had a silver signet ring but they took it off just now. Had to really pull it. Why?'

'OK, that's enough. Please don't worry, my love,' said one of the medics. 'Everything's under control now. You're safe with us.'

'And the rings?' Luc persisted. 'Where are they now then?'

'What?' a doctor said irritably. 'Er, I don't know. They're in here somewhere.' He was rifling through a small white bag with equipment in. He fished out a plastic bag wrapped into a ball. He unfolded it and held it out for Luc.

Luc peered into the bag it. There, at the bottom, in the corner, were their rings.

'OK,' he said. 'Let's keep them in there. But I will need to take them with me.'

The medics looked at him suspiciously but Maxine and McNeal nodded. 'Whatever,' said Maxine. 'Just make sure I get it back when my fingers have shrunk again. It's no use to me at the moment, is it?'

CHAPTER 22

TUESDAY 2.58 P.M.

SCOTLAND YARD, LONDON

Khan was pacing the room again. Bonati hated it when he did that. They'd interviewed several people together like this and the professor could never understand why he did it. He wanted to just shout at him to sit down, but if the inspector was infuriating, he was nothing compared to the sharp-suited man sitting across the table. Nicky Calder was dodging every question like a slippery eel. He seemed confident that he didn't have to answer any question if he didn't want to.

And he was right. He'd not been charged with anything and short of obstructing police inquiries (which was a charge they'd all love to throw at him if he carried on like this), technically he'd done nothing wrong – nothing that could be proved, at least. He'd not been arrested and did not have to provide any information beyond his name and address, and they already had this information.

They were waiting for his solicitor to arrive. Khan's attempts to 'have a nice little chat to save time before the lawyer came' fell on deaf ears. Calder was wiser than that.

'So, let me get this clear, Inspector,' Calder began again. It was as if he was running this interview. 'You have asked me here to help you with your inquiries. You have said I don't have to be here, but you gave me little choice but to come with you. You said if I resisted you'd have me arrested anyway. Well, let me ask you this. Arrested for *what*?'

'I thought you said you weren't going to say anything until your lawyer was here?' said Khan from across the room.

'I guess I'm getting impatient,' said Calder.

Khan came and sat down. He was quite happy for such an outburst of impatience. Questioning him without his lawyer present was fine with Khan.

'It depends on what you say,' he said. 'We may not have to arrest you at all, Mr Calder. You may be able to settle our concerns right here, right now.'

There was a knock at the door.

Damn and blast, thought Khan. Bloody lawyers.

A plain, unremarkable figure, mid-forties perhaps, with a bald head, silver glasses and a grey suit, entered the room. Calder stood up and shook his hand.

'Thank you for coming so quickly, Don,' he said.

The lawyer smiled and turned to Khan. 'Don Manton from Manton and King, Solicitors. Good morning, Inspector . . . ?'

'Khan. And it's Detective Chief Inspector.'

'Ooh, golly,' said Manton. 'We are honoured.' He looked at Bonati. 'And you are?'

'His assistant,' the professor lied.

Manton took a seat next to Calder at the table. 'Don't worry, Nicky. We'll get you out of here in no time. Right, gentlemen, would you mind telling my client and me what on earth this is all about?'

'We are investigating a multiple murder,' began Khan, solemnly. Bonati noticed the lawyer in the suit raised an eyebrow and he saw his Adam's apple move as he tried to hide a gulp.

'I see,' said Don Manton. 'And just what does this have to do with my client?'

'The victims have something in common,' said Khan. 'They all attended Mr Calder's launch party on Saturday night. It's now only Tuesday and two of the people on his guest list are dead, two are missing and another lies critically ill in bed.'

'And all of them live in London, yes? And all of them like jewellery, and all of them have expensive tastes, and all of them therefore are attractive targets for any killer,' said Manton. 'Please, Inspector, you can give us more than that, surely. I mean there must be a reason why my client is here.'

'Mr Manton,' replied Khan, calmly (he was well versed in dealing with lawyers). 'I have not charged your client with anything. I merely would like him to help us with our inquiries.'

Manton removed a notepad and a silver Parker pen from his leather briefcase. He scribbled the date, underlined it neatly and looked up in anticipation. 'OK, proceed,' he said.

CHAPTER 23

TUESDAY 3.14 P.M.

CRYPT, LONDON

'What do you mean, she's gone already?' Bex shouted, desperation written across her face.

'She told me her parents were in town earlier than planned,' said Stacey. 'They want to catch a West End show or something, so they're taking her out earlier.'

'When did she leave?' demanded Bex.

'Er . . . I dunno. Not long ago,' said Stacey. 'Maybe ten, fifteen minutes? You've only just missed her. What's happened?'

'And why doesn't she have her bloody phone switched on?' said Jud. They'd been trying to contact her since leaving Hatton Garden. 'Why can't we raise her?'

'Don't know,' shrugged Stacey. 'She's always forgetting it. Maybe she left it in her room. Or she's switched it off. Look, what's going on?'

'We think her parents have bought her a ring for her birthday,' snapped Bex. 'And it's from Calder's. It may be cursed!'

'Oh shit,' said Stacey. 'Let's hope not. I think she mentioned she was meeting them at The Ivy.'

'Yeah, that'll be right. It's where her parents always take her when they're in town.' Bex's voice was beginning to falter. 'She'll have turned her phone off. Oh, God, Jud. What if we're too late?'

Jud said nothing but grabbed her and left the room. 'See you in the car park in five. I'll get my bike keys. You go to the operations room and ask for Grace's parents' contact details. We may be able to get a mobile number or something.'

Bex did as she was told, though she was in a daze. Her head was spinning now and she could feel a sweat coming to her hands and a dryness to her throat. Grace was her best friend; she couldn't bear the thought of something happening to her. She ran off wearily in the direction of the operations room.

Five minutes later they were in the underground car park, mounting Jud's Honda Fireblade. 'Any luck?' he said as he fished his helmet out of the pannier.

'No,' said Bex. 'They had a mobile number for them but it's switched off. I guess they don't want to be disturbed.'

'Tough,' said Jud, squeezing the helmet over his head. 'They're about to be.'

Bex put on her helmet which she'd fished out of the pannier on her own bike next to Jud's. There was no point in taking two bikes and, though she hated to admit it, Jud was a faster rider than she was, even if it was a close call. And now was not the time to debate it.

'Hang on tight.' Jud's words were muffled as they mounted the bike. He looked back at her and his eyes were kindly. 'And don't worry,' he said through the headset, now connected. 'We'll get there in time, Bex.'

CHAPTER 24

TUESDAY 3.21 P.M.

SOUTH KENSINGTON TUBE STATION, PICCADILLY LINE, LONDON

Luc felt acutely alone. It was unusual for an agent to be deployed by himself – Bonati preferred them to work in pairs – but the CRYPT was stretched at the moment and Vorzek had insisted. The only other available agents, Nik and Stacey, had been told to keep researching in the labs – Bonati wanted his history lecture on the bubonic plague and he wouldn't be happy until he'd got it. And Grace was out having her birthday treat.

After interviewing McNeal and Sharp in the station café, Luc had made straight for the tunnel. The station officials had assured him that the stretch of line had been closed, so he was safe.

Despite these reassurances, he still felt nervous as the lights of the station dimmed behind him and he pressed on further into the blackness. McNeal had told him the recess in the tunnel wall was about a hundred metres down the track, the other side of a series of sharp bends.

Luc knew this stretch of line quite well as he often visited Hyde Park. He'd wondered several times in the past why the train on the Piccadilly line often seemed to lean and lurch more than others. Now, walking the tracks, he could see why. It was far from straight, bending in several places. At speed, no wonder it usually felt like you were on an underground roller coaster.

He couldn't help but imagine what would happen if the message to close the line had not got through to some quarters and a train came hurtling around the sharp bends.

Still he pressed on.

It felt colder, and he was sure it was getting colder. His eyes were scanning the walls as he went, looking for cracks or holes or entrances hidden in the shadows.

He'd decided to remove his Tri Axis EMF meter from his bag and he held it in his hand as he crept slowly along the tunnel. The needle was registering some detectable levels of electromagnetism, though nothing too unusual.

Onwards he walked, trying hard to ignore the thoughts in his head of an oncoming train, or of the myriad rats and spiders that his boots must be wading through right now.

He glanced at the EMF meter. The needle was rising: 23mG, 28, 32, 41mG. There was definitely some radiation here and he'd noticed yet another drop in the temperature.

He could sense a wave of sadness creeping over him like a mist.

Was it sadness exactly?

He paused for a moment and closed his eyes. He was connecting with his surroundings, using his extra-sensory perception to detect anomalies in the atmosphere of the place. Some residue of emotion that was lingering.

No, he decided, it wasn't sadness, exactly. It was abandonment. A feeling of hopelessness, of being forgotten about. He felt as if he was some kind of discarded rubbish.

He opened his eyes and looked about him. He could see very

little; the light from the station was long gone due to the bends in the track. He took off his rucksack and fished around inside it for his torch lamp with the head strap. He'd decided it was better to use that rather than his night-vision goggles, as they could be restrictive and he wanted to keep his peripheral vision unobstructed down here. Even the lightest change in light, detectable only in the very corners of his eyes, might mean an oncoming train, so he wanted full 20/20 down here.

He strapped the mini torch lamp to his forehead, placed the rucksack back on to his shoulders and straightened up.

He turned to his right, for a closer look at the wall he'd been following so closely. And then he saw it. Just up ahead, only a few feet away.

It was a dark hole in the wall, about three feet across and five feet high.

Was this what McNeal had been telling him about?

The needle on the EMF meter was going frantic now. It juddered like a high-speed pendulum and then settled on 103mG.

103! He'd never experienced readings like this before.

What the hell was inside that hole?

A few more tentative steps and he was there, outside the opening. Filled with trepidation but determined to find out what was causing this radiation, Luc stood to one side of the hole and peered around. His torch light swept into the dark recess like a miniature searchlight.

He jolted backwards. No matter what McNeal had said, no matter how detailed his description of this place had been, Luc was not prepared for this.

The torchlight had illuminated a nightmarish mountain of human remains – dark, earthy skeletons, stacked up like discarded mannequins, individual bones, crumbling ribcages, severed heads, headless torsos with remnants of flesh still clinging to them. And the stench. He had detected a rank smell earlier in the tunnel but had assumed it was a dead rat. Now, at the entrance to the gruesome cave, the potent smell of rotting human flesh made him retch.

McNeal was right. He'd not been hallucinating. But Luc had been the first one to believe him and come and explore – or maybe the first one brave enough to try.

He stared into the eyeless sockets of the skulls piled high in front of him. A wall of bones, so dense you could be forgiven for thinking you were looking at some ancient fence of willow branches and stones. It just didn't look human. Luc had read enough books on life science to last an eternity, and it was all fascinating. He knew that each and every one of us was nothing but a collection of minerals – calcium, iron, carbon, nitrogen, just like the earth itself. We were all made from matter that was once synthesised in nuclear furnaces deep inside the interior of stars, which exploded and formed the planets and life forms that surrounded it. He loved the idea that we were all made of stardust.

But down here, down among the spiders and bugs and bacteria and crumbling calcium bones that had melded over time with the soil around them, it seemed far from exhilarating. Hard to imagine stardust down here. Just soot and filthy dirt. Frightening to think of his own ancestors crumbling into soil like this.

But what the hell was this? And why was it here? He shook himself out of his morbid thoughts and allowed the questions to come at him, like the rapid fire of a machine gun.

How long had these bodies been here? Who put them here? And why? What did they die of? Was it some ritualistic killing? Or was it a mass grave for sinners, some unconsecrated land put aside for heathens centuries ago?

Whatever the answers were, he knew he needed forensics down here now.

But he had to take some readings first – Bonati would expect evidence. And what of the atmosphere? What did it feel like? He tried to concentrate but the startling sight of the decomposed corpses had eclipsed his emotions and he'd missed the fact that his feeling of abandonment had steadily grown, so that he now felt utterly rejected, searching for reasons to be alive.

He stared at the skulls, still intact. He could feel so deeply their abandonment. Though the skin had long since fallen off most of the heads and bodies, their sadness was palpable. Left here to rot.

But why? What *was* this place? And why, he suddenly wondered, had McNeal and Sharp been brought to this godforsaken place? And how?

He knew he needed to explore the site further, though every fibre of his being was telling him to get the hell away from the place.

He glanced back down the tunnel. Darkness.

He turned to face the cave entrance again and moved inside. His torch lamp flashed across the remnants of bodies as he moved his head around. The EMF meter was still going crazy. He set his rucksack down and took out the small video camera with night-vision sights. He had to film this for the guys back at the CRYPT.

He held the camera up to his eye with one hand, turned his head lamp off with the other and then pressed record. Looking through the lens of the video camera, the room was awash with infrared which made the decaying corpses look even stranger. Some skulls were facing outwards, their faces taking on an eerie character. If this had been a simulation in the SPA room, he thought to himself, full marks to Bonati for creating the scariest one yet.

But he knew it wasn't a simulation.

Still the feeling of abandonment seeped into his veins and mixed with the cold temperature to create the most inhospitable atmosphere he'd ever experienced as an agent.

And then he saw something towards the back of the cave. It was a gap in the wall of bodies. An opening?

He pressed on further into the shadows. Clutching the hand-held camera tightly, still on record, he squeezed past the mass of corpses and dirt and worms to find that the gap continued. It was, as he'd thought, some kind of makeshift tunnel.

Elation battled with disappointment inside him. He was pleased to have made the find. Perhaps this was indeed how the ghosts had brought some of the bodies into this place – perhaps even McNeal – but his heart sank at the same time, as he knew that the discovery meant he could not return to the safety and warmth of the station. Not just yet. He *had* to follow it.

CHAPTER 25

TUESDAY 3.27 P.M.

SCOTLAND YARD, LONDON

'So, let me get this straight,' said Manton. He'd been firing holes in Khan's theories since his arrival. It was why Don Manton was paid, after all. 'You are saying that the victims all purchased jewellery from my client's shop. Is that the only connection to my client? You have asked my client for his whereabouts at the times of each of the killings and he has answered you honestly. You have not sought to challenge his alibis so I am assuming from that that you do not believe he was responsible for the murders himself, correct?'

'Not directly, no,' said Khan.

'Well, what does that mean, Inspector?'

'Look, Mr Manton, I said at the beginning that your client is here voluntarily to help us with our inquiries. We have noticed a connection, a thread which connects all of the victims together. They have all purchased jewellery from Mr Calder within the last few days.'

'Yes, you've said that many times, Inspector. So the murderer was targeting rich people and where better to find them than at a launch party for a high-class jewellery store? The murderer was skulking outside and was able to identify and then stalk the rich customers who frequented my client's shop. Easy. I mean, really, Inspector, who is the detective here? I'm doing your job for you.'

'Rest assured we are exploring every line of inquiry, sir.'

'But you said "not directly" just then, Inspector. What did you mean by that?'

Khan looked uncomfortable. Frankly, this was a fairly ridiculous line of inquiry after all and he knew it. The suggestion that it wasn't Calder who'd caused the death of the victims directly but his cursed jewellery was too fantastical to mention.

There was no way Khan was going to raise the idea of cursed jewellery there and then. But he and Bonati wanted to watch Calder under these conditions, see his eyes, look for signs of discomfort or guilt even. But Khan knew that he wouldn't be able to hold him for long. He was a witness only – at the moment. He was the owner of a jewellery store, nothing else.

Besides, Calder had not shown any signs of guilt. Impatience, yes, frustration at getting embroiled in the case when all he'd actually done was sell some jewellery, yes, but guilt? He had explained his whereabouts at the possible times of the killings and it seemed plausible – the clubs he'd been to, the friends he'd been drinking with, and the times he'd closed the shop and returned home each day. He'd offered a string of names to whom Khan could turn if he wanted confirmation of his accounts.

And now, in the interview room, Calder seemed like anything but a murderer. He was of slender build, well-groomed, with flamboyant clothing and well-manicured hands.

Khan had waltzed into this man's little shop in Hatton Garden, closed it down for the day and taken the owner in for questioning on a thin hypothesis that he was selling rings that were cursed in some way. A theory so frail that it was too embarrassing to raise with him now, especially with his lawyer in the room.

Khan glanced at the rings on Calder's slender fingers. He

wore an ornate silver band on his little finger, left hand, and a thicker, plain silver band on his middle finger, right hand.

How could they possibly be cursed? It was ridiculous. Why wasn't Calder dying of this mysterious plague? The whole thing seemed so far-fetched.

Calder spoke first.

'I'm sorry, Inspector. We've listened to your questions and I've tried to answer them as best I can. I feel dreadfully sorry to hear what has happened to these people – the same people whom I saw laughing and joking in my own shop just a few days ago. It is chilling to think of it. But I can assure you, Inspector, there really is nothing else I can tell you. They came, they enjoyed themselves, they bought, and they left my shop that night. I haven't seen them since.'

'And,' interrupted Manton, 'you won't need me to remind you that my client closed his shop early, losing potential revenue I might add, in order to help you with your inquiries, Inspector. He could be in his shop now, selling jewellery, but instead he has done everything he can to help you. He has answered your questions honestly and consistently. It's time to let him go.'

Khan couldn't argue with that summation. He looked at Bonati, who returned the same look of resignation.

'You've said, Mr Calder,' Khan began, 'that the rings come from a range of suppliers across the country and beyond.'

'That's correct,' said Calder. 'My main supplier is in Italy, my homeland. I've been coming to England regularly over the years and have been planning this move for some time. Earlier this year I sourced the premises in Hatton Garden and moved over here to set up the business. I've been selling jewellery for my whole career. It is my life.'

'And your main supplier is in Venice?' replied Khan.

'Yes,' said Calder, calmly, despite being asked the same question several times since his arrival. 'I can provide you with contact details but, as I've said, you'll have to wait until I'm back at the shop. I don't have that information on me, and I don't carry a phone. Never have done.'

There was nothing left to say. The fact that Calder sourced his jewellery from Venice was, of course, of huge significance to the case, but then he hadn't tried to hide this information. He hadn't lied to Khan. He'd even said he would provide full details of the suppliers before being asked to do so. Khan knew he couldn't hold on to this volunteer witness for any longer.

He stood up slowly.

'One question, Inspector,' said Manton. 'Why the interest in the jewellery itself? I mean, you've asked several times for the origins of the items my client sells in his shop. Is there a reason for that? I've been wondering if you are more interested in the jewellery than in my client's whereabouts.'

Khan proceeded towards the door and Bonati stood up to avert Manton's gaze too.

'We like to examine every detail,' said Khan nonchalantly. 'You know, get the full picture.'

'Mmm,' said Manton, unconvinced. 'Well, I hope we have helped you.' He signalled to Calder to stand up and leave with him. 'Please don't hesitate to get in touch again if we can be of further assistance.'

'Oh, we will,' said Khan. 'We will.'

CHAPTER 26

TUESDAY 3.34 P.M.

WEST END, LONDON

The black Fireblade wove in and out of the traffic along Charing Cross Road like a needle threading its way through a particularly impenetrable fabric. Darting left and right, squeezing through spaces that seemed impossible to get through, Jud was on a mission. There was no way Grace was going to get that present, not if he could help it. Even if he had to ride the bike right into the restaurant, he'd do it.

Grace's life was at stake.

A large delivery vehicle up ahead stopped, its hazard warning lights bouncing off shop windows and reflecting off Jud's visor. Traffic flowed freely in the other direction but, as usual, no one was willing to pause and let the cars on Jud's side of the road overtake the stationary lorry. Not even for a few seconds.

Jud drummed his fingers on the handlebars and fidgeted in his seat.

Come on!

He could feel Bex was equally tense as she hugged his waist.

The pavements were lined with a torrent of pedestrians, flooding freely past the parked cars, some offering smug glances to the impatient drivers, going nowhere.

Some walked right in front of Jud's bike, high on the power they wielded at times like these, when two feet got you there quicker and you didn't have to take your life into your hands whenever you walked too close to the kerb and the speeding traffic just inches away.

Jud revved the bike's engine therapeutically – and received an admonishing look from a middle-aged lady, crossing with her teenage kids, fresh out of school.

'Pull over and I'll try Grace on the phone again,' said Bex through the headset.

'No point,' said Jud. 'I think we've established she's not taken it with her.'

'I should've called The Ivy!' said Bex. 'Could have got her to come to the phone. Why didn't I think of that?'

'Fair question,' said Jud. 'We were in too much of a hurry. We've got to think straight. I hate getting caught in traffic like this. We're stuck now.'

Bex was just about to get off the bike and fish through her pockets for her mobile phone when Jud gripped the clutch, kicked down the gear pedal and slammed the bike into first. Bex grabbed hold of his waist again just in time as they took off down the white lines in the centre of the road.

'Tell me next time!' said Bex. 'I was just going to get off and make the call.'

'Tell me when you're getting off next time, then,' said Jud. 'Right, squeeze in. It might get a bit tight here.'

She sat upright and squashed her legs snugly into the bike. The gap between the stationary vehicles and the oncoming traffic was barely wide enough for a person, let alone a Honda Fireblade with two riders. Luckily the oncoming cars were just able to swerve towards the pavement and miss Jud. The Fireblade passed through the gap to a fanfare of car horns and irate drivers, some objecting to Jud's reckless driving by wielding two fingers just as recklessly in his direction as they drove past.

Within seconds they were beyond the lorry and speeding down the now clear section of road.

'You're suicidal,' said Bex.

'Just determined. No point in phoning now, we're almost there.'

A few moments later they were screeching up West Street to The Ivy. Jud ditched the bike right outside and ignored the protestations from a passing traffic warden. 'Fill your boots,' he said as he dashed past him and entered the building with Bex in pursuit.

The paparazzi, gathered outside after a tip-off from some minor celebrities that they were about to arrive and didn't mind being 'accidentally' caught on camera, looked through their lenses at Jud and Bex. They were young and attractive. Should they have known them? Worth taking a few shots just in case.

Instinctively Jud put a hand to his face and kept his head down.

Soon they were inside the foyer, where the peace and tranquil music contrasted sharply with the taxi engines and shouts outside.

Jud was never going to get on with the maître d' at the desk. It was a fight waiting to happen, like a train heading in the same direction as another, hidden from view.

The smartly dressed girl, her auburn hair scraped back into a bun and a pair of trendy glasses perched authoritatively on her nose, looked Jud up and down disapprovingly. She wore a black suit jacket over a tightly fitted black top, like a swimsuit. Her face was tanned – could have been fake, hard to tell – and her nails were immaculately manicured. She was more striking than pretty.

Jud's hair was tussled in places and matted to his head in others, where the helmet had created its own inimitable style. He hadn't shaved for a few days now and the black jeans he was wearing hadn't seen a washing machine in weeks. The leather jacket, fortunately, gave him a rock star look, which may have excited the paparazzi but was certainly lost on the maître d'.

'Name? Do you have a booking?'

'No, we're here to talk to one of your guests – it's urgent,' said Jud.

'Well, if you wait outside, I'm sure I can fetch them for you. Their name please?' She shot a false smile in their direction and pointed to the door with a silver pen she was clutching.

'I'm not going to wait outside and you're not going to fetch them for me. We're going in to find them, OK?'

'I beg your pardon? I'm afraid—'

'Yes, well, we all feel afraid sometimes.' Jud interrupted, rummaging inside his jacket pockets, trying to find his identity card.

Bex could see he was fumbling, and sweating profusely, so she simply removed hers from her back pocket, placed it in front of the maître d' and said, 'We're here on police business. Either you let us in or we'll have you charged with obstructing an investigation. Got it?' And with that she shoved Jud towards the restaurant door and in they went.

The room was a sea of tables, each one filled with an embarrassing array of faces they knew instantly, faces they thought they might have seen in a sitcom ten years ago and faces they'd never seen outside the pages of *Heat* magazine.

But there, in a far corner, were Grace and her parents. They were poring over the menus and her father was in the midst of pontificating about something. His face was full of expression and his hands swept through the air demonstratively. He was in mid-sentence when Jud and Bex rushed to the table and stooped over Grace.

Bex grabbed her hands and scanned them. Nothing. No rings. Yet.

Relief.

'What the hell?' said Mr Cavendish, standing up and torpedoing a frown in their general direction.

'Sorry to interrupt you, Mr and Mrs Cavendish,' said Bex,

smiling and placing Grace's hands back on the table, patting them comfortingly.

'What? What is this?' said Grace's father. 'Do you mind? I mean, are we supposed to know you or something? Grace?'

His daughter was smiling. 'It's OK, Dad. I know these guys.' She turned to look up at Bex. 'What *are* you doing here anyway? Have you come to join us? I'm sure my parents won't mind – will you?' She turned to see a disgruntled expression cross the faces of them both.

'No,' said Bex quickly. 'It's OK. We don't want to intrude.'

'Too late for that, I'd say,' said Cavendish.

A tall, thickset man in a black overcoat was approaching from the doorway, followed by the maître d', looking excited.

'Quick,' whispered Jud to Bex, 'I reckon we've got about ten seconds left and then we'll be on the street with the cabbies and paparazzi.'

'Mr Cavendish,' said Bex hurriedly. 'I know this is a strange question to ask you, but have you recently bought Grace some jewellery?'

Now Cavendish looked madder than ever.

'Look, I don't know who you are, or what you're doing here, but I suggest you leave.' He beckoned to the bouncer approaching. 'Ah, good. Kindly remove these people, will you?'

'No!' shouted Grace, standing up. 'What is it, Bex? What's happened?'

The bouncer arrived and held Jud by his jacket.

Bad move.

Jud brushed his hand away.

Even worse idea.

He may have had more nerve than everyone in the building put together, but even Jud wouldn't win against someone who was almost a foot taller than him, with biceps the size of his thighs. But he'd certainly try.

Discreetly, silently, and with an expressionless face, the

bouncer extended an arm so that it enveloped Jud's shoulders and began bundling him towards the door. Bex quickly followed, with Grace at her side.

'Hey, come back here, young lady!' said her father.

'Oh, shut up, Dad!' she snapped back. 'Give me two minutes, for God's sake! I'm not a kid!'

'Charming,' said Cavendish to his wife. 'That's my birthday girl, right there.'

'Teenagers,' said a wise mother, shrugging her shoulders and smiling. 'Get on and choose the wine, darling. She'll be back in a moment.'

By the time they reached the doorway, Bex and Grace had become transfixed by Jud's hilarious attempts to reject his Goliath-sized escort. It was to no avail but Jud was never one to resist an opportunity for a fight.

'Go on, my son!' said one of the guests as they struggled past their table. ' 'Ave a go!'

Seconds later, Jud was deposited on the pavement outside. He was hot, he was angry and he was embarrassed. He was so ready to go back in there and do exactly what the guest had suggested. He'd have had a bloody good go. But fortunately Bex and Grace saw reason and they quickly talked him down.

'Leave it, Jud!' said Bex. 'It's OK now. It doesn't matter. We've found Grace. Emergency over.'

'Emergency? What emergency?' said Grace, anxiously. 'Honestly, will someone *please* tell me what the hell's going on. *Why are you here?*'

Jud wandered back to his bike, pausing to kick an empty Coke can across the pavement in anger. It bounced off the building, rattled back into the road and disappeared beneath the giant tyres of a Range Rover Sport.

'Right. Listen to me, Grace,' began Bex. 'You know some of the bodies on the new investigation were missing a finger?'

'Yes. I told you that,' said Grace. 'Luc and I saw the one at Knightsbridge.'

'Well, we think it was because of the rings they were wearing. We've traced them all back to a new shop in Hatton Garden – Calder's. All the victims, including the one you saw, were at the launch party on Saturday night. And we believe they all bought rings from there.'

'Yes? And?' said Grace becoming increasingly impatient.

'Well, we've seen the guest list for the party, Grace. Your parents were there. We believe they may have been there to buy you a ring . . . for your birthday.'

Grace looked puzzled. She stared back in the direction of the restaurant, where her parents were waiting, and tried to make sense of what Bex was telling her.

'And you think they're about to give it to me?'

'Yes,' said Bex.

'So?'

'Well, if it was from the same shop, and it's the same kind of jewellery then we're worried about it.'

'But why?' said Grace. 'It hasn't done any harm to my parents, has it.'

'I know that's true,' said Bex, 'but we think these rings are at the heart of it. It's the rings that may be attracting the ghosts in the first place. They *want* them for some reason.'

Had Grace not seen the victim at Gore Street, she would have scoffed at this idea. But now she pictured the woman, lying in the cellar garden, her ring finger savagely ripped from her hand. And she knew of the other victims too. If there was any kind of link, even one as strange as this, then she knew they had to take it seriously.

'But listen,' said Bex. 'That's not all. Jud and I were with the DG's wife. We saw what the ring had done to her – to her hand, to her body. We think it's . . . well, *cursed.*'

Grace's eyes opened wide. 'Cursed?'

'Yes,' said Bex, although hearing Grace say the word made her doubt it herself. Could the jewellery really carry some kind of curse?

'Well,' she continued, 'until we've conducted proper tests on it back at the lab, I'd say you shouldn't put it on, OK?'

'So I *can* accept it?' said Grace.

'Yes. We need it. Say thank you and bring it straight to the labs at the CRYPT.'

'But I shouldn't wear it?' said Grace, unable to hide the disappointment in her face.

'Up to you. I know I wouldn't.'

Grace's face was still confused. 'But if they *have* bought me a ring, and it has come from this same place, it doesn't seem to have affected them, does it?'

'Let's hope not,' said Bex.

'Oh great. Very reassuring,' said Grace. 'So what am I supposed to say?'

'You'll think of something,' said Bex. 'Just be glad we caught you in time.'

'Oh yeah, Bex. I'm delighted,' she quipped sarcastically.

Bex moved off towards the bike, where Jud was waiting impatiently.

'Oh, and Grace,' she said.

'Yes?'

'Bonati wants us back at the CRYPT by five. Another briefing. Don't be late.'

Grace tilted her head and smiled wryly.

Great birthday, she thought. Thanks, guys.

CHAPTER 27

TUESDAY 3.40 P.M.

HYDE PARK, LONDON

Cat and her boyfriend Jonny sat perched on an icy bench in Hyde Park, finishing the last stale crumbs of a cold burger and fries. The brown paper bag, having failed to keep the food warm, was now serving as a soggy tray for ketchup and mustard. Jonny dipped the last bundle of fries into the slippery mess at the bottom of the bag and stuffed the reddened morsel into his mouth.

Cat slurped noisily on her strawberry milkshake.

Jonny burped loudly and Cat slapped him. 'Pig.'

'I don't know what it is,' he said. 'Every time I see a burger on telly I think, "Yes please!" and every time I eat one I think, "Shit, never again!"'

'Well, I told you, marketing,' said Cat. 'It's the new art.'

Jonny finished his Diet Coke – he wasn't sure what the point of having a 'diet' Coke was when he'd just scoffed a giant burger and chips, but he always ordered one.

This was their regular haunt, their cosy place in a sheltered corner of Hyde Park, just a few minutes' walk from their respective respectable offices. He was a security guard (though his real job title was receptionist) for a large firm of business consultants near Paddington and she worked for a marketing company on the Brompton Road, at the other side of the park. This was the perfect place to meet up for a snack of dry burgers and limp chips.

Jonny belched again and rubbed his stomach as if in pain.

'What's that?' said Cat, looking in the direction of some bushes opposite them.

'What?' said Jonny, screwing the brown paper bag into a ball and hurling it towards the bin just feet away. 'Damn, missed.'

'Over there,' said Cat. 'Look. In the bushes. There's someone there, I'm sure there is.'

Jonny followed the line of her finger. 'No, I can't see anyone. It's just the wind pushing the bushes around, making shapes. Honestly, Cat, you've got such an imag—'

He stopped.

'Shit. I think you're right. What *is* that?'

They got up off the bench and walked towards the bushes and trees that lined the other side of the path. Jonny had seen it too. A dark, solid shape moved behind the bushes. The evergreen shrubs were still dense with leaves, despite the cold season, but they could see something which looked strange. Trees and shrubs sway in the wind; they don't up roots and walk. This had to be something else.

As they approached they could hear an odd sound too. It was like something was being dragged through leaves and over twigs. Sounded almost like a fox or a dog burrowing in a hole or rooting through leaves, on the scent of something. But the shape they could see passing among the shrubbery was the height of a person, not a dog.

'Wait a minute,' said Jonny, placing a hand across Cat's path. 'It's probably a couple of lovebirds. Leave 'em to it, I say.'

'Oh, come on,' said Cat, brushing his arm away. 'We've got to see what it is. Someone could be in trouble.'

Jonny didn't move. 'I gotta get back, Cat. I'm going to be late. I told them I wouldn't be long.'

'Wait,' she said, pulling at his coat sleeve. 'I'm serious, Jonny. I think someone is in there – maybe they're injured or something.' She went closer still. 'Hello? Anyone there?'

Silence.

'You see? They don't wanna be disturbed, and neither would I if I was doin' what I think they're doin'. I'm off, love. I gotta go. If I'm late again, I tell you there won't be any more afternoon snacks. That'll be it.' He started walking away. 'See you tomorrow darlin'.'

'Yeah, whatever,' Cat shouted back. 'Brave guy.' She refused to budge and walked up to the metal fencing that lined the path. The low branches of the trees hung over the fence and poked through the struts where she was standing.

'Hello?'

And then she screamed.

Jonny, now round the corner and out of sight, turned and sprinted back, faster than he'd ever run before. He was a big guy and he stumbled on the treacherous path, laden with slippery leaves. But he found his balance again and lumbered round the corner, slower than he'd have liked. But then fast food slows you down, as he always said.

'Cat? What's happened?' She was standing there, by the fence, staring into the trees with her hand over her mouth. There was no one else in this part of the park and the traffic from Kensington Road had drowned out her screams for anyone who wasn't close by.

'Well?' he said, reaching her and placing an arm around her shoulder. 'What've you seen?'

'There!' she shouted. 'In there!'

'What?'

'It was a . . . a . . . well, it was . . . horrible. Some kind of figure, all black. Then I saw its face.'

'And?'

'Terrifying. Like a mask of some kind.'

'Oi! Who's there?' Jonny shouted into the bushes and trees. 'Who is it?' He turned to Cat. 'If someone's playing tricks here I wanna know about it.' He looked into the dark shrubbery again. 'Get out here!' he shouted angrily. 'You can try and frighten *me* if you like.'

Silence.

Nothing stirred.

Jonny climbed over the metal railings.

'Don't!' Cat cried. 'Stop it!'

'No,' said Jonny. 'If someone's tryin' to frighten you, I wanna meet him.'

He brushed his way through the branches of the fir trees and on, deeper into the rhododendron bushes.

'Who's there?'

Still silence.

Jonny crept through the tangled bushes and twisted branches. Though he could hear the rumble from the traffic-laden roads outside the park, here, in the dark seclusion of the shrubbery, the city seemed a world away.

And then he caught sight of something. Up ahead, beyond the next bush, he caught a glimpse of black cloth. He pressed on, further into the greenery.

'Jonny, come back!' Cat shouted.

'I'm fine,' he replied. 'Back in a minute. I just want to—' He stopped, open-mouthed. His eyes had glimpsed a black figure, moving slowly away from him. But it was dragging something behind it.

A body.

Hard to make out but Jonny could see from the beige coat and the greying hair that it was an elderly woman. And by the limp way her body was being dragged through the muddy leaves, he could tell she was dead.

He hesitated. Should he return to Cat? Or should he press on and see what the hell this was?

He knew the answer. Jonny wasn't your average security guard. He'd only been there just over a year now. Thirteen months to be exact. Thirteen months since leaving the army. And after active service in Helmand Province, he wasn't easily scared now.

He crept on. Nothing could be as bad as the memories that still haunted him from Afghanistan. Whatever it was that had killed this woman, he knew he could take it on.

'Jonny! I'm coming in!' shouted Cat from the path.

'No!' he yelled. 'Stay where you are and call the police. I mean it. I'm fine.'

He was within a few feet of the figure now. The woman's body was small and frail. Whatever struggle she'd managed to put up, Jonny guessed it couldn't have been a match for the figure – whoever he was. He clutched her corpse like a rag doll.

Jonny caught a glimpse of the hand that was dragging the woman's arm. And it made him pause. It looked skeletal.

Skeletal?

As he stood there watching, the dark shape in front of him appeared to be sinking downwards.

Where the hell was it going? Had it found some kind of hole?

Jonny watched agog as the figure's body seemed to sink lower and lower. Disappearing into what looked like some kind of trench.

It was getting harder to follow the figure as the bushes became more compact here. Jonny dodged and weaved so he could keep sight of it, and then it was gone completely, as if the ground had swallowed it.

He heard panting behind him and quickly turned to see Cat.

'Don't you ever do that again!' she said. 'Jonny? What's wrong? What did you see?'

He gazed at her with a defeated expression across his face. His eyes were glazed over, impenetrable. She'd not seen that look since he'd left the army. And she knew it meant bad news. God knows she knew how hard it was to shift him from the nightmares that used to envelope his mind.

She held his arms. 'Tell me. What did you see?'

'You were right,' said Jonny. 'It *was* a figure. I saw it literally disappear underground. I didn't see this mask you were talkin' about, but it was dragging something with it. I could see that.'

'Dragging what?' said Cat, looking desperate.

Jonny's face was solemn. 'A body.'

CHAPTER 28

TUESDAY 4.03 P.M.

UNDERGROUND, SOUTH

KENSINGTON, LONDON

Luc trudged on, deeper into the tunnel. The camera had a limited life and he didn't know how far this filthy grave extended, or what he might find at the end of it, so he'd turned it off temporarily, placed it in his bag and switched on the lamp strapped to his forehead again.

He winced as he saw the brightly lit piles of discarded cadavers. He'd felt more secure looking at the images through the lens of the infrared camera. It had seemed more like a 3D movie. Now, in the stark, halogen light, he knew it was real. He was alone, acutely alone, and yet surrounded by bodies. The only living person in a tomb of skeletons.

He tramped onwards. The cold down here was finding its way into his own bones and they felt brittle and tender. He clasped his hands to his mouth and breathed on them heavily, his breath swirling around the tunnel like cigarette smoke.

Up ahead he could see the tunnel bending sharply to his right. He looked behind him and allowed the head lamp to illuminate the walls of corpses and the path leading back towards the cave he'd first entered.

The feelings of abandonment had not diminished, if anything they'd worsened. He could feel a lone tear forming in the corner of his right eye.

Come on, he said to himself. Get a grip.

Isolation was every agent's enemy. It went with the territory but it was always such a fierce opponent. It was a feeling no simulation in the SPA rooms could ever truly prepare you for. Whatever those SPA sessions threw at you, in the back of your mind you always knew that you were not alone – you were in the safety of headquarters, with your friends and colleagues just a short walk down the corridor or lounging in the rooms above you.

But, as every agent knew all too well, isolation was not the only foe; if anything, it was only the accomplice, the evil messenger that seized you and led you to the real enemy: panic.

And isolation was doing its work down here. It had captured his mind and was leading him down that familiar path to panic.

No matter how many simulations or training seminars or briefings you had, nothing – nothing at all – could help you build an immunity to panic. And if it did set in – as Luc could feel it was beginning to now in the dark, claustrophobic tunnel – there was little you could do to fight it. Your heart would race, a sweat would reach your palms and a dull ache would rise from the pit of your stomach and drive acid up your throat.

And then Luc committed the very worst of sin of all. It was the one thing other agents had always warned him not to do.

He started running.

It began as a slightly quickened step, punctuated by a few quick, nervous flicks over his shoulder. Then his feet were speeding up and his paces were lengthening.

He didn't know why. It was irrational. He could be running closer to his death, not to safety. He didn't know where the tunnel led, he only knew it was so far back now that surely it must be better to keep going – and quickly.

He reached the bend in the tunnel and ran on, now panting out loud as the rucksack on his back jostled and fidgeted to the beat of his steps.

And then he stopped.

What was that?

Up ahead, his torch had caught something, further down the tunnel. The halogen light, bouncing up and down as he'd run, had reflected off something pale. Was it a skull, brighter than the rest? Less decayed for some reason? The walls were lined with heads and body parts, after all.

No.

He stood still and let his eyes make sense of what he was now looking at. It wasn't a skull squeezed into the wall of other bodies. It wasn't in the wall at all.

It was a mask. A figure in black.

And it was heading straight for him.

CHAPTER 29

TUESDAY 5.00 P.M.

CRYPT, LONDON

The agents filed into Briefing Room 2, smaller than the main room but large enough for the assembled group: Jud and Bex, Nik and Stacey and Grace, just escaped from The Ivy, and from the gloomy fate that might have befallen had she put the ring on her finger. Her father, once he'd calmed down, had promised her he'd get her something else. But she'd taken the ring 'for research', still housed safely in its box.

'Where's Luc?' asked Jud.

'He's at South Kensington station,' said Bonati.

'Gone to check out this new sighting?'

'Exactly.'

'Who's he gone with?' asked Jud.

'We had to send him alone,' said Bonati. 'I know it's not ideal but we're stretched with so many cases at the moment. He said he didn't mind if he—'

'Alone?' Jud interrupted.

'Yes,' said Bonati quickly. He found Jud exasperating at times, especially when he interrupted him in front of the other agents. But he decided not to make a drama out of it, knowing that Jud and Luc were such close friends. 'Don't worry, Jud, he'll be fine.'

'So you've heard from him, have you?'

'What? Er . . . I don't know if he's reported in yet. I'm sure he will. Look, can we get on, there's much to discuss. This case is moving very quickly and it's going to spiral out of control unless we keep a calm head and stay rational. But I'm very grateful to everyone for your assistance and the rapid ways in which you've responded to this. I asked you guys to research the bubonic plague, which the hospital confirmed was what the missing McNeal was suffering from, and we've reason to believe it's what the other victims are all showing signs of. Anyone been able to do that? I know some of you have been dispatched to other places.'

Nik jumped in. He and Stacey had been poring over websites and history books while Jud and Bex had been trying on jewellery in Hatton Garden and Grace had been dining at The Ivy, so he'd now learned.

'It was bubonic plague that people were suffering from during what's famously called the Great Plague in 1665,' he began. 'It was by no means the first time Britain had been struck by a plague, sir, but it was the worst in terms of fatalities.

'The symptoms are exactly what we've all seen on the victims – sores around the neck and armpits and other areas. And blinding headaches too.'

'OK,' said Bonati.

'But it's only when we put the rings on' said Bex.

'Yeah. No sores, though – not yet at least,' Jud added.

'Anything else?' said Bonati.

'Yes,' said Stacey. 'We looked into where the plague originated from and how it came to Britain. There are mixed reports here. Some say it came from Holland, others say it came from Venice, which we know was very badly struck by plagues many times. It was the gateway to Europe in those days, a huge port, and giant galleys arrived there from Africa with the rats and fleas that carried the plague.'

Jud noticed Bex's expression had changed. She looked pensive, as if something had struck a chord. 'Well?' he said.

'I knew it! I knew I'd seen those masks somewhere before. The ghost we saw at the Waldens' place. That white mask with the long nose. It was Venetian.'

Nik was nodding. 'Bex is right,' he said eagerly. 'We looked into that too. It seems the masks were worn by plague doctors who operated in the city during the worst bouts of plague, rounding up the victims so the disease didn't spread. They covered themselves in long, black gowns laced with medicinal oils and a white mask to cover their face. The long nose was filled with health-preserving herbs, which they inhaled instead of breathing in the germ-filled air when they were in contact with plague sufferers, sir.'

'This is progress,' said Bonati.

'It's all coming back now,' said Bex. 'I went to Venice when I was a kid. We saw the masks in shops. I must have only been tiny, but I'm sure they were like that.'

'So the figures we've seen so far are the ghosts of Venetian plague doctors. And they're after victims of the plague, even here in London,' said Jud. 'I can see all that adding up, but what's the connection to the jewellery? It doesn't make sense. Why here? Why now?'

Khan spoke up. 'We can help you there, can't we, Professor?' Bonati was nodding and smiling. 'We've been interviewing Nicky Calder, the guy who runs the jewellery store. I'll give you three guesses where he's from and where he gets his jewellery.'

'Not Venice!' said Nik. 'You're joking.'

Khan looked deadly serious. 'No, I don't do jokes, son. Not where murder's concerned. Calder said he was originally from Venice.'

'That's great,' said Jud. 'So you're still holding him then?'

'On what charge?' said Khan. 'That he's selling jewellery that's cursed? I mean, I might be wrong, but I don't think there's a law against that. Not yet, at least.'

'So you've released him?' said Bex, anxiously.

'We hadn't arrested him, Rebecca! He came voluntarily to help us with our inquiries.'

'It didn't look that way at the shop,' said Jud.

'I didn't say he was happy about it,' replied Khan. 'But even he knew it was better to appear to be helping rather than hindering us. But look, we couldn't keep him and his solicitor knew that. So we had to let him go – for now. Believe me, he's under no illusions, he would be very unwise to leave the country. And there's no point in him trying, anyway. His name's with every border control officer by now. And, for good measure, I've got officers watching his every move. They'll call me if he tries to do a runner. But do you really think this jewellery can be cursed? I mean, how does that work?' As a policeman, Khan was still finding this whole 'cursed' thing difficult to comprehend.

Bex spoke first, before anyone else had time to answer. 'I'm convinced of it, Inspector. I mean, look at the evidence. Every victim bought a ring from Calder in the last few days. Some of the victims even had their ring finger ripped from its socket. So we know it's significant. What I want to know is whether Calder is aware of what his jewellery is doing.'

'Hard to say,' said Khan. 'If he's selling it knowing what damage it can cause then that's different. I mean, in some cases the victims have disappeared altogether.'

'Yes, McNeal in the hospital, of course,' said Bex.

Khan was shaking his head. 'But he's not the only one now. A woman has gone missing from Hyde Park. Kensington Road side.'

He filled them in on the details. A stony silence descended on the room as the agents looked at one another, a sense of foreboding etched on their faces.

'*Missing?*' said Jud. 'That could mean anything.'

'This woman. Has she visited Calder's shop?' asked Bex.

Khan nodded his head in resignation. 'Her mother said her daughter was wearing a new ring when they last saw each other.'

'And was she showing signs of the disease?' asked Luc.

'Well,' replied Khan, 'I'm told that her mother was worried, her daughter had been complaining of headaches recently and feeling unwell. That's why she'd come into town to meet up with her again.'

'But what about the rings themselves?' said Nik, getting impatient. 'I mean, we know they're desirable. We know that in some cases the victims' fingers have been ripped off, presumably still wearing the ring, but that doesn't necessarily prove they're cursed, does it?'

'When I held them in the jewellery store, something happened, I passed out,' snapped Jud. He disliked Nik's cynical approach to everything. Nik was always the first to try to find holes in his theories whenever he could.

Bex joined in. 'And the instruments told us they were giving off extreme levels of radiation, Nik. You should've seen it. Then you'd know. Why don't you go and spend some time wearing Grace's ring, huh?'

Bonati was keen to take control of this before the speculating and the arguing escalated. 'It is true that Jud and Bex felt something strange, but is it enough to prove the rings were actually *causing* the wearers to show symptoms of a plague not seen in this country for hundreds of years? Can a piece of jewellery carry a plague? Can it really be *cursed*?'

'Diseased bodies unearthed years later can certainly carry the spores of disease,' said Bex. 'No question. But there's something paranormal going on here. I'm sure of it. There's definitely a link between the rings and the ghosts we've seen and heard about on this case.'

'I think we need to discover the plague's origins before we can really answer your questions, sir,' said Jud. 'My gut instinct is that those rings are definitely cursed. But I know we need proof. We need to see where they're from.'

'Glad you said that,' the professor replied, smiling wryly. 'Because you'll be in Venice by tonight.'

Jud tried hard to hide his delight but it leaked out of the corners of his mouth, like a stifled smile. 'I'm going to Venice?'

'Yes,' said Bonati. 'You and Bex.'

Bex looked up. The other agents eyed her with envy. Bonati detected the mood.

'And if anyone would like to discuss my choice of agents in this deployment, do come and see me in my office after this briefing.'

As if they would.

'But don't think for one moment it'll be a holiday,' said Bonati. 'It won't.'

Somehow Jud knew he was right, though he was damn well going to try and enjoy it.

'So have there been the same ghost sightings in Venice?' asked Bex. 'I assume there have.'

'Well, that's what's strange,' said the professor. 'Khan has spoken to police over there and they said nothing's been reported. No one's gone missing in the last few days and nobody's seen any ghosts.'

'Or at least no one's reported it,' said Jud.

'Well, yes. It doesn't mean there haven't been sightings.'

'That's right,' said Nik. 'People don't always ring up the police when they see a ghost, do they?'

'That's right,' said Bonati. 'And in any case, I'm sufficiently convinced that there are real connections to Venice here. We have to check it out.'

'Oh, OK then,' said Jud, faking apathy. No one believed him – they could see the smile leaking out again.

'Well, come on then!' said Bonati, seeing them still sitting there, smiling. 'Get packing. You haven't got long. The taxi will be here to take you to the airport soon.'

Jud and Bex got up from their chairs and made for the door. As they moved past Bonati they heard his phone ring on the table next to him. Jud could see who was calling. It was the CRYPT control centre. And he recognised the number too – it was the line reserved for emergencies only.

'Wait,' Jud said to Bex. 'Hold on.'

The professor quickly picked up the phone.

'Bonati here. What? When? OK. We're on our way. Can you get a message to him?'

Bex looked at Jud anxiously as the other agents in the room all exchanged nervous glances.

'Righto. Well, keep trying. We're on our way.' The professor ended the call and stood up sharply.

'Sir?' said Jud.

Bonati looked uncomfortable. 'It's Luc. Code red.'

Everyone knew what that meant. Luc was in trouble. Serious trouble. The other agents stood up quickly and joined Bonati at the door.

'I'm coming with you,' said Jud. 'Venice can wait.'

'No!' Bonati retorted. 'Venice can't wait. I've given you both an order and you'll see it through. I give the orders here. Nik, Stacey, Grace, come with me. I'll call Dr Vorzek, see what other agents we've got available. See you in the car park. We'll take the Land Rovers. Now go!'

But Jud and Bex followed them too. There was no way they were going to get on a plane and leave the country while Luc was in trouble. Or so they thought.

Bonati stopped in the corridor. He walked right up to Jud and stared at him with a steely determination. 'You have been given your orders and you will obey them. You've been assigned to Venice and that's where you're going. I want all agents to keep a level head and think rationally. If you're unable to do that, you will both be confined to your quarters. Understood?'

Silence.

'I said, *understood?*'

'But, hang on a minute, sir. We're talking about Luc. We need to—'

'Don't tell me to "hang on" Lester. If you're suggesting, as I think you are, that we cannot cope without you, that we'll be unable to help Luc unless you accompany us then you're skating on thin ice, believe me. Besides, every moment spent arguing with you is delaying our journey to Kensington.' He saw the other agents still hanging around, watching the argument with relish. 'Now get going!' he said. 'All of you!'

He marched down the corridor in the direction of the lifts. The other agents followed him quickly.

Jud remained where he was. All the initial excitement of flying to Venice had now vanished. Suddenly it felt like a prison sentence. He turned to Bex. She could see he was clenching his fists by his sides. He let one hand fly and punched the doors behind him. His knuckles smashed into unforgiving metal but he barely noticed.

'Jud. Let it go,' said Bex, gently. 'Luc will be fine. Bonati's on it. And the others. You can trust them. Now come on. Let's go and pack.'

Jud stared at Bex. 'He better be all right, Bex. Or I'm leaving this place. I mean it.'

CHAPTER 30

TUESDAY 5.19 P.M.

SOUTH KENSINGTON STATION,

PICCADILLY LINE, LONDON

Luc was running again. Only this time he was going in the opposite direction. The masked figure approaching him down the murky tunnel had sent a shiver through his spine and he knew, instinctively, that without a whole army of agents all holding their EM neutralisers, he didn't stand a chance. What worried him most was that the ghost was carrying something. In the few seconds he'd watched it approaching, his flashlight had illuminated something dragging behind the figure. And he'd caught a glimpse of what it was. Bouncing unforgivingly off the ghost's skeletal legs was an old woman's face. Her frail body was being dragged behind, held firmly in the ghost's clutches.

It had killed – Luc could see that – and there was nothing to suppose it wouldn't do it again. Only this time a CRYPT agent would be its prize.

The rules when attending haunted crime scenes were clear: find out everything you can, sense whatever you can, take readings and make observations but do NOT place yourself in mortal danger. Weigh up the situation logically and look at the risk. If it was judged too high, and the chances of surviving were minimal, remove yourself as quickly as possible.

And that's what Luc was seeking to do now. Only there was a problem, and it came in the form of a sound. A low and steady rumbling that grew each second, somewhere up ahead, still some distance away but rising in volume, making the walls of bodies around Luc begin to shake to the increasing vibrations.

A train?.

It wasn't possible. Luc had received assurances from the station staff that the line had been closed until further notice.

He glanced quickly at his watch as he kept moving down the cramped tunnel. His body bumped into the filthy, death-ridden walls as he took his eyes off where he was going and stared at the tiny, illuminated face.

5.31 p.m.

He'd been down there for too long. Maybe the station staff had all assumed he'd returned to the platform unnoticed ages ago. After all, no one knew about the extended tunnel down here so they had no reason to think he would take this long.

But had they seriously reopened the line without double-checking?

If trains were now passing further up at the cave entrance, how the hell would he escape?

He paused and turned round to face the darkness of the tunnel behind him. He waited for a few seconds.

And there it was. The flash of white. The long, beaked nose and the ominous black shroud of the ghost, still dragging its prey behind it.

He *had* to keep going.

The sound of the train rose to a deafening, echoing growl. He knew he was close to the entrance to the hole by the level of noise coming from the tracks. It shook the walls around him. He stopped and put his arms out either side of him to try to prevent anything from crumbling. He shuddered at the thought of the walls of dead bodies caving in under the vibrations, sealing him inside this giant tomb forever.

He waited for the sound of the train to fade – it must have halted at the next station along – and then began to run again, his feet treading lightly but his face heavy with determination.

A few seconds and he was there, at the cave entrance. He could see the shiny metal tracks, reflecting the light from his head lamp.

Without waiting to calculate the risk, he ran on to the tracks.

This was madness, and he knew it. Any second now he could be sent into oblivion, struck by a passing tube train, his frame broken into bloodied, pulpy body parts.

But he knew from the evidence he heard so far, that it must have been possible to dodge the trains. After all, he'd spoken to the two witnesses in the café. They'd been spared from a brutal crushing. They must have leaned tight to the wall.

He promised himself that as soon as he heard a rumble in the distance he would stop, lean in hard to the dark, sooty bricks by his side and pray he'd be saved.

But, so far at least, there was silence.

Onwards he ran, stumbling occasionally over the slippery tracks and the uneven ground that lay between each strut. God knows how many rats and spiders he was crushing.

He paused momentarily to see if the ghost had left the cave too and was following him.

It wasn't. There was no trace of anything behind him.

He finally reached the sharp bend in the track, after which he knew he'd be able to see the soft spread of light coming from the tube station platform up ahead.

He made it.

There were figures standing on the platform and as he came closer he could see they were recognisable.

'Sir!' he shouted.

The people on the platform turned and looked blinkingly into the tunnel towards him.

Quickly Luc turned off the bright, halogen light strapped to his head and soon the onlookers could see him.

'Luc! Am I pleased to see you!' shouted Grace.

'It's good to see you,' said Bonati as he helped Luc up on to the platform. 'We were preparing ourselves for the worst. When we arrived just now we were told the line was active again – they'd started running trains, for God's sake.'

'So if I'd left the tunnel a few minutes sooner I'd have been mashed up,' said Luc. 'Great.'

'Yes, but as soon as we heard the trains were on again, I ordered them to stop and close the line down – which, luckily, they did. You timed your escape well,' said the professor.

'So what did you find?' said Nik, impatiently.

They were walking out of the station now, towards the black Land Rovers that had brought them there, abandoned on the pavement outside moments earlier. The blue lights fixed to the roofs were still flashing.

'Well,' said Luc, 'it's the weirdest place I've seen. I reckon it's a burial site. Hundreds of bodies, all stacked up like discarded wood.'

'Where?' said Vorzek.

'Just a few hundred metres down the track, inside what's almost like a cave entrance. And it led to a tunnel beyond.'

'Another tunnel leading off from the main shaft?' said Bonati. 'So that's how some of the victims were taken there.'

'Well, some may have been dragged down the main shaft, but I do know that others were brought down the smaller tunnel at the back of the grave.'

'How do you know?' said Bonati.

'Because I saw it happening.'

'What? You saw them coming?' said Nik. 'But you couldn't have seen McNeal or Sharp.'

'I didn't say it was them, did I?' Luc snapped. 'McNeal told me about the cave so I went down the tunnel to investigate. I found the smaller tunnel at the back of the cave and that's when I saw the ghost coming towards me. With another body. It was a woman – she was already dead, sir.'

The agents fell silent. Death always brought pangs of guilt and dismay that they'd not been able to get there sooner, to solve this haunting and banish the ghosts before another atrocity occurred.

'Did you say this cave thing was full of bodies?' said Stacey.

'Yeah,' said Luc. 'Packed. I've never seen anything like it. And the stench. Oh my God. It was putrid.'

'I think I know what this is,' said Stacey. 'Nik and I saw this online when we were researching the Black Death.' Nik was nodding now, he knew where she was going.

'Well?' said Bonati, clicking the first Land Rover with his remote.

'We saw several of these on websites. It's a giant plague pit. It's where they kept the bodies underground, away from the city. It's why that stretch of line has so many bends – the pits were so dense with bones it was easier for the railway engineers to go around them.'

'She's right,' said Nik. 'I'm afraid Luc has just met the victims of the Great Plague. They've been there for four hundred years.'

CHAPTER 31

TUESDAY 5.29 P.M.

TERMINAL 5, HEATHROW AIRPORT

The aeroplane doors closed and the engines fired up. Jud and Bex had been surprised at how small the plane had looked as they'd queued down the long, glass corridor from the departure lounge to the boarding tunnels, just moments earlier. They'd been expecting a much bigger one.

And Bex especially was not happy about it. She hated flying. Always had done. But somehow the larger planes felt less daunting on take-off. She could tolerate the 747s. It was, after all, like being inside a giant coach. It didn't feel at all like you were about to leave the ground. The seats, the newspapers, the luggage compartments – all reassuringly ordinary and coach-like.

But the interior of this plane consisted of just two rows of two seats with a narrow aisle in between. The roof was much lower and curved. There was no 'upstairs'. There was no way Bex could fool her senses into believing she was on a National Express coach. She was on a plane – there was no escaping that.

Her palms were sweaty and she'd begun fidgeting and rifling through the contents of the magazine rack in front of her.

'You OK?' said Jud.

'Yeah.'

'There's no TV screens on this little bird. Pathetic, isn't it?'

'Huh, yeah.' She was still trying desperately to distract her mind by flicking quickly through magazine pages, placing them back in the rack, rifling through her bag, checking her purse and her tickets, applying some lip gloss, sorting out her money, picking up a magazine again.

'Sure you're OK?' said Jud, amused by her constant shuffling.

'Yes,' she snapped.

'You don't mind flying, do you?' he said, half mockingly. 'I mean, you're not a nervous passenger?'

'No,' she bit back at him. 'I'm fine. Just leave it, OK?'

Jud smirked and went back to his own magazine, still splayed out on his lap at the same page. He'd not moved a muscle yet. He was grateful for the chance to sit down at last and rest.

The engines increased. Momentum was building, power thrusting beneath them. And then the wheels started moving. So that was it. No going back.

Bex pushed her head hard into the seat behind her and closed her eyes.

Jud glanced across at her but said nothing. She really was nervous. He wished he hadn't teased her now.

The plane finished taxiing and picked up speed as it reached the beginning of the runway.

Jud could see Bex's hands were clutching the arms of the chair tightly, her knuckles whitening.

Slowly he placed his hand on hers. She opened her eyes briefly and glanced at him. He just smiled gently. Didn't need to say anything. It was all out in the open now. Better just to get through it together and then he would tease her about it when they were safely on the ground.

The plane reached its optimum speed and the wheels left the ground.

Bex opened her eyes sharply. She needed to fidget again, find some way of distracting her brain and reducing the panic that was rising within her. Lots to do. Magazines to sort out. Her bag was a mess. Sort it out. Come on. Tidy it. Then do a crossword or a word search or a Sudoku. Take control.

That was just it. Control. It was always the same. She'd already lost control of her own fate, by placing her life in the hands of a pilot whom she'd never met, and now she was afraid of losing control of her emotions too. It was fear of fear itself that was beginning to eat away at her, like it always did in these situations.

The feeling of being in the air was deeply unsettling to her, and the idea that she was now – right now – climbing higher and higher into the sky was frightening but, like every other nervous passenger, control was at the heart of it. She hated passing control of her own destiny into the hands of someone else.

But what was she thinking? She couldn't fly a plane herself, could she? Thank God the one person in charge of her fate right now was an experienced and qualified pilot (or so she hoped). But still, sitting there quietly, without occupation, just wasn't an option. She needed to do something. And quickly.

'It's only a short flight,' said Jud calmly. 'We'll be there before you know it.'

It was strange to see Bex so nervous like this. Up until now Jud had only seen the fearless, adventurous girl he'd come to know. It struck him, watching her rummage around and fidget like a frightened school kid, how she had a vulnerable side too (just like he did). And, though it worried him beyond words – and it broke every rule he'd ever made since losing his mother – he knew deep down that Bex was becoming very important to him.

He turned back to his own magazine. It was his turn to seek distraction.

CHAPTER 32

TUESDAY 6.19 P.M.

CALDER'S JEWELLERY STORE,

HATTON GARDEN, LONDON

It had been a trying day to say the least. If anyone deserved a gin and tonic, albeit an early one, Nicky felt he did. The blinds were down in the shop window, the 'Closed' sign was on the door, the jewellery trays were safely removed from the front window and stowed away in the safe. And he had finally cleared up the mess left by his unwelcome guests. At last he could enjoy some private time – just him and Gordon (Gordon's finest gin). He kept a couple of bottles in the cupboard above the sink in the tiny makeshift kitchen at the back of the shop. The mini fridge had a small freezer compartment, just large enough to slot in a couple of trays of ice cubes and a tub of Häagen Dazs ice cream, chocolate chip cookie dough flavour.

He poured himself a generous helping of Gordon's, sloshed on some flat tonic from the plastic bottle in the fridge door and plopped in several ice cubes. Then he took the Häagen Dazs and a spoon from the cutlery drawer and settled down in the old armchair wedged into the corner of the kitchen area. Classic FM

– playing from the expensive Bose radio on his mahogany desk in the shop – was working its usual magic and soothing his mind.

He sat back into the chair and extended a long sigh.

He glanced through the open door into the shop and squinted at the luxury clock on the cabinet ahead of him – a mid-eighteenth-century clock from the famous Mayer family of clockmakers in Venice.

Twenty past six. He had forty minutes before he was supposed to be meeting friends in Soho. There was no point in going home first. He'd stay in his work suit. He wasn't overdressed – at least not for his friends, among whom he'd always enjoyed a reputation for being immaculately turned out. They wouldn't expect anything less from him.

His shirt was slightly discoloured at the collar and cuffs where the day's events had taken their toll and caused him to sweat. It was only a faint darkening but it was enough to bother him as he sat there, repositioning his cuffs into a neat, symmetrical shape around each cufflink.

Nicky Calder was a man of impeccable standards. The attention to detail he devoted to dressing was rivalled only by the fastidious way he ran the shop floor. It was immaculate. Or had been, before that inspector and his weird-looking officers had trashed the place. It had taken him hours. There was not a speck of dirt on the black and white tiles, or a grain of dust on the polished mahogany cabinets and stands. The whole place smelled of lavender – a combination of the lavender-scented wood polish he so liberally sprayed over the furniture every morning and the plug-in lavender air fresheners situated on opposite sides of the shop.

Forty minutes, he thought. Just time to check with his suppliers. The unexpected visit from the police had rattled him, far more than he'd chosen to let on at the time. Yes, he'd complied with that DCI Khan thug – he'd accompanied him to the station, as asked. Yes, he'd answered – eventually – any questions put to him. But the accusations flying around were troubling him.

To suggest that just because these victims had all visited a jewellery shop the owner of that shop must have had something to do with their deaths was ridiculous. It was like trying to make a big deal out of the victims all using the same washing-up liquid or going to the same supermarket, or visiting the same petrol station. They lived in London, for God's sake. They had money. They all shared the same impeccable taste in quality jewellery.

Big deal. It didn't make Nicky responsible for what happened to them after they'd left his shop. Khan would never make that stick.

But he sensed there was something that the Detective Chief Inspector had been keeping from him. Nicky had a gift for sensing when someone was not being honest with him – or at least not as forthcoming with their thoughts as they could be. And looking back, Khan had definitely seemed – what was it? Subdued? Elusive maybe?

Whether he liked it or not, Nicky knew he was going to get a return visit from Khan and his plodding cronies sooner or later. Bound to.

But what did he have to fear? In the eyes of the law he'd done absolutely nothing wrong. Nothing. All he'd done was sell some jewellery.

He chuckled at the desperate attempts of the hapless DCI Khan to pin something on him. What a loser, he thought to himself.

Buying a ring, as Khan knew very well, doesn't kill you. It might do some serious damage to your bank balance, but it doesn't end your life.

But even so, he thought, a quick call to his people in Venice would put his mind at ease.

He rose from the chair and made for the phone on the desk in the shop, glancing at the highly waxed wooden cabinets and display cases, so polished you could see your face in them.

He was proud of what he'd achieved – and so quickly too. It seemed like a decade ago that he was selling jewellery in Italy, and yet it was only a few months. That was all it had taken from beginning to end – find the property, apply for the lease, complete the visa applications and work permits, employ the shopfitters to work their magic and recruit the right staff to help him. Venice seemed a life time away.

And now here he was, the proud owner of Calder's, purveyor of the finest antique jewellery in London. There was no one who sold jewellery like he did. Of that he could be sure. And he didn't want it to end. Not for a long time yet.

He necked the final slurp of gin, picked up the phone and dialled. He'd already decided he was going to let his hair down tonight. He'd earned a few drinks, good conversation and a late-night dance in his favourite club. The gin tasted good at the back of his throat. He was looking forward to another.

There were too many rings down the line. But then there always were. His supplier was never quick to answer. Probably drinking again. He waited.

Eventually the monotonous ringing was ended by a low, gravelly voice.

'Si?'

'It's Nicky.'

'Si?'

'I've got some news for you. And you're not gonna like it.'

CHAPTER 33

TUESDAY 7.45 P.M.

(8.45 P.M. VENICE TIME)

FLIGHT BA2587, LONDON

HEATHROW TO VENICE

Bex peered out of the aeroplane window. It was often the same: the initial nerves – or terror, if she was honest – were replaced by courage by the time the plane was coming in to land. Her body just couldn't sustain panic for the length of an entire flight. The anguish and the fear and the constant need to keep herself busy usually dissipated by the time the plane had reached where it was going. And it was descending now, which helped. Landing was fine in her books. Take your time. It was the taking off she hated most.

The Venetian lagoon stretched out below them. It was dusk, and the islands and inlets were bathed in a pinkish hue. It was light enough to see by, but dark enough for the street lamps and romantic floodlights to have blinked into action.

'It's gorgeous, isn't it?' she said

Jud looked pensive.

'You OK?' she said.

'Yeah. I'm just thinking about Luc. Wish I'd been there with him when he was trapped.'

They'd been glad to have received a phone call from Bonati just as they were entering departures at Heathrow. Luc was safe. But his ordeal had sounded terrifying.

'Imagine it,' said Jud. 'Trapped in that underground grave with nothing but piles of putrefied cadavers to keep you company. I should've been there, Bex. Somebody should've been with him.'

'You can't be everywhere,' said Bex, gently. 'You can't save everyone.' She meant it kindly and Jud smiled at her.

'How are you now anyway? You survived the flight then.'

'I think so,' she said. 'Wait until we're on the tarmac, then I'll be just fine!'

Jud gazed past Bex and out of the window as the plane banked sharply, preparing for landing. They were close now and he could see the spires and roofs of Venice and the twinkling lights of the hotels and restaurants that lined the labyrinth of canals throughout the city. Bex was right, it really was gorgeous.

Or it would have been, had they not known what they now knew about the city below them. As Bonati had said, this wasn't a vacation after all. They were here to find out why the ghosts of plague doctors that roamed the city four hundred years ago had returned from the afterlife. Why now? And why London?

They both peered out as the buildings loomed larger and they could see the canals and pathways that ran across the city like veins on a hand.

'What do you think's down there?' Jud whispered. 'I reckon something or someone has stirred up old memories that should have remained buried deep down in the soil of the lagoon. There are too many connections for it not to be traced back to this place. It has to have started here. The plague, the doctors and their masks. The Venetian jewellery. What's going on, Bex?'

She shook her head slowly. They both could feel it – a real sense of foreboding.

Somewhere in this city, behind the ornate façades and beneath the calming waters of the Grand Canal, something evil had stirred and it was spreading like a septic wound.

CHAPTER 34

TUESDAY 7.58 P.M.

(8.58 P.M. VENICE TIME)

CANARY WHARF, LONDON

Kim Vorzek needed a break. Her boyfriend, Dougie, could not have timed his offer of dinner better. She was ready to let her hair down.

Managing the agents, especially while Bonati was secreted away with MI5 or DCI Khan or in meetings with Jason Goode, was not easy at the best of times. She was the technical guru, managing the machinations of the hi-tech equipment was infinitely preferable to managing the emotions of the agents. Humans were, after all, unpredictable. Equipment wasn't.

And recently the CRYPT had faced more challenges than ever before. It seemed almost as if ghosts in the city planned their hauntings to coincide with each other so that the agents were stretched. She knew that it was a ridiculous theory, but sometimes it really seemed that way.

And Bonati was so obsessed with keeping the DG of MI5 happy – and checking that his wife was still alive – that he'd not been able to keep his steely eye on the agents' progress like he usually did.

She'd sent agents to Wandsworth, where a disused factory building was now home to all manner of paranormal activity, some of which was violent when planning officers had entered it recently. The building was earmarked for demolition and the spirits were unhappy. She'd sent two agents over there, to take readings and sense what the hell was going on. She'd also got another back at the CRYPT researching what tragedy must've happened there in the past to make it such a significant site now.

And then there was the hotel in Shoreditch where the owners were being sued by guests after a particularly terrifying overnight stay in which one of their party had been so spooked by sounds and screams in the bedroom that she'd suffered a mild heart attack. The guests had gone to the police who'd contacted MI5 and sent the CRYPT agents in. The only problem was the hotel owners were less than welcoming – proof of ghosts was the last thing they needed.

And the giant warehouse in Clerkenwell was requiring agents on the ground too. Workers had literally downed tools until someone had rid the place of the violent poltergeist that was causing so many near-fatal accidents. The warehouse housed tools for the building industry and the packers whose job it was to box up the tools had refused to go on working until something had been done to stop the paranormal activity. A poltergeist loose in a tool store was not the safest place to be. One agent had already been injured.

And now the plague case too. Little wonder poor Luc DuBois had been left to fend for himself in the gloom of South Kensington tube.

She felt a strong sense of responsibility for these teenagers, as did the professor. Sending any of them to a violent haunting required courage and a very careful calculation of the risks involved.

Vorzek needed time out. Bonati was back in the CRYPT for the evening and he'd said she should go out – he could see the strain was getting to her.

She sipped her Jack Daniels and Coke and then rattled the shrinking ice cubes with the straw. The chink of the ice against the glass pleased her, though it always irritated Dougie, although he wouldn't say so, not tonight especially.

He'd been planning it for a while.

Unfortunately, as was always the case on an important night, he'd had to work late at the bank. There was just too much on at the office for him to be able to escape early, as he'd hoped, so he'd rearranged the plans and asked Kim if she'd be able to come to Canary Wharf, where Dougie, along with ninety thousand other workers, spent most of his waking hours. It was the nerve centre for so many international banks and businesses. A mini metropolis and as modern in design as any kid's picture of some futuristic world. Wall-to-wall skyscrapers, sculptures, fountains and piazzas. By night it looked space age.

But to Vorzek it was soulless and devoid of any kind of character. When Dougie's text had come in asking her to make her way to Canary Wharf instead of Soho, as originally planned, she'd been disappointed but not surprised. His bank owned him, like the CRYPT owned her. She knew he'd be working late. Always was. They were becoming strangers and they both knew it.

That's why tonight mattered so much. Dougie was going to get it right. Yes, Canary Wharf was his life, but there were some decent restaurants down by the water's edge and the piazza looked romantic enough tonight. Lights from the offices in the skyscrapers all around them provided a pleasant backdrop, like a stage set.

He'd chosen Carluccio's – always a safe bet. He'd even dashed down to the restaurant earlier in the day and reserved the best table, by the window with the nicest views over the wharf.

'So, have you had enough?' he said.

'Oh, Dougie, you're so impatient!' said Kim.

'Well, I'm just keen to move on to the next place, you know. The night is young, as they say.' He was never going to reveal the real reason why he wanted to get going.

She finished her drink, placed the napkin on the table and said, 'OK. I don't know how or why you eat so bloody fast, but let's go then. Where are we going next?'

'You'll see,' said Dougie, wryly.

A waiter appeared as if from nowhere, thanked them and then brought them their coats. It was a cold night and they'd both dressed wisely for the brisk winds that so often whipped around the wharf. It was a blustery place at the best of times and tonight it was especially bracing.

The cold air pushed into their faces and turned their eyes watery as the waiter held the heavy door open for them.

'Have a good night,' he said in a light Italian accent.

'We will,' said Dougie, smiling.

They walked across the pavement, between the giant clocks that stood on stilts like one-legged giants across the vast expanse of pavement outside. Metal installations were as common as trees in this part of town.

'Where are we going?' said Kim.

'Oh, just for a stroll,' said Dougie, nonchalantly.

'But it's cold!'

'Don't worry, we'll get a drink at one of the bars and then maybe wind our way back into town if you like.'

'But the bars are that way, darling,' said Kim. They were walking away from the buildings towards the water's edge.

Dougie stopped at the railings and turned back to face the giant buildings and a million office windows twinkling like fireflies.

'Come here, you,' he said and grabbed her for a cuddle.

'Get off, you soppy thing. I'm cold!' she said.

Then he took something out of his pocket.

She'd clocked it already – something angular distorting the shape of his jacket pocket. But she pretended she'd not noticed it.

He held her hand.

'Look, darling, this has gone on long enough.'

'What has?'

'You and me. The way we live. The way we're ships that pass in the night. I never see you. I want to be with you. I know we're both stupidly busy in the day, but I want to feel I can see more of you. I want to . . . well, come home to you.'

'What are you saying, Dougie?' Come on, she thought, spit it out.

'Well, erm . . .' He produced the box in his hand and carefully opened the lid.

'Marry me,' he said.

She thought for a while. It was only a few seconds but to Dougie it was a lifetime. The very fact that she had to think about it at all unsettled him.

'How?' she said.

'How? By becoming my wife. I think that's still how it works, or do they call it something different now?'

'No, no.' She chuckled. 'I mean how can we live together? You know about my work. You know it's not a nine-to-five job. I live there, for goodness sake. And there's no room for you!'

'Then leave.'

'What?'

'Leave,' he said, a fixed expression on his face that told her he meant it. He wasn't being his usual flippant self. He was asking her to choose.

She stared at the ring, gleaming up at her, its jewels shimmering in the glow of the street lamp nearby.

It was gorgeous. Not just because of its inherent beauty, but because of what it represented. Security. A home life. Together-ness. Maybe even a family . . .

Her head was in a whirl. She'd still not answered him but he was being patient – for once. He just gazed at her sympathetically. He brushed a few locks of her hair away from her eyes. She had let it down tonight – gone were the work-like chignon and the office specs – and as she turned and leaned back against the railings next to him to take in the romantic vista, the wind caught her glossy black hair and gave her the dishevelled look of a model.

'Go on,' he said softly. 'Put it on. See how it fits. If it doesn't then it doesn't. But you won't know until you try.'

And she knew he wasn't just talking about the ring. He was talking about marriage.

With her head spinning now – and it wasn't the Jack Daniels, though God knows he'd been buying her enough of them tonight – she stared lovingly at the glistening jewel surrounded by the white, velvet cushion inside the box.

It was stunning. A delicate silver band holding the most elaborate diamond cluster she'd ever seen.

'You shouldn't have,' she lied.

He took it gently from the box and held it up for her. He watched her eyes twinkling, watched every move in her face, every line, every dimple, to judge her reaction.

She stared back at him. He looked proud.

And then his expression changed. A frown. A grimace.

'Dougie?'

He groaned as his head dropped to his chest.

'Darling? What's wrong?' she said anxiously. 'Dougie!'

'It's my leg!' he shouted. 'It's . . . ouch, something's holding it. God, it's like a vice.'

They looked down.

She screamed.

There was a hand, rising from the water's surface on the other side of the metal railings that ran the full length of the dockside. A grey, mottled, skeletal hand and it gripped Dougie's leg and began pulling him – smashing him into the railings like a piece of meat.

Another hand, shoulders . . . a head. Frozen with fear, they stared at the white mask, black eyeholes and a chilling, elongated beak. The ghost grabbed Dougie and lifted him over the railings. He was shouting and kicking and lashing out at the figure. With the jewellery box still in his hand, he'd formed a fist around it and smashed his knuckles into the ghost's face. But the mask was as solid as concrete. The figure didn't even flinch.

Vorzek, too, was wrestling with it, trying valiantly to prize its iron-like fingers off her fiancé's body. She kept shouting for help from someone – anyone who could hear.

In the distance some people heard her shouts, shot a glance in her direction and immediately began running towards them.

But it was too late.

Vorzek's chest and stomach were in agony as she bent over the thin, metal barrier to save her man on the other side. He was crying out to her, 'Help me, help me!' But he was sinking now. Down into the dark, murky depths, the jewellery box still clasped in his trembling hand.

CHAPTER 35

TUESDAY 8.16 P.M.

(9.16 P.M. VENICE TIME)

WATER TAXI, VENICE

The water out in the lagoon was choppier than they'd expected. The little wooden taxi was being tossed around as they sped off in the direction of Venice.

It was a beautiful boat – polished wood, brass fixings, gleaming windows and a spacious, leather-upholstered interior. The owner, like every boatman on the jetty outside the airport, was proud of his prized possession, the source of his income and his pleasure. He'd been ferrying eager tourists to the island for fifteen years now and still he loved it. He was, after all, the first true Venetian most of them had met. He was the gatekeeper, the one who introduced them to the magic of Venice. And he played the part well. OK, so he wasn't a gondolier but that was hard, gruelling work. He preferred to entertain his customers from the comfort of his luxury boat. And he could pack more people in it anyway. The rewards were higher.

There was an earthy chug in the distance and soon they were holding on to the sides of the boat as a giant water bus went past.

It was the cheapest method of transportation between Venice and the mainland, and Jud and Bex could have waited for one leaving the airport but they were glad they hadn't. It was dirty, functional and jam packed with people. Like any city bus.

'So you've been to Venice before, huh?' said the driver. His face was lined and weather-beaten. He had a shock of black hair, greying at the sides, and a moustache to be proud of.

'Yes, I've been,' said Bex. 'But that was many years ago.'

'Ah,' he said. 'And you've returned to us with your *bambino*, huh? *Bene.*'

It was obvious what he meant and Bex flushed a little at the suggestion that Jud was her boyfriend. Jud pretended not to hear and gazed out over the lagoon and the rooftops and landmarks of the city on the horizon – the bell tower in the Piazza San Marco, and the giant domes of the elaborate Basilica. It seemed like a fairy-tale city, or a mirage appearing through the evening mist that rolled across the water.

The salty smell was not unpleasant as it wafted across the lagoon. The evening air was a blessing after the stuffiness of the aeroplane and it was helping the headache that Bex had developed during the panic-stricken flight.

'There are one hundred and seventeen islands in the giant saltwater lagoon that stretches along the coastline here,' said the driver, his Italian accent adding a certain charm to the usual patter he'd delivered day after day for so many years. 'And every one of them is *bellissimo*.' He raised his dark eyebrows as he said the word. Bex couldn't help but giggle at this theatrical Italian. 'You will love your stay, my friends, in the most famous city in the world – the *città dell'amore*.' The eyebrows went into overdrive.

They both knew what he meant. Ease off on the whole lovebirds bit thought Jud to himself, but he pretended he'd missed the man's words for the chug of the boat's engine.

They glanced up ahead as they drew closer. Ornate, luxury houses with balconies and arches lined the waterfront – as they had done, unchanged, for hundreds of years – their fancy façades welcoming the millions of guests that flocked to Venice each year and helped to prevent the city from sinking into debt, and into the lagoon itself. Reading a guide to Venice on the plane, Jud had been surprised to read that the city was literally sinking. Built on giant wooden piles driven into the marshy ground at the bottom of the saltwater lagoon, the city had sunk by twenty-four centimetres in just the last hundred years alone, evidence suggested.

But the weight of millions of tourists flocking to its attractions each year was worth enduring if only for the money they left behind. Without it the city was unsustainable.

'You couldn't make it up,' said Bex, sounding excited now.

'What?'

'I mean, look at it. If you drew something like this as a kid, people would say it was fantasy – a city doesn't look like this. But it really does.'

Jud nodded his head. He couldn't disagree. It was breathtaking, especially in the warm glow of dusk. The sun was setting to the West and many of the buildings were bathed in a pinkish light. He'd never seen such elaborate architecture.

The taxi was heading for what had seemed like a tiny gap in the land but was in fact the start of the Rio di Noale, a canal which led them to the world-famous Grand Canal. The boat's chugging echoed from the elaborate buildings, disturbing the peace. The pleasingly symmetrical and extravagant Ca Pesaro stood proudly at the end of the canal, earning its role as the first elaborate building you see as you enter the historic Grand Canal.

As the boat swung left and joined the main waterway, Jud and Bex gasped at the majesty of what they were seeing.

There were gondolas, their perpendicular owners in their black and white stripes, with biceps the size of Jud's legs. There were other water taxis, their heavy polished brass rails catching the last moments of sunlight, and along the banks there were intimate archways through which they could glimpse the twink-ling lights of bistros and bars and hotels. It was a labyrinth of indulgence and hedonistic holidays.

'Heaven, don't you think?' said Bex.

'It's amazing,' said Jud. 'Like a stage set. I can imagine the buildings only having a front façade and just being propped up by scaffolding behind.'

'I know,' smiled Bex. 'But it's real. Believe it.' She saw his expression become pensive. 'Thoughts?'

'I'm just wondering,' he said, 'what this place must've been like in the plague.'

'Brilliant,' said Bex. 'Spoil the moment, won't you?'

'Well, we're not here for a holiday, Bex.'

'I know, I know. I just wanted . . . I don't know. I just . . . whatever.'

Jud looked at her, puzzled, and then said, 'We need to get to a restaurant or something as soon as we land, yeah? I mean it's nearly ten o'clock.'

The boat turned a corner to the right and then they saw the view so recognisable it seemed like a cliché. The Rialto Bridge.

'It's stood here since 1591,' said the driver, proudly. 'Lasted well, huh?'

'Stunning,' said Bex, dutifully.

The boat slowed to a respectful cruise and they went under the arches. Jud looked up just before they entered and was blinded by a thousand camera flashes from the myriad of tourists all poring over the bridge like insects.

Through the other side they could see rows of gondolas, their gleaming black hulls and extravagant leather seats and drapes enticing rich tourists to come and spend ludicrous sums of money on thirty-minute rides.

And the posts to which the boats were tethered were driven down into the murky depths of the canal, and looked like rows and rows of giant pencils.

The restaurants and bars that lined the canal banks were heaving with customers. Wine glasses were shimmering in the light and the Italian waiters, dressed smartly in black, were pandering to the needs of the wealthy visitors. It was a factory – but a glamorous one, that was just the point.

The boat gently pulled up to an available pencil and a precarious-looking wooden jetty. A burly guy with a bald head and a red face shouted some Italian very quickly to the driver, who answered in an equally theatrical way, and a rope was pulled into the bank and secured.

Jud paid the obligatory one hundred euros. He'd claim that back, for sure. He jumped off the boat, rejecting the hand of help from the driver. Bex was quite happy to be helped on to the jetty by her charming host, who winked cheekily and said, 'Enjoy yourselves.'

They pulled their wheeled suitcases behind them, the little plastic casters rattling over the old cobbled pavement, and wandered in the direction of the nearest bistro.

'I'm starving,' said Jud. 'Pasta here we come.'

A few moments later they were sitting at a riverside table at La Porta D'Acqua.

'Fill your boots,' said Jud, glancing at the menu. 'Whatever you want.'

CHAPTER 36

TUESDAY 9.11 P.M.

MILE END HOSPITAL, TOWER

HAMLETS, LONDON

Bonati raced in through the doors and up to the receptionist.

'Dougie Pincent,' he said, anxiously. 'He was admitted earlier this evening. Where can I find him?'

The receptionist looked at him curiously. 'Visiting hours have finished, sir. You can visit him in the morning, from eight o'clock onwards.'

The professor was having none of it. He showed her his identity card and said it was part of an investigation. This was not the time to argue.

She directed him to the right ward and a few moments later he was peering into Dougie's private room. He could see Kim Vorzek was at his bedside. A gentle tap on the door and Vorzek looked up to see his smiling face at the window.

'Thanks for coming,' she said. Bonati could see her eyes were red and puffy from crying.

'What the hell happened, Kim? What you told me on the phone was hard to believe.'

They sat down in chairs either side of the bed and talked in whispers over his sleeping body.

'One minute we were standing there, Giles, by the water, and the next minute there was a ghost at my leg. Dougie tried to fight it off but it went for him. I mean *really* went for him.

'Giles, I thought I'd lost him.'

Bonati extended a hand over the bed and held hers.

'I'm so sorry,' he said. 'You must be shattered. Have you eaten? Do you want some coffee?'

'No, I don't want anything.' She sniffed and tried to force a smile. 'I just want to be here, you know, for when he wakes up.'

'So how did it happen?'

'Well, he was sucked down into the water by the ghost. I leaned over the edge of the railing and tried to grab him. But he was gone.

'I turned away and must've collapsed with shock. There were others there by then. When I recovered I told them what had happened and they couldn't believe it. Thought I was hysterical, or drunk.

'And then there was this gurgling sound and a shout. We looked at the water and he was there, his hands were gripping the jetty. I couldn't believe it. He's a fighter, you know.' She gazed at him, still sleeping in the bed beside her. 'Well, we grabbed him and just pulled as hard as we could. He was coughing and spluttering and he had this massive bruise on his head, but he was alive. We got him out.'

'And the ghost?' said Bonati.

'I dunno. Maybe it had had enough. Truth is I don't think it was after Dougie anyway.'

'No?'

'No.' She looked forlornly at the bedside cabinet beside her. She picked up a small jewellery box and opened it to show the professor. 'I think it was after this.'

174

Bonati's eyes opened wide. 'No! It's not . . .'

She was nodding her head. 'I asked Dougie in the ambulance where he'd bought it and he said a new shop in. Hatton Garden.'

'My God. You've been through hell.' Bonati looked again at the ring. He guessed what it meant. 'It's an engagement ring, isn't it?' he said gently.

She nodded. 'I haven't answered him yet. Don't worry. I will. I'll tell him I can't. It won't work. I know what you're going to say.'

Bonati was shaking his head slightly and staring at her with sympathetic eyes. 'You don't know what I'm going to say, Kim. Because you don't know how I feel. I'm tired, Kim. I'm tired of being alone. My family is the CRYPT, and so is yours. But you're younger than me. We can't expect you to devote your life to us – and to no one else.'

'But my work, Giles. I can't leave it. It's my life.'

'Who said anything about leaving?'

'But . . .'

'No. Look, you need to concentrate on making sure Dougie's OK. I can see he's had a nasty blow to the head and the mental scars of what happened tonight will run deeper still. But eventually, when you're ready, come and talk to me. There is no rule that says you have to live with us, Kim. Get yourself a flat round the corner. You're too special to be alone, but you're too precious for us to lose. Can't we share you, huh? Marry Dougie and work for us.'

She managed a smile. She grabbed a tissue from her pocket and wiped her nose.

'We'll see,' she said. 'But thanks, Giles.' She held his hand again. 'I mean it. You're the best boss anyone could wish for.'

'Stop it,' he said, smiling. 'I just don't want you to make the same mistakes I've made. I had my chances but I devoted myself to my work. I lost sight of what really matters.'

'You're loved, Giles. What would the agents do without you?'

'Mmm, I wonder,' he said.

There was a vibration from the phone in his jacket pocket.

'Look, I've got to go,' he said softly. 'You stay here as long as you want to. Take all the time you need. I'd like to say take some time off, but—'

'Now you're being stupid,' said Vorzek. 'We're busier than we've ever been right now . . . Or maybe I should take advantage of this sudden generosity!'

'Well, anyway. Do the right thing for Dougie.' He stood up and walked over to pick up the jewellery box. 'I'll have to take this, Kim. It's too dangerous and you know it.'

'The ring or marriage?'

Bonati smiled sympathetically, patted her shoulder and then left the room. He walked slowly down the corridor, wondering how many other people were here visiting their loved ones. What would happen to him if he fell sick? Who would come and visit him? Who would they write down as his next of kin on the forms?

He seldom thought of growing old. It was always work, work, work. He'd never stopped to ponder life after CRYPT. Whom would he share it with?

He brushed away the morose thoughts and took his phone from his pocket.

It was a text from DCI Khan.

Call when you can.

He quickly left the building and went to his car. That was it, he thought. He'd share his retirement with his Mercedes. And he'd buy more when he had the chance. He'd spend his last few years driving stupidly fast on the roads he'd always wanted to drive: the alps, the autobahns, Route 66.

He opened the car door, got in and pressed the number for Khan.

'Ah, Professor. How's Dr Vorzek's partner? I heard what happened.'

'OK, I think. Khan, we've got to stop this before someone else is taken.'

'Too late.'

'What?'

'We found three more bodies down in the plague pit at South Ken. We'd sealed it off. And we had someone in Hyde Park, where you told us to patrol.'

'So what the hell happened?' Bonati sounded angry. 'Did your officer fall asleep or something? I mean, why didn't he see the ghosts coming through?'

'Oh, he would have seen the ghost all right. He would've seen it close up. Just before it killed him.'

'Shit.' Bonati said quietly.

'We found DC Stricker's body lying in the bushes just near the tunnel entrance that leads to the plague pit.'

'I'm so sorry, Khan.'

'Yeah, well, the Commissioner is asking some serious questions, I can tell you. And he's told me to do a press conference in the morning.'

'A *press conference*? Why? I mean, why does the whole world need to know?'

Khan's anger was building now. 'Why?' he said sharply. 'Because we've had multiple fatalities in one day, and not only that but people are now reporting sightings of these bloody ghosts right across London. The switchboard's been jammed. The world *already knows!*'

'OK, OK, I'm sorry,' said Bonati. 'We've been busy too. MI5 have been calling. But we only have so many agents. When's your press conference then? Do you need me?'

'Of course I bloody need you! Don't worry, you won't be on camera, but we need to talk and get the script right. Thirsty?'

'Yeah. Where?'

'I'll come to you.'

'OK,' said Bonati.

'See you at your place in half an hour then. Will Goode be there?'

'Try stopping him,' said the professor.

CHAPTER 37

TUESDAY 9.38 P.M.

(10.38 P.M. VENICE TIME)

GRAND CANAL, VENICE

'So, what do you notice here?' said Bex. She had tomato sauce on her chin, from the delicious meatballs and spaghetti she'd ploughed through. Jud thought it was fun not to tell her. He polished off his lasagne and wiped the plate clean with the last remnant of garlic bread.

'Do you mean do I feel anything?' he said.

'Yeah.'

He thought for a moment. He gazed out at the romantic vista – the gondolas gently moving down the water under the Rialto Bridge, the gondoliers' songs blending with the soft lapping of the water at the jetties, the floodlit buildings on the opposite bank, and the dark, starry sky beyond.

'There's a lie here.'

'What?'

'I don't know. It's like there's two halves of Venice.'

'Of course there is, look – it's bisected by water!'

'No, that's not what I mean. Look at it this way, there's the side we see – the romantic view of the city, the picture-postcard stuff, you know – but then there's a darker side, and it's buried beneath us.'

'Literally?'

'Well, kind of. It's like London, isn't it? You've got the buildings, the landmarks, the attractions, but beneath the sites there's some darker stuff they don't want you to know about.'

'Such as?'

'Well, the more gruesome history. The crime and punishment, the practices that went on when we had different values, different customs. Look at Marble Arch, for goodness sake. Look at what happened when some rich guy tried to dig up the ground round about there. You know what happened. He found thousands of buried souls, hanged on the same site at Tyburn and flung in great pits. They were there all along, in the same patch of ground people walk over everyday.'

'And now the plague pits we're finding.'

'Exactly,' said Jud. 'Ask Luc.'

'And you think Venice is the same?'

'I'm sure it is. Cities always have a darker edge to them. They don't just represent man's achievements, they represent our failures too. You only need to start digging and you find evil is buried alongside good. It's called humanity.'

'You're getting very philosophical, Lester.'

'Not really. It's a fact. Just think about this place. Think of the power, the money, the glamour. You don't imagine these things aren't fought over and hard won? There's greed here, real greed. And I reckon there's some dark secrets buried in the marshes below us. With so little land, after all, where do you think they hurl most of the bodies?'

'And can you imagine what this place must've been like when the plague struck?' said Bex, gazing up at the bridge, still packed with people, all moving slowly like a train of ants. 'It must've always been crowded here.'

'Exactly. I bet if you showed signs of the plague here you'd be dealt with pretty quickly. Imagine how it would spread.'

'But why are the plague doctors in London, Jud? It just doesn't make sense.'

'Well, you know we've got the jewellery as a link – it's Venetian, at least that's what Khan said. Apparently this Calder guy said his main suppliers were here in Venice.'

Bex was screwing her face up and looking puzzled. 'But there's something missing. Jewellery is an inanimate object, it carries no residue of emotion or evil intent. Can it really be cursed?'

'I've got a feeling we'll know that soon,' said Jud.

'And do you think the ghosts are here too?'

'It would be strange if they were only operating in London, wouldn't it?'

'And there are plenty of shops here selling Venetian jewellery, after all,' said Bex. 'Oh God, I just hope they haven't been seeing the same brutal attacks we've seen in London. The police say there's been nothing, but can that be true?'

'That's what we've gotta find out,' said Jud, yawning. It had been a day to end all days. CRYPT agents certainly knew how to fill each hour with action. There was never a dull moment. He swung back on his chair and looked at the sky. 'I don't know about you, Bex, but I'm shattered.'

But Bex was just getting into the conversation now. She wasn't ready to go. And besides, opportunities like this, to have Jud to herself, were rare.

'It's always amazed me how violent ghosts can be. I mean, the destruction they can cause – to people, to their families.'

Jud was only half listening, he was gazing at the ripples on the water as it gently flowed past. The charm of Venice was slowly working its magic and he was close – only close – to relaxing.

'You don't need to tell *me* what ghosts can do to families. I know,' he said.

'What?' said Bex.

'Er? What?' Jud rubbed his eyes and tried to stay alert. He realised he'd just said something he shouldn't have. Whether it was the city, or the company, or just plain tiredness he wasn't sure, but he felt vulnerable to attack. 'I can't remember what I said.'

'You said, "You don't need to tell me what ghosts can do to families." '

'Yeah,' said Jud nonchalantly, trying to backtrack, 'well, I mean I've seen it, you know – so have you – we've all seen what ghosts can do to people. And the fallout for the victims' families must be devastating.'

'Mmm,' said Bex, nodding and staring at him. But she could tell, she'd seen it, a slight flicker in his eyebrows, a melancholy gaze in his eyes – and she knew somehow that he had been talking about something else, something buried deep inside him. A pain that, for one brief second, had risen to the surface from where it had been festering, like the salty marshes at the bottom of the canal beside them.

'Come on,' Jud said quickly. 'It's time we found the hotel. Drink up.'

CHAPTER 38

TUESDAY 10.55 P.M.

CRYPT, LONDON

Jason Goode was pacing the floor, like he often did when he was deep in thought. He'd had a busy day, just like Bonati and the agents, although most of his time had been spent on very different pursuits, many floors up in the global headquarters of his IT empire.

Running an international business like Goode Technology PLC required stamina and huge levels of fitness. Luckily Goode was blessed with limitless reserves of both. He was an enigma – everyone at HQ thought that. The hundreds of employees who travelled to Goode Tower every day knew that it was a privilege to be working right at the hub of the global business. No one took their job for granted.

But that wasn't to say it wasn't fun or exciting working for a creative, innovative entrepreneur like Jason Goode. Life could certainly be unpredictable. He was a human dynamo, an endless source of ideas and strategies. He would try to visit most of the people in his vast headquarters at least once a fortnight. They'd always know when he was on their floor – there was a buzz about the place. Whether it was in logistics or research or human resources or accounts, the staff were always secretly thrilled to be getting a 'royal visit', as they often called it.

And today had been one of those days, those 'stir frying' days, when Goode tried to keep abreast of how several departments were doing. He called them 'pit stops' – those meetings which he would schedule to catch up with senior figures in each section and do a morale-boosting tour, followed by some straight talking in one of the many boardrooms, with senior executives. A chance to motivate and energise his family.

And now, pacing the floor in Professor Bonati's office, Goode had to switch hats again and turn his attention to something quite different that lurked below ground. His precious CRYPT. Quite how many staff actually knew about the CRYPT was questionable. Officially only a handful of senior executives were aware; to all others, the floors beneath the building, if they existed at all, were used only for car parking and storage.

Most employees arrived and left on foot, catching trains and buses back to their homes outside the city. A few drove to work and they parked their cars below ground, often blissfully unaware that just the other side of the walls was a vast labyrinth of laboratories and accommodation all specially designed to support the work of the Covert Response Youth Paranormal Team.

When agents entered or exited the building by car or motorbike, they did so via a ramp at the rear of the building. It led to a barrier that required a secret pass code, then a separate floor of parking spaces, buried deep underground. If they wished to leave the building on foot, which they seldom did, they would do so via a tunnel that ran beneath the car parking ramp and led away from the building, to an electronic exit a few feet away, down an alleyway. It would be almost impossible for an employee of Goode Technology to meet a CRYPT agent. That's how Jason Goode preferred it.

And although he had enjoyed a very positive day of meetings

and morale boosting with his team above ground, it was here, in the heart of the CRYPT, that he felt most at home and revitalised, with his closest family of all.

It was just as well that he had such large reserves of energy and stamina. It would be a long night.

DCI Khan knocked back his first whisky and Bonati offered him another.

'I'm still not convinced that a press conference is advisable or even necessary at this stage, Inspector,' said Jason Goode.

'I understand your reservations,' said Khan, 'but we have to say something. We cannot risk being seen to be doing nothing. We have to respond to calls when they come in and, believe me, we've been getting many now.'

'So the ghosts – these plague doctors – have been sighted where?' asked Goode.

Bonati was able to answer that one. 'Kensington, Knightsbridge, Chelsea, Hyde Park.'

'And news just in,' said Khan, 'is that further sightings have been reported in Bloomsbury, Chiswick, and now over in Richmond.'

'These are all rich, up-market places. I'm guessing they are where people with expensive tastes in Venetian jewellery live,' said Goode.

'Exactly,' said Khan.

'Well, at least we've closed Calder's down for now.'

Khan and Bonati looked at one another nervously.

'I mean, we have, haven't we?' said Goode.

Khan shook his head.

'What?' Goode looked incredulous. 'You mean to tell me this guy is still being allowed to sell cursed jewellery? You're not serious?'

'But how do we stop him?' said Khan. 'Believe me, we've tried to come at this from every angle. We've had Calder in, we've questioned him, but it boils down to this, you can't arrest and charge someone with selling cursed jewellery. His lawyer would have a field day.'

Goode was still unimpressed. 'So this man is still selling the stuff? And punters are still buying it?'

'Well, we still don't know if—'

'Don't even finish that sentence. You were going to say that we still don't know if my agents are right and that the rings have anything to do with the hauntings. Detective Chief Inspector, not only are the rings a very real and obvious link to the victims, it has been confirmed by my agents that they do indeed emit extraordinarily high levels of radiation – and we know what that means. Besides, one of my agents, Jud Lester, so the professor here told me, experienced strange sensations when he held the rings in Calder's own store.'

It was true. Bonati had been relaying the events of the day to him, as the professor always tried to do whenever he was in the building. And he'd been dismayed to hear that his own son had foolishly played with the jewellery.

'Hang on, Jason,' said Bonati. 'The inspector has a point. We can only work within the law. We can't invent new laws just so that people we target can break them and we can then arrest them. That's not how it works.'

Goode sat down at the cherrywood dining table and slammed his own whisky tumbler on the surface. A small ripple of the amber liquid splashed on to the polished tabletop and he wiped it away with his sleeve.

'Giles, don't take his side, for God's sake. We're standing on the brink – no, we're already knee deep in – a major haunting in the city and the root cause of it is still at large, even though we know who it is and where it's coming from. This is madness.'

'We're on it, Jason, as I've been telling you all day.'

'Yes, Giles, and as Khan is now telling *us*, people have been *dying all day*! Look, either you go in there and arrest this guy or

I'll go and get the bastard myself and you can arrest me for it. I believe my agents . . . even if you don't.'

'That was unnecessary,' said Bonati, in that professorial tone he sometimes used with his oldest friend when Jason had let his anger and emotion get the better of him.

'Look, gentlemen,' said Khan, 'I can promise you my officers and I are poring over this man's accounts, his movements, his acquaintances, everything about the guy, in the hope that we can find some reason to haul him in again. But until we do, we cannot close him down on a whim. We just can't.'

'Jesus!' said Goode. 'He thinks it's a bloody whim, now. Brilliant.'

'Please, let me finish,' said the inspector. 'But we will take him. We'll go and get him in the morning. Even if I have to make something up myself and then let him go once this has all ended and be sued for wrongful arrest. It'll have been worth it. But in the meantime, the Commissioner has told me we have to hold a press conference first thing tomorrow because, whether we like it or not, the rumours of these hauntings are spreading. We all know what happens when word of paranormal activity gets out. Panic spreads like the plague – sorry, bad analogy – and before we know it we have hysteria on the streets. You know how it escalates.'

And they certainly did know. Goode and Bonati's early attempts to create a Paranormal Investigation Team (or PIT as they'd called it) were thwarted in those early days by too much exposure and too many members of the public catching on that they were investigating *real* ghosts. They'd ended up causing more fear than they'd prevented. The real enemy of the city was not ghosts, it was panic. Fear itself. And as anyone in the CRYPT knew all too well, ghosts fed off human fear. They harnessed the energy given off when humans' emotions were running high. Fear could be a killer – literally.

Maybe the Commissioner was right. To say nothing at all, as

Goode would have preferred to do, could be counter-productive.

'But what the hell are we going to say to the public?' said Goode.

'That's why I'm here,' said Khan, feeling frustrated that they'd been going round in circles and, as usual, humouring Jason Goode and allowing him to get his frustrations off his chest.

But, as Bonati knew very well, Jason Goode had a habit of cutting through bullshit and saying it like it is. That was why he was both infuriating and inspiring to work with.

'OK,' said Goode, standing up again to launch into another round of pacing. 'We say this: yes, there have been some fatal attacks in the city, but these have all been premeditated and focused. They have not been random killings – that's what the public want to hear. Random killings are the thing people fear most.'

'Yeah,' said Khan, 'and the other thing is ghosts.'

'OK,' Goode continued. 'So we say that the killings have been committed by members of the same gang – a group of violent jewel thieves, dressed in black and wearing masks to protect their identity.'

'Do we need to focus on the jewels?' said Bonati.

'I'd say so, yes,' said Goode. 'Look, some have had their fingers ripped off, and some members of the public have seen that, haven't they?'

'Yeah, a few,' said Khan.

'And we can say that all the victims have attended the same shop and so were wearing the same kind of jewellery – which must be highly prized by this gang of lunatics.'

'Can we mention the shop?' said Bonati.

'Yeah, sure we can,' said Goode. 'Why not? It's true, isn't it?'

Khan nodded. 'It is true, yes. And we're not suggesting for a moment that Calder is responsible either. Maybe that'll work.'

'Well, one thing is certain,' said Bonati. 'You can expect a lawsuit from Calder for loss of earnings. No one will ever visit his shop again.'

'Which is exactly what we want, ain't it?' said Goode. 'Besides, if this turns out to be wrong and we've got the wrong guy, then I'll pay the bastard off myself – I'll give Calder his lost earnings. That'll shut him up.'

Bonati agreed. 'And at least that way we can stop anyone else buying this jewellery and bringing the curse to their own doors.'

'Oh, well done, Columbo,' said Goode, smiling at his old friend. 'That's the whole point!'

CHAPTER 39

WEDNESDAY 2.48 A.M.

CHARTERHOUSE BUILDINGS,

CLERKENWELL, LONDON

It had been a rousing night, just what the doctor ordered. Nicky Calder stumbled through his front door, having spent the last five minutes trying to get the little brass key into the Yale lock. It was hard when you were drunk. Eventually, fed up with seeing two keys and two locks, he'd closed one eye and screwed his face into a shape resembling a walnut. Got it.

Now inside, he made straight for the coffee machine. It was, after all, going to be an even longer night still, with no prospect of bed – not for some time yet.

He'd decided he needed a holiday. Everyone at the club had advised him it was a good idea.

'You look awful,' they'd said when he'd pitched up at the beginning of the evening. 'Everything all right, Caldy?'

He'd told them that he'd had a difficult day, though he'd omitted to say exactly why. His friends had reminded him that he'd not had a day off since moving to London. There had been the flat to sort out, and the shopfitting to manage. He'd been meticulous in his requirements and there was no way he was going to leave it to shopfitters themselves. He'd been on at them every day right up until the store had opened.

And since then, he'd still been in overdrive. He did, after all, want this to work. He had so much riding on it. But this business with the police had rattled him, there was no use denying it.

His friends had spent the evening persuading him to treat himself to a well-earned break and so that was exactly what he'd resolved to do.

Right now.

Perhaps it was the drink or the protestations of his equally drunken friends, but Nicky was fired up and ready to make the break. Just a few days was all he needed. A few days of relaxation, of reading his favourite novelists, drinking his favourite gin and doing precious little else.

But he knew he had this silly police investigation going on. Had that ghastly Inspector Khan really meant it when he'd advised him not to go anywhere? After all, he'd done nothing wrong.

Just for good measure Nicky decided it would be better if he didn't chance his arm and leave the country altogether. Not right now. You never knew. Khan might not have been bluffing and may have alerted border control and customs. It would be so very awkward if he was to be detained at an airport. He couldn't face the embarrassment.

But there was one very obvious place he could go. A place where he could be assured of a relaxing time and warm hospitality. He had a friend he'd known for years now, since their days working together in the jewellery shops of London as apprentices all those years ago, when he'd learned his trade. When Nicky had returned to Venice, his friend, Sebastian, had moved to Scotland, where he was still living. When Nicky came back to London, this time to open his own shop, he had promised Seb he would visit him. And now was the perfect time.

That was it. He was going to Glasgow.

He staggered into the bedroom and reached up to get the suitcase from above the wardrobe. He lost his grip and it thundered to the floor. 'Shush!' he said, giggling like a school kid, his finger at his lips.

A few minutes later he was packed. Just a few clothes, his iPhone charger and his precious Kindle e-Reader. He went into the tiny bathroom and prepared his black, leather toiletry bag. He was a stickler for presentation and he wasn't going to be without his shaver and vast array of skin care and hair products. The bag was bursting at the seams but he managed to zip it up and placed it in the suitcase.

He grabbed his wallet and keys left abandoned on the worktop in the kitchen and headed for the door. The excitement of leaving on the spur of the moment was sending a rush to his head. He was almost giggling again, like a naughty truant.

But why shouldn't he go?

It had only just sunk in (mainly because his friends had spent the evening trying to tell him) that, at last, he was his own boss. If Nicky Calder wanted a few days off, then he should take them. If he didn't show for work in he morning, who cared exactly? It was his shop, his business, and provided he could make up the sales when he came back – which he knew he could, given that the Christmas season had not even started yet – then why shouldn't he escape for a day or two?

The door slammed decisively behind him and he took the suitcase downstairs to the entrance.

There was the sound of a chain rattling behind the door of the flat next to his. It opened slightly and Calder saw a pair of eyes staring at him through the gap.

'Good morning,' Calder said, drunkenly.

The neighbour just rolled her eyes and shook her head slightly. She was about to tell him to keep the noise down but was relieved to see him holding a suitcase. At last, some peace, she thought. He was forever coming back to his flat late at night and giggling and fumbling with his keys. She ignored him and shut the door promptly.

It was 3.30a.m. The next train wasn't until 5.30a.m. from London Euston, so he had plenty of time to catch a taxi – if he could find one. The night's heavy drinking and smoking had left him feeling dry-mouthed and hungry so he was looking forward to a pastry and a moccachino from the station café. Besides, he loved London stations in the early hours of the morning. They were filled with optimism as the shops twinkled into action and the smell of hot bagels and griddled bacon filled the air.

He strolled down the dimly lit street, his wheeled suitcase jarring on the paving stones. There was a taxi rank up on the main Clerkenwell Road – it wasn't far.

The juddering of his suitcase wasn't loud enough to penetrate through the closed car window of PC Stringer, who was sitting, head on chest, snoozing and dribbling, a *Top Gear* magazine splayed over his knees and peppered with the crumbs of a sausage roll.

Stringer had pulled the short straw at the station and had been ordered to watch this odd little man all evening from afar. He'd waited outside his favourite bar, outside his favourite restaurant and then his favourite club. He'd shadowed him home and then watched him stagger through the front door of his apartment block. He had felt relieved when the front door had slammed shut and he was, at last, free of this man for a few hours, while Calder slept off what would be a raging hangover, judging by the way he was staggering and stumbling at the end of the evening.

Stringer had thought he'd treat himself to forty winks. His target was going nowhere. He'd be snoring like a pig by now up there in his little bachelor pad. Packing a suitcase and reappearing half an hour later, bound for Euston, was the last thing Stringer expected his man to be doing.

So he slept on. And Calder tottered freely down the road, reached the junction, and was gone.

CHAPTER 40

WEDNESDAY 6.09 A.M.

(7.09 A.M. VENICE TIME)

HOTEL CAVALLETTO, VENICE

The jarring sound of glass bottles rattling and metal barrels rolling across cobbled floors burst unexpectedly through Jud's window.

He opened his eyes and glanced quickly at the clock beside his bed. His body clock was still on British time and he was surprised to see it was past seven already, it had felt earlier than that.

He got up and went to the window. What the hell was that noise?

Pulling the curtains wide, he peered sleepily down to the ground. So that was it.

There was a small canal running right up to the rear of the hotel and it was a traffic jam of delivery barges. There were laundry boats, steered by huge, burly men who picked up giant linen sacks as if they were small shopping bags and hurled them on to the pavement. There was lots of theatrical shouting and gestures, jokes and laughter. It seemed that dramatic dialogue accompanied every job in Venice. It was how the workers passed the day – last night Jud had assumed such theatrics were for the benefit of tourists, all eager to see a 'real' Venetian boatman at work. But here, there were no onlookers, only Jud. It was how the locals were built, Jud assumed. It was one of the things that made them Italian.

Jostling for position were other barges, each one heaving under the strain of cases of wine, soft drinks and large, metal beer barrels. One of the boats housed a small crane which was now being handled skilfully by its adept driver – the arm swinging across, lifting up deliveries and depositing them on the cobbles like some metal grabber in an arcade machine.

Two men were standing on the pavement, puffing on cigarettes and engaged in deep conversation that seemed to require much shaking of heads and remonstrating with large hand gestures and plenty of gusto.

Venice was not a place for a leisurely lie-in, it seemed.

Jud showered and dressed. No doubt he'd be getting a call or text from Bonati soon and he'd tried and failed enough times in the past to fake being up – the professor could always guess when he was still in bed.

He went downstairs to the dining room, now laid decoratively for a sumptuous breakfast of pastries, fresh fruit, scrambled eggs, all manner of cereals, natural yoghurt, prunes, and a strange, salty meat that proved to be a tastier equivalent of Danish bacon.

He sat at a table in the corner, overlooking the rear of the hotel – he was still transfixed by the logistical challenges of manoeuvring large canal barges and exchanging giant bags of fresh laundry for old ones. If this was the rush hour in Venice, then it was infinitely preferable to squeezing on to a London tube. Jud couldn't imagine these Italian giants sitting quietly on a bench seat, reading a newspaper with a million other commuters.

He'd read the night before that the boatmen of Venice were

the last of the true, indigenous Venetians. You had to be a native of Venice to work on the boats, especially the gondolas. There were few other residents of Venice who'd been born there. The vast majority of the workers in the lagoon had travelled to the city to work in hotels, restaurants, kitchens and shops. It was a tourism factory run by migrant workers.

He ordered coffee, nice and strong, and some toast. The waiter, whose accent was anything but Italian, smiled and told him to help himself to the buffet.

As the waiter trundled off, Jud saw Bex in the doorway of the restaurant. He stood and waved to her.

'Morning. Sleep well?' he said.

'Yeah, not bad. A rude awakening though. Have you heard the noise outside?'

'Yeah, brilliant, isn't it?' said Jud, smiling.

'Mmm,' said Bex, rubbing her sleepy eyes. 'You eaten?'

'No, not yet. Shall we hit the buffet?'

A few moments later Jud was tucking into a large plate of scrambled eggs and smoked meat. The waiter chuckled when he asked for ketchup.

'So what's the plan?' said Bex.

'Well, I say we get out there, before the crowds, and have a wander about, see what we sense.'

'Sounds dreamy. Best excuse for sightseeing I've heard yet,' said Bex.

'There's sightseeing and there's sightseeing,' said Jud. 'I don't do the usual tourist sites. I want to get down into the backstreets and canals. Where it's quiet. Get a feel for the place.'

'Fine by me,' she said.

'We still haven't got the name of Calder's suppliers. It's the place I wanted to start.'

'No, but I guess Khan will get that from Calder today. He knows we need an address and I doubt he'll let Calder get away without telling him. In the meantime?'

'Well, in the meantime, I guess we check out the jewellery stores. See how it goes. And I want to talk to some locals – you know, get some local gossip. Bonati and Khan said there's been no reports of violent hauntings lately, but that was the official line. We don't know what goes on behind the scenes. You don't always turn to the police when you think you've seen a ghost, do you?'

'No, exactly.'

'But finding a real local is going to be hard, I'm sensing. That's why I want to get into the backstreets – the cafés and bistros where the locals eat. I don't want the usual touristy rubbish from some official tour guide or brochure. I want to know what's really happening.'

Bex finished her pastry and downed her last drop of coffee. 'Let's get going, yeah?'

'OK. We get out into the streets while it's quiet, then we come back here and do some research on the laptops. We've got to have some news for Bonati if he rings.'

'*When* he rings' said Bex.

They left the restaurant and agreed to meet in the lobby in five.

It was still early – early enough for the narrow cobbled streets to be relatively free of tourists with their cumbersome rucksacks and cameras, pausing every minute to hold up the traffic and take yet another shot of a shop or bridge or monument. This morning the path was clear and Jud and Bex could cover some serious ground.

There were still the traces of an early morning mist that rose from the canals and filled the adjoining side streets, turning them even more mystical than they already were.

'You could get lost in this maze of alleyways and canals,' said Bex.

'I think that's the whole idea, or it would be if we were on holiday. I'd say that's the perfect vacation for me – getting lost in Venice.'

'Me too,' said Bex, and she was so close to saying, 'We should come back and try it sometime,' but she decided not to. The city's charm was working its magic again, just like last night, though she knew Jud was immune to such emotions.

They walked on, through narrow streets and over quaint little footbridges that traversed thin waterways, stopping at the crest of each bridge to take in the stunning vistas.

But there was a melancholy rising in Jud. There was something about this place. He'd read several guide books and magazines on Venice in the last twelve hours and they'd given conflicting reports on the atmosphere of the city. The more honest ones, perhaps, had said that many people, over centuries and centuries, had felt a deep sadness when walking along the streets and beside the waterways. The city of love was not, it seemed, able to capture the hearts of everyone who visited it. Some had described Venice as a smelly, decaying monument to greed. Others had said the harsh truth that Venice was slowly dying, sinking into the murky waters of the lagoon, could play with your mind and evoke feelings of hopelessness and abandonment, especially in the quieter times, when the armies of tourists were in bed.

Here, as the mist continued to roll around the empty streets like an unwelcome stranger, Jud could see what they meant.

'Odd to think we're walking on a city that's dying,' said Jud.

'What?'

'Well, it is, isn't it? The old wooden piles supporting it are not going to last forever, are they? The whole place is manmade and it's sinking further into the swamp.'

'Oh, you're such a romantic!' said Bex. Why did he always have to spoil the mood? she thought. Why couldn't he just enjoy the views for a little while and let the place seep into him?

But that was exactly what Jud was doing. He was 'tuning in', detecting a mood, finding residues of emotion everywhere he went. It's what made him such a good agent – the best.

'I don't know,' he said, 'it's attractive and cool and artistic and there's a stunning view at every street corner but there's a truth behind all this, Bex. The city's suffering.'

Sounds just like someone I know, Bex thought to herself, but averted her gaze.

'Suffering?' she said.

'Yeah. Can't you feel it? It's almost like the city is ill. It's decaying.'

Jud's morbid mood was beginning to grate with her. She, too, could sense tones and atmospheres – she wasn't impervious to them, far from it. But she was detecting a very different mood right now.

'But for every person who's described this place as depressing,' she said, 'there's a dozen who say the reverse – it's uplifting, inspiring, romantic.'

'Maybe.'

'Well, perhaps this city just accentuates the mood we're in at the time,' she suggested, gently.

'Oh, great. So it's me, is it? It's back to me and my moods,' said Jud. 'Well done, Sigmund Freud.'

They walked on, down the Calle Dei Fabbri, and joined the Sestiere San Marco. The great arches of the Procuratie Vecchie seemed to run for miles down the street, an incredible architectural feat, and each one providing a tantalising glimpse of Piazza San Marco – the world-famous St Mark's Square. The Basilica was still hidden from view, to the left, but they could see the giant bell tower rising above the buildings that lined the square.

They walked through one of the arches, pausing to look left and right down the long, elaborate corridors, like cathedral cloisters, but with decorative tiles on the floor, marble Romanesque carvings and fancy café bars and shops running into the distance. How different it must have looked in the sixteenth century when the Procuratie housed the offices of the Procuraters of Saint Mark – the leaders of state who helped to run the Republic of Venice.

They stepped into the giant square, still relatively quiet save for the vast numbers of pigeons waddling around, stabbing at the ground like hammers, for the discarded crumbs of a previous day.

They looked south, at the waterfront and the two giant columns that stretched into the misty sky, housing the two symbols of Venice: St Mark's winged lion on one and a statue of St Theodore, patron saint of Venice, on the other.

'It's gorgeous, isn't it?' said Bex.

'Yeah. Of course, that's where the public executions always took place – between those two columns.'

'Lovely,' said Bex. 'Thanks for that.'

They looked left and saw the majestic Doge's Palace, a master-piece of Gothic architecture, and then the Byzantine landmark of Venice itself, the Basilica di San Marco.

'I've never seen anything like it,' said Bex. 'Stunning. So elaborate.'

'It is, isn't it?' Jud couldn't help but agree. It really was impressive, with its beautiful domes, intricate carvings and gold-leaf frescos. It was unique.

'Strange how buildings can affect you – I mean, you know, affect your emotions,' said Bex.

'It's like all art, I suppose,' said Jud.

'No wonder so many people flock here. Imagine this place at midday, Jud. How busy would it be!'

'Yeah. I just hope there's no sightings of ghosts here. You can imagine the panic.'

'Oh God, yeah.'

They walked past the Doge Palace and on towards the waterfront. The mist had still not cleared but it added a mysticism, a magical feel, as if they were on the stage set of some fantasy film.

They walked left and over the Ponte della Paglia. Bex stopped.

'I know what that is!' she said, pointing further down the canal that ran from the waterfront back into Venice, passing the back of the Doge's Palace.

'Yeah, me too,' said Jud. 'It's the Bridge of Sighs, isn't it?'

'Exactly,' said Bex. They'd both read about it. 'They say it was the last view of Venice that prisoners would get as they were marched over the bridge from the courtroom in the palace to the prison cells on the other side.'

'That's right. It's enough to make you sigh.'

'Of course,' said Bex, a cheeky smile appearing on her face, 'legend has it that if two lovers kiss on a gondola just beneath the bridge, they'll enjoy everlasting love and happiness.'

'Yeah. Whatever. Shall we get a coffee?'

They returned to the square and walked briskly across it, back towards the north side from which they'd come. There were a few locals shuffling across, en route to work – not a bad commute, thought Jud – while café owners set up tables and umbrella stands, with giant heaters gently warming up.

'Let's get a drink and see if we can get chatting to someone,' he said. 'I have a feeling the cafés here are going to be expensive – and will soon be full of tourists anyway – so let's find somewhere quieter, shall we?'

They left the square and returned to the comforting intimacy of the tiny cobbled courtyards and winding backstreets.

'Let's find the Street of Assassins, Jud.'

'The what?'

'The Street of Assassins. In Italian it's . . . now what is it?' Bex screwed her face in thought and Jud could see dimples at her cheeks. 'Rio Tera . . . Dei Assassin, or something like that,' she said. 'It's just a little backstreet but because it's quite hidden, it was where a lot of murders and muggings occurred. It's tucked away, so if you walked down there hundreds of years ago, you'd be mugged for sure – or worse.'

'Sounds good. Let's find it.'

They called into a tobacconist's shop for a miniature guide map. As luck would have it they were not far away from the street.

When they found it, it looked pretty much like any other backstreet in Venice, but they were relieved to find a café bar on the corner that was open.

They entered the little shop, the door rattling behind them. Immediately their nostrils were treated to the enticing smells of warm croissants and pastries and though they'd only just eaten breakfast, they couldn't resist one more.

'Two coffees and two croissants, please,' said Jud, reaching into his wallet for some euros.

'Stunning Italian,' said Bex.

'Can you do any better?' he said, smiling.

'*Due caffè e due . . .* erm *. . . cornetti?*'

'*Sì, signorina,*' said the man behind the counter, flattered and excited by this young woman's attempts to speak his language. She had a fan now, no question.

'OK, OK,' said Jud. 'Is there anything you can't do?'

She just smiled and watched him struggle over the right coins.

They sat at a small, wooden table in the window. Workers were swelling in numbers and they walked briskly past, anxious to get to their shops and offices before the tide of tourists flooded the streets.

'Let's talk this through,' said Jud. 'If Calder's jewellery really is laced with some kind of curse and is attracting ghosts from this city – the ghosts of plague doctors, we think – then the jewellery must be from here.'

'Yes, we know that,' said Bex.

'But that's not enough, is it? I mean the city is full of Venetian jewellery shops. It's big business. And we've already seen that the streets aren't lined with bodies and ghosts.'

'No, at least it doesn't seem that way.'

'So, what is it about this particular jewellery? I mean, why should the rings that Calder's been selling be so dangerous? Where did he get them from?'

'Well, we should get a call from Bonati to tell us that this morning.'

'Yeah, hope so. Do you think this guy speaks English?' said Jud, glancing in the direction of the man behind the counter.

'Don't know. It's likely, if he wants to make money from the tourists. I doubt many of them speak his language.' She rose and walked to the counter.

'*Lei parla inglese?*' she said.

'*Sì, signorina.* Yes, of course.' His native accent was thick and oozed charm. 'What d'ya wanna know?'

She beckoned for him to come to the table, which he did, gladly. He was always keen to speak to a pretty face.

'What do you know of the plague doctors?' she said.

The man looked confused. 'Eh?'

'The plague doctors. The . . . erm . . . *medici.*'

'Doctor? You need doctor, *sì*?'

'No, no. I mean, the doctors with the masks. You know, the plague.'

'Ah, yes, the men with the white faces, *sì*?'

'Exactly,' said Jud. 'What were they like? What did they do?'

The man pulled up a rickety chair and sat down, a little too close to Bex for comfort, but she was too keen to hear what he had to say to object.

'You see, *miei amici*, this city has some dark secrets. A lot of people who come to this place, they spend their money, they buy their masks. They wear them and they laugh. But no one knows what those masks – you know, the ones with the big noses, *sì*? – no one really knows what those people were like.'

'The doctors, you mean?' said Jud, sitting on the edge of his seat.

'Sì, the *peste medici*.'

'*Peste?*' said Jud.

'I think it must mean *plague*,' said Bex. Her Italian lessons in school and infrequent holidays to Italy had never required her to use 'plague'.

'Yes, *signorina*. You call it the plague. Well, they were not men you would – how do you say – argue with.'

'But why? I thought they were doctors?' said Bex.

'Oh, *sì*, *sì*, they were doctors, But they were working under – what is the word – orders. Yes, they were given their orders. It was the law.'

'What was the law?'

'That they should collect up anyone suffering from the plague and remove them from the island. Take them away from Venice.'

'What, not just the dead bodies then?' said Bex.

'No. Not just the dead ones. The ones who were suffering. The leaders had to keep the disease under . . . under *control*, you see. They didn't want it to spread, like it had in the past. We've lost thousands and thousands of people over the years. Venice has had the plague more times than anywhere else.'

'So what happened? Where did the doctors take them?' asked Jud.

'Well, I'll tell you. They came and—'

The door rattled again and a young woman, dressed smartly, entered.

'I'm sorry, *miei amici*,' said the man to Jud and Bex. 'Please, *un momento*.'

He rose and went behind the shabby counter, smiling hospitably at the young woman.

'*Posso aiutarla, signorina?*'

'*Sì, un caffè per favore.*'

'*Naturalemente. Ecco.*'

She left with the takeaway cup of steaming coffee and their host was soon back at the table. It was rare to have such eager listeners and, like all Venetians, he was proud of his city's history.

'What was I saying?' he said, scratching his head. Bex chuckled. He was a character – tanned, wrinkly, weather-beaten skin, and breath that smelled of tobacco. His eyes were hazel and a little red in the corners, with heavy bags beneath them, the kind of eyes Bex sometimes saw on Jud's face after a night playing his Xbox or watching too many movies.

He must have been at least sixty, but he was as spritely and energetic as a man half his age. He was slender but his arms were strong and sinewy, from cooking and serving all day. And he had charm in bucket loads. Italian charm – the best kind.

'You were saying about the plague doctors, *signore* . . .' said Bex.

'Signor Aliprando. Signor Ali to you.' He gave a grin which showed nicotine-stained teeth. 'Aliprando is an old Venetian name. For an old Venetian, huh? So, yes, what I was saying, they came in the night sometimes. The *peste medici*. They would find out where you lived. And they would come to your house. They would take you away, so the disease did not grow – or did not . . . how you say . . .'

'Spread,' said Bex.

'Yes. So it would not spread. They would take you away in boats. The doctor would sit in the end of the boat and stare at you and take you away from your home. You would never come back.'

'Imagine that,' said Bex to Jud. 'The last thing you see is the doctor, in a black shroud and white mask, staring at you from the end of the gondola.' She shuddered. 'And the mask was for protection?'

'Yes. The long nose – you've seen it, huh? – that was filled with, what do you call them, erbes?'

'Herbs,' said Bex. She wanted to say, 'Seen them? Of course

we've bloody seen them. In London!' but she kept quiet.

'They didn't want to breathe in all the bad things, you know, so they sniffed the 'erbs and they were OK.'

'So where did they take the plague victims?' said Jud, getting impatient. He didn't want to spend all day in this café, but he sensed they were getting somewhere, if only this man would speed up!

Signor Ali looked around him before he spoke. Then he leaned in closer to the table and spoke in hushed tones.

'Poveglia. They took them to the Island of Poveglia.'

Jud's eyes lit up. 'Oh my God! Of course!'

'What?' said Bex.

'I've heard of that place. I've heard the name, Poveglia. I read it somewhere – years ago. I didn't realise it was here. It's haunted, isn't it?'

'Haunted? What is *haunted*?' said Signor Ali.

Bex spoke quietly. 'Ghosts . . . erm . . . *fantasmi*?'

'*Fantasmi*, yes. Ghosts. You say "haunted", *si*? Yes, it has the ghosts.' He spoke even quieter now. 'The Island of Poveglia has lots of the ghosts. And we cannot go there.'

'Why?' said Bex.

'It is – how do you say – forbid . . .'

'Forbidden,' said Jud. 'Why is it forbidden?'

Signor Ali shrugged his shoulders. 'I guess it is because it is cursed. Very bad things happen to people who go there. Very bad.'

'So what did they do with the plague victims when they got there, Signor Ali?' asked Bex.

'They threw them in pits! They threw the people, alive or dead, into the big holes in the ground. And they left them there.'

'My God,' said Jud. 'No wonder the place is haunted.'

'Some people say it is the most haunted place in the world,' said Signor Ali proudly, but in a hushed whisper, his eyes offering the drama that his voice was unable to convey. He stared wildly at the two of them then sighed and they got another whiff of tobacco mixed with strong coffee. 'Even the fishermen in the lagoon, they won't sail near the island. They fear they will catch human bones in their nets.'

'*Human bones?*' said Bex.

'Oh, *sì*. The bones of the bodies left there. The stinking bodies with the plague, *sì?*'

'But I don't get it,' said Bex. 'I mean, why would you be prohibited from going there because of the ghosts? Surely the police don't believe the story, do they?'

He looked confused. 'What you say?'

'I said, surely the police don't believe there are ghosts there? Do they actually keep you away from the island?'

Signor Ali shook his head and shrugged. 'All I know is there are signs everywhere saying it is a dangerous place. And when people have been there, very bad things have happened to them. Very bad.'

'Such as?' said Jud.

'What?'

'I mean, what kind of bad things happen to you if you go there?'

'Lots of stories of violence. Hauntings. It is the island of death. A cursed place.'

'And where is it?' said Jud, half excitedly. Bex could see already where this was leading. 'Is it far?'

'No, no. It is a short boat ride away.'

'And do you have a boat?'

Signor Ali nodded and smiled wryly. '*Sì*. I have a little boat.'

'So? Will you take us there?' said Jud.

Bex shot him a glare. 'Jud, you can't expect Signor Ali to break the law for us. We've only just met him and, besides, we might get caught.'

The old man patted her arm comfortingly with his weather-beaten hand. '*Non temere, bella signora*. Do not worry. Signor Ali will look after you.' He looked at Jud and spoke in a throaty whisper, glancing furtively out of the window. 'I hate the stinkin' police. I'm not frightened of them, they are weak men. I will take you to Poveglia. I will not walk on it, but I will take you to its shores.' He grinned a cheeky grin and they saw his stained teeth again. 'For the right price, of course.'

CHAPTER 41

WEDNESDAY 8.41 A.M.

(7.09 A.M. VENICE TIME)

SCOTLAND YARD, LONDON

'What do you mean, he's gone?' Khan shouted down the phone. The young officer at the other end gulped.

'I'm sorry, sir. I thought he was in bed. I don't know how it happened. I saw a neighbour leaving just now and I asked if she'd seen Calder this morning. I couldn't believe it when she said she saw him leaving with a suitcase in the early hours. About half past three. She didn't ask him where he was going.'

'So why the hell didn't you see him leave, Stringer?'

'Er . . . I'm sorry, sir. I, er . . .'

'Fell asleep? Fell *bloody* asleep. Brilliant. So our only suspect in this case, at least the only living one, has done a runner. I'll remember this, Stringer. Now get your arse back here, pronto.'

'Very good, sir.'

Khan slammed the phone down on his desk. In less than thirty minutes he was due in the conference room, facing the country's media and having to answer questions. If anyone asked him for the whereabouts of the owner of the jewellery store in question, he was sunk. He resolved to make damn sure it wouldn't get to that stage.

He collected his things together and paced off to the conference room.

A few minutes later he was facing rows of reporters, already in position and all eager to get the latest on what they were now calling the 'Masked Murderers' story.

Khan had felt relieved that no one had yet suggested there were ghosts involved. But it was still going to take some explaining. The prime objective was to reassure people that these were not random killings, but specific attacks, with theft in mind – theft of one kind of jewellery from one specific shop. A shop which now, thanks to Calder's disappearance, was fortunately shut.

'Morning, ladies and gentleman,' he began, in a tone that was less than hospitable. He hated these conferences, always had. These parasitic reporters fed not on what he said but the little snippets of what he nearly said, or shouldn't have said, or someone else told them he said. The truth was always so difficult to get out there, to the public, because the truth didn't always sell newspapers. Although in this case, if they knew the *real* truth – that the ghosts of five hundred-year-old Venetian plague doctors were roaming the city's streets – it would certainly sell enough newspapers to keep them all happy.

He'd have to choose his words carefully.

'Thank you all for coming.' (As if they needed an invitation, he thought.) 'I am able to give you more updates on the recent attacks we've seen in London. Firstly I want to assure the public that we are doing all we can to protect them. We have many, many officers working on this right now and I have no doubt that we will find the perpetrators and bring them to justice soon.'

'So who are they?'

'Where are they now?'

'Are they still in London?'

'Has there been another killing yet?'

The reporters had started already, with their usual interruptions and heckling. Press conferences were bun fights at the best of times and, as Khan knew better than anyone, when there were multiple murders involved, no one kept to any kind of protocol. It was usually a free-for-all.

'Please,' said Khan, managing to hold his temper, for now, 'I will answer your questions at the end, but first I would like to give you the latest information. We have identified a link between the victims. All of them were wearing expensive jewellery, all of which was purchased very recently from the same shop.'

'Where?'

'Which shop?'

'Please! I'm just about to tell you. The victims all recently visited Calder's – a new shop in London's jewellery district, Hatton Garden. We have discovered that the store sells a unique kind of jewellery, Venetian in origin. The items are very expensive and, it seems, highly prized. We believe that the perpetrators of these brutal attacks were actually after the jewellery. They were not – I repeat, *not* – random killings. They were premeditated, planned and focused. So there is no need for panic. The public should remain vigilant and cautious, but there is no need to be fearful. Anyone who has purchased jewellery from Calder's since its opening last weekend *must* inform us immediately.'

He looked straight at the audience and the many cameras pointing intrusively at his face. 'Under *no* circumstances wear the jewellery. Put it in its box and call us. We shall collect it from you and keep it safe until this is over. I repeat, do *not* wear the jewellery, and especially not in public.'

This was not what the reporters were expecting and there was an excited buzz in the room, as everyone started firing yet more questions at Khan.

'But what about Mr Calder? What does he say?'

'Is he a suspect? Have you taken Calder in for questioning?'

Khan raised his hands to try to quieten the crowd. 'We have interviewed Mr Calder and he is not a suspect. The shop is now closed until further notice.'

He couldn't say that he'd told Calder to close it. Neither could he say where the hell Calder was right now, but at least no more jewellery was being sold.

'So, this Calder guy,' said a reporter in the front row. 'You're closing him down, Inspector, putting him out of business, are you?'

'Our prime objectives are to prevent any more attacks and to identify the perpetrators and bring them to justice,' said Khan, decisively. 'Mr Calder's business is of secondary importance right now. But we will ensure that he is compensated for any loss of earnings.'

'So where is he? Is he at home?'

'That's all I can say for now, thank you very much.'

'You don't know where he is, do ya?'

'Thank you, thank you. This conference is over.'

'I think he doesn't know where this guy's gone. I reckon he's done a runner.'

Khan was moving swiftly to the door. This was exactly what he, Bonati and Goode had wanted to avoid. Best to get the hell out of there as soon as possible.

As he left the room, he was bombarded by yet more questions as reporters thrust their microphones into his face and demanded to know more.

'No further comment. We'll keep you updated. No more. Thank you, thank you. No more.'

And then he was gone. Until the next time.

As he paced down the corridor, he whispered to one of his officers, through gritted teeth, 'Bloody well find this guy. *Now!*'

CHAPTER 42

WEDNESDAY 10.21 A.M.

(11.21 A.M. VENICE TIME)

HOTEL CAVALLETTO, VENICE

Jud and Bex had walked miles now, almost the entire length of the city. They'd waited until the shops were open and then, on the instructions of Bonati, begun the painstaking task of visiting every jewellery shop in Venice.

The news from Bonati had not been good. Calder had been allowed to disappear. The professor had sounded furious. But the instructions were clear. If it was no longer possible to find out from Calder himself where he got his jewellery from, then the only way would be for Jud and Bex to make inquiries themselves. Khan's officers had returned to the shop but had found no records at all of any suppliers.

And so it had fallen to Jud and Bex, to ask every jeweller in Venice if they'd heard of Nicky Calder, recently moved from Venice to London.

No one had.

'This is weird, Bex,' said Jud as they paused in the Campo

San Luca and looked again at the map Jud was clutching. 'I mean, Venice is not a big place.'

'No? It's beginning to feel like it is!'

'No, I mean it's small enough for everyone to know each other – at least within the same industry. I mean, you go to London and I'm sure most of the main jewellers know each other. They're in the same business, they'd have met each other, or heard of each other's shops. But here, no one's heard of Nicky Calder. And yet he claims to be from Venice.'

'He was lying?' said Bex, with tired resignation in her voice.

'But why should he, if he's done nothing wrong? He had nothing to gain by lying to the police. It would only rouse their suspicions once they found out he was lying.'

'Well, we haven't searched everywhere yet. I reckon there's still more left.'

They looked again at the map. After Bonati's phone call, they'd quickly returned to the hotel, opened a laptop and searched for jewellery shops in Venice. The map had displayed more little red arrows than they'd ever imagined and they knew then it was going to take a while. They'd asked the hotel to print it off for them, saying they were there to buy a very special ring for Bex – which had aroused some excited looks from the receptionists.

'Come on,' Bex continued. 'We've still got a few left on the other side of the Grand Canal. We haven't searched there yet.'

The crowds had swelled now and it felt like a rugby scrum, trying to squeeze through the mass of bodies, all moving irritatingly slowly, and pausing every few moments to take yet another photograph of a house or shop identical to the last one they'd photographed.

But they made it to the Grand Canal and began the trudge left, still in the traffic of tourists, all heading like pilgrims towards the Rialto Bridge.

The enticing smell of cooked garlic bread and pasta was

wafting into their nostrils and their bellies. Bex could see Jud's face twitch in the direction of a restaurant.

'Soon!' she said. 'After we've finished searching.'

They were up on the bridge eventually, where the view really was a living Canaletto. The image had been so firmly printed on most people's minds from the world-famous oil paintings that it seemed strange not to see it fixed, motionless now. The gondolas and barges were drifting and the people lining the canal were moving like insects. Somehow they expected the view to be frozen in time. Jud secretly wished everyone could just stand still for a moment. But he was shoved forwards by a large American tourist, wearing a body warmer and a mass of cameras and lenses.

Eventually they made it to the other side, where the pavements were no less crowded, but there were quieter backstreets here, and they ran off at right angles from the Riva del Vin, each one punctuated by quaint footbridges that gently rose over miniature canals.

They took one side street and followed it to Campo San Silvestro, one of the many tiny squares that served as intersections for the labyrinth of alleyways and streets.

'There!' shouted Bex. She'd seen a small shop in the opposite corner of the square. As they approached, they could see its red paint was peeling from the wooden struts either side of the door and the glass was cloudy in places and cracked in others. Either the shop had been there a very long time indeed or it had not been looked after, or both, which was likely.

The doorbell clanked as they entered. The ceilings were low and Jud found himself ducking in places. There were antique cabinets dotted across the old, tiled floor, which was chipped and uneven. Each cabinet housed a few antique rings embedded and pinned to fading blue velvet.

There was the sound of feet shuffling. Soon a small, frail-looking woman tottered out of a back room. They couldn't decide if the frown she was displaying was as a result of being disturbed or because they didn't look wealthy enough to her. But she didn't seem overwhelmingly pleased to see them.

'Sì?' was all she said.

Bex attempted to explain. They were trying to trace a jeweller – a Signor Nicky Calder. They believed he was from the city, and wondered if she knew him.

The old woman's frown deepened, almost enveloping her dark, wrinkled forehead, as if her eyes were imploding.

'Calder?' she said in a strong accent. She shook her head. 'No. *Non lo so* Calder. I know Calderario. *Sì?* Niccolo Calderario. *Bello uomo.*'

'What's she saying?' said Jud.

'Handsome man,' said Bex.

'Who?'

'Niccolo Calderario. It's obviously someone she knows. And the name sounds similar.'

'Very similar,' said Jud, 'especially when *you* say it.'

The old lady was nodding and shuffling around the shop, polishing the tops of the cabinets with a cloth that was dirtier than the cabinets themselves. 'Sì, Niccolo Calderario and his brother, Lorenzo. *Ma lui è andato.*'

'Niccolo? *Andato?* Gone? Where? Er . . . *dove?*'

'Sì, Niccolo. *Si recò a Londra.*'

'What? Tell me what's going on,' said Jud. He hated being in the dark like this. 'What's she saying?'

'She says Niccolo Calderario had a brother, Lorenzo. But Niccolo isn't here any more. He's gone.'

'Where to?'

'Guess.'

'London.'

Bex nodded. She thanked the old lady and asked if she knew anything else about the brothers.

The woman told her that Niccolo had always been interested in jewellery. They lived not far away from her shop as children.

Lorenzo had never been interested in coming to the shop. He was a tough kid, always getting into fights and things, but his brother, Niccolo, had been a gentle boy – and helpful too. He'd worked in her shop some days and he always said he would have his own shop one day. He went to Rome or somewhere to work for jewellers there.

Bex asked her how she knew Niccolo had now gone to London. How did she know he'd left Rome?

She said it was because he'd been home again earlier this year. He'd even been into the shop to see his old friend. He'd told her that he was opening a shop in London and would be very rich. Selling precious jewellery from Venice to rich London people.

'And the brother?' asked Bex.

The woman shrugged her shoulders. She didn't know what had happened to Lorenzo. It looked as if she didn't much care either.

Bex asked her if she knew where Niccolo was buying his jewellery.

She shrugged again and shook her head. She explained that Niccolo had not wanted to buy any of her own rings – he said he'd found a better supplier, in Venice, one who would make him a very rich man.

Bex thanked the old lady again for her time and they left the shop quickly before she had a chance to sell them some of her wares.

They walked briskly across the square and down a side street in the direction of the Grand Canal. They found a small footbridge to perch on. The small canal stretched out below them, squeezing like a worm between the backs of apartment blocks, their balconies filled with washing and plants and old rusty bicycles. The air was thick with a heady cocktail of salty water, mould, washing detergent and the distant wafts of coffee and garlic from the apartments above them.

'Well?' said Bex after she'd translated as much of the

conversation as she could remember, and had understood. 'What do you think?'

'It's gotta be him,' said Jud. 'It's too much of a coincidence otherwise. And the name fits perfectly. Niccolo Caldera . . .'

'Calderario.'

'Yes, Niccolo Calderario becomes Nicky Calder when he gets to London. It kind of makes sense, doesn't it?'

'OK,' said Bex. 'So we may have identified Calder, we've found someone who knows him and can trace him back to Venice. So that part of the story fits. But what about the source of the jewellery? We're no closer to that, are we?'

'No,' said Jud. 'Not yet. But it's a start. Now we know his real name we can ask around. And I wonder if we can trace his brother. This Lawrence guy.'

'*Lorenzo!*'

'Yeah, that's what I said,' Jud replied, smiling cheekily. He was beginning to like it when she spoke Italian. 'When are we meeting Signor Ali?'

'I think we said ten o'clock, didn't we? We need to wait until it's quiet and there's no light in the lagoon.'

'OK. Well, that's ten hours we've got to find out more about these Calderario guys. Where do we go next?' said Bex.

'Online, I guess. We can start researching the names and see what comes up. Might find out where he's getting his jewellery too. Worth a try.'

'OK. But can we eat first? I know we've been eating all morning, but the smell of this garlic bread is doing my head in. I've *got* to have some.'

Back in the Campo San Silvestro, a man with a baseball cap pulled low over his face and a long jacket zipped up to the neck left the little jewellery shop.

Inside, the old lady lay prostrate on the cold tiled floor which led to the little back room.

Blood oozed slowly from the slash across her throat.

CHAPTER 43

WEDNESDAY 12.16 P.M.

(1.16 P.M. VENICE TIME)

GRAND CANAL, VENICE

Bex watched the passers-by as she finished her last mouthful of salad, a stray rocket stalk still poking out of her mouth.

'It seems hard to believe that there've been no reports of the plague doctors here – at least not in the papers or on the news.'

They'd asked the hotel staff about any possible sightings reported in the media but had come up with nothing.

'Well, as we know, that doesn't mean there haven't been any. Khan may have had reassurances from the police over here that nothing's been reported but that doesn't mean it hasn't happened, Bex. We don't know. And why should they tell a British copper what's going on anyway? What's it got to do with him?'

Bex wasn't so sure. 'If the sightings of ghosts in London had matched the description of something that's been seen over here then you'd have thought the Venetian police would have told him.'

Jud shrugged. 'Maybe.'

They finished their meal and decided they'd brave the crowds one more time and make their way back to the hotel. Now they had the real name of Nicky Calder, it was going to be just as easy to find out more about him online as it was trudging around shops and houses. They'd find an online telephone directory or at least the number for a records office and Bex could try calling them.

Jud signalled to the waiter for the bill.

'Before we leave for Poveglia,' said Bex,' let's have another walk around the backstreets tonight and see if we can sense any paranormal activity. You never know, we might see some ghosts.'

A young couple on an adjacent table turned and looked at them. The girl looked as though she'd been crying. Her eyes were red and puffy and her face looked drained. Her boyfriend looked tired too, as if he was suffering from a hangover.

'Did you say ghosts?' said the young man, wearily. Though his Italian accent was evident, he obviously spoke fluent English.

Bex looked across at him. 'Yes. Why?'

The two diners shuffled their chairs over to them. The waiter brought the bill and Jud paid, but waited to hear what they'd got to say.

The man looked nervous; he was glancing about him, checking he wasn't being overheard. They could see dark shadows beneath his eyes, which blinked heavily.

'I saw a ghost last night,' he said solemnly.

'You did?' said Bex.

'Yeah, sure. This is my girlfriend, Maria. We live together in Dorsoduro in the south side of Venice. It was last night. We both saw it, didn't we, Maria?'

She nodded silently and looked down at the table with an expression of grief.

'So what did you see exactly?'

'We saw someone taken. I heard screaming outside my window. Maria was sleeping at the time. It was late. Maybe midnight? I went to the window and opened the shutters. The screaming stopped but I looked down and saw a *ghost*. It was wearing some kind of black cloak. And . . .' the man was looking at the table now, fiddling with a paper coaster. His eyes flickered across the café tables. 'And it was carrying someone. A young woman, I think. And her body was just – how do you say – lifeless?'

'She was dead?' said Bex, looking shocked.

He nodded solemnly. 'The ghost was dragging this girl. I ran down to the street. I wanted to see if I could help her. But the ghost had gone by the time I got there.'

'You keep saying "ghost", but how do you know it was a ghost?' said Jud. 'I mean, surely it was a man – an attacker?'

The man shook his head. There was a defiant look in his eyes. 'That's just what the police said to me.'

'So you reported it?'

'Yes, of course I reported it. I called the police straight away. They came around to my house. They interviewed me.'

'And they told you it must have been a man? Did you see his face?' said Bex, gently. She could see from his face that it was still painful to recall. The memory of the sight was clearly haunting him still.

'I didn't see its face,' he said, his voice faltering as emotion took hold, 'because it was wearing a mask.'

Jud and Bex were silent for a moment, allowing him to compose himself. They stared at one another. Was this it? Was this a link?

'So why are you so sure it was a ghost and not a man in a mask?' said Jud, quietly.

The young man stared straight into Jud's eyes. He spoke softly but decisively. 'Because it wasn't walking,' he said. 'You understand? It was . . . how do you say it? *Floating.*'

Jud stared at Bex across the table. 'And you said this to the police?'

'Sì. I told them exactly what I saw.'

'And they didn't believe you?'

'They said they'd investigate – I mean they have to, don't they? But they said I'd been drinking – which I had, but I mean, I know what I saw. And I know that the thing that took that woman, whatever it was, it *wasn't* human.'

Jud scribbled the name Hotel Cavalletto on to a napkin, with the hotel telephone number he got from his phone. He wrote down his own mobile number too. 'Keep in touch,' he said, handing the napkin to the young man. 'Call me if you remember anything else.'

They rose from the table. Bex patted the girl's shoulder as they left. 'We believe you,' she said.

'Who are you, anyway?' said the man. 'Are you tourists or ghost hunters?'

Jud hesitated and then said, 'Oh, just tourists. But we're interested in ghosts. Always have been.'

And then they were gone.

A few minutes later the young couple rose from their table, paid for their lunch and left the restaurant.

The man in the baseball cap, who'd been sitting close by, rose quickly and followed them out, watching them like a hawk as they mingled with the crowds heading for Rialto Bridge.

CHAPTER 44

WEDNESDAY 1.48 P.M.

(2.48 P.M. VENICE TIME)

CRYPT, LONDON/HOTEL

CAVALLETTO, VENICE

'They've found Calder,' said Bonati.

'Thank God for that,' Jud replied down the phone. 'Where was he? How did they find him?' Jud was perched on the edge of the hotel bed, staring out of the window at the building opposite, where an old lady was battling with a large sheet she was trying to hang on a makeshift line out on the balcony.

His mobile phone – supposedly the new brand with the best reception signal ever – was proving temperamental and dipping in and out of signal in the city. So the hotel phone was a better, if less discreet, choice.

'Well, a neighbour saw him leave early this morning with a suitcase,' said Bonati. 'So they viewed all the CCTV footage in London stations and saw him at Euston. He caught a train to Glasgow. The police were waiting for him by the time he arrived in Scotland. They met him on the platform.'

'Ha, I bet he was pleased with that!' said Jud.

'Well yes, quite. He said he was just catching up with a friend up there. But officers accompanied him straight back down to London again. Khan wants to hold him this time. For questioning.'

'At least the shop is closed now – no more jewellery sold?' said Jud.

'That's right,' said Bonati. 'For now. But unless he charges him with something, Khan won't be able to hold him forever. You've got twenty-four hours to find something on this guy. Or at least find where he's getting his jewellery.'

'Hasn't Khan asked him that yet?'

'Yes, of course, but Khan says he's refusing to answer any questions now. His lawyer's advising him to keep his mouth shut until Khan shows his cards and actually accuses him of something.'

'Well, we may have made some progress on that front,' said Jud.

He filled the professor in on the real name of Calder and his brother.

'We're going to go to the police to see if they can help us find the brother.'

'Well, go carefully there, Jud,' said Bonati. 'I heard from Khan that they were anything but cooperative when he spoke to them yesterday. They didn't exactly sound like they were in helpful mood.'

'Why is that, do you think, sir?' said Jud.

'Who knows. Maybe they just think it's a case of British police interfering, stirring up trouble, sticking their noses in, you know. They denied any knowledge of ghosts or plague doctors. I think, between you and me, they thought Khan has a screw loose.'

'Mmm,' said Jud, cheekily. 'Well, we can tell you there *has* been a sighting in Venice. Last night.'

'Go on.'

'A young couple, living in the south side of Venice, saw a masked figure seize a young woman and drag her off.'

'And are they sure it wasn't a man?'

'They said it was floating, sir.'

'Really? So if the police try to deny there's any paranormal activity, we know two things. Firstly, they're lying, and secondly they have something to gain – or something to lose – in this.'

'There's more, sir.'

'Well done, Jud. Go on.'

'We've traced the origins of the plague doctors – how they seized plague victims and took them to the island of Poveglia.'

'Yes, I've heard of that place. I hadn't realised it was in Venice.'

'Yeah, it's a small island in the Venetian lagoon here. It was used as a quarantine station during the plague. The doctors, in their masks, would take victims over there and leave them in giant plague pits.'

'And you're going there, yes?'

'Well, that's the weird thing, sir. You're not allowed to go there.'

'What do you mean?'

'Just that. People are prohibited from visiting the island. The police won't let you go. They say it's too dangerous.'

'Too haunted?'

'Well, that's what the locals tell me. But don't worry, we're going there tonight, sir,' said Jud, excitedly.

Bonati could sense his eagerness. 'Well, just go carefully, Jud. Look after each other. Don't run into trouble.'

'Oh, don't worry about us, sir. Bring on the ghosts, I say.'

'No,' said Bonati. 'I was talking about the police.'

CHAPTER 45

WEDNESDAY 4.59 P.M.

(5.59 P.M. VENICE TIME)

HOTEL CAVALLETTO, VENICE

Research in Jud's room, via the laptops they'd brought with them, had unearthed all manner of stories and legends associated with Poveglia. It seemed it wasn't the only island in the lagoon used as a quarantine for plague victims, but it remained the only one out of bounds to visitors. It still wasn't clear why it was forbidden to travel there.

But one thing was clear, the levels of paranormal activity there would be higher than anything they'd encountered before, and Jud couldn't wait to get there.

The television was droning away in the corner of Jud's room – some local station, which Bex had insisted on to help her polish up her Italian. To Jud it was just inane rambling but Bex was able to pick out some words. A cookery programme, like any other celebrity chef programme back in England, was drawing to a close.

They stared at their laptops and continued to search for as

much information as they could find on the *peste medici* – the plague doctors of Venice.

A news programme was beginning on television.

'*Titoli di oggi: Tre persone sono trovate morte nella città.*'

Bex looked up and stared at the screen, her mouth open.

'What? What's happened?' said Jud.

'Sh!' she said, listening intently.

'Come on, what?' said Jud impatiently.

Before Bex had a chance to reply an image flashed up of a woman. They recognised her instantly.

It was the old lady from the jewellery shop.

'What's happened to her?'

Two more faces appeared. It was the young couple they'd spoken to in the restaurant.

'Eh?' said Jud. 'Why are they in the news? What's happened?'

Bex looked across at him, fear printed across her face. 'They're dead, Jud.'

They sat in silence for a moment, staring at the screen, Bex trying valiantly to pick up any snippets of phrases she understood.

'Their bodies were found this afternoon. Police suspect murder. And they think it's the same person.'

'Who?' said Jud desperately. 'Who do they think's done it?'

Bex didn't need to answer. A photo came up which chilled them both to the core. Jud stood up and stared at the screen, his hands at his face.

It was a slightly blurred photo, probably taken on a mobile phone, but you could see what was going on, and who was in shot.

They were.

It was a photo taken in the restaurant by the Grand Canal. Jud and Bex were seen talking to the young couple. The newsreader, from what Bex could understand, said something about these people being seen at the jewellery shop too. And sure enough, the next photo, even more blurred and out of focus, showed Jud and Bex from behind, walking across the Campo San Silvestro.

'*Ha veduto queste persone?*' said the newsreader. '*Chiama questo numero . . .*'

'Well?' said Jud, his eyes darting across the room at Bex.

'She's asking if viewers have seen these people – seen *us*, Jud,' she said nervously. A telephone number flashed across the screen. 'Anyone with information has to call that number,' she continued. 'We're in serious trouble, Jud.' Her voice was cracking now as the enormity of the situation enveloped her.

'No!' said Jud defiantly. 'We've done nothing wrong, Bex. *Nothing.*'

'So what do we do?' she said, moving swiftly to the window and closing the shutters. 'Do we go to the police? We've got nothing to hide, so do we go and tell them that?'

Jud shook his head. 'Wait. Let's stay calm. We've got to *think*. Somebody's obviously framing us. They want us out of the way. Someone must have overheard us at the restaurant, talking about ghosts. Maybe the same person, I don't know, who visited the jewellery shop just after us and questioned the old lady. Someone knows we're on to them.'

'OK, but what do we do now?' said Bex. 'Seriously, Jud, they'll be at the hotel any minute. You gave the man the name and number of the hotel, for God's sake. And your own number! The police will have that now.'

'Not necessarily. Only if he was carrying it.'

'Which he was. How much time did he have to lose it, Jud? I mean, that couple must've been followed from the café.'

'Probably. I can't help thinking it's got something to do with what that guy told us. About the ghost he'd seen. He said the police didn't believe his story. And there we were, the next day, talking to him openly about ghosts – God knows who was listening.'

'So?' said Bex anxiously.

'If we hand ourselves in now and try to explain, do you think the Italian police are going to say, "OK, that's fine, you can go"? Of course they're not! They want suspects and they're probably quite happy for them to be foreigners, rather than their own people. So if we go there now we're going to be locked up at least overnight and we'll *never* crack this.'

The idea of incarceration was abhorrent to Jud. For so many obvious reasons, most of which he just couldn't say, he *had* to avoid that. He had too much to lose, too much history that would inevitably unravel if they were caught. They had to avoid that at all costs.

'So what are you saying?' said Bex. 'We should make a run for it? Oh yeah, that's going to make us look innocent, isn't it?'

'We've no choice, Bex. We *have* to sort this. And we're not going to be any use to anyone stuck inside a cell. We hide, and then we call Bonati and Khan – we get them to pull some strings, you know, get in touch with whoever's in charge over here. Get our names off the bloody hit list. MI5 will sort it. We don't need to go into the police station and tell some local copper we didn't do it. We'll lie low until it blows over and they start looking for the real suspect. If we don't find him first.'

It made sense, Bex had to admit. Let Bonati and Khan get the police off their backs so they could get on with the job. If someone was really trying to frame them, then wandering into the police station was playing into their hands.

But Bex was still worried. 'Yeah, and where are we going to hide?' she said.

'Where is there that no one goes? Think about it. Where's the best place to hide without anyone bothering us?'

Bex gasped. 'Of course! Poveglia!'

'Exactly. It'll give us some time. And it means we can get on with this investigation. I'm sure that place is significant. If we can just get to Signor Ali.'

'But if he's seen the news he'll know it's us and turn us in straight away, Jud! Are you mad? He'll never take us to Poveglia now.'

He shook his head. 'No, I didn't get the feeling that he was a fan of the police at all, Bex. He said he hated them, didn't he? I dunno, maybe he's had run-ins in the past. It's worth a try. If we tell him we're being framed, he might believe us.'

'And if he doesn't?'

'I'll handle that,' said Jud. 'He's an old man. He's never going to be able to keep us there, is he?'

They grabbed their rucksacks, still packed with the standard-issue equipment for detecting paranormal activity. If Poveglia was as haunted as people said it was, they were going to need everything they had. And who knew how long they were going to have to stay on there, until this news story blew over. But if the choice was between being arrested and charged with a triple murder or evading capture by hiding on the world's most haunted island, they knew which was the better option.

But would it prove to be the right one?

It was worth the risk.

CHAPTER 46

WEDNESDAY 5.28 P.M.

(6.28 P.M. VENICE TIME)

ALIPRANDO CAFÉ, VENICE

'So someone is trying to – how you say? – *frame* you, is that it?' said Signor Ali, his old, lined face ringed with tobacco smoke. Jud and Bex nodded.

They were squeezed into the back room of his café, a Closed sign up at the window and the lights turned off.

Jud and Bex had managed to leave the hotel via the fire escape. Jud had worn a hoodie which he'd brought with him and Bex had covered her face by placing a hand to her hair, pretending to prevent it from blowing in the cool breeze. Luckily the little streets and promenades of Venice had still been busy when they'd slipped out of the hotel and they blended into the crowd quickly.

Without pausing once to look at a map they'd somehow managed to remember the way to Signor Ali's little shop, safely tucked away in a quiet part of the city, on the corner of Rio Tera Dei Assassin.

Signor Ali slurped from the tiny metal coffee cup, filled with rich and strong espresso, its aroma filling the little room. Jud and Bex were still waiting for him to offer them a drink.

Fortunately for them, their host didn't own a television – he didn't believe in them – so he'd been blissfully unaware of the situation when they'd returned to his café, though he'd taken some convincing to shut up shop and hide with them out the back.

But Signor Ali was a lover of stories and this was quite a tale they were telling.

He sat back on the old wooden chair, took a final, long drag from his cigarette and then stubbed it out in the dirty ashtray on the table between them. Bex saw that his fingers were yellow with nicotine stains.

'So, let me understand, my friends. The police think you killed these people, they have proof that you were the last people to see them alive, *sì?*'

'Well,' said Jud, 'they have photos of us with the victims a short while before they were found murdered.'

'Who found them?' said Signore Ali.

'We don't know,' said Bex. 'Why?'

'Well, who knew they were going to be dead?' said the old man.

'I suppose another customer entered the shop, and found the woman,' said Bex.

Signor Ali was unconvinced. 'I bet that woman has one customer a day, if she's lucky. It seems strange that someone would have entered just after you and found her lying there. I mean, it all happened so fast, *sì?* The news story came quickly.'

They nodded.

'And what about this young couple, huh?' he continued. 'Who found them? And where were they?'

It had been hard for Bex to understand much of the news report, but she'd heard the word 'Dorsoduro', which was where the couple were living.

'So they were found at home, *sì*?' said Signore Ali.

'We don't know that,' said Jud. 'They may not have made it as far as home before they were attacked.'

'Well, I bet they were killed in their home.'

'In that case,' interrupted Bex, 'how were they found? Did someone just happen to visit them and find them there? Signor Ali is right. It's all very convenient.'

'It's not convenient for the victims, Bex,' said Jud.

'You know what I mean,' she snapped back at him.

The strain of the last few hours was taking its toll on the two of them. Their faces looked tired and their patience was running thin. They'd not fallen out once since arriving in Venice, but they were on borrowed time and they knew it. Sooner or later they'd let rip at the other and vent the frustration and fear that was building inside each of them.

'I say we leave all that to our defence lawyers if we get caught. Right now, I just want to get the hell out of this place.'

The old clock on the wall behind Bex chimed half past the hour and it made them jump.

'Jud's right, we've got to get off this island,' she said to Signor Ali. 'They'll be at the hotel by now. They'll have realised we're not there and they'll be searching the streets.'

'So you're going, huh?' said Signor Ali. 'Where are you going? You cannot go to the airport. They will find you!'

Jud and Bex looked at each other. 'Well,' said Jud, across the table, 'that's where you come in.'

Signor Ali screwed his face up as if in doubt. He started to shake his head and their hearts sank as the painful truth revealed itself – they were truly alone in the city.

'You won't help us?' Bex said desperately.

He stared at her, stared at her deep, brown eyes, glistening with the onset of tears. These two kids looked tired and lost. Jud was clearly trying to hide his fear but the old man could see through that. They needed help.

He struck a match and lit another cigarette. He continued to peer at them through the cloud of smoke that lingered before drifting up, towards the already stained ceiling.

'I cannot help you,' he said.

Their faces fell.

'Why?'

'I have too much to lose. I have had problems with the police before. I don't need to tell you about it but I cannot afford to be in trouble again. Signor Aliprando has to be a good boy.'

'All we are asking for is a boat ride,' said Jud.

'Let me guess,' he said. 'You're going to hide away with the ghosts, sì?'

'On Poveglia, yes.'

'Well, good luck, my friends. I do not know who will get you first, the ghosts of Poveglia or the police of Venice!' He gave a throaty laugh that descended into a coughing fit.

'So you'll take us to Poveglia?' said Bex, her eyes staring imploringly at Signor Ali.

'Sì. How can I refuse such a *bella signora*? And you can come too, if you must!' he said to Jud, with a wry smile. And then his expression altered. 'But I warn you, if I see the police in their little boats, I turn straight back and I hand you over, OK? Signor Ali does not like the food of the prison. And I am *not* walking on to Poveglia. You understand? I am *not* coming to that island. It is not for Aliprando. I like my life. I want to keep it.'

Jud flicked a nervous glance in Bex's direction who returned his worried gaze. Was this really the right thing to do? They must be the only people in the world who would travel to the world's most haunted island to find sanctuary.

'When do we leave?' said Jud.

'As soon as the sun has left the sky,' said Signor Ali, gazing thoughtfully out of the tiny window in the back wall. 'Darkness will be our friend tonight.'

CHAPTER 47

WEDNESDAY 7.15 P.M.

SHOREDITCH POLICE STATION,

LONDON

Nicky Calder stared at the plain, colourless walls of the small police cell. His face looked haggard – he'd not slept for twenty-four hours, after all. The impromptu dash up to Scotland for an unplanned holiday had backfired. It had not taken long for the police in Glasgow to find him. He'd not even made it off the platform. He'd matched the description they'd been given perfectly.

There'd been a struggle. He wasn't going quietly, that was for sure. Commuters had found it quite entertaining watching this small, theatrical man battling with three burly policemen, his cries echoing around the giant station. 'Why? What have I done?' he kept shouting. 'Tell me what I've done!'

But the officers had kept quiet and just manhandled him into a small office at the end of the platform where they'd sat and waited with him for the return train back to London.

'Our instructions are to escort you back to London, sir,' they'd said.

'So am I being arrested?'

'You could put it like that, sir, yes.'

'On what charge?'

'You have not been charged with anything, sir. Yet.'

'So why am I being arrested?'

'You are being arrested on *suspicion* of committing an offence. That's how it works.' The officer's tone was expressionless though it seemed patronising.

'What offence?'

'Receiving and selling stolen goods.'

'*What?*' Calder had said incredulously. What the hell were they saying? 'Where's your proof?'

'All in good time, sir. All in good time. I'm sure DCI Khan will be happy to answer your questions at Scotland Yard.'

Calder had known there was no point in resisting arrest. That really was a crime and he'd not wanted to fall into that little trap. So he'd complied and returned with them to London. What choice did he have?

But he'd been sitting in this cell, in Shoreditch Police Station, for several hours now and still had not been given any more details. He'd protested in the strongest terms through the little window in his cell door to the custody sergeant several times but to no avail.

He had to face it, he was alone.

There was a rattle of keys outside and the door handle turned. Khan entered the little room.

Calder stood up and began shouting.

'What the hell do you think you're doing? I mean, what am I being charged with? You *cannot* just—'

'Oh yes we can, sir. We can hold you here for twenty-four hours before we have to charge you with anything. And you're going to answer our questions, sir. This time, you're going to answer every one.'

'I want my solicitor. Is he here yet?'

'Yes, there is a lawyer for you in the waiting room. Don't worry. You'll have legal representation. And you're going to need it.'

'Don't threaten me, officer,' said Calder. 'There are rules you have to follow. You have to—'

'Shut up.'

'I beg your pardon?'

'You heard me. I said shut up.'

Khan entered the room, made straight for Calder and stood over him like a teacher poised to admonish a petulant child.

'I reckon I've had just about enough of your temper tantrums. We all have. The custody officer here says you've been bothering him too. You need to cool it, son. You need to calm down, take a look around and remember where you are.'

Calder ignored him and moved to the other side of the small room. 'Why the hell am I here, Inspector? Tell me that. I hear you've closed my business down. Told everyone to stay away. My lawyer told me on the phone. And we want some answers, do you hear me?

'You've dragged me away from a holiday. You've locked me up in a cell. You won't just get a rap over the knuckles when my solicitor's finished with you. You'll lose your bloody job. You will.'

Khan smiled. This little man's tantrums were amusing. And he could tell, from the way his eyes were twitching and his hands were fidgeting with his jacket, that he was nervous. Very nervous. This guy had something to hide – a great deal, if Khan's hunch was right. There was just something about him. Something false.

'You say *your* solicitor. I think you might be surprised, sir.'

'What?'

'The man standing in the foyer outside is from the usual firm down the road, the one that supplies lawyers for those who don't have them. But I'm sure he's very good.'

'What? Where's Manton. Where's Don?'

Khan shrugged. 'Called to say he's no longer representing you. Didn't say why.'

A flash of fear leaked from Calder's face – he couldn't hide it. Manton, gone? Jumped ship? He'd have some serious questions to ask him as soon as he was out of here. How dare he desert him like this!

He composed himself. 'So, the interview?' he said to Khan in as dignified a voice as he could muster.

'Delighted,' said Khan, showing Calder the door and mocking his suspect's attempt to retain his dignity. 'Shall we proceed?'

A few moments later they were sat in an interview room no bigger than the one they'd just left. Calder was attended by a young solicitor – recently out of law school, by the looks of him, and as nervous as his new client.

There was a small, frosted window in the corner of the room, through which they could see large, coloured blobs sweep past as the traffic moved down the uniquely named Shepherdess Walk. The ceiling hung low – the usual square panelling into which were fixed long, harsh strip lights. It was a functional room, devoid of character. The kind of place that unsettled Calder, so used to the finer things in life. The luxury of his little boutique seemed a million miles away now.

'Shall we begin with your name?' said Khan.

'Nicky Calder?' said Calder.

'I mean your *real* name, sir.'

The young lawyer looked confused. What had he got himself into?

Khan continued, straight-faced. 'It's Niccolo, isn't it? Niccolo Calderario.'

Calder looked uncomfortable. Khan watched his eyes flickering as he considered what to say next. He had guilt written across his face, there was no hiding it.

Khan looked across at the lawyer who'd raised his eyebrows. He'd not expected that. He noticed Khan looking at him and quickly pretended to write something significant down on the cheap pad of lined paper he'd brought with him in his shiny new briefcase.

'Is that a crime, Inspector?' said Calder. 'Is it a crime to change your name?'

Khan shook his head. 'Not at all, sir. Not at all. I just think it's a fine name. I don't know why you changed it.'

Calderario smiled at him, though Khan could see he was rattled.

'So that's why you've brought me here, is it? Because I've changed my name?'

'Oh no. I think we have more important things to discuss.'

'Such as?' he said less confidently. He seemed to have shrunk. Gone was the bravado and the temper. He'd sunk lower in his chair and was drumming his fingers nervously on the little table. He'd not once looked at his new lawyer – and did not intend to. As soon as the interview was over he planned to call Don Manton and find out what the hell was going on.

'Jewellery,' said Khan. 'Let's talk about jewellery.'

'Go on.'

'Well, I've seen your shop. You have a very fine selection of pieces, Signor Calderario.'

'Don't patronise me,' he snapped.

'Oh, I don't intend to, sir. If by patronise you mean become one of your patrons, one of your customers. I wouldn't buy one of your rings if you were the only jeweller in London.'

'And I wouldn't sell you one.'

'Well, that's a relief.'

'Will you get to the point, Inspector?'

'I will, in good time. Let's talk about what you sell. I'd like you to begin with where you get your pieces from. Who's your supplier?'

'I've already told you this. My jewellery is Venetian. It's antique. Very rare. I've been in the business a long time,

240

Inspector, and I know quality pieces when I see them. I can't say I have one supplier. No one in antiques has one supplier. We are collectors of fine art. We travel far and wide for the right piece. This is not some cheap factory, Inspector, I sell rare gems.'

'OK. I understand,' said Khan, smiling. He'd already decided to play it soft and gentle to begin with. There was no point in setting off another of Calderario's temper tantrums, as much as he'd like to wind him up again. But he could see from his appearance that his will was being steadily broken. 'So perhaps you could tell me just some of the names of your suppliers then. Just give me a few.'

'I buy my rings from across Italy.'

'Names, please.'

'Over the years I've dealt with many dealers and collectors.'

'Just the names.'

'Oh, really, Inspector. You just don't appreciate the way this profession works, do you? It is not the supplier that matters, it is the beauty of the piece.'

'Names?'

'Fabio Esposito, Adele Costa, Salvatore Bianchi, Erico De Luca, Benedetta Lombardi, Natalina Rossi, Sandro Marini . . . any more?'

Khan stared at Calderario. He was bluffing. These were just names he was reeling off. If he'd lived in Venice for most of his life he could list as many names as he liked. This could take all day. And how many of them were real people – or still alive – or actually supplying him with jewellery? Probably none of them. And how long would it take to check?

His stomach was aching again. He'd taken his ulcer medicine already and he knew he couldn't take any more. But this man was getting to him. There was something about him, something that ran deep. He could feel his blood pressure was dancing again – the old, familiar palpitations in his chest, the sweat in his hands.

He was a mess and he knew it. It was punks like this who'd be the death of him. But what else could he do? He knew he had to keep working.

He exhaled deeply and stared back at Calderario, who by now was grinning.

'More names, huh? You want more, Inspector?'

Khan shrugged. 'I want the names of the people who supply your jewellery, yes. I want you to write them all down and my officers will verify them. If we find you are lying to us, then we shall add that to the list of offences you will be charged with. Rest assured, sir, you're going nowhere.'

'Fine,' said Calderario. 'I quite like the tea here. And I'm saving on my heating bills. Gas is so expensive these days, isn't it?'

CHAPTER 48

WEDNESDAY 8.01 P.M.

CRYPT, LONDON

Bonati was exasperated. It was proving to be the busiest time for the CRYPT since its inception. He had agents across London at several hauntings, all of which were proving harder to solve and were showing no signs of abating.

And the plague cases were not slowing up – anything but. Since the incident at South Kensington, there had been several more sightings across town. And yet more fatalities. Despite posting agents at every site and at every suspected haunting, they were no nearer to controlling this.

And MI5 was asking questions. The Director General was in no mood for excuses. His own wife had been attacked, after all. This was a case in which he was taking a very personal interest. Though Lady Walden was now responding well to treatment, her condition had deteriorated after they'd visited her at home. Just like the other victims, who were now safely in hospital. She'd been admitted to hospital too and now the DG wanted real answers from South Kensington.

Down in the CRYPT there was an atmosphere about the place, a tension. Bonati was walking the corridors in Sector 1, the living accommodation, the place the agents called 'home'.

But it was anything but homely tonight. Most of the agents were still deployed on cases, hiding out in various haunts across London, taking readings, sensing atmospheres, communicating with spirits.

The zombies' lounges were empty. Of people at least.

But there was a residue of emotion lingering. You didn't have to be an agent to detect it. It was like when you visit someone's house and they're not there – something of them remains. Their mood, their state of mind just before they left. Bonati could see it here, in the discarded drinks cans, the half-eaten food. The abandoned magazines. The agents – the teenagers he was responsible for – were in a state of flux. Especially the new recruits.

Was it really the right thing to do? To put these kids through such horrors time and time again. Didn't they need security, stability? Was the CRYPT way of life what they really wanted?

You're damn right it is! he said to himself. They loved it. If he knew teenagers at all – and though he had no children himself, he had taught students for years and now lived here with them – he knew that routine and a predictable way of life was the last thing they wanted. They loved the thrill of being here, the assignments that came, and the need to abandon what they were doing at the drop of a hat and get to the next haunting.

But here, in the unusually quiet rooms, their occupants out fighting ghosts, Bonati felt a twinge of sympathy for them.

Where would it end? he thought. What would they go on to after this? Would they ever be able to hold down regular jobs and families and have a normal life after this?

But it was no different to life in the army, or the emergency services. And these organisations were never short of recruits.

How far he and Goode had come since those early days and those research projects up at Goode's castle. This was a real outfit now, a secret branch of MI5. And though it didn't look like it, from the discarded Coke cans and clothes hanging off chairs, his agents were providing a vital service to the country.

He knew the truth was that it was only going to get bigger and bigger. CRYPT had an impressive success rate that was not going unnoticed by the security services and ultimately the government. Soon they would need to recruit. They would expand their reach. There might even need to be CRYPT bases in other cities, other countries. Ghosts, after all, were everywhere.

He brushed all thoughts of the future away. They'd deal with expansion if and when it came – and at least in Jason Goode they knew they were never going to run out of funds.

He pressed on, determined to finish his rounds in time for a quick snack before the scheduled meeting with Khan and Goode. He often patrolled the premises. He liked to keep abreast of what was going on, see how the agents were living, working, see what state their rooms and their laboratories were in. This was his institution and it would be him who carried the can if something happened.

He moved past the main dining room for Sector 1, through the central atrium and on past the games rooms. All was quiet. Up towards the skulls' dorms and lounges.

Still quiet. There really was no one here.

He pressed his fingers up to the small pad on the right of each door as he went. The fingerprint recognition system was activated and the doors slid open each time. Downstairs, in the high-security Sector 3, they'd installed retina-recognition systems, but up here fingerprinting was enough.

Bonati walked along the east corridor and pressed his finger up at the next door. It was Jud's room.

The door slid open.

Chaos, as usual. An eclectic assortment of clothes, magazines and drink cans littered the floor and lay abandoned on his desk and table.

The door to his wardrobe was ajar.

What was that, on the other side of the door? It had swung open and there was something behind it, in the corner. Against the wall.

Was it Jud's dressing gown? He doubted whether he ever wore one. He wasn't a kid for paisley pyjamas and slippers. He probably didn't even own a dressing gown.

So what was it?

The professor stepped into the room. It was unusual for him to be in any of the dorms. A quick glance from the corridor was all he usually did. Just to check everything was OK. Messy, but OK.

He approached the wardrobe and gently pulled the door back towards himself.

The dark shape turned round.

Bonati only had a second to see the white mask coming for him. Only a second before the hard, skeletal fingers had scratched at his face. He put a hand up to try to protect his eyes and kept his head bent low.

The blows were coming thick and fast. Like arrows they jabbed at his head and his chest. He was propelled backwards against the wall, stumbling over a small table as he went and knocking a glass lamp to the floor.

He fought back. He tried to hold the ghost's arms at bay, but it was too strong. Immensely strong.

All the time he was thinking, why the hell was it here? In the CRYPT? And how? And why Jud's room?

But the ghost was too much for the professor. He was fit and strong and healthy for a man of his age but no match for the plague doctor. He shouted at it, kicked and jabbed, tried to overpower it but it was no good. He must have shocked – and angered – the ghost as much as it had surprised him, and the energy levels seething through its body were soaring, solidifying it, increasing its strength by the second. Bonati slumped to the floor, his back sliding down the wall.

As he placed his hands over his head in a faint effort to protect himself, he caught a glimpse of something on Jud's bedside table. He knew instantly what it was.

Stupid kid. Why the hell did he keep it in here? Why not locked away in the labs? he thought to himself.

It glistened under the automatic lighting that had blinked on when the door was opened.

And it was what the ghost had come for.

The ring from the Waldens' house.

CHAPTER 49

WEDNESDAY 8.29 P.M.

(9.29 P.M. VENICE TIME)

PORT CHANNEL OF LIDO, VENICE

The little fishing boat was rocking, far more than either Bex or Jud had expected. The trip across the lagoon from the mainland, at the other side of the island, had been a bumpy one the night before, even sitting in the luxurious water taxi, but now, in the choppier waters of the Port Channel on the south side of the island, Signor Ali's little wooden boat was being tossed around like a piece of driftwood. Which was what it would soon become if the wind kept rising.

It was dark, at last, and the lights of Venice twinkled behind them. Up ahead, the island sandbar of Lido Di Venezia stretched out before them – ten kilometres of private sandy beaches, luxury hotels and casinos. And home to the world-famous Venice Film Festival.

'Poveglia is up ahead on the right,' shouted Signor Ali. He was standing at the wheel, his hair blowing in the evening wind. Jud and Bex were stowed away inside the tiny cabin, out of sight of any unwanted search lamps from patrolling police boats. 'Not far now.'

Jud slowly peered up out of the window above him. Darkness had worked its magic and, so far at least, they'd managed to keep out of sight, though the trip from Signor Ali's café to the jetty where he kept his private boat had been harrowing.

They'd waited in the back room of his shop for what had seemed like days, though it was only about three hours. They'd filled their time drinking and listening to Signor Ali's tales of Venice and fishing and drinking and gambling. He had a captive audience, after all, and he was never going to run out of stories. How many of them were true was debatable, or would have been had either Jud or Bex cared, especially the usual fisherman's tales of giant catches of grey snapper, striped mullet and king mackerel, all caught by his own reel in the rich, salty waters of the Adriatic.

But their minds had been on other things. Jud had managed to crank up Signor Ali's ancient computer and accessed the internet to research the island they would soon be heading to. Though Jud had brought his own laptop with him there was no wi-fi and the antiquated lead connecting Signor Ali's computer to the phone line was never going to work for Jud's. Though the online connection was slow at best, and it dipped out occasionally, which was exasperating, Jud had managed to find out more information on the place they called the world's most haunted island.

And pretty soon he and Bex could see why it had earned that name.

Signor Ali had been right. It really had been used as a quarantine island during the periods in history when Venice had been struck by the bubonic plague. Some said that as many as 160,000 bodies may lie in shallow graves dug into the filthy soil on the island. And there had been many sightings of human bones washing up on the shores of neighbouring islands, for the soil on the island was rich with human remains and flooding was common.

No one had lived on the island for many years. In the 1920s an asylum was built there, and its poor patients were often experimented on by an ambitious doctor, keen to make a name for himself for curing insanity. His methods were as insane as the actions of his pitiful patients. He conducted crude lobotomies with hand drills and even put many through various tortures up in the giant and depressing bell tower that looked over the island.

The asylum closed down in the late 1960s due to lack of funding (Jud thought it was amazing it had lasted that long). The last person ever to live on Poveglia was an old caretaker who resided there in the 1980s, making a home for himself out of the abandoned and overgrown ruins of the asylum, with nothing but the ghosts of the mental patients and the plague victims before them to keep him company.

The same ghosts whose screams unsettled the fishermen when their boats strayed towards the island from time to time. They soon sailed away from it as fast as they could.

And now here were Jud and Bex, sailing *towards* the wretched place. Not just for a quick ghost tour but for research *and* for safety.

The idea seemed ridiculous even to Jud, but it was infinitely better than getting arrested. Not even Bex knew how much he had to lose if he was to face trial for murder. Again. Bonati and his father would have to work hard to see him right a second time.

He was surprised Bonati hadn't replied yet. He'd tried calling several times just before they'd left Venice but had been unable to raise him. And the other agents were all working at locations, no doubt, or buried deep in research (or Xbox games!). His father, Jason Goode, had been unavailable too – but that was no surprise. He never was.

They'd resolved to try again as soon as they arrived on Poveglia. Their standard-issue CRYPT mobile phones enjoyed the best reception of any phone on the market – another of

Jason Goode's personal missions, to create a phone that you could literally use anywhere, anytime.

Suddenly a sharp light burst through the tiny porthole in the cabin and swept across the little space Jud was sharing with Bex. They kept low, as low as they physically could, though it was uncomfortable and cold and damp, and now Jud had to contend with cramp that was rising up his leg.

'Head down!' they heard Signor Ali whisper loudly from outside. 'It's a police boat.'

A few seconds later they could hear the sound of other male voices outside – deep tones, talking quickly and in unusually monotonous tones for Venetians.

Signor Ali was speaking hurriedly back.

'Well?' whispered Jud. 'What are they saying?'

'Jud, I can barely hear them, let alone translate! I'm not superhuman.'

They were squashed together like sardines in a tin. Now was not the time to fall out.

'OK, I'm sorry,' said Jud.

'Sh!' said Bex. 'Let me try and listen for something.'

She heard the word '*pesca*' mentioned several times, which she was pretty sure was 'fishing'. Signor Ali's idea of fixing his usual fishing nets to the back of the boat had been proved wise. It was the cover they were using – some late-night fishing in the lagoon, when the harbour was quiet. He worked in his café all day so evenings like this were the only time he could fish anyway. It seemed plausible.

They waited with bated breath as the rapid exchange continued above them.

'What the hell are they still talking about?' whispered Jud.

'I don't know. I've just heard the word *licenza* so I guess they're checking to see if he has a valid fishing licence.'

'I sure hope he has.'

She nodded reassuringly. 'He will have. He was boasting in

the shop, wasn't he, about the fish he catches and sells. All that stuff about king mackerel's. Of course he'll have a licence.'

'Does he look like your honest law-abider to you?' said Jud doubtfully.

'Hmm,' said Bex. 'I see your point.'

They waited with baited breath.

There was the sound of feet above them. Scuffling. And more shouts.

Were they coming in? Were they about to make the finest catch of the season – two suspected murderers?

Jud and Bex stared wide-eyed at the little hatch that was all that separated them from arrest and a prison cell.

And then the noise seemed to fade. The police officers must have left the boat and climbed back on to their own. There was the sound of chugging; the lights swept across the little cabin and disappeared. The boat had gone.

'Blimey, that was close,' said Bex, relieved.

'Yeah. Don't get too comfortable, though,' said Jud. 'I think we're nearly there. Look.'

As the search lamps from the police boat slowly inched away and their eyes became used to the dark again, the faint and ugly outline of an island appeared on the horizon.

'Poveglia,' a voice shouted down to them. 'You can see it now.'

CHAPTER 50

WEDNESDAY 9.20 P.M.

CRYPT, LONDON

'So where the hell is he?' said Jason Goode. He was drumming his fingers on the desk, fidgeting in his chair. 'Do you know, Khan, I sometimes wonder if adults are harder to manage than teenagers.'

'Tell me about it,' said Khan. 'I just hope he hasn't fallen asleep like one of my men did the other day. Bloody idiot.'

'Oh, I heard about that. Lost your man, didn't you? Hot-footed it to Scotland.'

'Yeah. We've got him now though.'

'Is he talking?' said Goode.

'Full of bullshit,' said Khan, miserably. 'We were shovelling it around like dung beetles. I didn't believe anything he said.'

'But you know his real name. Bonati told me it's Niccolo Caldera ... or something.'

'Calderario. Yes. And I've already contacted the Venetian police to help us trace his history over there. If you guys are right and that jewellery he's pedding really is cursed, then I'm damn sure we're going to find out where it comes from.'

'Well, that's what I was hoping we'd be finding out now. Bonati's supposed to be giving us an update. Where *is* he?'

Goode went to his drinks cabinet again and refilled his glass of bourbon. 'Another drink, Inspector?'

'Please. God knows I need it.'

'So what did the Venetian police say?' asked Goode. 'I mean, any sightings at all? Have they seen what we've been experiencing here?'

'No. That's the weird thing. According to the police, not a thing. No reports of ghosts at all. I'm due to speak to them again later tonight and I'll see if there's been any change. But so far, no help at all.'

'So where is this Niccolo guy now? Still in the cells?'

'Yes. But we can't hold him for much longer without something to charge him with. I've talked to the Commissioner about an extension but he's nervous. We need some hard evidence. Or at least a bloody theory instead of all these hunches.'

Goode was staring out of the window, at the city lights that stretched across the dark sky. The building slowly revolved, giving them a full panorama.

He'd spent thousands on regular refits and refurbishments of his penthouse suite, but try as he might, he just couldn't create the sense of home he was so badly missing in his life.

Of course, it didn't help that he was so rarely there – always travelling to meetings in Europe and back across the pond to the States. It felt more like a hotel room than a home.

He spun round and looked at Khan with an agitated expression on his face. 'Right. He's nearly half an hour late. Let's go down and see where he is. I've been calling and texting him and received nothing. I've called Vorzek and she doesn't know either. This isn't like Giles. Something's up.'

He slammed his glass on to the table and headed for the door. Khan finished his drink – he wasn't about to waste top-quality bourbon – then hurried after him and down the long glass corridor that led to the lifts.

A few minutes later they were down in Sector 1. Goode had

called Vorzek on the way down and arranged for her to meet them at the lifts.

'So still no sign of the professor?' said Goode.

Vorzek shook her head.

'By the way,' said Goode more gently this time, 'I'm sorry to hear about your partner, Kim. What's the latest?'

'He's still in hospital. They're keeping him in for observations as he had a really nasty blow to the head, but he's going to be OK. He's been lucky.'

'Luckier than some of the others,' said Khan. 'The body count is piling up.'

'Charming, thank you, Inspector,' said Goode. 'So have you searched Bonati's suite?'

Vorzek nodded.

'And the labs in Sector 3?'

She nodded again. 'He's not down there.'

'What about the meeting rooms?'

'Well, I've asked some agents to help us with that. They're searching them now. But nothing so far.'

'So he's gone out?' said Khan.

Vorzek shook her head. 'Unlikely, Inspector. He wasn't scheduled to be out this evening and in any case he's left his keys and his phone and wallet in his office. I saw them on his desk. He would never do that normally.'

'No wonder he wasn't returning my calls!' said Goode. 'Never takes his bloody phone with him! But if his keys are still here, then so is he.'

'You did try his private rooms, didn't you, Kim? I mean, he's not taking a nap or something?'

'I did, and he's not,' she said.

'Right. If you've tried Sectors 2 and 3, then he must be up here. Let's get going. You try the dining room and kitchens – maybe he's feeling peckish. Then try the zombies' quarters at the end. Khan, you try the games room and dorms on the left and

I'll work my way down the right. He's got to be here somewhere.'

'I can't get access, can I?' said Khan. 'I mean, these fingerprint scanners and all that.'

Vorzek handed him a small, plastic card. 'Use this,' she said. 'It's a pass key that overrides the fingerprinter. Just place it over the square panel beneath the scanner. It'll work.'

'OK,' said Khan. 'And what if the agents are in their rooms?'

'I don't care!' said Goode. 'Tell them to bloody well come and help us!'

They proceeded from the central atrium. Vorzek went left and headed down the corridor to the games rooms, though she thought it highly unlikely Bonati had chosen now to play snooker. Perhaps he was in the storerooms or kitchens for some reason.

Khan and Goode began searching the rooms at the other end of the building.

They were gathering a steady trickle of agents in their path, all anxious to know where their leader was hiding. Agents often hid themselves away, either to research or just get some personal space to 'download', as they often put it, but the professor? He'd never stowed away before. And besides, he had a complete suite of private rooms to hide away in. And he wasn't there.

After several dorms, Goode moved towards the stretch of corridor that housed Jud's.

He was nervous. He'd never gone into his son's room uninvited – not since Jamie was small, anyway, and they were living together as a family.

He pressed his index finger against the scanner and the door slowly slid open.

'Oh, God,' he said.

The room looked as if it had been turned upside down. There was furniture tipped over and clothes everywhere and in the corner nearest the door, the professor's body lay slumped against the wall. His face was barely recognisable. His eyes were swollen and bruised like a boxer's after a prize fight and there were gashes to his cheeks which had leaked tracks of blood that covered his face like war paint. His silver hair was damp and matted with more blood – he must have had a cut to the head too.

But most worryingly of all, he was not responding.

'Giles? Giles? Can you hear me?' Goode was holding his bloodstained hand and squeezing it. He found a pulse – just. He gently raised one of his eyelids to see if he could get a reaction. There was no reaction from the pupils.

He'd lost a lot of blood, no question. As Goode pulled his friend away from the wall, he could see it was everywhere.

'Hello! Somebody! Over here. Come on!' he yelled towards the open door.

Grace was the first to get there. She stopped and put a hand to her mouth as she stood in the doorway.

'Oh God.'

'Go to the medical lab. Get a stretcher. Hurry!'

Grace just stared at the professor.

'*Now*, Grace!'

She ran off, tears in her eyes.

A few more agents arrived and they, too, stood staring at Bonati. It wasn't supposed to be like this. The professor was the rock around which they all tethered themselves. They'd all seen injuries, sometimes fatal ones, but not here, in the CRYPT, and not the professor. It was wrong – a violation. Somebody – or something – had penetrated the fortress and attacked the very leader that inspired them.

'Giles!' Goode kept calling his name and patting his face. 'Can you hear me?' He was panicking now. His heart was racing and there was a sinking feeling in the pit of his stomach.

He couldn't do this alone. Bonati was his rock too.

'Giles!'

There was a faint movement in the professor's left hand. Then a twitching in his right eye. His lips moved almost imperceptibly, but Jason had seen it. The congealed blood at his mouth cracked and shifted like solidified lava.

'Giles? Hello? It's me, Jason.'

The professor tried to open both eyes, though the swelling meant he could only squint. His whole body ached. And the wounds on his face stabbed him again, as they had before.

He nodded his head.

'What the hell happened?' said Jason, still holding his hand.

'There was a ghost,' he said wearily. 'In here.'

'What? Actually *in the* CRYPT?'

Bonati nodded slowly.

'Where is it now?'

The professor shrugged. 'It's gone. But not before it had a good go at me.'

'You had me worried, Giles. Thought I was going to have to run this place alone!'

'You'd never manage that!' choked Bonati. He was weak and battered and bruised but he was alive.

'You've lost a lot of blood. We need to get you sorted out – and quickly.'

'Yeah. The ghost kept puncturing me like a pin cushion. Jason, they're so strong. *So* strong.' He winced again, and his head felt dizzy. Goode could see his colour was not returning yet – his face still looked pale beneath the blood splatters and bruises.

'Lie down,' said Jason. 'There's a stretcher on its way.' He turned to the agents, gawping in the doorway. 'Where's that bloody stretcher?' he shouted. 'Find it, now!'

Khan ran to the doorway. He'd been at the opposite end of the corridor when he'd heard the shouting.

'Oh blimey. What's been goin' on here?'

He brushed his way past the agents at the door and helped Goode support Bonati's head on a pillow which he grabbed from Jud's bed.

'It was after it,' Bonati whispered. He was pointing a shaking hand towards the bedside cabinet.

'After what?' said Goode. 'Say it again.' The professor was barely audible.

'After the ring,' whispered Bonati. 'Jud brought the ring over from the Waldens' house. It was in here. The ghost had come for it.'

Goode and Khan glanced quickly at the bedside cabinet. The ring was still there.

'But it didn't take it,' said the inspector.

'No. I made sure of that,' Bonati croaked. 'But as you can see,' he wiped his face and winced at the pain, 'it wasn't happy about it.'

CHAPTER 51

WEDNESDAY 9.39 P.M.

(10.39 P.M. VENICE TIME)

ISLAND OF POVEGLIA, VENICE

Even from a distance the island seemed ugly and unwelcoming. The trees were dense and thick, and at irregular intervals the crumbling roofs of abandoned buildings were just visible above the woods. At the side nearest to their boat a group of foreboding buildings carved ominous shadows in the moonlight. A solid block of brick edifices, resembling a Victorian hospital or school, stood guard over the beach, and a giant, ugly bell tower soared over the site like a prison watchtower. Row upon row of black square holes formed open windows in the walls, the glass now long gone.

The trees and shrubs surrounding the campus were straggly and unkempt, brambles and thorns creeping their way across the crumbling brickwork. It was uncared for, abandoned and inhospitable. So different to the welcoming lights of the Lido just a few miles behind them, the vast casinos and hotels enticing tourists in. This place was lonely, neglected. Like an unwanted guest at a party or a tramp in a busy park. The one no one approaches, or speaks to, or loves. The blot on the landscape.

The odour wafted towards them before they'd even landed.

'What *is* that smell?' said Bex, as she thrust her head above the hatch for a closer look at the island looming closer.

'Dunno. It's putrid,' said Jud.

'Rotting flesh,' said Signor Ali, raising his eyebrows as if to say, I told you it was scary. 'It is human bodies you can smell. Very old and very – how you say? – decayed.'

'But why can we smell it?' said Bex. 'I mean, when you go in a graveyard, you can't smell dead bodies, can you?'

'Ah, *bella*. This is no graveyard. These people were not buried in the coffins. They were thrown into big holes in the ground. And sometimes the island gets flooded. The waters come up the beach and disturb the graves.'

'So it's a giant grave,' said Bex, staring out at the island's silhouette, the moon rising behind it.

'Sì. Some call it the island of no return,' said Signor Ali.

'Yeah, you're not helping,' said Bex. 'Now I understand what you meant about the fishermen worrying they might catch human bones in their fishing nets.'

'Sì. I have many friends who say they have found skulls and bones in their catches. It is always when they are fishing near this place.'

'Well, if that website was right,' said Jud, 'there may be over a hundred and sixty thousand bodies buried there. No wonder there's bones around. They've been burying people on the island since Roman times. The plague doctors in the seventeenth century weren't the first people to dump bodies on here and use it for quarantine, you know.'

'Great, thanks,' said Bex, sarcastically. 'You know, Jud, you should become a tour guide.'

The boat was closing in now, just a few hundred metres away from the makeshift harbour and precarious-looking jetty.

Jud looked startled and jabbed Bex, standing closer to him, still staring out of the cabin's hatch.

'Hear that?' he said.

'Hear what?' said Bex. 'Don't do that!'

Jud's eyes were darting across the skyline – he was tuning in, sensing. 'Hush, there it is again. Hear it?'

Bex shook her head. Signor Ali was chuckling up ahead at the wheel. 'You hear the bells, sì?'

'Yes!' said Jud. 'You hear it too?'

'What bells?' said Bex. She was feeling frustrated that she couldn't hear anything above the steady throb of the boat's little engine and the waves lapping against the hull.

'It is the bells of the bell tower,' said Signor Ali, smiling wryly. 'Many of my friends have heard this from time to time. The bell tower is ringing.'

'But there's no one in it,' said Bex.

'Exactly,' said Signor Ali, grinning.

She listened in carefully. If Jud could hear it, so could she, she thought to herself. She knew it wasn't a competition about who could sense the most activity, but if it were, she was not about to lose it.

And there it was, just detectable over the engine's hum. The faint but recognisable ringing of a huge bell, emanating from the cluster of buildings at the water's edge. And from one structure in particular – the giant tower that thrust upwards like a blunt dagger.

'Are we landing there?' said Bex.

'Are you mad?' said Signor Ali. 'There is no one on the island but there are plenty of people on the ocean, and some of them have the binoculars. We will sail around to the other side and find somewhere beneath the trees. You can jump out before I hit the beach. You might get wet feet, but at least you'll be hidden. I am not coming with you.'

'You sure?' said Jud. 'It'll be a ball.'

'What's that you say?'

'Don't worry,' said Bex. 'He's just teasing. He loves his ghosts – he's stupid like that.'

'Well, in that case, he's come to the right place. Enjoy it, *il mio ragazzo*.'

'And you? Will you get back OK?' asked Bex.

'Of course. *Sì*. Signor Ali knows this place better than anyone. I have never been lost!'

'No,' said Bex, 'I mean will you get back without being seen? I hope no one sees you leaving this island.'

'That is why we are sailing to the other side. I will sail as close as I can and then you will have to jump out. I am not stopping.'

'You're worried the police will see you?'

'No. I'm worried the ghosts will have my boat.'

Jud and Bex looked at one another. Something told them he wasn't joking.

The boat slowly chugged its way around the coastline of the forgotten island. Gnarled, ugly tree trunks and jagged shrubs grew right down to the water's edge in places, like nature's own barbed-wire fencing, prohibiting anyone from stepping foot on the island. The beach rose and dipped at irregular intervals, sometimes throwing up just enough sand to walk on and then disappearing into the depths, to be replaced by jagged rocks that thrust through the ripples like angular fists.

Eventually they were at the other side of the island, in a quieter stretch of the lagoon, far from the comforting lights of Venice to the north and the exciting neon displays on the Lido to the east. But the smell was even stronger here, like stagnant water, filled with corpses.

Signor Ali pulled the boat in close, but not too close – there were rocks on this side of the island too, and great branches that hung low.

'You're going to have to jump out,' said Signor Ali, wincing at the stench. 'I will get as close as I can, but I am worried for my boat. If I break it on the rocks, no more fish. No more food. And anyway, the police will be around patrolling again soon. We must be quick.'

Jud and Bex looked towards the island. Jump here? Was he serious? How deep was the water? And it smelled rotten. And what about the rocks? It was impossible to tell from this distance, especially in darkness too.

But what was the alternative? They could hardly sail back round to the main jetty of the island, near the cluster of abandoned buildings, in full view of the busiest section of the lagoon, could they? The police or a passing water taxi would see them landing on the island and soon they'd be found. They *had* to approach it from over here, but they'd both expected to see at least some beach.

The sound of the engine dropped to a lull and the boat slowed down.

'Right, are you going or not?' said Signor Ali. 'We must be quick.'

They were going to have to swim for it. They'd be cold and wet for hours after swimming in this giant cesspit, with no way of warming up – they could hardly light a fire for warmth without attracting attention – but at least they would be free.

'What about the equipment?' said Bex, glancing across the cabin at the two rucksacks in the corner. 'We can't get it wet, it'll be useless.'

'We'll hold it up, you only need one hand to swim,' said Jud nonchalantly. Then he glanced up on to the deck and saw a lifebelt hanging on a peg. 'No, even better. We'll put them in that and push it along. Signor Ali? Can we use the lifebelt?'

'What? Now you tell me you cannot swim? You English, huh!'

'No, no. We need to keep our equipment dry. Our bags. We could stack them on top of it and push it to the island.'

'OK, OK. But I want it back, you hear . . .' But they could tell from the resignation in his voice that he thought he'd never see it – or them – ever again.

Suddenly the idea of stowing away in this ghostly place – the 'island of no return' as Signor Ali had called it – seemed crazy and they both felt a faint panic rising within them. They were at the point of no return – the term was apt; they could hardly tell Signor Ali they'd changed their minds and could he sail back to Venice with two fugitives in his cabin. He *had* to get rid of them. They'd managed to sneak away from the main island; there was no chance of sneaking back to it again undetected.

But that stench was rancid.

This was it. They had no choice. No turning back. The cold, dark, stinking waters of the lagoon beckoned, and the mysterious unknowns of Poveglia awaited them.

But this was why they were agents. To face up to the challenges, to conquer that tiny voice inside them, inside all of us, that says 'retreat'.

Jud was first to move. He turned, grabbed the rucksacks from the other side of the little cabin and then climbed up through the hatch on to the deck. Bex quickly followed. They had little time. Signor Ali was convinced that the patrol boats would be round soon.

Jud balanced himself on the edge of the deck and lowered his legs into the water. It was cold – far colder than he'd expected. But this wasn't Venice in the height of summer, it was winter. And the icy wind that whipped across the lagoon from the ocean was bracing. The cold cut right through his jeans and into his legs as he kept moving them around under the surface, trying to keep the circulation going. If he stayed still too long he knew he'd be in trouble.

'Come on, Bex, it's fine,' he lied.

She passed the large, red and white lifebelt down to him and then climbed into the water too. It was like plunging into an icy bath. The extreme temperature took her breath away.

'Bloody liar,' she said, panting. 'Jud Lester, you're a madman. This is *not* one of your better ideas.'

'Oh, so suddenly it was all my idea, was it?'

'Duh, yeah!' said Bex, her body jerking in every direction, as she frantically kept her legs moving through the freezing waters. 'It was.' But his smile told her he was trying to wind her up. Yeah, great time for jokes, she thought. What was it about this guy? Didn't he *ever* take life seriously?

And it why did it have to be so bloody cold?

Signor Ali handed down the lifebelt. 'Good luck,' he said. 'I wish I could say this lifebelt will save your lives on the island, but I don't think it will.'

'Gee, thanks,' said Bex. 'Very comforting.'

'Yeah, whatever,' said Jud. He held on to the boat with one hand and stacked the rucksacks on to the lifebelt with the other. Signor Ali helped him tie them on with a short piece of old rope he'd found in a cluttered toolbox on deck.

'Right, now *go!*' said Signor Ali, impatiently. 'I can see some lights up ahead. It might be a patrol boat. I must leave you . . . *buona fortuna.*'

'What's he say?' said Jud.

'Good luck!' said Bex.

'So will he come and get us?' said Jud.

Bex asked him and he nodded.

'*Domani notte,*' he said.

They'd only just managed to push themselves away from the boat before it sped off out to sea. Signor Ali wanted to create some distance between his boat and the forbidden island before he returned to the main island. He would say he'd been out fishing in open sea. It wasn't unheard of.

Treading water in the shivering cold, they watched him for a second and both wondered if he would keep his promise and return tomorrow night.

Then they swam as quickly and aggressively as they could,

panting furiously, not even sure if it was the cold sending their hearts racing or the thought of what they might encounter in the next twenty-four hours. Exhilaration mixed with trepidation, sending adrenalin racing around their bodies as they pushed on, closer to the branches that hung down to the water's edge. Nearly there.

There was a ringing in the distance.

'Do you hear the bells again?' said Jud.

'Yeah,' said Bex. 'And somehow I don't think it's a welcome. More a warning.'

'Whatever. It's just a bell, Bex.'

But then, through the wind and the lapping of the water and the faint ringing of the bell, they heard a new sound. And although their bones were already chilled, it froze them with fear.

It was the sound of screaming.

They approached the nearest low-hanging branch, grabbed it and stared at one other. They knew from each other's faces that they'd both heard it.

'This place has earned its reputation,' said Jud, still out of breath from swimming. 'It's certainly living up to expectations.'

Bex let out a scream herself.

'What?' said Jud. 'What's happened? Is it the screams you don't like? Don't worry about—'

'No!' she shouted. 'It's my leg. I must've hit a rock. Bloody hell, it hurts. I caught my knee on something. Ow!'

'We'll strap it up. As soon as we get on there. I'll find something in the bag and we'll sort it. You've done really well.'

'Don't patronise me!' she said. 'I'm probably a faster swimmer than you!'

There was a scream again. It was unlike anything they'd heard before. Not even in the SPA rooms had they heard such an animal-like, guttural noise. It was the sound of real terror, the screams of someone in agony. The ghosts of Poveglia's grisly past were making themselves known.

Undeterred, they clung on tightly to the branch and pulled their way in towards the bank, the rope from the lifebelt hanging over Jud's shoulder.

The stench had not abated. A foul, putrid cocktail of salt water, tree bark and the remains of rotting cadavers wafted into their nostrils. No wonder people stayed away. If you didn't hear the ghostly screams, like they had, the rank smell alone was enough to put you off.

But something told them this was not going to be the only assault on their senses. If they thought the smell was bad, they knew somehow it was only the beginning.

Things were about to get much, much worse.

CHAPTER 52

WEDNESDAY 10.01 P.M.

CRYPT, LONDON

Bonati sat back against the pillow, propped up behind his bruised head. The CRYPT's own medic had been fussing around him since he'd been carried there. He just wanted some peace and quiet. But he was not going to get it. Not now. He'd been prodded and poked and tested like a piece of meat. The medic was looking for signs of the plague. The professor had not even picked up the cursed ring but after such close contact with the ghost, they couldn't take any chances.

At least his face looked better now. The gashes had been wiped and treated with a strong antiseptic that had stung sharply. He'd regained some colour to his cheeks now. There was no doubting it, he'd had a lucky escape. Things could have been *so* much worse (as everyone kept telling him).

The medical suite at the CRYPT was not extensive – optimistically small, you might say. And so far it had been enough.

Jason Goode was sitting beside Bonati's bed, one of just three in the room, the other two being recently vacated by agents on the mend. Dr Vorzek was seated at the other side, looking relieved at the professor's fast recovery and hoping that her fiancé would be as lucky. He, too, didn't like being made a fuss of and had pleaded with Vorzek to go back to work and leave him alone. 'Stop fussing, will you!' was all he kept saying. 'You're worse than the nurses!' And now here she was at someone else's bedside.

'That was a close run,' said Goode. 'You were lucky, Giles.'

The professor nodded slowly. 'Yes, I know, I know. Horrid to think the ghosts could penetrate into here, Jason. I mean, right into the CRYPT. Is nowhere safe?'

'Well, at least we know it was only here for the ring. Bloody stupid of J to leave it in his room like that. Why the hell wasn't it locked away in Sector 3? Its energy would have been undetectable in storage down there. They'd never have traced it. We'd have been safe. I'll kill him when I see him!'

The door was pushed open suddenly and a grim-faced DCI Khan walked in. He was pale and they could see he was clutching his stomach. Something was up.

'What's happened, Khan?'

'Bad news. I've just spoken again to the Polizia di Stato in Venice. There've been developments since we talked to them earlier today.' He stood over the bed and looked at the professor. The three faces glanced gloomily in Khan's direction and braced themselves.

'You haven't heard from Jud and Bex yet, have you?' he asked, hopefully.

'No,' said Bonati. 'Why do you ask? What's happened?'

'Well, it seems there have been some incidents in Venice since we last spoke. Very serious ones.' His face looked grave as he stared at the professor. 'Three people have been murdered in Venice today. Violent deaths.'

Bonati and Goode stared at the inspector.

'Go on,' said Goode, ominously.

'The police have sent us over some film footage – it went out on the national news this evening apparently. It shows two people leaving the scene of each crime just moments before each of the victims was found dead. They're saying they believe the two people are the culprits. And . . . well, I've seen the pictures.'

'And?' said Bonati.

'I'm afraid it looks like Jud and Bex.'

There was silence in the room while they looked at one another. Jud and Bex wanted for *murder*? It was ridiculous! This wasn't happening. Somebody somewhere was getting confused. Mistaken identity perhaps.

'This is nonsense! What the hell are the police playing at over there? When did anyone hear from Jud and Bex last?' said Goode, looking around the room anxiously. He was feeling frustrated. This was not how he worked. Not how his company functioned. At any given time, he knew where his employees were, what they were doing, who they were meeting and why. Some said he was a control freak. He'd live with that.

But the CRYPT was different. Investigations took longer, and were less predictable than meetings. Agents were harder to tie down, they had more freedom than employees of Goode Technology PLC. Much more freedom – and trust.

But these things came at a price. At times like these it was so frustrating not being able to keep tabs on them. Especially when one of them was your own son.

Vorzek shook her head. 'I'm sorry, gentlemen, I've not heard from them since they left the country. We went through an equipment check before they left for the airport. They were in good spirits. But I've not heard from them since.'

'I spoke to Jud earlier today,' said the professor. 'About lunchtime. I filled him in on the Calder situation. He told me he'd discovered his real identity. Niccolo Calderario. Jud said there had been a sighting, and it matched the ghost descriptions over here. But he didn't say anything about a *murder* case. Nothing at all.'

'So this has all blown up since lunchtime?' said Goode. 'This is too fast – too convenient. Something's gone seriously wrong here. And where the hell are they now? No one has spoken to them since lunchtime? Really? Have they been arrested, do you think?'

'No. That's why the film footage of them was broadcast on the news, they said they're still searching for them,' said Khan.

'God knows how they must be feeling,' said Dr Vorzek. 'It's worrying they haven't called in since it happened.'

'You bet it's worrying, Kim,' said Goode. 'Are you *sure* they haven't called you, Giles?'

'Well, to be fair, Jason, I haven't checked my phone since I was attacked, I left it in my study when I went on the rounds before we were supposed to meet. I would've checked it as soon as I'd finished but was brought straight here on a stretcher. What was I supposed to do? They may have been trying to call, I don't know. There's been no call to the emergency CRYPT line, otherwise we'd know about it.'

'Kim, can you go and get the professor's phone from his study?' said Goode.

'Of course,' she said and quickly exited, glad to be out of the room when Jason Goode was in mercurial mood.

'So, let me get this straight, Khan,' snapped Goode. 'You're telling me that the Venetian police have found three people dead and they genuinely believe that Jud and Bex did it? Is that what you're saying? Because this is *fantasy*. Pure bloody fantasy.'

'I agree it's ridiculous, but the problem is the footage clearly shows them either talking to the victims or leaving the scene a short time before they were found. I'm sure it's them.'

'Well, we'll have a look for ourselves in a moment,' said Goode. 'But are they the only people to have seen the victims? It's Venice, for God's sake! It's a busy place. Were there others there too? Who found them? Bit of a coincidence they were found just after they were killed, don't you think? And someone just happened to conveniently film J and Bex moments before that. There's a conspiracy here, Khan. I can smell it.'

'But still no real link to this Nicky Calder and his jewellery,' said Bonati. 'Which is why they went there in the first place. We're no further forward on that, are we?'

Khan shook his head. 'When I tried to question Calder on the names of his suppliers, he just reeled off a list of Italian names. They might have been real people, might even have been proper jewellers, we don't know, and of course we're on it now but I suspect he was just stalling us.'

'Jud and Bex must have been on to them,' said Goode, his eyes darting across the room as he tried to think this through. 'They must have got too close for comfort and now someone is trying to get rid of them by framing them with three murders.'

'Possible,' said Bonati, 'but we're getting way ahead of ourselves here. We need much more proof. The two things need not be linked at all.'

'So where are these rings coming from?' said Khan. 'Why so much protection and the secrecy? I mean, it sounds like people have been killed now. If there is a link between the murders and the jewellery then, these rings must be special.'

'People will do anything for money. You know that,' said Bonati. 'And if Calder's found a way of sourcing stolen jewellery then he'll do anything to protect that source.'

'Never mind the jewellery! Where the hell are Jud and Bex?' said Goode.

Vorzek returned with Bonati's phone. She handed it to the professor, whose face dropped as soon as he clicked the unlock button.

Three missed calls. All from Jud's phone.

Goode could see his expression. 'We've missed him, haven't we?'

Bonati nodded.

'Well, try him again!' Goode shouted. 'Now!'

The professor called but there was no connection. 'He must be out of range,' he said miserably.

'Don't be stupid,' said Goode, seizing the phone from Bonati. 'Do you know how sophisticated these things are? They never drop out of signal. My scientists told me—'

'Well, your scientists were wrong!' said Bonati, angrily. 'There's no bloody way we can get in touch with him and Bex now. We have to wait for them to call us again if they can. There's nothing we can do but wait.' He was angry with himself for not having his phone on him at all times. Angry and embarrassed. They all knew how significant those missed calls were. But there was no point in his oldest friend losing his temper like this. It helped no one. Sometimes Bonati wondered if the whole CRYPT would function better without Jason – except it would be penniless, of course.

'When did he ring?' said Khan.

Goode threw the phone back at Bonati, scowling. The professor hurriedly checked the calls.

'Earlier this evening,' said Bonati, disconsolately.

'Voicemail?'

Bonati shook his head. 'Nothing. Just missed calls.'

Khan's face looked grave. 'Well, wherever they are now, it sounds like the whole of the Venetian police force is after them. God help them both.'

Goode stood up and walked towards the door.

'Come on,' he said. 'Let's not leave it to God alone, shall we?'

CHAPTER 53

WEDNESDAY 10.55 P.M.

(11.55 P.M. VENICE TIME)

POVEGLIA ISLAND, VENICE

Jud and Bex were soaked. Their bodies shivered and their boots squelched as they trudged across the mud. The coast was some way behind them now and at least they had the trees for cover. They stared ahead into the gloom of the abandoned island. It was a cloudy night and the moon provided little relief. It was raining too, heavy droplets pummelled their already sodden heads.

A light flashed across the trees ahead of them. It was coming from behind them somewhere, on the open sea. A boat.

'Get down!' said Jud.

They fell to the muddy ground. They couldn't get any wetter so there was no point in trying to find a dry place to hide any more.

Jud glanced through the trees at the water. The lights of a boat were passing from left to right.

'It's a police boat, isn't it?' said Bex. She'd recognised the shape and colour of the lights.

'Yeah, guess so,' said Jud. 'I'm glad we're on here. They'll never see us.'

But their relief was short-lived as they saw that the police boat was towing something. In the mottled light of the moon they could just make out the shape of the little fishing boat.

It was Signor Ali's.

'They've got him,' said Jud, ominously. 'It's only a matter of time now before he talks.'

'Not necessarily,' said Bex. 'He said he was going to tell them he'd been fishing.'

'So why would they tow in someone who was fishing legally?' said Jud.

Bex knew he was right. Signor Ali had some explaining to do. And was it really in his interests to hide the truth? Why should he lie for two people he'd only just met? Two people who could be murderers, if the reports were true. And there was no doubt the police would try to convince him of that.

But the boat was not slowing down as it passed the island. It was heading for the lagoon – back to Venice, they hoped. They watched in silence as the patrol boat, towing Signor Ali's fishing boat, moved beyond the edge of the island and disappeared around the corner, in the direction of the Lido. The sound of the engine faded and soon all they could hear were the waves at the shore and the wind whistling through the trees. Although it was a relief to see the boat pass, they felt acutely alone once it had gone.

'It's only a matter of time before they come and search for us,' said Jud. 'We don't have much time.'

'Great. Because we don't even know what it is we're looking for, do we?' said Bex.

'We'll know when we see it,' said Jud. 'There's something on this island that links all the hauntings. I can feel it. The plague doctors have been appearing in London and taking bodies, just as they did all those years ago right here, in Venice. They brought them here, to Poveglia, so there has to be a link. If we can find that, and expose the truth, we'll be safe. Now let's go.'

They stood up, collected their bags and disappeared into the darkness. The lifebelt they'd used to float the rucksacks lay discarded in the mud.

As they walked on, deeper into the island, they failed to look back the way they'd come. If they had, they'd have seen the red and white lifebelt slowly disappearing into the sodden earth. Something was sucking it under. Soon it had gone – buried with the bodies.

As the agents' eyes re-acclimatised to the dark after the bright lights of the police boat, they could make out the silhouette of the collection of buildings in the distance – the old mental asylum, now derelict. But they knew that between there and where they now walked, there must be dozens of plague pits.

Jud looked down at the sodden earth and wondered what his boots were walking over. The stench was truly awful. The ground was squelchy and uneven. There must have been some kind of farm here once, but it was long abandoned. Now it was just a sea of mud with the occasional island of stones, weeds or turf. It felt like the marshy bogs of Dartmoor. But the stench was putrid and they'd both come close to gagging several times already.

As the wind rustled the leaves in the trees that surrounded them like grim reapers, they could just make out the faint ringing of bells again from the ghostly tower in the distance.

There was a flutter just beside Bex. She ducked quickly and shivered as a flurry of bats swooped past and disappeared into the blackness.

'How do you feel?' said Jud.

'How do you think I feel?' said Bex. 'Bloody cold, soaked through and hungry. Next question.'

'No, I mean, what do you sense?'

They stood still for a few moments. And looked at one another. Bex's dark eyes penetrated into Jud. They were connecting with the landscape, sensing. Catching the wave of emotion that poured over the island.

'Abandoned,' said Bex, mournfully. 'Discarded. Like we've been thrown away.'

'Me too,' said Jud. He closed his eyes – Bex's face was a distraction, she looked beautiful even in this light, with her straggly wet hair and her dripping face. 'You're right,' he said. 'It's like being on a scrap heap – a rubbish dump. Only it's bodies. And we're standing on them.'

'Do you think so?' said Bex.

He opened his eyes. 'Definitely. They're all over the island, aren't they?'

'So what now?'

Before Jud had a chance to answer, something knocked into Bex and she went down like a bowling pin.

'Woa, Jesus!' said Jud, spinning round to see what was on them.

Nothing.

'Bex? Bex?'

'I'm OK,' she said.

Quickly Jud stretched out his hand and pulled her up to him. She stumbled on the slippery mud and he grabbed her with both arms and held her tight.

For a brief moment they were both acutely aware of being so close and Jud backed away.

'You OK now?' he said.

She nodded.

'What the hell was that then?'

'Don't know,' she said. 'I was pushed over by something.'

'Was it an animal?'

'It would have to have been pretty big to floor me like that,' she said.

'Come on, let's move,' said Jud. He held on to her arm and together they ran across the boggy ground, losing their feet occasionally but determined to keep pushing on.

There was a wall up ahead. About four feet high, but it was enough for some shelter. They'd felt exposed in the middle of the dark field.

Quickly they sat down against the wall and stared keenly into the darkness.

And then they saw them.

It was like a scene from a movie, only it was real.

The field they'd been walking over had shapes appearing across it – spaced out and running.

One, two – four – six . . . there were too many, moving too quickly to get a proper count.

What were they?

'What's going on?' said Bex. 'What the hell are they doing?'

'Sh!' whispered Jud. 'Get the video camera – and the goggles.'

She fished around in her rucksack and presented the camera to Jud. She placed the infrared goggles on her eyes and Jud looked into the infrared sighting on the video camera.

'Oh my God,' said Bex.

Jud remained silent. They could hear each other's panting as they struggled to make sense of what they were seeing.

There were several ghosts, just like the ones haunting London. Dark cloaks, white masks. And they were sweeping across the open field, sometimes stooping to burrow in the ground like giant rats, before moving on again to another patch of soil.

'Are they digging?' said Bex.

'I dunno. Perhaps they're—'

'Jud!' Bex shot up and turned to face a ghostly mask peering from the other side of the wall. There was an arm clinging on to Jud. By the throat.

He grabbed the hand and pulled as hard as he could. He freed his throat and kept pulling. Bex joined him and together they wrenched the figure over the wall. It landed in the sunken mud at their feet but scrabbled to its knees and clung on tight to Jud's legs.

He jabbed at with his fists and struggled to get his legs free, punching into the body with his boots. Bex grabbed its shoulders and pulled hard.

She saw the video camera in the mud, quickly seized it and smashed it into the figure's head.

There was a cry.

A deep, throaty, man-like cry, but muffled and masked.

The figure scrambled to its feet in the slippery mud and ran off into the darkness, across the field to the others.

Jud and Bex turned and stared wide-eyed at the crowd of dark figures that now assembled and began moving in their direction.

'Run!' said Jud. 'This way.'

They grabbed their bags and vaulted the wall. Sprinting now, without stopping to look over their shoulders, they headed for the shelter and secrecy of the ominous-looking buildings in the distance.

Their feet were pounding and as they went they glanced down at the uneven ground beneath them.

'Oh God!' said Bex as she stumbled.

'What? Come on!' said Jud, grabbing her arm and pulling her up.

'Look!' she said, pointing to the ground just beside her left boot.

There was a skull, half buried in the earth. And a shoulder bone too. Their eyes darted across the ground and they saw other remains.

They were running right through another plague pit, only this one was more exposed. And their feet were now crunching as they went, bones being ground together under their weight.

'We're running over people!' said Bex.

'They're dead. We don't want to join them. Just keep running!' said Jud. He glanced quickly over his shoulder and saw the dark figures sweeping towards them. The agents were outrunning them – they'd make it, as long as they kept going. They'd find cover in the buildings. Somewhere to hide. And get their breath back.

Just a little further. *Come on.*

Soon the giant edifices of the old asylum loomed above them. They crouched low as another colony of bats fluttered frantically past them and ascended into the eaves of the building.

'Quick,' said Bex. 'Let's go in here.' She'd seen an open doorway that led into a dark chamber. 'It's gotta be better than out here.'

'Hope you're right,' said Jud as they disappeared into the black.

CHAPTER 54

THURSDAY 1.20 A.M. VENICE TIME

MARCO POLO AIRPORT, VENICE

The Ispettore from the Polizia Di Stato in Venice stared through the window of the airport arrivals lounge. The smart private jet taxied to a halt and the portable stairway was driven up to the cabin door. The lights of the airport cascaded on to the tarmac and he counted three men and two young agents leave the plane.

What is it with these British? he thought. Always meddling. Always wanting to be there, interfering. As soon as you even suggested that one of their countrymen was wanted for a crime they descended on you like a plague of locusts, to ensure you gave them a fair trial.

And now, just as his Sovrintendente had warned him, here they were. Ready to ask questions, no doubt.

But Britain was a friend to Italy, and the number of tourists that flocked to Venice from that little island in the cold North Sea meant that it wasn't worth creating a scandal. He would be charm personified – as his superiors had instructed him to be.

A few moments later, Khan, Bonati, Goode, Luc and Grace were in a police boat, speeding across the lagoon to the headquarters of the Polizia Di Stato. In different circumstances they might have marvelled at the sight of the lights in the distance, the elegant spires, the dome of the Basilica and the majesty of the giant tower in St Mark's Square. And then the romance of the Grand Canal and the famous Rialto Bridge as they pulled up along the bank. But tonight was different and they were too anxious to find Jud and Bex. This wasn't a pleasure trip.

Jason Goode had been in a nervous mood throughout the flight. They'd still not been able to raise either Jud or Bex and he was getting ever more restless. Luc and Grace had wondered if he would be so concerned if they were lost in a foreign city. It seemed sometimes to them that Jud was favoured by just about everyone, especially Mr Goode.

But tonight they shared his concern. Where the hell were they? Why weren't they answering their phones? Was the whole of Venice out of signal? A quick glance at their own phones proved that it wasn't. Bonati had already called Dr Vorzek back at the CRYPT to say that they'd made it. She had volunteered to man things in London while they were away, and besides, she didn't want to leave her fiancé alone after their experience. Despite his protestations to the contrary, she knew he was still shaken up after his ordeal.

They left the police boat and followed the Ispettore through the narrow streets to a large building close to San Marco. They spoke little on the way and tried hard to keep pace with the Ispettore who strode unhelpfully fast.

Once inside the building, they were shown down a long corridor of closed offices to the end, where the light from an open door was shining onto the black and white tiled floor.

'Good evening, gentlemen,' said a man in a uniform even more impressive than the Ispettore's, rising from his desk and welcoming them in. 'I am the Sovrintendente here. You had a good trip, *si*? Some coffee?'

They all nodded their heads and soon the office was filled with the aroma of real coffee beans.

'So,' the Sovrintendente began, 'you have been informed of the investigation. And you will know that we are looking for two suspects in particular.' He picked up a remote control set, pointed it at a television monitor and soon they were all looking once again at the footage of Jud and Bex leaving the Campo San Silvestro.

'I am grateful to you for coming,' he said. 'I thank you for your cooperation. I am sure, like me, you will want to see justice done. If your two people are innocent, then I am sure, with your help, we can clear this up very quickly.'

'Thank you,' said Bonati, smiling, or attempting a smile – his face was still painful and badly bruised after the attack in the crypt. He was as keen as this policeman to keep things cooperative and polite.

'But,' said the Sovrintendente, his tone altering, 'if they are guilty of a crime then we must bring them to justice – and quickly. And so far, I am afraid to say it is not looking good.'

'Why?' said Goode quickly.

'Because they have disappeared.'

'Gone to ground?' said Bonati.

'If that means disappeared, yes. My officers are searching the entire city, but so far they have not been found. We do not believe they have left the island as we would know about that. We have officers on alert at stations, airports and harbours. Our coastal guards are in position and checking every boat in the lagoon.'

He looked straight at Khan and chewed his lip thoughtfully. 'In the meantime, Inspector, could you please tell me once again who these people are and why they are in Venice? You are the same man who called me about the ghosts, sì?'

'Yes, I am, Superintendent. I shall explain again, of course.'

It was a pre-planned script, and it was not too much of a departure from the truth. Bonati had insisted they should keep the Venetian police as well-informed as they could, without scaring anyone or allowing talk of paranormal activity to leak too far. Fear of ghosts could spread through Venice as fast as the plague did. And no one wanted that. Khan's first call to the police to inquire about hauntings had been met with some ridicule. Better to avoid any talk of ghosts altogether – for now.

'They are special agents, working for the British Security Forces,' said Khan. 'We are engaged in a large-scale investigation into some serious crimes that have occurred recently in London. Crimes that have led us to Venice.'

'How?' said the officer.

'We have reason to believe that the perpetrators of the crimes were all concerned with one thing – jewellery. The same kind of jewellery, to be exact. We have discovered that the victims of these crimes had all purchased antique jewellery from the same shop in London. The owner is Venetian and, by his own admission, the jewellery originates here. Agents Lester and De Verre were sent to investigate for us – low key.'

The officer's expression had become less hospitable. 'Inspector, are you saying that they were here investigating a crime without our knowledge? Why did you not ask for our help? There are rules, Inspector. Very clear rules. If a police investigation takes you to a foreign city, then you must involve the police authorities in that city. You know that.'

'Rest assured, Superintendent, we were planning to do just that. Our agents only arrived late last night. I have no doubt at all that they were about to approach you. That was their brief. But then this happened.' He pointed to the freeze-frame on the monitor, which had captured Jud and Bex talking to the young students in the riverside café.

'So why have they disappeared?' said the Sovrintendente. 'I mean, it does not make sense, don't you think? If they are law enforcers, like us, then surely they should have come straight to us and explained that they are not responsible for these crimes. Don't you agree they should have done this?'

Khan wanted to admit that it did indeed seem strange – and bloody frustrating – that Jud and Bex had disappeared but he didn't want to make matters worse for them than they already were.

Before Khan had a chance to reply, Jason Goode spoke up. 'Superintendent, what I think – what we think, and the reason we are here – is that our agents have not got in touch with you yet precisely because they too are in danger. They have not contacted us either. That is the reason for our concern. And the reason why we have come to you. However you look at this, one thing is sure, they need to be found, and quickly.'

'Well, we can agree on that one, Signore Goode. So where do you think they may be? They are not in their hotel, this we know.'

Bonati and Goode exchanged glances. They *had* to tell the officer. There was simply no point in hiding it any longer.

'There is one place we believe they might be,' said Bonati, cautiously. 'You will not like it, Superintendent, because I understand it is not permitted to go there, but we have reason to believe they may have gone to the island of Poveglia.'

The officer was unable to hide his surprise.

'Poveglia?' he said, incredulously. 'What are they doing there? There is nothing on Poveglia. Do you not know that? Do they think they will find the answers to their investigation on a dead island? An island with nothing but corpses? Why would your "special agents", as you call them, travel to a stinking place like Poveglia for clues?'

Bonati sensed there was no point in unravelling the whole connection to the plague pits at this time. That would entail trying to convince this officer that the ghosts in London were real – the disembodied spirits of Venetian plague doctors – and something told them that he would take some convincing.

'We believe they are there in hiding, Superintendent.'

'Hiding? From us? They have something to hide, *sì*?'

'Hiding from the killers!' Goode snapped.

'Easy,' said Bonati softly to Goode. God knows, the last thing they needed now was another outburst from a member of the Goode family. Like father like son he thought to himself.

'In the circumstances, Superintendent,' Bonati said calmly, 'may I suggest we begin with Poveglia. We would be very keen to help you, of course.'

The officer nodded, though not without reluctance judging by the expression on his face.

'Sì, sì. I am as keen to find these people as you are, gentlemen. And if you believe they may be there, for whatever reason, then we must begin our search.'

Bonati gave a look of relief in Goode's direction.

'In the morning,' the officer added.

'Why the wait?' said Khan.

'There is no point in searching that place until the sun rises. You would need all the – how you say – *torches* in Venice to light up that place. There is nothing there, no street lights, no lamps, nothing. It would be like trying to find a bird in a forest. Or a fish in the sea. We wait until the morning.'

'I'm sorry, Superintendent,' said Bonati, authoritatively. 'We feel it would be beneficial for everyone concerned if we find these agents as soon as possible. We believe they are in danger. If we cannot have your support then we shall proceed alone.'

The officer smiled. 'You do not understand, you English? This is our country. These are our rules. Visits to the island of Poveglia are prohibited. You are now telling me that you are going to break the law? You will be arrested.'

Khan waved an arm in Bonati's direction. 'It can wait, Professor. It can wait until the morning. If we can have the super-intendent's full cooperation in the morning then we wait until then. He is right anyway. It will be black as pitch out there tonight. You'll never find them – and that's even if they are on there, which we don't know.'

Jason Goode stood up from his chair and approached the

officer's large, mahogany desk. 'I'm sorry, officer. This is *not* good enough. I demand to be taken—'

'Jason,' said Bonati, getting to his feet. 'Leave it. The inspector is right. We need to work together. And we cannot break the law as soon as we've arrived. We shall be no good to Jud or Bex if we are arrested before we even try to help. The superintendent has already kindly offered to take us to Poveglia in the morning. And that is only a few hours away.'

Goode lowered his head in submission. He knew very well that they were right. But he was already regretting coming to the police in the first place. He could have hired a boat at the drop of a hat. He knew people everywhere – or he had the money to buy people. They could have found the island under the cover of darkness. But he knew that posed dangers, and they just couldn't risk getting arrested.

'I just hope our agents are safe,' he said.

Luc and Grace, seated behind Goode, knew exactly what he meant. They, too, had been researching the 'island of no return' and they could only imagine what Jud and Bex might be going through.

'Very well,' said the Sovrintendente. 'I shall see you at the docks in . . .' he glanced at his wristwatch – an impressive silver band and a lavishly decorated face, 'shall we say five hours?'

Reluctantly his visitors agreed, said goodnight and left the room via the open door, still wedged wide open as it had been when they entered, the lights of the office illuminating their path down the black and white tiles.

As they left the room, not one of them noticed the small, brass name plate on the open door. It read, SOVRINTENDENTE LORENZO CALDERARIO

CHAPTER 55

THURSDAY 2.19 A.M. VENICE TIME

POVEGLIA ISLAND

Their clothes were still sodden, their muscles were tight from the constant shivering that had come over them since entering the freezing waters of the lagoon, and the chilling atmosphere of the asylum was dragging their spirits to the depths of despair. If Jud and Bex were looking for a new challenge, they'd certainly found one. The island of Poveglia was living up to expectations.

They had been inside the tiny room, hidden deep within the empty asylum, for more than two hours now. Two long, lonely hours of waiting for the ghosts to appear around the doorway, without being able to move for fear of attracting attention. The chase from the plague pits outside had been fast and furious but at least it had raised their adrenalin and sent their hearts pumping. Now, sitting here, in the dark shadows of the forgotten room, their inactive bodies had stiffened in the cold.

They'd managed to remove some equipment from their bags, and, as silently as possible, set up the instruments to take some readings.

It had been incredible. Rarely had either of them seen such high measurements of electromagnetic radiation or such sudden drops in temperature. Though the motion detectors had picked up nothing yet, it was clearly an active site, no question. But so cold. So *damn cold*.

It was a wretched place – a forgotten, abandoned place with a palpable feeling of death and decay.

Jud watched the cloudy swirls of breath leave his mouth and mix with the chilled air, slowly dispersing into the gloom. How many more breaths did he have in him? How many did Bex have? Or any of us? he thought. Do we ever know which one is our last?

Does fate hand us an allotted number of breaths – an allowance which you cannot change? Could you ever find out that number? Would you want to?

Oh shut up, he told himself. The macabre, morbid atmosphere was getting to him – a sharp reminder of his own mortality.

He turned to Bex and watched the warm air leave her still lips. Her eyes were closed. Was she sleeping? He didn't want to stir her and see.

A small shaft of moonlight clawed its way through a window opening and lit up part of her face. She looked tired and cold. There were tiny mud splatters on her cheek. Jud could see dark shadows beneath her eyes and her lips were chapped from the freezing salty water and the whipping winds that swirled around the fields outside.

Was he actually breaking the very rule he'd placed on himself during those bitter, lonely months in prison? The rule that he'd never, ever expose his heart again. He would *never* become emotionally attached to anyone. Never. Self-preservation was all that mattered – be strong, fence in your feelings and that way they'll stay intact.

Affection had crept up stealthily on him, it seemed. They'd become such a strong partnership without him even noticing.

There was a gust of wind outside that whistled through the window opening and drew Jud away from these arrogant thoughts. How dare he believe she'd planned to be with him all along! Was he really *that* special?

He glanced away from Bex, up at the window in the opposite corner of the room. It was still night-time. The shaft of silver moonlight on Bex's face had disappeared behind heavy storm clouds and the room was in near darkness.

It had been a lucky escape, no question. Bex's idea to leap through the first open door they'd seen and hide in the shadows had been the right one. They'd stowed away, in the corner of the dark room, and had remained there ever since, neither of them wanting to tempt fate by exploring other parts of the asylum just yet and risk being seen by something or someone. There was no question at all that this place was filled with all kinds of paranormal activity. They could both feel it. Sense it. Hear it. The feelings of abandonment, the distant ringing of the bells and the chilling screams coming from the floors above them – the long, hollow wards once home to the mental patients on whom the staff conducted their evil experiments – all combined to create an atmosphere more potent than anything they could experience in the SPA rooms back at the CRYPT.

But what – or who – had attacked them in the field? And who were the figures they had seen in the dark?

The cry from his attacker in the mask had seemed human. So they weren't alone on the island. The threats they faced on this wretched place weren't only from ghosts, it seemed.

There was a noise from outside.

Jud looked up at the cracked window again and held his breath.

Footsteps?

He listened intently. It *was*. It was the sound of someone walking. Soon the footsteps stopped.

'Bex,' he whispered. 'Bex! Listen.'

She stirred beside him – he felt her leg press against his and watched her arching her back and stretching her arms upwards.

'Sorry,' she said sleepily, 'I must have drifted off. Was I asleep for long?'

'There's someone outside,' he whispered.

She was startled and woke up instantly.

'*Listen.*'

Silence. And then footsteps shuffling again.

'Do you think it's the one who attacked us in the field? The ghost?' she said.

'I don't believe it *was* a ghost, Bex,' said Jud. 'I don't think any of those figures out there were ghosts, you know.'

Before Bex could argue with him, his suspicions were confirmed. They heard a voice.

It was faint and muffled and deep, but it was definitely human. The sound of a man talking to someone – perhaps on the phone? There was only one voice audible.

Quickly but silently they rose to their feet and approached the cracked window in the corner. It was impossible to see anything on the ground as the window was too high, but they could hear the man's words more easily from here.

'Lorenzo? Sì. It's Marco. OK.'

'*Lorenzo?*' whispered Bex. 'Not Lorenzo Calderario, surely?'

'It's a long shot,' said Jud. 'There's probably lots of Lorenzos in Italy.'

'Listen,' said Bex.

'*Sì*' the voice continued in Italian and Bex tried hard to translate.

'They're here,' the man was saying. 'On the island. I've seen them. What? No, don't worry. We'll take care of them. They can't have escaped. We'll find them.'

Jud and Bex stared at each other through the gloom, trying to make sense of what she was translating.

'Who is this guy?' said Bex.

'Dunno,' said Jud. 'And who's he talking to anyway? It can't be Calderario, it just can't – can it?'

'I get a feeling we're going to find out soon,' whispered Bex. 'But what's he doing here in the first place? Do you think he's the same guy we saw in the field? The one who attacked us? What makes you think that was a human anyway?'

'Just a feeling, and that noise it made. This could well be the same man. But I don't really know any more than you do. We've gotta follow him, Bex. See exactly what he and his men are doing here. Listen. What's he saying now?'

The man continued and Bex whispered in English as best she could. 'You don't need to come. No! We can handle it . . . What? OK, OK . . . If you don't trust us . . . Bring your own men, Lorenzo. You're the Sovrintendente so I can't stop you. So come! Come and . . . get them yourself. But . . . they'll be dead by the time you get here. You'll see.'

She stared at Jud incredulously. They remained still and silent as they listened to the sound of footsteps once more. After a few moments the footsteps faded and all they could hear was the lapping of the waves and the whistling of the wind.

'It's Lorenzo Calderario,' said Bex. 'That's who he was talking to. It *has* to be. And he's a *sovrintendente*!'

'A what?' said Jud.

'Superintendent!' said Bex, excitedly. 'Police chief!'

Things were beginning to fit into place.

'Although we still don't know why he's so keen on protecting this place,' said Bex.

'Maybe he's not protecting it at all, he's just after us,' said Jud. 'You heard the guy. The police are trying to frame us with the killings in Venice. We know that already. That's why he's looking for us.'

'Yeah, I know that,' snapped Bex. 'But think about it. Why does he want us out of the way so much? What's he trying to hide? And how does Lorenzo know this man on the island anyway? This Marco guy. Who is he? What's the connection? Are they working together?'

'They must be. But doing what?' said Jud.

'Exactly. Who knows.'

They stood up. Their legs were stiff and cold and their jeans had still not dried properly. If either of them had been alone they would have removed them and shook them vigorously, but they were both too embarrassed. There was no way they'd risk the indignity of standing there in their sodden pants, even if it was dark. Better to let the warmth of their skin dry the clothes gradually from within – although it felt more like the reverse was happening and their clothes were slowly making their bodies colder and wetter. They'd never experienced cold like it. The spare coats they'd brought in their rucksacks had been a godsend, but by now they, too, were damp from hours spent holding them close to their wet bodies.

'We need to get moving,' said Jud. 'Get the blood pumping. Let's go back outside and see if we can watch these people. I want to see what they're doing. If entry to this place is illegal, they must have a serious reason to risk being here. I wanna know what that is.'

'OK, let's go,' said Bex, grabbing her rucksack as Jud heaved his own on to his shoulders. 'But just remember it's not a fact-finding mission any more – we're being hunted. It's about survival.'

'Whatever.'

He followed her silently out of the dark room and into the night. The clouds had parted again momentarily and there was a brief respite from the gloom as the burnished moon lit up the jetty and the giant buildings behind them.

The asylum complex was vast – great, square buildings, large expanses of concrete and tarmac and metal railings everywhere, presumably put there to prevent the sick patients from staggering out of the buildings and straight into the lagoon. What must this place have been like? Bex wondered to herself. More like a prison than a hospital.

But then maybe that was just the point. Perhaps the people of Venice a hundred years ago wanted clear of the sick, mental patients as much as they did the plague victims centuries before.

Bex knew from her history lessons at school that, even in London, Victorian methods of treating 'madness' were questionable at best. Asylums often held chilling stories of cruelty and neglect. It was a brutal time for some people. She knew that. Venice was no different, she supposed.

A fragile-looking wooden jetty stretched out into the makeshift harbour at this end of the island. It was the place where the patients would have been brought to the asylum and, perhaps, the place where the plague doctors, generations before them, would have brought the dying victims from the main islands. It was anything but welcoming – so different to the neon lights and hotel façades of the famous Lido harbour just a short sail further down the lagoon.

This was a woefully sad place, a desolate, isolated part of Venice that was no longer spoken of. If it could have been removed from the landscape altogether it would have been, long ago. Instead it was left to rot, sealed off and kept out of bounds. But there was anger here. Jud and Bex were not wanted – there was no question of that. The great bell tower was ringing again, a foreboding knell bidding them leave.

Jud was impervious to its call. He'd no intention of leaving this island yet. There were still so many more answers to find. And besides, anything was better than getting arrested and flung in a Venetian jail while a case was prepared against them both. He had more to lose than most.

There was a noise behind them, from the direction of the asylum buildings.

'Hear that?' whispered Bex.

'Yeah. Get down.'

They crouched low to the cold, solid ground. The waves lapped against the wooden jetty to their right and the wind was howling through the empty windows of the giant edifice to their left. They stared through the darkness towards the building, trying to trace where the noise had come from.

It had been a cry. A human cry, or at least it had sounded like one.

The figure they'd heard outside had moved on – they'd heard his footsteps fade, so they felt sure it couldn't have been him. Besides, the noise they'd heard had sounded shrill, like a young child or a woman's shriek.

There it was again. This time it lasted longer, like a wail.

'I don't like the sound of this,' said Bex. 'Someone's in pain.'

'It's the asylum,' said Jud. 'It's the ghosts of the patients. It's gotta be. The levels of energy in that place were off the scale.'

They slowly rose and began walking again. Then stopped abruptly.

And stared.

The faint image of a figure was appearing from one of the doors on the ground floor, just a few feet from where they were standing.

It was a wretched sight, a dirty, shivering woman, dressed in nothing but a long, tattered nightgown of thin cloth. Her hair was dark and matted together in unkempt clumps, straggly and wild.

But it was her face that struck them as they watched, wide-eyed. It was so thin and pale. From this distance you could see the bones through the wafer-thin skin that seemed stretched across her face. Her eyes seemed out of proportion to the rest of her body – too large, as if the cheekbones beneath them were struggling under their weight.

And her mouth was open, from which there came a pitiful cry. No words, at least not that they could recognise, just a wail that combined with the whistling wind which rattled around the broken windowpanes and doors of the building that had once housed this girl like a prisoner.

She was escaping. A mental patient from another era. Unacceptable to the people of Venice, brought here and thrown away.

Just like in life, she'd dreamed of fleeing the island – swimming away. If the rocks and the tides and the cold took her, then it would be a mercy.

Jud and Bex watched in silence as the ghost drifted away from the building, pausing occasionally to glance over her shoulder, furtively.

'She's looking for the guards – for the nurses and doctors,' said Bex. 'She's running away, isn't she?'

'Yes,' said Jud. 'It's desperately sad.'

They watched her frail body sweep across the ground and on towards the side of the wharf. Her wails were fading now, as the wind took up and blew her bedraggled locks around and whipped up her baggy nightgown. They saw glimpses of her bony, almost skeletal body beneath.

Her head was shaking now, moving in all directions. If this was how she'd been in life, no wonder she'd been brought here – or perhaps it was this place that had caused the madness.

And then she was gone.

Dropped like a stone into the icy waters.

Plunged into oblivion. Another soul lost.

'Why did she return for that?' said Jud. 'I mean, why bother?'

Bex stared pensively at the spot where the ghost had been standing just seconds earlier. 'Perhaps it was the escape she'd never managed to achieve in life. Perhaps she died in the hospital and never had the chance to swim away. Imagine, she'd probably gazed out of those windows for years, dreaming of escaping.'

'So she returned to fulfil her dream, you mean?'

'Yeah. The cries weren't of pain but of freedom, maybe.'

'Sad all the same,' said Jud.

'This whole place is sad,' said Bex.

They returned to the muddy path that led them out to the open fields beyond the asylum. It was almost impossible in the dark to see exactly where they had been before, but they both guessed that most of the island was filled with shallow graves, so it wouldn't be long before they heard the familiar crunching of bones beneath their boots again.

Bex stopped. 'What was that?'

'Not another noise. Where?'

'That sound. I'm sure it was an engine. Listen.'

They stood there, the wind lapping around their pale faces, their eyes darting through the trees and over the wild entanglement of shrubs to the water beyond.

'You're right,' said Jud. 'It *is* an engine. And by the sounds of it, it's moving fast. Look!'

There was a flashing light, far in the distance, across the lagoon. Police? Was this the same boat that they saw towing Signor Ali away?

'It'll be Lorenzo. He wants us off this place,' said Bex.

'Yeah, but why?'

'I dunno, but I think we're about to find out,' said Bex.

They stared across the lagoon, trying to make sense of what was unfolding around them. What was going on here? There was no question that this place was significant, and their instruments had told them the paranormal activity here was intense. So why would humans come to the island at all? They reckoned the figure in the nightgown was unlikely to have been the first ghost to have appeared on Poveglia. There had probably been hundreds – thousands – of sightings over the years.

'So what's this Marco and his team doing here?' said Bex. 'Are they hiding something?'

'It would certainly be a safe place to stow something away, I suppose,' said Jud. 'It's against the law to travel here, after all.'

'Yeah, and who *is* the law around here?'

Jud nodded. 'Exactly. Lorenzo Calderario – if we're right.'

'I tell you, Jud, the Calderarios have found something on this island and Lorenzo protects it by forbidding anyone from travelling here.'

'So what have they found?'

'That's what we've got to discover,' said Bex. 'Before they find us.'

They heard the sound of the engine rising. They crouched lower, behind the shrubs that stood between them and the shoreline in the distance, and waited for the searchlights of the boat to come back into view again from behind the dark silhouette of the asylum buildings up ahead.

And sure enough, they saw it again, lit up like a Christmas tree. Not only did the boat display the usual navigation lights, there was a giant searchlight on deck too, which someone must have been operating as it now swept across the lagoon like a lighthouse and soon pointed in their direction.

Instinctively Jud and Bex ducked, even though the boat was still some distance away and there was no way their faces could be seen from there, especially through the trees. But they felt exposed all the same. Like rabbits caught in headlights. Caught. Snared.

The searchlight on the boat swept away again to a different part of the island and they looked at one another.

'Well?' said Bex. 'What now? Hide in the asylum again?'

Jud shook his head. 'Too obvious. It'll be the first place they look. And we've got to find what it is they don't want us to see. I don't believe it's in the asylum. I want to see more of the island.'

'Maybe we're better off in the open fields anyway,' said Bex. 'As long as we can get down, into the ground.'

'Oh, sure,' said Jud. 'Let's join the bodies, shall we?'

CHAPTER 56

THURSDAY 2.45 A.M. VENICE TIME

POVEGLIA ISLAND

They trudged their way through the boggy ground, sometimes slipping into unexpected holes and recesses, other times stumbling over great stones that rose from the mire like macabre monuments. It was a cursed ground. But it was a place that might, just might, provide them with the cover they needed to secrete themselves away from the police officers and their searchlights. At least the foul stench of decay would mask their own human scent from the police sniffer dogs, they hoped. And they knew they'd be coming soon, their barks would soon be stabbing the silence of the forgotten island and disturbing what little wildlife had chosen to roost there.

Jud gazed across the field. He could see shapes again. There was a dark figure, quite close, stooping low as the others had done before.

Was it another of the men, the ones this Marco guy was talking about? Or was it a ghost?

And what *was* it doing? It looked almost as if it was searching for something on the ground.

'Do you see it?' Jud whispered to Bex by his side.

'Yeah, of course. What's it doing?'

'I wish I knew. We've got to get closer.'

'But Jud, the police. They'll be here soon.'

'We've got time. I can't hear them yet. We'll know when they're here. I've got to know what it's doing. Come on.'

They edged closer to the dark shape, now slumped on the ground. Or was it kneeling? They could see movement from what must be its arms. As they approached they could see the figure had its back to them and was hunched over, scrabbling around in the mud.

Jud stood still and tugged Bex's arm. 'Tell it to turn and face us. Say we don't fear it.'

They edged a little closer to the bent figure and Bex stepped in front of Jud, defiantly.

'*Gira!*' she commanded. '*Verso di noi. Non teme!*'

Nothing.

And then slowly the figure turned.

The face was hidden by a dark hood, pulled close over the head. But she could see no white mask.

And what was that? Skin?

'*Parla!*' said Bex, standing firmly and refusing to show any fear.

The figure suddenly launched itself at Bex, pushing her to the ground. She landed on a stone in the small of her back and the pain ran right through her. In anger she fought back, fists and legs flailing at the shape in front of her. Jud quickly piled in and then he stopped.

And they saw it.

The figure's hood fell back in the struggle, revealing the face of a man.

A human. It was no ghost. But he made straight for Jud. Within seconds he had him in a headlock. Jud was choking.

Bex lost no time. She picked up a rock from the stony earth and slammed it into the man's head.

The attacker released Jud and slumped to the ground, where

he lay motionless in the boggy earth, his face now splattered with mud and his mouth open. A thin line of red was trickling from his bruised forehead.

'Oh God!' she yelled. 'I've killed him! I've killed him!'

Jud stood up and grabbed her. 'Stop it! You did the right thing. You had no choice, Bex.' He kept holding her and trying to catch her eyes as she shook her head violently and put her hands to her face.

'Look at me. Look at me, Bex! You did the right thing. He was going for us. I could hardly breathe!'

He quickly knelt over the body and felt for a pulse at his neck.

'He's alive anyway. You've knocked him unconscious but he's alive. He'll have a headache, but he'll come to. Wait a minute, what's that?'

'What?' said Bex, bending down to see what he was looking at.

'Look!' said Jud, pointing to where the man had been digging.

There was a discarded trowel on the ground and a small, brown bag. Jud quickly picked it up and fished his hand inside.

There was something in it – several things. He pulled them out.

Though they were dirty and encrusted with mud, Jud could see exactly what they were. He held them up to Bex, smiling.

'Rings?' she said incredulously.

Jud nodded. 'Get your flashlight out, quickly!'

Bex produced the torch from the rucksack and shone it at the ground beneath their feet.

'Oh, shit!' she said.

There were skeletons – two skulls and a mass of bones. As she swept the torch along the filthy ground, they saw another body and another, more complete this time. They ran towards it and shone the torch closer.

They could both see it. There, on the left hand of the skeleton, half buried in the soil but with enough fingers protruding to see what it was.

A ring.

Their minds were racing now as the magnitude of the find revealed itself to them.

'My God, Bex. It's jewellery. It must have remained on the plague victims. They must've been brought here so hastily, all those years ago, and buried so quickly they didn't even remove the jewellery.'

'They wouldn't have wanted to,' said Bex. 'No one wanted to touch them. They wanted rid of them, didn't they? Rings and all, I suppose.'

'So this man is . . .'

Jud was nodding. 'A grave robber. Exactly. He finds the jewellery among the human remains, and . . .'

'Ships it off to London?'

'Exactly.'

'Where Calder – or Calderario – sells it for some stupid price to unsuspecting buyers.'

'That's right,' said Jud. 'And seals their fate. These rings carry the curse of Poveglia.'

'And the ghosts,' said Bex. 'The plague doctors appear because the plague is spreading. And they're doing just what they were ordered to do in life – find the source of the plague and *get rid of it*.'

'Yes,' said Jud. 'And that might mean getting rid of the rings or doing away with the victims altogether.'

'It's a theory, Jud. So this Marco guy really is working for Lorenzo – the brother. But how do they get away with it? I mean, how do they keep it from the authorities?'

'Sovrintendente, remember? It's him. It's the brother.'

'My God. What a racket,' said Bex. 'If it's true, they've got it sewn up between them. And it explains why the police are trying to frame us with the murders in Venice. It's because they didn't want us getting near the island to investigate. They had to make something up, some reason why they could lock us up.'

'Exactly,' said Jud. 'And stop us from ever coming here and exposing their little operation.'

'We've got to stop this, Jud. We've got to let these people rest in peace – with their jewellery. This place has to be sealed up and left alone.' She looked around her and Jud caught a glimpse of the whites of her eyes darting across the landscape, catching the moon. 'It's cursed, Jud.'

CHAPTER 57

THURSDAY 3.02 A.M. VENICE TIME

POVEGLIA ISLAND

There was no way Lorenzo Calderario was going to pass up an opportunity to get to Poveglia first and find the fugitives, while those British investigators slept in their beds. That was why he'd been so reluctant to bring them here tonight. He *had* to get here first. The delegation from London had confirmed his suspicions that the two agents might have gone to the island. And the call from Marco proved it. His plan to trap them in Venice had backfired. It wasn't as though his contacts hadn't done their jobs properly – they had. The killer had done exactly what he'd been asked to do: follow the two agents, take photos, take out the people they speak to – two or three would be enough, they agreed – then link the two foreigners with the killings. That way Calderario and his officers could – legally – conduct a manhunt and lock up the agents before they found their way to Poveglia and disrupted the operation there. An operation that had proved so successful until now.

It was only a matter of time. But the team from London had confirmed his worst fears – they'd made the link to Poveglia sooner than he'd expected. And they'd found a way of getting there too. He knew exactly who was to blame for that.

He'd suspected that the old fisherman, Aliprando, had not been straight with him when he'd accosted him out in the lagoon. He'd known something was up but if Aliprando was not going to spill the beans, there was little he could do. The old boy could sit in the cell in the station overnight. Sovrintendente Calderario would deal with him in the morning. And deal with him severely.

Aliprando was well known to the police, and he could hardly be relied upon to tell the truth. He never did. How many times had they taken him in for smuggling? And drug-related charges too. Aliprando was one of the main sources of work for his young officers. Like a training ground for new recruits.

What was it he'd said this time? Some late-night fishing? A likely story. He was too lazy to do anything so strenuous these days. Aliprando had promised he would return to Venice after his 'fishing trip'. But when they'd found him later returning from the other side of Poveglia, Calderario knew it was time to take him in. They'd towed his boat back and locked him up. But the stubborn old man had refused to talk.

The sovrintendente stood on deck while one of his juniors steered the boat. He moved to the bow, where he could gain some privacy from the army of officers he'd brought with him. He was feeling anxious after Marco's call.

What if they were unable to catch the two fugitives from England?

And, in any case, what if his officers found Marco and his team before he did? The police, like the residents of Venice, believed the legend that the island was haunted and should be avoided at all costs. That's why so many of them were tucked away in the boat, staring out at the island with fear in their eyes. He'd had to insist that they accompanied him.

But bringing them risked spoiling the whole damn operation. There was nothing else for it. He was going to have to call Marco again and tell him to abandon everything and get the hell off the island – for now at least. Once this business with the foreign agents had died down, then they could return.

'Come on, come on!' he shouted into his walkie-talkie. 'Marco. Speak to me, Marco!'

Nothing.

The sovrintendente glanced at the officer at the helm. How long would it be before the boat would be pulling into the island? How long did Marco and his men have? If his officers found Marco and his team, he'd have to deny all knowledge of them and take them into custody.

At least Marco was expendable. It wasn't as though he was family. At least, not close family like his brother. Marco was a distant cousin, along with Alberto, the shady face beneath the baseball cap. The killer. He'd soon be wanting his payment. Lorenzo knew it was only a matter of time before Alberto would come wanting his cut. And this time it would be substantial. Three killings in one day? He'd drive a hard bargain.

And now Niccolo wasn't answering his calls in London either. Where the hell was he? Had he been taken? The Englishmen had not mentioned anything about his brother.

Calderario felt alone suddenly. Were his team slowly deserting him? *Where the hell was Marco?*

At last, there was a crackly voice on the end of the line.

'Sì. Marco here. What do you want?'

'Have you found them?'

'No! Of course not, Lorenzo. You only spoke to me a few moments ago! Give me more time.'

'Change of plan,' said Lorenzo, anxiously. 'If you cannot find the fugitives, forget them! Get off the island. Do you hear me? *Get off the island!*'

'You told me to find the two—'

'Never mind what I told you! Get yourselves to the southern end of the island. We're coming to search the place. So for God's sake get out of the way. If my men see you they'll shoot. They don't know about you so they won't wait and ask questions. Understand? Tell the others. Get yourselves down to the southern end. Then get in the boats and disappear. We'll start at the northern end and give you time to get off – if you're quick. Now get going!'

'But the men are spread out,' said Marco. 'They're not all here. They're—'

'Well, find them then!' bellowed Lorenzo. 'Get yourself down to the boats now! Or I won't be responsible for what happens to you. I've warned you. If my officers see you first then God help you. You've got twenty minutes. Now *go!*'

He ended the call, slipped the walkie-talkie back into his pocket and headed for the little hatch that led through to the cabin below deck. His army of gunloaded officers were waiting and staring out at the ugly island that loomed closer on the horizon.

'Listen, men,' said the sovrintendente, squeezing into the cramped space. 'We're nearly at Poveglia. When we get there we'll search the main buildings around the northern jetty. Then, if we don't find what we're looking for, we'll move on – do a sweep of the island beginning with the fields around the asylum. Take your time. Start from the northern side. Don't rush. We want to find these fugitives. I'm not returning to Venice without them.'

They glanced solemnly at the chief and nodded their heads in obedience. Not one of them had been happy to take the mission – not that they'd had a choice. The rude awakening by the sovrintendente in the middle of the night; the phone call to say they were needed for an exciting mission and must report to the station immediately; then the disappointment and nervousness when they discovered on arrival that the setting for this secret mission was Poveglia, island of no return.

And now, as their boat approached the jetty, and the ominous landmarks of the bell tower and the giant, derelict buildings of the asylum loomed overhead, they felt something deep down in the pit of their stomachs. Something felt very rarely among their ranks.

Fear.

CHAPTER 58

THURSDAY 3.09 A.M. VENICE TIME

POVEGLIA ISLAND

Bex stopped running. 'D'you hear that?'

Jud shook his head.

'Listen!' she said.

There was the sound of shouting in the distance and the barking of dogs. With all the distraction of the grave robber and the discovery of the rings, they'd lost focus. They'd forgotten the police were coming. And now they were closing in.

'Turn the bloody torch off!' said Jud.

Quickly Bex fumbled for the switch and the light went off. They crouched down low and looked around them. Soon they could see the lights of the police officers' own torches in the far distance, on the fringes of the neighbouring field.

'Dig!' said Jud. 'Come on, help me.'

'Dig?' said Bex. '*Run* you mean! Surely it's better to make a break for it.'

'They've got dogs, Bex! We'll never outrun them. We've no choice. We have to go *down*. Get among the remains. This guy's already dug a hole. We just need to keep digging. We can hide down here. They can't cover every field. They'll only come in if they see something on the ground. So lie down and dig!'

They lay in the soil and dug. Bex used the trowel and Jud used his fingernails, pulling away great clumps of damp earth, like a wild animal. His hands found thin, brittle bones and the curvature of the top of a skull. The stench was almost unbearable.

Bex's metal trowel struck something hard. It was another skull. And then the remnants of a ribcage.

'Oh Christ, I can't do this!' she said.

'You can. You *have* to,' said Jud. 'We're almost out of sight.'

He was right. They looked up and realised that they were inches away from being below the surface of the ground. A few moments later they stopped and lay still, among the bones and the skulls and the countless maggots and worms that inhabited this rich soil.

'Cover yourself in mud,' said Bex.

'I am!' said Jud.

'No, do some more,' she said. 'It'll take away any smell of you. And you won't catch the torchlight either.'

She was right. They both plastered as much mud over their faces as they could. They were soon not only invisible from the edge of the field, but up close they were blending with the soil – camouflaged, the outlines of their bodies merging with the dead corpses around them.

They lay there motionless, buried alive among the wretched plague victims, trying hard not to breathe too heavily and send clouds of warm air spiralling from the ground. Any trace and the police would be on them in an instant.

They could hear the sound of voices coming closer, and the barking of dogs, and the sound of heavy boots squelching over sludge.

Jud moved his hand slowly through the mud towards Bex. He found her hand and gripped it tightly as they each held their breath.

CHAPTER 59

THURSDAY 3.41 A.M.

POVEGLIA ISLAND, VENICE

'Where's Adrione?' said Marco.

The men just shrugged their shoulders and glanced back at him with exhausted expressions on their faces. It had been a strange and frustrating night. Just when they'd stumbled across a particularly bounteous pit, the order had come in from Marco to get going to the boats at the southern end and leave the place. Their shift was aborted.

'Maybe he didn't get the signal,' said someone.

'I beeped all of you and you got the message. It doesn't make sense.'

'Maybe his radio's died.'

'Well, we've gotto go. We can't wait for him,' said Marco, impatiently.

'You're saying we leave him here?' said another man, angrily.

Marco walked up and stared at him. Marco was tall and muscular and built of granite – compared to this little slug. He wasn't about to have any trouble from his men. And least of all from this one. 'Yes. That's exactly what I'm saying. Got a problem?'

The man shrugged and sloped off towards the boat that was hidden beneath some low-lying branches at the water's edge.

'Come on then,' said Marco. 'Get in the boat. We don't have long.'

Half a mile inland, through the mist and the darkness, Sovrintendente Lorenzo Calderario and his men were sweeping the fields with their searchlights and their dogs. The chief would not accept failure. There was too much to lose. Some of his men thought he'd become obsessed with this forsaken place in recent months. He was always talking about how they should protect it 'for the safety of the people'. No one was allowed to set foot on the island, *no one*, not even the farmers or fishermen. The place was strictly out of bounds. And the sovrintendente had increased the number of boat patrols recently too – he accompanied them whenever he could. People at the station were saying he spent more time out on the water than he did on land these days.

And here they were again, only this time he'd dragged his men on to the island itself – unwillingly in most cases. He'd talked so much about the violent injuries people had sustained in the past at the hands of the 'Poveglia ghosts' that many of his officers believed him. The rumours had swept around Venice too – Poveglia was a place to avoid at all costs, not just because of the exorbitant fines you'd face if the chief's men caught you, but because of the dangers on the island itself. People being thrown from buildings, hanged from trees, buried alive in giant pits – or just driven mad from the constant screaming that never left your ears long after you left the island. The stories abounded. Even the most hardened cynics, the ones who didn't believe in ghosts at all, avoided this place.

But now, armed with guns and giant torches, here they were, trudging through the mud on yet another of the sovrintendente's wild goose chases to rid the place of trespassers.

'Are you *sure* there's people here, sir?' someone said, clearly unimpressed with this night-time raid. Just a few hours ago he'd been safely tucked up in bed. Now he was searching a damp, malodorous bog with the barking of dogs ringing in his ears.

'Yes! Keep searching!' Calderario shouted. 'We *will* find them. And bring them to justice. Come on, move!'

They continued their search of the long stretches of open fields that ran across the island. They'd already conducted a search of the abandoned asylum. Traipsing around those empty corridors and wards had been chilling, to say the least. Some of the men had not wanted to enter the place, though they'd been given no choice. Some had heard screams, others had talked of the ghostly bells, while the dogs had rushed in blissfully ignorant – and bloodthirsty.

But still no trace of the fugitives.

And similarly out here, in the bleak landscape of bogs and pits, the wind ripping into their faces and turning their knuckles numb as they clutched their guns and flashlights for dear life, there was still no sign of anyone.

Were they wasting their time? Was the chief slowly going mad?

'How much longer should we search, sir?' said an officer, tentatively.

'Until we've covered the entire bloody island,' Calderario shouted. 'Now move! Follow the dogs. They must be on to a scent.'

They marched on through the grime and the sludge. Their dogs seemed braver than they were, happy to run off into the blinding gloom and bury their noses into the foul pits and troughs in the boggy fields around them.

There was a sudden barking off to the left. One of the dogs had found something. The men ran towards the sound, their torches lighting up the patch of field ahead of them.

'What's up, boy?' shouted one of the officers. 'What've you found?'

CHAPTER 60

THURSDAY 3.59 A.M.

POVEGLIA ISLAND, VENICE

The awkward angle of Jud's body, as he lay in the soil, was causing cramp to surge through his thigh and down into his leg. And the cold of the earth wasn't helping either. But thank goodness the sound of boots had passed now. The men searching the place must have moved on. A little longer and they'd be able to get up.

'You OK?' he whispered to Bex as he squeezed her hand.

'Yeah,' she said, though her voice was weaker now. Jud could feel her body was shivering, sending vibrations through the earth. 'How is this going to end?' she whispered.

'The men will go, they'll leave the island and we'll be alone again.'

'Yeah, alone with the ghosts.'

'But we'll be safe, Bex. We'll get through this.'

'And when they've gone? What then? How're we going to get off this place?'

'There'll be a boat somewhere. You'll see. We'll find one. And we'll get back to Venice and contact Bonati and the others. They won't believe what we've found. Bloody grave robbers! We've cracked it, Bex. We just need to wait until—'

He stopped.

What was that?

There was the sound of footsteps again. Even closer this time. And it didn't sound like one person either. There were too many boots.

'Oh God,' whispered Bex, squeezing Jud's hand until it ached. 'They're back.'

They held their breath and stayed as still as they could, waiting for the light of a torch to sweep over their faces, or for the snout of a dog to come sniffing.

Sure enough their eyes, through their death masks of mud, could see the orange glow of a torch – and another.

This was it. They braced themselves.

They heard a voice.

It was familiar.

'This way,' it said. 'Over here. There's something buried in the ground.'

Their bodies were relaxing. Bex stopped shivering. Through the cracked mud on their faces they both broke into a smile.

The lights intensified and they saw Bonati's face peering down at them.

'I see,' he said. 'Finding somewhere to cuddle up, eh?'

They sat up – and saw a crowd of faces staring at them through the gloom. Luc, Grace, the professor and Jason Goode. Jud could see the relief on their faces, especially his father's, who dashed forward and held out a hand for him to grab hold of. He pulled him up out of the quagmire and held him. Quickly he let him go and made sure he hugged Bex too, who'd been pulled from the earth by Bonati.

'You didn't think we'd leave you here, did you?' Goode said, smiling. 'We were supposed to come in the morning – the Venetian police said they wouldn't bring us here until then – but we discovered something that might surprise you. We thought the police chief was kind of strange. I mean, why wouldn't he bring us here tonight? So we checked him out. And his name?

No wonder he didn't give it to us when we met. You won't believe it. It's—'

'Calderario?' said Jud. 'Lorenzo Calderario?'

'How did you know?' said Goode.

'You should hang around with us agents more often, you know. You might learn a little,' said Jud, smiling cheekily. And then he checked himself and added, 'Er . . . Mr Goode – sir.'

Bex couldn't hide her amusement. She'd never have got away with that. She exchanged looks with Grace who was stifling a smile too.

Bonati raised an eyebrow and glanced surreptitiously at Goode who, fortunately for Jud, was grinning.

'They're in it together,' said Bex. 'The brothers have a nice little racket going here.'

'Doing what?' asked Luc. 'I mean, why is this place so special? Why are the Calderarios so keen to protect it?'

'I'm sure they'll tell us everything as soon as we're off this island,' said Bonati. 'Come on, we don't have much time.'

'Are they still here then? Lorenzo and his men?' Bex said anxiously. 'Shouldn't we get out of sight?' She went to move away quickly but Goode grabbed her arm.

'Don't worry,' he said, more relaxed than the professor, as ever. 'They've moved off – we waited and watched them go beyond that hedge in the distance. They're heading in the opposite direction. But you're right. We should get going. Back to the boat, everyone.'

They set off slowly, keeping their heads down so as not to attract the eyes of officers in the distance.

'But how did you find us?' asked Jud. 'I mean, how did you know we were buried here?'

'Tracks,' said Luc. 'I've always loved tracking. Back when I lived on the vineyard in France. My brothers and I used to track each other through the woods. I could see your footprints a mile off. You hid yourselves well, but you forgot about your footprints. They led us straight here!'

'So the police would've found us too?' said Bex.

'Oh yeah,' said Grace. 'In time. They just haven't done this field yet.'

They turned off their torches and allowed their eyes to get accustomed to the darkness once again. Goode led the way across the fields, through the hedges and down the tree-lined track to the shore again.

Everyone felt a keen sense of excitement at the reunion. They allowed themselves the luxury of relaxing their minds as they ran through the darkness.

But a faint glow in the distance, over to their left, ended their premature celebrations. It was Calderario and his men. They must have caught a glimpse of their torches in the field.

'Damn it,' said Goode. 'They must've turned round and headed back our way. I'm sorry, J. I was sure they were headed away from us.'

'What now?' said Grace. Getting caught on the island of no return was the last thing she'd expected to happen to her just hours earlier.

'What now?' said Goode, rhetorically. 'We run! Come on!'

They pounded the pathways, slipping and staggering on the uneven ground, but determined to move onwards.

The boat was moored some distance away. Luc led the way. He hadn't lied about his tracking ability, and his in-built sense of navigation was impressive. He had a photographic memory, which helped. He'd programmed into his mind the shapes of the trees, the walls and the curvature of the land since leaving the boat. Now it was just a question of reversing the process. But the dark sky and the sporadic moonlight didn't help. Onwards they ran.

Jud paused to glance over his shoulder.

The officers were following them. He could see their torches bobbing up and down as they ran towards them. And the barking of the dogs. He felt like a fox chased by hunting dogs.

'Come on!' said Goode. 'Pick up the pace. *Run!*'

They were panting now and their breath swirled into the cold night air as they staggered and stumbled frantically on the uneven ground.

'How much further?' asked Jud.

'Not far. I'm sure it's close,' said Goode. 'We're near the water now – I can smell it.'

He was right. The foul, decaying stench of the open graves was mixing with the salt water of the lagoon now.

Suddenly there was a growling in the bushes and one of the police dogs burst on the group and began tugging at Grace's rucksack, its breath gushing from its nostrils in the cold air.

'Hey, get off!' she shouted, pulling on the straps now lodged in the dog's vice-like jaws.

Jud stopped in his tracks. He picked up a fallen branch lying on the ground and pushed it hard towards the dog's hind legs. It fell on its belly in the mud but quickly spun round to face Jud, growling viciously. He waved the branch in its face and then hurled it into the undergrowth and, miraculously, the dog pelted after it.

'Just proves there's not a dog in the world that doesn't chase sticks,' he said, a note of relief creeping into his voice. 'Even a search dog needs some time off, I guess.'

'Hmm,' said Bex, unconvinced. 'What kind of dog was it?'

'Dunno,' said Luc. 'A hound of some kind.'

'*Move!*' shouted the professor. 'Whatever it was, there'll be dozens of them in a minute. And they won't all chase bloody sticks!'

They turned and fled as fast as they could manage in the gloom. Luc tripped over a gnarled tree root, but quickly staggered to his feet and ran on.

'You better have a fast boat,' said Jud, exhilaration ringing in his voice. He loved a good chase. Fear just didn't seem to register with him – at least, not often.

'Oh, you know me,' said Goode, smiling wryly. 'I don't think you'll be disappointed.'

They ran out on to the small, pebbly beach on the western side of the island, flanked by a rocky outcrop on one side and a wooded bank on the other where splayed branches reached down to the water's edge.

'It's here,' said Luc. 'Come on.'

The boat was hardly small enough to hide beneath the branches, but it was long and sleek and dark in colour. The matt black of the deck resisted the moon's reflection so it remained quite hidden to the unsuspecting eye. It was obviously a high-powered speedboat.

'Where did you get this?' asked Jud. 'I mean, this is a serious piece of kit.'

'You didn't think we'd bloody row here, did you?' said Goode. 'I've got friends. It belongs to a pal of mine on the Lido. He owed me a favour anyway.'

They jumped into the boat and Goode started the engine. It boomed out a throaty roar as the stern backed further into the branches and the bow swung round to face the open water. Goode geared up, the bow rose a few inches above the waves and they sped off.

Bex glanced over her shoulder and saw the police officers spilling out on to the secluded beach. Within seconds they were tiny figures in the distance as the boat swept out into the Adriatic.

Their faces were pelted by the bracing wind but they didn't care. It was refreshing to be away from the muck and the grime and the putrid stench of death. The speed of the boat was exhilarating as it cut through the choppy waters and crosswinds like a sharp knife. There was a faint pinkish glow on the horizon ahead of them. The sun was finally beginning to show, at last, bringing a sense of hope and rejuvenation to the battered team.

'We're heading east,' said Jud. 'That's away from Venice. You're going the wrong way!'

Goode shook his head and glanced over to his son. 'We're going the *right* way,' he said. 'You'll like Porec. It's beautiful.'

'Porec?' said Jud. 'Where's *Porec*?'

'Croatia,' said Goode. 'I've got friends there. You know, J, you really should brush up on your geography.' He pointed eastwards in the direction they were going. 'It's about sixty miles in that direction. We'll be there in under an hour.'

'What do we do when we get there?' said Bex.

'My pilot's already moved the jet to Pula Airport, it's not far away.'

They sat back on the dark leather seats and held their coats close to their necks to shut out the bracing wind. The island slowly shrank into the distance.

'So, come on then,' said Goode. 'Explain the fascination the Calderario brothers have with that place. I mean, why all the effort to keep people away? It's haunted, after all, why would anyone want to go there?'

'Ah,' said Jud. 'We know *some* people who like to visit it. And regularly.'

'That's right,' said Bex. 'Grave robbers.'

'Grave robbers?' said Goode.

'Don't tell me, stealing from the bodies of plague victims?' said Luc.

'Exactly right,' said Jud. 'And I think you can guess what they're taking. Fortunately for them it's something that needs a little longer to decay than human bones.'

'Jewellery!' said Bonati. 'So that's it. The Calderario brothers must have found out that the pits were full of jewellery worn by the abandoned bodies and they set up this nice little operation. Lorenzo protects the island from intruders while their gang of grave robbers set to work. Is that right?'

Jud nodded and smiled. 'Then his brother, Niccolo, sells the jewellery to unsuspecting buyers in London. Very lucrative,' he said.

'Now you can see why Lorenzo was so keen to frame us with crimes in Venice,' said Bex, 'to keep us away from here and throw us in the slammer.'

'It'll be them in the slammer soon,' said Bonati. 'The prosecutors will have all they need. The Venetian authorities will throw the book at the Calderarios. I'll call Khan again now.'

'And I suppose the plague doctors will disperse now,' said Bex. 'I mean, now that the source of their anger has been identified and stopped.'

'Let's hope so,' said Luc. 'If the jewellery is returned here, then there's no reason for them to come back from the dead like before, is there? Their job is done.'

The professor nodded and was about to get up and find his phone when he saw Jud fumbling in his pocket. He fished something out.

It looked like a lump of dirt but Jud brushed off some of the mud and slowly held it up to the others.

'Want to buy a ring, anyone?' he said, grinning.

Bex leapt at him, grabbed it from his hand and hurled it into the ocean.

And as the cursed ring sank forever into the murky depths of the Adriatic, the black powerboat cut a rippling wake of white crests as it bounced its way over the waves and raced on into the sunrise.

Crypt:
The Gallows Curse

Andrew Hammond

When a brutal crime is committed . . . but there's no human explanation . . . who can the police turn to?

CRYPT:
Covert Response Youth Paranormal Team

This secret MI5 division recruits teenagers with extra sensory perception. CRYPT agent Jud Lester and the team crack these cases using their innate talents and state of the art technology.

Terror has seized London. People are dying in vicious attacks. But those who survive agree: the killers, bearing the scars of the hangman's noose, materialised out of thin air.

CRYPT has been dispatched.

The hunt is on . . .

978 0 7553 7821 0

headline

Crypt:
Traitor's Revenge

Andrew Hammond

When a brutal crime is committed . . . but there's no human explanation . . . who can the police turn to?

CRYPT:
Covert Response Youth Paranormal Team

This secret MI5 division recruits teenagers with extra sensory perception. CRYPT agent Jud Lester and the team crack these cases using their innate talents and state of the art technology.

A security breach at the Houses of Parliament fuels bizarre rumours, whilst reports of horrific sightings ignite panic in York . . .

CRYPT has just landed its most explosive case yet!

978 0 7553 7822 7

headline